# ROCKY NOOK TEA ROOM

by

Laura J. Wight

Published by Weir River Press —USA—
Hingham, Massachusetts
Second Edition October, 2016

Wight, Laura J./Rocky Nook Tea Room
ISBN-10 0989433358
ISBN-13 978-0-9894333-5-8

PUBLISHER'S NOTE:
This book is a work of fiction. Names, characters, places and incidents either are the product of the author's imagination or are used fictitiously, and any resemblance to actual persons, living or dead, business establishments, events, or locales is entirely coincidental.

# Prologue

*Boston Globe*
*Present Day*

*Hingham-*

*Human remains are being exhumed today from a well located under the barn of an antique property on East Street. The couple owning the property discovered the body while excavating the well for irrigation purposes. During the cleaning out process, what appeared to be a human hand was uncovered. Authorities were immediately notified and the barn subsequently sealed off as a potential crime scene. Forensic experts have been called...to investigate.*

# Chapter One

April 1924

Gertrude Edmands sighed in frustration. She had performed with both the Boston Symphony Orchestra and the Handel and Haydn Society. She had sung in front of thousands of people over her long and illustrious career. A few more performances, even though she had long since retired, were not the problem. Her problem was Fred. He was going to abhor everything about this.

She reviewed the elegant handwriting on the thick stationary a second time.

*Dear Miss Edmands,*

*After reviewing your outstanding career resume, I am honored to add you to our repertoire of vocalists appearing at the resort this summer. As a special request, would you sing a reprisal of your role of Pteecha in The Sphinx? One of our board members witnessed your performance at Boston's Jordan Hall some years ago and recalls it as an experience he will never forget.*

*If it fits with your schedule, we have you appearing on the third Friday and Saturday nights in the upcoming months of June, July and August. If you would be so kind as to confirm this by return mail, I will make the necessary arrangements, advertising etc.*

*I look forward to meeting with you and, of course, hearing your most celebrated voice.*

*Sincerely Yours,*

*George Cornell*

*General Manager*
*Magog International Resort*
*Magog, Canada*

"You know, Annie, I haven't given a public performance outside of the tea room in years." Gertrude rubbed the spot between her brows.

"But that's not what's bothering you." Annie shrewdly assessed her employer.

"Of course you're right." Gertrude carefully folded the letter and put it in the pocket of her faded house-dress. She brought her head up. "I don't suppose you know where Fred is?"

"In the strawberry beds behind the barn." Annie had the answer ready. She stood, tapping her foot.

Gertrude continued to sit. Logistically, plans for the upcoming performance would unfurl seamlessly. She had a month and a half to get her repertoire in order and to make travel arrangements. She had time to shop for the proper clothes. And with Annie taking the helm at home, the tea room would be left in competent hands. None of those things were issues. The stumbling block was Fred. When she apprised him of the plans she'd made, the ensuing confrontation was sure to turn ugly.

For the past several years Fred had taken charge of their lives and finances, and Gertrude had felt only relief, relinquishing control after what seemed like a lifetime of responsibility. But now she was attempting to take charge again…for Fred's own good, of course. The result? He would be angry and shocked, but the actions she'd fomented were necessary, and there wasn't a damn thing he could do to stop what she'd put into action.

Gertrude didn't believe in happily-ever-afters. Her life had never worked that way. From the outside, some would say her existence looked charmed, and when she was much younger, she might have agreed with them. But now, and for too many years, things had been about survival…and since meeting Fred, subterfuge. It was time to change all that. But not until she completed this one last, grand venture.

She pushed herself back from the table and rose to her feet.

“If I'm not back in half an hour call the police.”

Even though she couldn’t see it, Gertrude knewAnnie rolled her eyes as she strode out the back door. Part of the young housekeeper wanted to hear the conversation between her and Fred, but the other part knew she was safer inside. Once they got going, it could be all out war. Shaking her head, Gertrude wondered for the thousandth time why Annie kept this job.

The crush of tiny May flowers beneath Gertrude's feet released fragrances and small insects into the air. She was nearly oblivious. The sun was bright but the deep breaths she took of spring air did nothing to warm her suddenly cold chest. Things would be so much easier if Fred wasn't utterly intransigent. But wasn’t that one of the things that set her heart a flutter? That made them so compatible? He never gave in without a fight. Hell, he never gave in. It was one of his finer attributes, but this time it was going to make them both miserable.

Gertrude passed the chicken coop which occupied the lower level of her red, three story barn. From atop the pen, one of the outdoor mouser cats jumped down and came to rub around her ankles. She paused and stooped to scratch a ragged ear, momentarily enjoying its contented cat sounds while she gathered her courage. Eventually she gave up her dawdling and moved purposefully toward the back field.

She spotted Fred right away. An imposing figure in the midst of the strawberries; tall and broad of shoulder, head bare of his normal hat, and sleeves rolled up to show the silhouette of hard-used muscles. His whole demeanor was one of contentment as he concentrated on the plants at this feet. The patchwork of greenery was punctuated with flashes of bright red from ripening fruit. She watched as he bent to pick a crimson berry, rising to pop the small, tart offering into his mouth. He puckered with appreciation before Gertrude made a slight movement and called his attention to where she paused, watching.

What little confidence she'd gathered, wavered.

"Hi," she called, tentatively.

"Gertrude." Was there a young, spring eagerness in his voice? She nearly snorted. Why not. She hadn't destroyed his morning yet. "I wasn't expecting a visit from the boss." He grinned, knowing how much she disliked it when he gave her that title. But this time she didn't rise to the bait.

"A boss can't come and check up on her farm manager?" She countered, not so steadily.

"That would be depending on what the boss would want from the farm manager, now wouldn't it?" He smirked and chewed suggestively on the crushed orb in his mouth. She grew warm, watching. He had so much power over her that a single look had her flushed and wanting. Would his raw appeal never grow old?

She tightened her face, refusing to be distracted. He noticed the change, right away.

"What's the matter?" The way he asked, it was barely a question.

"Nothing," she hesitated. "Well, nothing yet. There will be when…" Her courage momentarily gave out. "We need to sit in the arbor."

He walked toward her, keeping the rows of strawberries to his right and left, his features becoming more distinct as he neared. His face was strong, square chinned and deeply tanned. Sweat stood out on his forehead, and he gave her a puzzled look as he used his upper arm to wipe it away.

"Can it wait until lunch?" He grunted, then drawing alongside, reached for her hand. With ingrained habit, she snatched it back.

"There's no one to see us," he grumbled.

Fred always hated her caution, but that wasn't what drove

the need to keep her distance right now.

"It's not that," she allowed.

Fred raised an eyebrow but defied her request. He grabbed her hand firmly and sighed. "Okay. Then tell me. What's got you so rattled?"

Dark auburn hair fell forward across his face and his green eyes never left hers. "Come on." He led her to the arbor, where the spring grape vines were beginning to weave tendrils through the cut lattice work, and a coarse wooden bench waited beneath the delicate leaves. He sat and caressed her knuckles with his callused thumb until she settled beside him, feeling the heat where his leg pressed into hers. Gertrude struggled with words, but there were none that would be easy. Instead, she drew the letter from her pocket and handed it over.

"Open it."

Carefully Fred unfolded the letter, smoothing it on the well worn denim covering his thigh as he quickly read the contents. Gertrude watched his face harden. His jaw clenched and the muscles in his neck tightened as he came to the closing lines. With exaggerated deliberateness he crumpled the paper in his fist, gritted his teeth and let one controlled syllable escape from between thinned lips.

"No."

"Fred, you must understand…"

The inevitable explosion detonated.

"No! You won't do this."

"You know as well as I do that it's the next logical step…"

He interrupted again. "There is nothing logical about this," he growled. "You're not going. This…all of this we've built, is my responsibility and ultimately it thrives or fails on my decisions."

"No Fred. That's where you're wrong. Up until now you *have* made all the choices, and taken all the risk. So now it's my turn. And if you would look at this solution reasonably, you would realize this is the safest way, much safer for me than for you. And if you weren't so stubborn…"

"Stubborn." Fred ground out an incredulous laugh. "That's what you think? Well isn't that just the pot calling the kettle black? Okay. You want stubborn? I'll show you stubborn. Listen to this. I won't allow it," he yelled. "This was my idea and I refuse to let you put yourself in danger."

"Fred, please." She placed her hand over his, attempting to quell his agitation. "Up until now you've assumed responsibility for me, your sister, for all of us. But the way you want to proceed with this is filled with peril, and I can't sit back and let you do it alone any more."

His glare turned her heart to ice, and in response she stiffened her spine. "I can see that you're not going to behave reasonably." She would do what she had to do, despite his anger. Her voice became hard, resigned. "I'm sending a return letter today. I'm taking the job."

He threw the crumpled letter to the ground and abruptly stood. "If that's the way you'll have it," he ground out, "good luck to you then."

Fred strode across the lawn without a backward glance, rage in every step. Gertrude sat watching and shaking and knowing that there was nothing she could do differently.

# Chapter Two

December 1867

Gertrude Edmands passed her fourth birthday when the auspicious day came that her family realized she was never again to be considered a normal child. But then, her household was far from normal.

Her father, Thomas Edmands, slept a great deal of the day, awakening at noon to eat his first meal. He would then promptly disappear into his study where his unique voice would be raised and lowered in octaves throughout the afternoon. Gertrude was admonished never to bother him or interrupt.

Each evening, after an early supper, he would dress in a splendid, dark formal frock coat, double breasted with peaked lapels, paired with impeccably pressed trousers. He would rush out into the night, enveloped by a swirling cloud of bay rum cologne, papers clutched in his hand.

Gertrude's mother, Hannah, quite liberated for the day, taught music at a nearby private school for girls in Cambridge. She would arrive home at the end of each day, partake of the early dinner repast, then retire to her bedroom directly from the table, bringing with her a thick leather satchel of school work that rarely left her side.

The four year old's sisters, Eva and Alice, were eleven and nine years older than her, respectively. Both teased her as an unkempt and undisciplined minx, but were quick to shower her with hugs and treats smuggled home from the finishing school they attended daily.

Gertrude cheerfully skipped through her very young years in Somerville, Massachusetts. Her only companion for much of the time, Miss Martha Smith, the housekeeper cum nanny charged with keeping the engine of the odd household running and seeing that Gertrude wasn't too much of a nuisance.

This, it turned out, was not such a hard task, as Gertrude was a child who could entertain herself most days with a plethora of characters flitting through her overactive imagination. Dress up and role playing were two of her favorite pastimes and she had no need of an audience with which to spin her tales.

Twelve rooms made up the family's ample Gothic Revival style home, the exterior of which was mellowed brick and featured three cross gables with pointed arch windows, each decorated in green pendant trim. The interior was equally as ornate.

Each opulent room available to Gertrude provided a myriad of settings for her fantasies. The dining room with its heavy green damask drapes and muted sunlight became deepest Africa. Her sister's room, frilly with pink tulle, perfectly befitted a Paris dance-hall, and the kitchen with its cast iron stove belching heat, converted easily into the belly of a transatlantic ocean liner.

Gertrude couldn't remember the exact day she stood outside of her father's office and began taking notice of the sounds within, but she did remember the first tentative and seemingly harmonious notes that emerged from her throat in imitation of what she was hearing. It seemed effortless and fun to wait for her father's vocal explosions and imitate them, albeit at a softer volume but accompanied by lavish movements of her limbs. It soon became an integral part of her daily routine to emulate his sonorous offerings and quickly became the most enjoyable aspect of her solitary existence.

Eventually, after weeks of mimicry, confidence high, her orchestrations grew more flamboyant. She forgot the need to be circumspect while her father toiled within, and her volume rose.

One bright afternoon, deeply involved with the latest aria her father was practicing, she didn't notice the door opening up a small crack. The notes, this day, had come to her especially strongly. She threw them from her depths. Dredged up and flung out into the air where they hung, dramatically, like small winged vessels.

****

Thomas Edmands stood, transfixed in the doorway. Was this his small, innocuous daughter, and was it possible those full and seasoned sounds emanated from her little body? Surely this was not normal. That ripe huskiness; was it a fluke, or perhaps a single musical phrase that inadvertently resonated in her tiny lungs?

An experiment was necessary. He closed the large door, and leaning on it heavily, let forth a new range of notes once, twice and again before reopening the portal to observe Gertrude's concentration. And then she echoed forth. Ah, yes! There is was again. His daughter, his own lovely infant daughter, was sending the same music he'd just vocalized out into the room with more feeling and intensity than he could imagine possible. His whole being shook and he closed the door with a quiet click to spend the rest of the day puzzling over what should be done about this amazing occurrence.

****

That evening, as her mother entered through the front door, something unprecedented happened that brought

Gertrude's head sharply up from the small blocks she was stacking on the fine Persian Sarouk that covered the golden pine floor. Her father burst from his office and without a word, took her mother's arm and pulled her into his inner sanctum, where-after muffled voices rose and dropped behind a firmly closed door.

Martha, alerted by the change in household rhythm, came out of the kitchen smelling of lamb stew, wiping her hands on a serviceable white apron. She exchanged confused glances with Gertrude.

"Did your mother arrive home?" she asked in puzzlement.

Gertrude nodded and pointed to the study. "She's in there with Papa."

"Hmmph. There's a strange thing for you. I wonder if this will affect the supper hour?" she groused. Martha remained in the room, straightening things that were already in place while inching her way closer and closer to the office door. Gertrude observed as her nanny strained to hear what was being said inside, but the stout old oak door refused to let out any secrets. She sighed.

"Well, come and help me set the table. I suppose we'll find out soon enough."

Gertrude arose from the floor and followed Martha into the kitchen. She was handed the Gorham silver that was used at the table every day and a small pile of wine colored linen napkins. Martha, in turn, loaded her arms with Mrs. Edmand's best Limoges china. They headed into the dining room and began laying things out in a familiar pattern just as Gertrude's sisters arrived home.

"Hey tadpole." Eva cried out affectionately, bringing the smell of fresh, cold air with her. She dropped a gentle kiss onto the mahogany curls of her youngest sister. "How was your day?"

Gertrude looked conspiratorially at her sisters.

"Mama and Papa are in the study." Her eyes felt extra large as she waited for their reaction.

"Ooooh. I wonder what's going on?" Alice took off her white kid gloves and speculated. "Remember the last time they had a chat in Papa's office? We all ended up going on holiday to that lovely place in the Berkshires to hear him sing with his orchestra." She clapped her hands together, "Wouldn't that be marvelous."

"Yes, but remember two years ago?" Eva, in contrast, looked pensive. "It was before you would remember, Gertrude, but Papa was home quite a bit at the time and when he and Mama came from his office, it had been determined that Mama would seek to resume teaching, as she had done before she and Papa were married."

Gertrude shook her head. "But Papa is quite busy now," she reasoned. "He's been gone every evening."

"That's very true, my sweetling," Eva agreed. "I guess we'll have to be patient and wait to see what's going on." The girls, as one, removed their heavy woolen coats and hung them on the brass tree by the door.

Alice paced. Eva sat and studied her nails. And Gertrude went back to her blocks. Martha hovered, hoping for a sign that would let her know when she could put food on the table. It was generally accepted that Mrs. Edmands would arrive home and within minutes of the girls' subsequent arrival, dinner would be served. This upset of the schedule was a disturbing occurrence that was unprecedented. Thankfully, it lasted only another quarter hour.

Mr. and Mrs. Edmands emerged from the study suffused in smiles and "tut-tut's" as they surveyed the expectant faces of their children and housekeeper.

"Food?" Mr. Edmands questioned Martha. "It might be a good idea to set it upon the table before we allay your obvious curiosity." Mr. Edmands beemed with alacrity, raising his hands and shaking out his cuffs in the direction of the dining room table. The children had no choice but to follow his lead, and Martha ducked back into the kitchen to serve the meal quickly.

What happened next was even more unexpected than anything that had gone before. Mr. Edmands, having presided over everyone being seated, waited for the large tureen of soup to be placed on the table, then burst out into song.

"Now Papa," Mrs. Edmands admonished, "don't you think this could have waited until we all finished eating?"

"Nonsense. Look at this crew my dear, and tell me that digestion would be properly accomplished while they are all on such tenterhooks." He winked, then gestured toward Gertrude. "Come and stand by me, daughter, and see if we have a surprise waiting."

Gertrude, thinking that this could mean the rare occasion when there was candy in his pocket, jumped from her seat and stood obediently next to her father.

"Now Gertrude, pay close attention. This is an enchanting piece that I've been practicing today from Rossini's *Stabat Mater*." He tapped her nose gently and his rich tenor once again filled the room. He sang, perhaps, five bars and then turned toward his daughter who had watched his cravat wiggle with the movement of his Adam's apple. "Gertrude. Can you copy that? Can you sing that for me?"

Gertrude blinked up at him. She could feel the importance of the moment from the expectant look on his face. Although puzzled at his request, she put her mind back to earlier that afternoon when she had been singing the very same notes that had just left her father's throat. She took a deep breath and turned her face heavenward, unleashing her voice.

The room went deathly still, and at her conclusion Gertrude looked up at her father and slowly around at the faces staring toward her. Suddenly she was nervous. "Was that all right, Papa?'

He grabbed her in the fiercest of hugs. "Oh my darling, my dearest girl. That was perfection Gertrude. Perfection indeed."

Her mother seemed suddenly to emerge from her trance. “A contralto, Thomas? Am I hearing correctly? And the intonation, how….I just don't see that it's possible.”

“A gift,” Mr. Edmands beamed, still holding Gertrude closely and stroking her hair with gentle fingers. She leaned into him and absorbed his praise. “A gift from God. And it is our duty to see it nurtured and cherished and shared with the world.” He turned his face down to her, then. “Do you understand, Gertrude? You have something very special here my child.”

She methodically worked through the strangeness of the situation, the unaccustomed attention and the praise, determining what answer might be expected and what she should do next.

Her father gave her a little nudge. “Well, what do you think?”

Gertrude pondered a bit, still wondering if there was the possibility of a little candy to accompany the acclaim, but when it wasn't forthcoming, she looked up to her father and said the first thing that came to mind.

“I think it makes me feel good to sing.”

The whole table burst into laughter. The exquisite tension broken by Gertrude's simple statement.

“It makes her feel good to sing,” Mr. Edmands repeated, and smiled down at Gertrude. “Well my sweet prodigy, it makes us feel good too.”

# Chapter Three

December 1867

On Dana Street in nearby Cambridge, the Torrey household was subdued. Robert and his two year old daughter sat quietly on the flowered divan where Edith surreptitiously sucked her thumb and thirty year old Robert pretended to concentrate on his new copy of Mark Twain's *The Celebrated Jumping Frog*. Usually Twain could distract him from most anything, but his wife's muffled cries from the upstairs room had him on edge. Even young Arthur, recently turned one and normally full of energy, sat quietly in his playpen chewing the ear of a tattered stuffed dog.

Sarah had been in her bedroom with the doctor for almost twelve hours now. This was, by far, the longest labor that she had endured. When Robert had dared poke his head into the darkened room several hours earlier, Sarah had assured him, sweating and panting, that things were going swimmingly and would he please absent himself post-haste. Glancing at the doctor who was calmly attending, Robert had no choice but to retreat back to his two young offspring and continue an uneasy vigil.

He had married Sarah only four short years ago, and this was to be their third child. This many children, at the beginning of his wage earning years, should have been a burden, but God had been generous, and provided them with the security to procreate comfortably with a sound roof over their heads.

Robert had worked his way up to a lucrative position as senior clerk in the highly successful architectural firm of Ware and Van Brunt. Two years previous, as he was just starting out with them, the burgeoning company had won a competition to design a building for the Harvard campus to be known as Memorial Hall. The office had instantly exploded in size and importance which had moved Robert up the ladder at breakneck speed. Although the cornerstone of the building had yet to be laid for the vast project, the office was constantly bustling with all the activity and planning that preceded a ground-breaking. His job looked secure, and expanding his family was not to be considered a hardship.

If only Sarah would deliver this baby before Monday. Time was fleeting and it was fast approaching dusk on Sunday. Robert desperately wanted to be present for the birth of this child. He had missed the other two children's entries into the world by several hours, and sought a more tangible connection with this child's debut.

He should, for all intents and purposes, be by his wife's side, but that was not possible. This morning their in-house help had sent a note that she could not attend her job, citing illness. And just an hour ago, Robert had summoned the neighbor’s twelve year old son to go and hunt down the absent girl to find if she had recovered, but he had yet to see results. Truly he held no hope of seeing her before her appointed shift next morning. On a weekend, the slatternly girl enjoyed tippling at some of the Boston waterfront establishments and was probably sleeping the day away to make up for excesses of the previous evening. She was not one to inspire confidence at the best of times, so even if she miraculously appeared, Robert would, most likely still end up watching and caring for his little ones.

With a huff, he got up from the divan and bent to pick Arthur from his crib.

“What do you say, old boy, shall we get a little fresh air?”

Fresh air was badly needed. Arthur was, once again, decidedly damp and aromatic in the diaper region. Robert had valiantly changed the babies' nappies several times during the day, but had not been able to perfect the art of rendering the cloth snug to the infant's body. Having pondered with displeasure the thought of repeating the process, he instead chose to ignore the fragrant saturation, at least for the time being. He needed outside. Robert bundled first Edith and then Arthur quickly into their winter coats.

“Come, Edith.” Robert, with the door open and Arthur firmly gripped against his ribcage, held out his free hand to his daughter who obediently popped the thumb out of her mouth and joined them.

They walked out onto the side porch and down the stairs into the yard…his yard. Robert was proud of the fact that just last spring he had been able to come up with the down-payment to purchase this comfortable home, having rented it the two years before.

He gazed up at the modest dwelling. It had a smattering of ginger-bread embellishments that were popular in current Victorian architecture, and, interestingly enough, it sported a mansard roof; a throwback from an earlier time but very flattering on the elongated back section of the house. He took a long look at the wooden clapboards, and silently confirmed his opinion that the house was pink. His wife, of course, had assured him over and over that the color chosen for the siding was rose-beige. Loving her as he did, Robert had easily agreed as the painters had smirkingly wielded their brushes. Strangely, it didn't bother him. And he had no intention of changing it.

Inside the house, the downstairs consisted of a formal sitting room in the right front quadrant, flanked by two small bay windows that overlooked the tree-shaded street. A formal dining room sat to the other side of a central staircase, and a very large kitchen opened up to the rear, allowing the children a warm space where they could be fed and even play. The overlarge room could retain its slightly chaotic air without notice from guests or visiting relatives.

The upstairs had the luxury of five bedrooms, his and Sarah's being the largest at the front with the smaller nursery attached, and three more extremely small and modest rooms along the side and back of the house. Sarah laughed, chiding they would all be full within a few years.

Their furniture was a hodge-podge of odds and ends having been passed down through his family and Sarah's. The mismatched items strangely suited the house and created a lived in warmth that could never be reproduced with new Sears and Roebuck furnishings.

The outhouse, a pride and joy of his own architectural design, stood grandly in the back yard, painted a matching pink to the house. He'd adorned it with transom windows high up on all sides, and ornate, scrolled trim painted in delicate cream. On the door, resplendent and not to be missed, gleamed a glorious polished brass knocker. This last was Roberts' final addition, as he had been interrupted on several memorable occasions and wished to avoid any future invasions to his privacy.

He walked the circuit around the house—happy there was no snow yet this year—accompanied by his two children. Glancing at the Simmons' house to the right and the Bentley's house to the left, he caught the eye of Mrs. Bentley peering out of her parlor window, which she clearly took as an opportunity to bustle out her side door, breath puffing in the cold.

"How is Sarah doing?" she queried, her blond eyebrows pointed in a line of concern. Laurel Bentley was his wife's best friend and confidante, and the tension was evident in her voice.

"The doctor has come out to assure me several times that things are progressing slowly but properly." He shifted drooping Arthur to a more secure position on his hip.

"Why do you have the children, Robert?" Laurel looked puzzled. "Where is your girl?"

"Oh, I thought you knew. I bade your son go look for her over an hour ago. She sent a message this morning that she was indisposed for the day. She couldn't have picked a more rotten time to take off."

Edith chose this moment to begin pulling on him from her two and a half foot height.

"Oh, Robert," Laurel scolded. "Why didn't you come to get me? You know I'm more than happy to help out." She competently approached and relieved him of his youngest burden.

She cooed at Arthur while her nose twitched at his obvious aromatic, sagging state. "Why don't I go in and change him?" She said practically, then arched a brow down toward Edith, still tugging. "Do you and the children want something to eat?"

Robert ignored the second question and answered the first. "I didn't bother you earlier because my wife reminded me that you were entertaining your in-laws and I didn't want to intrude."

"Oh please. You could have interrupted any time," Laurel chuckled. "My dear mother-in-law took offense that I hadn't brought out my best Spode china and my father-in-law complained that the beef was stringy and undercooked." She paused to look at Arthur's diaper. "I would have been grateful for a legitimate distraction."

Edith was whispering more insistently now and frantically pulling at her father. Although Robert was oblivious, Laurel, it seemed, was not.

"It looks like Edith needs to make a call to the loo. Is that right Edith?"

The two year old nodded emphatically, but, taking matters into her own small hands, also answered the question her father had not. "And I'm hungry, too."

Laurel laughed. "Well run along with Papa and take care

of business. Then meet me in your kitchen. I'll find something to fill the hole in your tummy." Wasting no time, she whisked Arthur off in the direction of the Torrey home with—Robert imagined—the intention of setting a diaper to rights and seeing for herself just how Sarah was faring in her labor.

Robert heard the shout just as Edith was finishing up in the outhouse. He scrambled with her dress and coat then grabbed her up in his arms. In his haste, he nearly fell out through the door. His long legs gobbled up the yard and he was almost at the porch when Laurel met him. Her face was wreathed in smiles and his insides unclenched for the first time in hours.

"You have a new son, Robert." She beamed, adjusting Arthur onto one hip. "Edith." She reached for the little girl. "Stay with me while Papa goes to see your new brother."

"But I want to see my new baby," Edith pouted.

"You will, my dear. But your father is going to see your mother first." She gestured with her head toward the house, while plucking Edith from Robert and filling her free arm with the second, larger child. She then angled her body back to her own yard. "Go," she mouthed at Robert, not allowing time for any of the Torrey's, large or small, to argue.

Robert took the porch steps in one bound and reached the door to his bedroom moments later. He knocked gently, his eyes focusing on the white and blue Privy Council flock wallpaper in the hallway as he waited anxiously.

"Robert?" The questioning voice broke his spell. "Come in and see your new son." His wife's voice was tired but jubilant.

As Robert entered, the gray haired doctor stood by the four-poster bed, rolling down the sleeves of his previously crisp white shirt. He moved to clap Robert on the back.

"Congratulations." He fussed with his cuff-links, but when he was unable to secure them in the dimming light, he popped them into his trouser pocket instead, and reached for his coat. “I'm sure I'll see you again next year.” He chuckled at his own joke. “If you need anything just send your girl around to get me, but everything went very well once your son decided it was time to make his appearance.”

He smiled over at Sarah, shook Robert's hand and quietly took his leave. Robert stared after him with a foolish grin, and only as he disappeared did he turn his gaze to his glowing wife.

A small bundle was tucked snugly against her side, swaddled in the yellow coverlet that she had so painstakingly embroidered over the last few months. He smiled at her. Sarah had never looked more beautiful.

“Have you thought of what we should call him?” his wife asked. They had never picked names for any of the children before they were born.

“I have, just now.” He knew the old goat would be pleased when it was time for another house call. “We should name him for the doctor. I've always admired him, and Lord knows he’s become a familiar fixture.”

When he saw Sarah pondering, he led her a little more. “And didn't you have a grandfather with his name as well?” He lightly stroked the baby's cheek and glimpsed bright blue eyes that hinted at the promise of becoming green. Robert leaned down to kiss his wife, waiting for her decision.

She smiled up at him, then gestured to the empty embroidered heart on the yellow quilt that was waiting to be filled.

“I like it.” She glanced lovingly back and forth between him and their new addition. “Welcome to the world, Frederick Lawrence Torrey.”

# Chapter Four

November 1887

"Mama. Where are my gloves? I'm going to be late." Gertrude flung clothes around the room, searching in vain through piles of petticoats, combinations and corsets. Her bags were already packed and those projectiles were the discarded items she had deemed inappropriate for her trip. Her mother stood in the doorway, looking at the brightly colored mess, shaking her head in exasperation.

"Your train doesn't leave for another two hours, and your father already has the carriage waiting out front. Slow down, child." Hannah clearly refused to become flustered. "Which pair are you looking for, white or green?"

"I'll take either at this point. I just can't find anything," Gertrude grumbled.

Her mother walked to the dressing table beside the crimson draped bed and extricated the soft green kid gloves from under an opened hat box. She handed them to her flustered daughter.

"Now let's go over your list again. Calmly this time, to make sure that you haven't forgotten anything." Gertrude knew her mother was trying to be the voice of reason, but in reality, was as anxious as she at the upcoming trip. This was the first time Gertrude would tour unchaperoned, an auspicious feat at the age of twenty four, but there was simply no one to accompany her this time.

Gertrude's sisters, Eva and Alice had long since married and moved away. Papa had a busy singing schedule for the upcoming week, and Mama was in the middle of giving exams at school. Even Martha, whom they had called upon in the past to accompany Gertrude, was busy taking care of her daughter's children and was not available.

Gertrude blew a stray piece of hair out of her face with a puff of breath. "I've gone over my list too many times, and every time I do, I change my mind and swap something out. I won't open my bags again. If I've forgotten anything, I'll just purchase it once I've arrived." She suddenly became aware of the apprehension in her mother's face, and sought to mollify her.

"You know I'll be fine." Gertrude forced herself to quiet the hurricane she had become and willed her body to lower calmly to sit on the bed. "Besides, Idell will be there to keep an eye on me."

Gertrude could tell that her mother barely refrained from rolling her eyes. Idell Miles, the soprano in the program and thirty years old, held most of the responsibility for Mrs. Edmands' worries. Kind and bright but far too racy, Idell was the type of newly emancipated woman who fascinated Gertrude and gave her mother megrims. Lately, Hannah fretted that there had been signs Gertrude might be trying to emulate her friend. Gertrude didn't know what to say, for her concerns were not unfounded.

Her mother continued. "Just send us a telegram and let us know when you've arrived safely." She continued her list of requests, clearly wondering whether Gertrude would remember to comply. "And make sure you take all your meals with the rest of the company, and don't leave the hotel unaccompanied."

Gertrude sighed. "We've been over this a thousand times, Mother. I'll be very careful, and I'll be home in six days. It's not like I'm headed to Timbuktu. It's only a two hour train ride to New Bedford."

Gertrude hefted her matching bags from the bed and headed out the door. She was met by her father in the living room, who relieved her of her burden and stared purposefully into her eyes while twitching his head in the direction of Gertrude's mother.

Gertrude interpreted the the signal.

"Okay," she whisperingly agreed. "I'll meet you outside, Papa."

She turned and walked back to her mother, lovingly patting the older woman's cheek. "I promise I'll be in touch every day, and I'll follow your guidelines explicitly. But you have to stop worrying about me. I'm old enough to be on my own. Heavens, mother, you were married by the time you were my age."

"Exactly, my dear." Gertrude's mother crossed her arms over her chest and nodded as if she'd won a point.

And here was an area of concern that Hannah frequently harped upon. When would Gertrude find a nice young man and settle down? Not that her career wasn't taking up most of her time. She had made hundreds of appearances in choral productions around the state and was amassing a fine portfolio and bank account for herself.

But according to her mother, that self-sufficiency was beside the point. She thought Gertrude needed a husband to guide her and watch over her. Since her parents were not getting any younger and constantly complained how exhausting it was trying to keep up with the young contralto, they were hoping to put her care into the hands of a worthy male.

Gertrude thought that was hogwash, as evidenced by the sparkle in her eye as she kissed her mother goodbye, contemplating her immanent release from parental rules. She fairly skipped out of the doorway and onto the circular drive that was littered with the last of the brightly colored leaves having fallen from the mighty elms flanking the house.

Gertrude lifted her skirts and stepped up into the carriage

her father had brought around. Their old horse, Buster, waited patiently for all the fussing to be complete, until with a click of her father's tongue, he set off at a stately trot toward the train station.

Gertrude never got tired of the trip into Boston. They lived less than five miles from the Old Colony Depot, but the enjoyable drive took them across the West Boston Bridge and eventually to Tremont Street before they turned onto Kneeland. As they skirted the Boston Common, she craned her neck to catch a glimpse of some of the imposing mansions breathing old money onto the public promenade. Gertrude sighed. She had sung in some of those luxurious edifices, bricks and brass with manicured greenery framing imposing front doors. The well-heeled of Boston were great patrons of the arts. Gertrude wondered whether she would always be the visiting contralto, or perhaps, some time far in the future she would aspire to owning one of the grand residences.

The station, when they arrived, bustled with travelers and vendors, newspaper hawkers and food carts. A myriad of culinary odors assailed her olfactory senses. Her father flipped a coin to a boy who would look after Buster for the few minutes it took to get Gertrude settled.

Steam rose up from the grates at their feet, imparting small bursts of warmth as they moved amidst the crush of bodies. She glanced up at the enormous clock overlooking South Street and saw that less than an hour remained before her departure. Excitement washed over her in great waves and she moved with confidence through the crowd toward her waiting train. Mr. Edmands tipped a porter, and handed him Gertrude's bags before turning with some final instructions.

"Keep an eye out for pickpockets, my dear. You are a woman alone, and someone may try to prey on you as you change trains in Taunton." Mr. Edmands cleared his throat. "I'll be waiting for you right here, next week. Please try to be safe." He smiled then, allowing the pride in his eyes to show. "And let them all bask in that marvelous voice of yours."

"I will Papa," Gertrude returned, her face suffused with love for her greatest devotee. "I'll do fine, won't I?" She searched his eyes for confirmation.

"You will perform splendidly, as always," he beamed. "Don't let this new company intimidate you. You will have your friend Idell to lean on, and I daresay she will guide you well enough." It was the closest he would get to meddling. He always left the meddling to Gertrude's mother, who was much better at it.

"Now run along, and I'll see you in a few days." He picked up her hand and gave it a quick, reassuring squeeze before helping her up into the rail car.

She turned at the top of the stairs. "I love you Papa." It was out before she could stop it, and she could see that the public proclamation both embarrassed and pleased him in a most heartfelt way. She gave a quick wave and disappeared into the car.

Gertrude settled into a high backed seat, relishing the sun that streaked through the window and warmed the embrace of the butterscotch leather. This was not her first trip to New Bedford, but it was her first journey there by train, and certainly her first one alone. Although nervous, she was looking forward to it, and the views she would have of Boston Harbor and the ocean vistas in Quincy before the train turned inland.

The train lurched into motion after what seemed like no time at all, and shortly following, Dorchester Bay came into view, the water a steel gray and the chop covered in frothy white. It looked cold, even in the bright sunlight. Gertrude realized that it would not be long before winter iced it over, sending shelves of frozen salt wedges to pile on the shores. And the thought made her happy. She so loved winter.

Changing trains in Taunton, and seeking help from a

porter to move her large bags, her father's words about pickpockets came back to her. But holding her purse closely, she found nothing of a disturbing nature, and after tipping the helpful man, happily settled in for the rest of the journey.

It seemed like the train had barely left Taunton, when they pulled into the station at New Bedford. Of course, her light nap had certainly helped pass the time.

She wrestled with her own bags this time until a liveried young man offered his assistance. Upon explaining her destination, he quickly showed her to the proper spot under a brightly striped green tin roof where she would wait for the next conveyance to her hotel.

There were several other young people waiting with her, and she had a feeling they were chorus members, well acquainted with each other as they chattered like magpies amongst themselves. She smiled at the group and it wasn't long before they included her in their youthful enthusiasm. A lovely young man in the assemblage gave her a hand up when their transportation arrived, and the short trip was ever so jolly.

Bancroft House was just ahead according to the driver of the horse car that took them from the station. Gertrude craned her neck to get a first look. The hotel was an imposing edifice of brick; three floors rising up from the street. It wasn't particularly inviting, but she knew that many times the plain exterior of these hotels gave way to luxurious accommodations.

It was exciting to Gertrude that the hotel was on the same street as the New Bedford Grand Opera House. Gertrude dreamed of performing at that august venue some day.

The group alighted from the trolley and a hotel porter was quickly at their side to retrieve luggage. She tried to appear worldly as she was swept from the street into the—much to her delight—splendidly appointed lobby, but truly her excitement was so great that everyone around must hear her heart beating hard and loud in her chest.

Bumping around amidst the group she wondered what to do next. But as the chorus members dispersed, being welcomed by other exuberant voices, she was left with a clear view of the registration desk.

She approached the check in counter, ornate with Purbeck marble and gold filigree, and waited, second in line while the young clerk finished up with a mustachioed older gentleman attired in a fine dove colored cutaway morning coat. She noticed the more stylish dark ditto suit on the clerk as the previous guest moved on, and the nattily attired employee turned and gestured her forward.

"May I be of service to you, Ma'am?" His smile became more genuine as he, perhaps, gave more attention to single, women guests.

"I'm here with the singing company performing for the New Bedford Choral Association. I believe we have a block of rooms under reservation?" She'd been told by Idell that her low, husky voice was attractive, almost as beguiling as her heart shaped face, chestnut curls gathered at the back of her neck, and pure, deep brown eyes. If that was bunk, Gertrude couldn't prove it by the warm attention she was receiving from the young man checking her in.

"If I could please have your name, I will be more than happy to look up your room number." The clerk poured on the charm and grace.

"Gertrude Edmands. Miss Gertrude Edmands." She managed a bit coquettishly. She could see that the young gentleman was taken with her appearance and again, Idell had taught her to respond to these situations with a just a touch of shy flirtatiousness. Laughingly, it seemed to come naturally for Gertrude.

"Miss Edmands. Yes. We have your reservation. You, and the rest of your group are staying on the third floor. Your rooms overlook the park so as not to be disturbed by the street noises." He seemed very pleased to report this to her and she dimpled up at him, flashing him a smile with her perfect, white teeth.

"Thank you for your thoughtfulness." Her eyelashes swept down to hide any look that hinted at her surety that he had nothing at all to do with the company's room placement, while he continued.

"You will be sharing a room with a Miss Idell Miles, and I see that she has already checked in. I'll have the bellhop bring your baggage." He made a gesture and a spotless youth appeared from nowhere.

"If you will be so kind as to follow him to the lift, Miss Edmands, he will show you to your room. And please do not hesitate to let us know if there is anything additional that you require." With a cheeky grin, the clerk handed the bellhop a room key and was almost successful in suppressing an appreciative sigh as Gertrude turned and walked smartly across the deep plush carpet of the lobby.

The lift doors closed behind Gertrude and she felt her confidence bubble up. There was nothing like a little male attention to raise the spirits and make one feel on top of the world. The only thing that gave her greater satisfaction was her singing. When she was in full voice, there was nothing on earth that made her feel more alive.

She had been singing professionally for seven years with various choral societies and before that, her life had been all about lessons and recitals and private party debuts. She knew she had a unique gift and was pleased to be able to use it, especially now that her mother and father were slowing down in their careers. Her father was still singing, but the venues were smaller and the work more sporadic. Her mother seemed tired and Gertrude didn't think that her teaching would continue much longer.

Suddenly she felt a burst of homesickness and realized that for the first time she would have no one to give her a quick, good luck squeeze before she went on stage. Nor would there be a family member—of whom she counted Martha as one—in the audience to cheer her on. The reality of being alone sobered her up, but then the lift door opened and suddenly there was Idell, vivaciously chatting up an elderly woman. And just like that, Gertrude's short, introspective mood lifted.

"Gertrude." Idell practically threw herself into her friend's arms as she stepped from the elevator. "I was just telling Mrs. Stone, here, about our glorious new group and how she must come see us do Handel's *Messiah* as she has never seen it done before."

Gertrude took in Idell from the top of her head to the tip of her toes, and as always, everything about Idell was over-the-top: her colorful dress, her midnight black hair and snapping gray eyes, but mostly her unbridled enthusiasm. Idell could make something out of nothing, and she was intent on ringing all of the glory possible from their upcoming nights singing at the Pleasant Street Church. Mind you, it wasn't a small venue. There were three nights of performances organized by the New Bedford Choral Association and they had been told that the shows were nearly all sold out. This, of course, was due primarily to the fact that they had obtained the services of George Parker, a most illustrious and well known tenor, along with the Boston Symphony Orchestra to headline.

Gertrude had yet to meet Mr. Parker. He had recently been performing with the Handel and Hayden Society, so the *Messiah* practices had required a stand-in. Idell was familiar with him, having sung with him on different occasions and she assured Gertrude that he would bring magic to the production.

Idell practically danced her way back down the heavily tapestried hall to the room she and Gertrude would share.

"Wait until you see our swank accommodations." She grabbed Gertrude's hands, spinning around mid-hallway. "Green and gold brocade everywhere you look, and the feather bed is divine. Most of the chorus is already here and it's a good thing because the conductor has called a meeting in the private dining room in two hours. I wonder if George will show up on time." She threw the words up in the air, willy-nilly, to be considered by Gertrude or not. Her mind worked so rapidly that she was always on to the next thing before allowing comment.

Using her key, she opened their door and the bellhop deposited Gertrude's bags in the entry way. Gertrude fumbled in her reticule for a coin but Idell was quicker and tipped the youngster, giving him a quick, playful, peck on the cheek before pushing him out the door. "Off you go, huckleberry." She winked at Gertrude. "Don't call us, we'll call you."

She closed the door behind his reddening ears. "That will give him something to talk about with his friends tonight." She paused briefly. "Why don't you have a good look around and unpack your things. I'm going down the hall to use the woman's water closet. I've taken a peek at it already. It's quite lovely. Completely decked out with copper fixtures." She grabbed her purse off of the bed and exited in a blur.

Gertrude slowly unpinned the hat from her head and shook her curls out in relief. She removed her gloves, and then with an impish disregard for propriety sat on the sinfully soft bed and quickly discarded her shoes. She wiggled her toes in glorious relief and let them hit the bare floor with a satisfying slap before tackling her bags. She had almost finished when a knock came on the door.

Thinking that in her haste Idell must have forgotten her key, Gertrude skipped to the door and pulled it open. Her mind went blank, then synapses began firing wildly. Oddly, the only word that came to mind was a piece of Idell's slang that Gertrude had never used before. "Fizzing," was the word that rang in her brain. Simply fizzing.

"Well hello there." The voice that emerged from the dapper man was smooth and cultured. "I'm looking for Idell, but I'm assuming you must be the esteemed Miss Edmands?"

When Gertrude finally found her voice, she addressed the stunning gentleman in front of her and extended her hand.

"Yes, I'm Gertrude Edmands," she whispered, with none of the sauciness that had come to her so easily with the hotel clerk. "And you must be Mr. Parker."

Mr. Parker, indeed. Why hadn't anyone thought to warn her of how handsome the singer was? He stood tall, perhaps six feet, with natty clothes hanging easily on his lanky frame. One well-placed sandy curl dipped sinfully across his tanned forehead, making him look like he'd just come in from a sail, and bright blue eyes held her mesmerized.

Gertrude's lips moved without emitting a sound before she shook herself and was able to speak further. "It's a pleasure to meet you."

He raised one perfect eyebrow, and gave her a heart-stopping smile. "I assure you, Miss Edmands," He perused her slowly, from the top of her mussed curls to the bare toes that peeked out from beneath her frock while she held her breath. "The pleasure is all mine."

And instead of shaking her hand, he lifted her knuckles to his lips. Gertrude was instantly lost.

# Chapter Five

June 1888

Twenty years old and feeling invincible, Fred Torrey perched atop one of the highest points in Boston. The final pieces of steel on the nine story structure had just been secured and Fred made sure he was one of the first to stand atop what was soon to become the Tudor Apartments on the corner of Beacon and Joy Streets. The Queen Anne style architecture was starting to take shape and would blossom as the brick work progressed upwards. He gazed down and across the street to the Boston Common, waving jauntily as a pedestrian gaped up at him. Turning almost 180 degrees, he found himself with a bird's eye view of the Charles River, not too far in the distance. He fancied breathing a fresher, salt tinged air from his high vantage point. Certainly, he thought, it was grand to be young and involved with the construction industry in Boston.

After finishing high school three years ago, Fred hadn't been sure what his next step would be. His father, working as a senior clerk for the renowned Henry Hobson Richardson, had offered him an office boy position, but Fred already knew he was not cut out for an indoor existence.

Therefore, after some discussion, and using his connections in the industry, Mr. Torrey found Fred an apprentice position with a major construction firm.

He had started out picking up scrap lumber and nails from

the heights of various projects where other helpers dared not go, then moved on to making cuts and sizing materials while working far above street level. Fred eventually opted to work longer and later than the other apprentices and by doing so, gained experience. The older men on the job began to trust him and eventually imparted the secrets of their craft. Now, three years later after his introduction to the trades, he was part of a crew who was responsible for building this imposing edifice. And every day, at the end of 10 hours, Fred went home tired and proud.

Home was a one room, cold water walk-up with a shared privy in the back, at 130 State Street. He had a surprisingly well appointed room—thanks to his mother and a family penchant for hand-me-down furniture—all to himself for the sum of two dollars and fifteen cents per week. Considering that his wages had risen to nine dollars and forty eight cents for his week of work, he was living well, eating steak and potatoes at the local pub every night for twenty cents and then sending the rest of his pay home for his father to put away. If he saved just five dollars a week, in two years he would have a down payment on a home of his own, which pleased him no end

But at the moment, Fred was not thinking of home or family or savings. They were the farthest thing from his mind, as he balanced and monkeyed his way down the framed structure to reach street level. His work day was through and it was time to find both food and camaraderie.

He headed off at a brisk pace to his favorite spot down by the wharves where he could count on his friends to poke fun at him for his aversion to seafood. He could also count on them to tease him about his current fixation on a young lady who, last month, had begun coming into the eating establishment every night with a group who looked to be her co-workers.

Each evening he would watch her covertly while enjoying his steak and his friend's lively conversation. Fred's buddies could clearly see the direction of his interest, but as several of them were working on assignations of their own, none wanted to put the kibosh on Fred's luck.

This evening seemed to be starting out luckier than most, as Fred's arrival time at the stone fronted pub coincided with that of the lady in question. She brought up the rear of her group of friends who proceeded, single file, through the red wooden door that was so small, it would have better accommodated a twelve year old. It almost looking like an afterthought, carved out of the mortar. Fred got as close to the woman as he could without causing her alarm, and imagined that he caught a whiff of lavender perfume. His heart sang.

All but two of the ladies passed through the door when a sudden commotion from within rattled the others who were trying to enter. A large inebriated gentleman—who refused to wait his turn—barreled out into the group, attempting to emerge onto the street before the doorway was clear. One women in the group was instantly knocked to the ground, and the hand bag of the lavender smelling beauty in front of him hit the walkway.

Fred, without a second thought, grabbed the offending man by the lapels and wrenched him out of everyone's way, throwing him clear of flailing petticoats. In a seamless move, he scooped the first fallen girl up into his arms at the same time snagging Miss Lavender's purse from the ground.

Soft curves crushed into his chest as he shifted his suddenly pleasant burden. One hand stayed firmly around a slender waist, while the other, from beneath bent knees, eagerly offered the retrieved bag back to the woman of his dreams.

Mere moments before, Fred would have been ecstatic at any interaction with his lavender girl, but now, dammit, he was thoroughly distracted. His attention toggled back and forth between his dream female and the rescued damsel, whose weight seemed somehow to fit perfectly in his arms.

"Miss?" Fred gave up the purse, less reluctantly than he might have previously imagined, and lowered his eyes to his warm burden. "Are you injured?"

He was completely oblivious to the gaggle of her friends crowding around until they began to speak.

"Maude. Are you all right?" More than one voice raised the question.

Maude seemed to be having trouble catching her breath, lost under the twisted weight of her bonnet. She struggled to free herself from the lace and ribbons, finally able to suck in a great burst of air when her head covering was no longer askew. It was now Fred's turn to have trouble with his breathing. Staring up at him was the face of an angel, and it was ablaze with anger.

"What the devil was that all about?" She cursed unwittingly. Then realizing she was suspended by an unknown male, made a noise that Fred interpreted as "Eeep."

His arm tingled where it was now making contact with her lush behind, and just like that, the previous object of his desires completely faded away. Fred let himself be swept up in this new and unexpected development.

"Begging your pardon, miss," he soothed down at her. "I didn't mean to be so familiar, but I needed to get you out of harm's way." Fred nodded in the direction of the stumbling drunk, and reluctantly, before she could take exception to his contact with her rounded bottom, he let her feet fall gently to the ground and uncurled his other forearm from around her waist after deciding she was well enough to stand.

"That's quite all right." She coughed and studiously avoided his gaze, attempting to calm herself while pulling her short jacket down into place. "Thank you for coming to my aid." She raised deep, brown eyes slowly to his and Fred captured her look with his appreciative green stare.

She shook herself free of his steady regard. "What an awkward way to bring about an introduction." But circumstances had clearly made her bold and she thrust her hand forward. “My name is Maude Lindsay.”

Fred shook the proffered hand with vigor. “I'm Fred…Fred Torrey.” He gestured that she should move ahead of him and into the pub where her friends had retreated to reconvene. Once they reached her group, Fred couldn’t stop himself from making an offer. “Would you and your companions care to join my group for supper?” The invitation came out spontaneously but he knew his buddies would be all for it. Odd, but he didn't seem to be able to keep his grin under control, nor his eyes off of the enchanting Miss Lindsay.

“What do you say, girls?” Maude intoned to the rest of her party. “Should we join Mr. Torrey’s group of gentlemen?”

With affirmative nods all around, both factions, male and female moved from the doorway where the young men had been keeping an interested eye on the goings-on. A quick shuffling of chairs and introductions all around led to a shedding of coats. Before long everyone was seated, had ordered, and a lively discussion ensued encompassing the discovery of shared friends, who knew whose sister, and what one did for work.

Maude and Fred sat a little apart from the rest of the group, their chairs close but not touching. Smiles and shy glances indicated their mutual attraction, and Fred’s world seemed once again, larger and more fortuitous than one man clearly deserved. His future fairly crackled with possibilities.

# Chapter Six

August 1890

"He's married." Idell hissed across the small, Queen Anne style table, drinking morning tea in yet another hotel dining room on their tour.

Gertrude had the good graces to blush under her friend's unexpected tirade.

"I can't believe you would even contemplate such a thing," she added.

"I've told you," Gertrude assured Idell. "He means to leave his wife. He's sworn to me that there's no love in their relationship. He only married her to procure someone for his daughter's care after his first wife died."

"I know what he told you, Gertrude, but I've met the woman. She is a force to be reckoned with. I know for a fact that George can't do without her. She organizes his life while he cavorts on the road. She doesn't just care for his daughter, she also runs a successful boarding house on Commonwealth Avenue that gives him enough money for his extravagances. Listen to me. You cannot do this and you mustn't."

Gertrude fretted but with a firm resolve. She'd thought that Idell, of all people would understand. Idell, whom she had performed with, night after night starting with that wonderful week in New Bedford, and culminating with this cross country tour. Idell, who had seen her through emotional upheavals and storms concerning this very same issue as, over the ensuing passage of time, it continued to eat Gertrude alive.

This was not a situation that Gertrude was rushing into. It had been three years since she'd met George, and even though she had been smitten immediately, she had behaved herself all this time, not rising to his blatant flattery and overt attentions.

Three years she had worked hard at ignoring him, throwing herself into her craft and trying to get thoughts of him out of her head. But now, now he had come to her and promised that he was leaving his wife; that if Gertrude would simply give him the surety that he needed, the commitment he was looking for, he would go ahead with plans for a divorce and then undertake arrangements for their future. Together.

"Gertrude, I know you're tired, we're all tired. It's been a long trip and we're not even close to going home. George is just lonely, you know, like men get. He's just a fancy Dan looking for a fling. Do you understand what I'm saying? Please don't do this."

Gertrude was twenty seven years old, and even though her experience with men was very minimal, she had been on the road with the Boston Festival Orchestra for nearly three months now and witnessed all of the nocturnal comings and goings that went hand in hand with such a trip. Of course she knew what Idell was saying, but she was tired of listening. This was her time and this was her man, she was sure of it.

"Idell, while we were down south, I listened to you. You told me to wait, that my feelings would change and that I would become interested in someone else. I did as you said. I waited. But you have to know that my mind hasn't changed. I still love him and it's time for me to tell him."

Idell groaned and put her head in her hands.

"I can't believe you think he returns your feelings. I'm

telling you right now, he will never leave his wife. You will be his distraction on the road and as soon as we get back to Boston you'll be dropped like a hot potato."

Gertrude picked up her delicate tea cup and took a long sip to hide her face. She wanted her friend to think she felt strong and secure in her decision. Because, yes, she was going to go ahead with this...affair. But, no, she was not sure of anything where George was concerned. She simply knew that she wanted him in a way that was completely impossible to ignore and she was tired of waiting. At her age, most of her friends were long since married. Even Idell, although she had kept her stage name, had been happily married for two years, and kept herself faithful while on the road. As much of a smart aleck as she appeared on the surface, Idell was a traditionalist when it came to relationships.

Gertrude knew her friend could never approve of what she was about to do. As much as she needed a confidante, she would try not to involve Idell in any way, from this point on.

"I'm sorry you feel that way, but it's my decision to make, isn't it?" She put her cup down with more authority than she felt and changed the subject abruptly. "I understand we'll be getting some new chorus members arriving today."

Idell sighed but went along with her red herring. "Scuttlebutt has it that we're in need of more depth. Some of the local reviews we've received recently have been less than stellar, so Mr. Chadwick has called up more voices from Boston."

Mr. Chadwick was the director of their tour, and they all trusted him implicitly when it came to direction and public relations. The new recruits would be arriving shortly. They had been practicing back in Boston for several weeks. The existing company all hoped that the integration would go seamlessly. Idell was optimistic.

"I'm looking forward to a few new faces." She sighed purposefully. "Perhaps there'll be some nice young man in the group who will sweep you off your feet."

Idell's sarcastic snort didn't register. Gertrude's head was already in another place. "I'm going to head out for a bit. I noticed a lovely hat shop just a few blocks down the street, and I'm anxious to get a fitting." Gertrude knew her excuse to leave the table and the hotel was transparent. During the last of their one sided exchange, George had emerged from the lift and now lingered near a small news stand while glancing across the lobby, her way.

"Go then." Her friend's eyes were troubled as they looked up at Gertrude. "But be careful, will you?"

Gertrude's quickening heart allowed for only the briefest smile at Idell. She was caught up by another pair of eyes, beckoning through the wide double doors of the breakfast room. She quickly discarded her napkin on the table and rose to her feet, fairly floating across the room. When she reached George, his hand briefly brushed Gertrude's before he wordlessly enticed her around the few stragglers in the lobby and out onto the street.

Idell made a moue of displeasure as she watched her friend depart. "You have no idea, the heartbreak you're letting yourself in for." She took a last sip of her tea and made to head upstairs to her room, taking the grand staircase instead of the elevator. The carpeted stairs, wide at the bottom, swept in a semi-circle across the front of the hotel, windows opening up the vista of the main street below. She glanced out of the large panes at the top and, looking down, witnessed Gertrude's animated face turned up in the direction of her companion, as if for a kiss. She wondered if it were the glass or her emotions that distorted the scene.

Vaguely, she became aware that a commotion was occurring in the lobby. She turned from her vantage point, high above, and saw a dozen boisterous young people elbowing their way amongst each other to be first to reach the front desk. It was the new recruits. At that moment, she felt very old. Sighing, she went down the stairs to be a self-appointed welcoming committee, hoping it would take her mind off of troubles.

"Children, children," she yelled loudly over the din. "I'm Idell Miles and I suggest that you save some of this enthusiasm for the show later." The group tittered but yielded to this new authority. "Unfortunately, there's not enough room at the inn, as they say, so each of you will be rooming with some of the company that are already here. I am eagerly expecting a third in our room." This accompanied by an eye-roll that evoked the proper response from the crowd.

"Get your assignments and we'll meet in the lobby at 6:00PM sharp to head off to the Opera House. Do not be late." The last, she said in an imperative tone, then leaned back against the nearest wall to see which one of the youngsters she would be claiming.

One by one, they moved through the queue until there remained only one woman, certainly not in the first blush of youth. She looked about the same age as Gertrude. Dressed stylishly, but obviously within modest means, she had a secure, no nonsense posture which Idell was drawn to immediately. The woman signed in, smiled prettily and turned to where Idell was waiting.

"Well, it looks like you are stuck with me," she said. "But I'm very quiet and you'll hardly know that I'm around."

"That will be great for a room-mate, but won't go over quite so well in the show. I'll just be fine if you don't snore."

The new woman laughed.

"No snoring that I know of." She held out her hand. "I'm pleased to meet you. I've followed your career for some time now."

"Oh, so you are a fan?" Idell used the popular new slang term and received a puzzled look in return. "Don't mind me. I like to keep up with the kids." Still not quite understanding, the woman gave Idell a shrug, and bent to her suitcases.

Idell offered a hand. “I think we should go up and get you settled.” She grabbed one of the bags from the floor. “I didn't catch your name.”

The petite, but far from mousy brunette, trolled her eyes around the ornate lobby, ogling the splendor before settling back on Idell.

“I'm Edith Torrey… from Boston,” her voice was just a little breathless. “And I have to tell you that, so far, this is probably one of the most exciting moments of my life.”

“Is that so, Edith Torrey from Boston.” Idell winked. “I'm just glad you said, ‘so far’.”

# Chapter Seven

April 1891

*For Sale: Gorham-Lincoln estate in Hingham at Rocky Nook. Nine room home, barn and three and one half acres of arable land. Nearby Boston train. Please inquire by post to Mrs. Catherine K. Lincoln, East Street,*
*Hingham, Massachusetts.*

Gertrude clutched the advertisement from the Boston Herald and knocked gently on the study door. She entered and looked fondly toward the now balding head of her father, leaning distractedly over some new musical scores.

"Papa, may I speak with you or are you too occupied at present?" Gertrude knew her voice held just enough hesitation to bring her father's gaze away from his papers.

"What is it, child? You know I always have time for you." He smiled affectionately and gestured to the upholstered chair across from his imposing mahogany desk and she sat, albeit on the very edge.

"Hardly a child, Papa. I'll be thirty in a few years." She scoffed.

"Well then, my ancient one, I'd better make time for you now lest you whither away to nothing before my eyes." He spied the paper, much abused, in her grasp. "Would it have anything to do with that worn out scrap that you've carried in here?"

"Yes Papa, it would. You see I've been thinking about branching out a bit; making use of my savings." She stole a glance to gauge his reaction. Mr. Edmands' face remained characteristically neutral, which was his tendency with all things until pertinent facts were revealed.

"I've found this advertisement for a house in Hingham. You know I've been doing quite a bit of singing on the South Shore lately, and I'm really quite taken with the area. This particular residence is close to the church where I've performed for the Musical Association of Cohasset. It is also a very short distance to Melville Gardens where *you've* played numerous times in the past. I was interested in your thoughts on the matter."

She had many more things to add, but decided to wait for her father's response. She thrust the advertisement across the desk and held her breath while he perused it carefully.

"We've been very content having you live with us Gertrude." He glanced up over his glasses and smoothed the paper absently on his blotter. "I would hate to think that this reflects an unhappiness on your part to continue living here," he paused, "with us."

"Papa, no. Of course not." She sought to soothe feelings she had not meant to ruffle. "You know I have always enjoyed being here with you. It's just that I feel the need to try something new. I have been coddled and spoiled by you and Mama and Martha for so long, I'd like to discover what it's like to manage a household of my own." Her eyes pleaded understanding, and as her father clearly struggled to come to grips with this new turn of events, Gertrude continued.

"This might not even be the right residence, but I know you and Mama have talked about retiring to the country in a few years time, and this house would be big enough to accommodate all of us if, eventually, you wanted to join me." Gertrude added the last with a sincerity that obviously touched her father since he became slightly melancholy.

“Well, I'm not ready to give up things in the city just yet, my dear. And you know your mother still enjoys the amenities of our fair metropolis.” He most likely reflected on the corner market and the dress shop within a block that Hannah had frequented for more years than Gertrude had been alive.

Her father steepled his fingers. “I realize that life moves on,” he sighed, “sometimes more rapidly than one would like. In any case,” he brought up one hand to rub his eyes, “this isn’t about me, this is about you, my model daughter. And you are correct. It is past time for you to explore your own path in life.

“If you want to take a look at this property, I'd be pleased to go with you. I happen to know that you and I both have an unencumbered weekend on our schedules in two weeks time.”

Her father kept track of everyone's engagements.

“The spring buds will be blooming heartily by then.”

He surprised her with his quick capitulation. She had a dozen more persuasive arguments to which she had yet to resort. “Thank you, Papa,” she responded with sincerity. “That will be grand.” She clapped her hands. “I'll write to Miss. Lincoln today and see if I can arrange a meeting.” She leaned over and kissed his cheek before practically dancing from the room. Her father, clearly witnessing her less-than-modest exit, was left chuckling.

Gertrude hurried to her room and immediately penned a letter to Hingham. She included her dates of availability, sealed the envelope, and then trusting no one with her missive, walked the letter a half a mile to the post office and posted it herself. It was possible her letter could reach Hingham by water mail packet in just a few days, but then it would depend on which day or days of the week Miss. Lincoln went into town to pick up her correspondence. Gertrude would start checking her post office box for a reply as early as the beginning of next week.

Her happy thoughts stilled for a moment as she remembered the last conversation she'd had with Idell. Her friend was not one for letting her off the hook, and when Gertrude had run the "buying a house in the country" by her, Idell had scoffed and guessed, rightly, that part of the attraction would be having a remote location in which Gertrude could entertain George. Their trysts were becoming difficult to maneuver with Gertrude living at home and George still residing with his wife. And the various companies with whom they traveled were, on the whole, not slow-witted, so they'd had to become as discreet as possible with their liaisons on the road as well. George was inordinately worried for her reputation, something that they disagreed on. Gertrude was sure that her reputation would suffer no consequences as soon as George announced he would be leaving his wife, but George was vehement that they keep their affair secret. Oh, wouldn't he be pleased if she purchased a country property and began feathering a nest for the two of them? A country estate for the distinguished Mr. and Mrs. George Parker. She could hardly wait.

****

When Gertrude and her father arrived in Hingham on a warm spring Saturday morning a few weeks later, the town livery picked them up at the Old Colony House train station, and Gertrude could hardly contain her excitement.

The cart started off slowly, but as they cleared the platform, the horse picked up speed and trotted briskly over Broad Bridge, affording them their first breathtaking view of a vast salt marsh. The grand marsh—Gertrude knew—was at one time part of Hingham Harbor, but some enterprising souls had reclaimed land from sea by erecting flood gates to turn a mill. Now a meandering salt stream with marsh grasses and marine vegetation, well known as either The

Home Meadows or Hingham Meadows, stretched beyond those gates from the central village to stately Main Street. It enchanted Gertrude as it did every time she visited the South Shore.

"Isn't it lovely, Papa?" She enthused. Her father wrinkled his nose at the rotten egg smell.

"Certainly daughter. There is nothing more appealing than the odor of mud flats in the morning." His smile let her know that he was enjoying the scenery as well, but was reserving judgement on the whole enterprise.

The carriage continued up the rise of Summer Street to the top of Neck Gate Hill where they were witness to a dazzling view of the harbor below dotted with its many cottages. White, billowing sails caressed the breeze off the sparkling blue water and gave the whole of it a fairy land guise. If Gertrude was not truly taken before, she was now ecstatic and not to be put off.

"Father, you can't tell me that there is a more beautiful vista anywhere between here and Somerville."

"You mean besides Boston's Castle Island, May Pole Hill in Quincy and Hunts Hill in Weymouth?" he quipped, but then agreed with Gertrude.

"Lovely." He emoted. "Quite lovely and unrivaled, I'm sure."

The driver turned sharply onto Summer Street and headed inland, eventually crossing the train tracks and approaching the rear of the property on East Street.

"That will be the house you're looking for." The driver pointed to a red colonial style residence nestled comfortably into the trees just ahead.

"Could you stop for one moment?" Gertrude questioned, already moving from her seat.

The driver brought the hack to a stop with a tug on the reins and hopped down to assist Gertrude who alighted with alacrity. As he regained his perch, she surveyed the back of the property with a keen eye, taking in the varied roof-lines, crooked chimney and flower gardens—still tangled with the previous year's detritus—encroaching up the back of the house. Her gaze wandered toward the barn, noting that it needed paint but was impressive in size. It would be an artist's dream to capture the asymmetry of the euonymus vine clinging to the weathered wooden shingles. A half sigh escaped her.

"Bigger than I thought," she muttered, mostly to herself. "But not unmanageable. Older than I imagined, as well." Her finger tapped thoughtfully at her lower lip. "Well, there's only one way to find out."

She waved the driver off as he made to climb down and assist her, making her own way back up into the conveyance, and declaring, "Carry on."

The handler brought them around to where the house in question fronted on East Street. It sat no more than fifty feet back from the road with the lush spring-green lawn that rolled up to the front door complementing the muted red of the clapboards. A few of the black shutters leaned slightly askew, but the charm of the house was in no way diminished by their disorderliness.

"Maybe yellow with black trim," thought Gertrude to herself. "But not necessarily right away because I might get used to the red."

The driveway lay to the right of the house front, and as the driver turned in Gertrude was given a lovely first look at the edifice of the barn. There was a large, central door—also black like the house trim—that stood open, rolled that way upon an upper track. Smaller, double doors to either side of that were clearly used more often, and large enough for horses and other livestock. Gertrude hopped down as the driver pulled close and had a quick look in, observing a deep, planked space on the ground floor, backed up by a partial upper story.

Moving her eyes outward, the land to the left of the structure swept away, past a fieldstone retaining wall, and revealed what was most likely a basement level. Certainly, she snickered to herself, there was plenty of room to do anything "barn-like" that might come to mind.

Several, smaller ancillary out-buildings dotted the property, for which her city breeding could come up with no name. She assumed that all would be revealed in a guided, extensive tour.

Gertrude rounded the corner to the left of the barn—careful not to tumble off the retaining wall—and perused an obviously well tended field out back, although it was impossible to tell the nature of the crop from her vantage point. She strained to see more when a small upright figure with wispy gray hair caught her attention. The elderly woman made surprisingly good speed across the back yard and was headed in their direction.

"Hello," the small woman called out, waving her hand as she approached. "Hello."

From what Gertrude could see, she was dressed completely in black, right down to her serviceable shoes and there was no hesitation in her step as she advanced up the incline toward the group.

Gertrude had already moved in the woman's direction as her father alighted from the carriage, paid the driver and asked him to return in two hours time. The livery man agreed, happy to have a paying fare on a slow weekend day, and departed down a winding back driveway that deposited him onto Summer Street once again.

Gertrude smoothed her skirts and turned toward the older woman as she reached them. "You must be Miss Lincoln." Gertrude put her hand forward to have it immediately captured by two small dry ones that did not let go, as sharp black eyes pierced into hers. Gertrude tried not to be affronted by the frank perusal being conducted, but instead continued. "I am Gertrude Edmands, and this is my father, Thomas Edmands."

"Yes, I received your letter inquiring about the house."

The strange little greeter paused for another look at Gertrude. “You are an unmarried woman then?”

“I am.” Gertrude spoke forthrightly. She was used to the initial judgment of people, questioning her unmarried status as she advanced in years, and she waited for the plethora of insensitive questions that inevitably followed. Mrs. Lincoln surprised her.

“Good.” She nodded, then gestured with her arm. “Would you and your father care to see the inside of the property first or the land and out-buildings?” She continued as if she had not just completely flummoxed her company. “Oh, no. That’s wrong. I've completely forgotten to offer you refreshment after your trip from Boston. We'll start off inside then, shall we? I have some cakes put aside as well as a freshly brewed pot of tea.”

Miss Lincoln began walking toward the house. “Come on then.” Without looking back, she led them across a small expanse of lawn, through a back, screened door and into a long, cool room which boasted a massive fireplace along one wall. Smooth and golden, the pumpkin pine surrounding the fireplace looked ancient by any standards. Each highly polished board was easily sixteen inches wide. To one side of the main, bricked chamber, a small, iron door had been left open to reveal a large, beehive oven which looked like it might still used for cooking bread.

“We've shut down the fire in the main house for the season. It’s normally used from October to May to heat the house and to cook, until the room becomes unbearably hot with the weather, and then we rely on the summer kitchen.” She preceded them to the right, and straight through a passageway with stairs leading upward on one side and another doorway outside to the left. Although neither Gertrude nor her father were very tall, they both fought the urge to tuck their heads as they walked into the room Miss Lincoln had deemed the summer kitchen.

The room was long, like the one where they had first

entered, but unlike its predecessor which was enhanced with fashionable eight foot plaster ceilings, this kitchen had low, dark beams running its width in intervals of two feet. These beams were suspended at less than six feet and anyone taller than that would be unable to remain upright. Miss Lincoln, short of stature, seemed oblivious to this and they quickly discovered why.

"I've been in this house since I was born," she began as they found chairs around the scarred oak table in the center of the room. "I know every inch, and every nook and cranny." She chuckled, "I also know quite a good number of scandalous events that have occurred here during my lifetime and the lifetimes of my ancestors. I want you to know that owning this house is not for the faint of heart."

Gertrude and her father exchanged surreptitious glances and were both clearly amused.

"My Great-Grandfather, Stephen Cushing, built this house on the land of his father in 1751, and brought his bride here. Their daughter, Mary, married Gorham Lincoln and continued to live here and were blessed with many offspring, one of them my grandfather who married Catherine Kilby. I am the youngest of my parents' brood, my mother being born a Thaxter. That makes me Catherine Kilby Thaxter Lincoln, although you may call me Kate. I am the last one of my brothers and sisters remaining on this earth." She paused to take a sip of her tea. "I am still quite young at sixty-six years of age—Gertrude had pegged her as older—and have a mind to do some traveling, which I cannot to do as long as I am bound to this house."

Gertrude's father spoke up, politely. "Am I to understand that this residence has been in your family for five generations?" Somehow he had kept track.

"Six, if you count the fact that one of my nephews briefly inherited the house before he took himself off eleven years ago to assist in the construction of the Panama Canal and has never been heard from, since." She delivered this last piece of startling news quite matter-of-factly, but Gertrude supposed that she'd had sufficient time to get used to the idea.

During Kate's monologue—which continued—Gertrude perused her surroundings.

A small fireplace to her left was lit, giving off a cheery warmth, and at her back was a small alcove which she could only imagine held an unusual indoor well, if the bucket and wheel hanging above the opening was any indication. The floors, ceiling and walls were all of wood in various mellow shades, but the room did not seem dark, just inviting. Gertrude was amazed at how comfortable the place made her feel. The house seemed already to be wrapping itself around her. She shook off the strange feeling, and brought up the question of the opening behind her.

"Is that a well?" Gertrude inquired, pointing to the corner of the room.

"It is. Although we don't have to draw from it with buckets any more. It has pipes that connect it to the kitchen sink, and now all we have to do is use the hand pump to obtain our water."

The Edmands, being from the city, had long since gotten used to running water in their house. They had a large cistern at roof level and a steam-run pump that made water available to all of the taps throughout. It even more than adequately supplied two water closets they had installed just a few years back.

"Your next question will probably be about our sanitary facilities," Miss Lincoln laughed. "I'm sorry to say that we still use the outhouse, but there is plenty of room inside if you care to update and install indoor plumbing."

Gertrude knew this would be one of her first improvements if she purchased the home. Cold treks out of doors at night or in the winter offended her sensibilities, not to mention her personal idea of modern hygiene.

"May we see the rest of the property?" Gertrude asked,

putting down her empty teacup, anxious to see if her good feelings continued throughout the tour.

"Certainly," Kate Lincoln replied, then added cryptically, "And there's no need for you to keep a straight face. I can already see that you're drawn to the house."

With a wide eyed shrug to her father, Gertrude followed their hostess' example and rose to explore the remainder of the rooms.

The first floor consisted of the summer kitchen, and off that—toward a back end—a step-down, dirt floored room that held wood for the fireplaces and, by the smell, some sort of animals in colder weather. They headed back to the large keeping room, or winter kitchen, and at Gertrude's question, Kate assured her that they still did, indeed, make bread in the brick oven. Mr. Edmands stuck his head into the opening and jokingly asked Gertrude when the last time was that she had made a loaf of bread. She endured the joke with humorous aplomb and was quick to assure her father that she would hire someone to keep food on the table.

A music room stood at the left front of the house, and a large parlor on the right. Three staircases rose to the second floor: one by the summer kitchen, one in the middle of the house, and one in the great hallway opposite the front door that bisected the two front rooms. Miss Lincoln chose to lead them up the front staircase, which took two turns before emerging into a small center hallway at the front of the house.

Off the hall they found an array of bedrooms: two to the left, two to the right and one large room in the middle of them all— above the winter kitchen—that held an enormous wooden loom. All of the rooms, so far, had full fireplaces to keep things cozy during the winter, and were paneled with more of that glorious pumpkin pine paneling. As much as the fireplaces were welcome, Gertrude knew that a brand new coal fired furnace in the basement would be another amenity on her list of improvements.

In the back part of the house, over the summer kitchen, were two more bedrooms, oddly shaped and obviously used only in the warm months as neither had a fireplace. Heat and indoor plumbing would turn them around as well.

Miss Lincoln continued the tour. “We have a walk up third floor, and although it has always remained unfinished, it's a nice place to put children and bedrolls when too much company arrives.” She opened the heavy wooden door with its wrought iron latch and peered up, but declined to ascend. Only Gertrude decided to make the climb to the top of the stairs.

Amazed at the amount of unused space at the top of the house, she envisioned adding several more rooms for the household staff she would need to engage.

Gertrude walked to a center chimney which dominated the space and was about to leave when her eyes were drawn to a window set at an angle into the side of the roof. She went over to it, and bending slightly, got her first glimpse of the scope of the property outside. The barn, the yard and the fields stretched out before her, and in the silence she almost heard them beckon; the house, the land. She shook her head to dispel the momentary fancy, but it seemed, instead, to settle around her like a comfortable mantle.

Before she made it back to the second floor, Gertrude had already made her decision. This house was hers. It might take weeks to finalize the small details, to hammer out the paper work, to make everybody happy, but she knew in her heart that she would never walk away without it.

*Boston Evening Transcript, May 29, 1891*

*“Miss Gertrude Edmands, the well-known contralto, has recently purchased the Gorham-Lincoln estate at Rocky Nook, Hingham, which was recently occupied by Mrs. Catherine Kilby Thaxter Lincoln. Miss Edmands will not occupy it this season, but will eventually, after renovations, make it her permanent residence.”*

# Chapter Eight

June 1892

Fred whistled as he walked briskly through the mud left over from the quick summer storm. His trip took him from Pier 2 at South Bay back to the main office which fronted on Albany Street. His new position as a lumber surveyor for the firm of Curtis and Pope Lumber was a dream come true. As much as he had enjoyed being part of the hands-on building in the construction trade, he could sense—at twenty-four year's old—that his time being comfortable and unaffected by the elements in the great outdoors was fast waning.

Once again aided by his fathers' connections in the industry, he had been given the opportunity to try himself in this new arena. So far, in the two months that he had been here, Fred had proven an asset to the company with his hard work and quick assessments, already devising faster means to move lumber from ship to rail car, or steamer to local packet ship. His skills at improvising were finally proving to be a great advantage. He hoped that his good fortune would carry through to this evening, when he would be meeting Maude after they both got through with work.

His hand went, once again, to the small box in his pocket that he rubbed as a good luck talisman. He had been carrying it around for a week just waiting for the proper moment to bring it out and ask Maude for her hand in marriage. He didn't doubt their love for each other, it was just that Maude was very distracted lately by matters at her family home in Waltham. Maude's mother had, earlier in the year, become ill and left her job as a secretary at the Waltham Watch Company. She had, many weeks after quitting, been diagnosed with an incurable cancer and Maude's father had fallen apart. Now Maude was sending money home to help out and was also absent most weekends, taking the train out late on Friday nights and not arriving back in Boston until the last train in on Sunday. She was beginning to look drawn from all of the worry and travel. Fred had held off on his proposal before the final diagnosis in hopes that things would improve. But now, because Mrs. Lindsay's constitution could only decline, Fred thought it might be prudent to ask for Maude's hand in marriage before the inevitable happened, and perhaps bring her mother some joy knowing that her daughter's future would be assured.

Fred checked the large clock on the exterior of the shed as he passed, and saw that it was only ten minutes before quitting time. Many nights he worked late, but this evening would be the exception. Tonight he would head down Dorchester Ave to meet Maude at a little restaurant they had discovered halfway between his work and the Oakman Manufacturing Firm on Mercer Street where Maude carefully packed glass insulators all day.

Fred began whistling again, this time more from nerves, before grabbing his hat and heading out the door.

They met under the striped canopy, as was their habit, and Fred brushed a quick kiss across one cheek which caused the color to bloom in Maude's face.

"Fred, you know it's not proper to show affection in a public place." She looked around her to make sure no one had seen the exchange.

"I couldn't help myself. You look so charming this evening." And indeed she had donned a pink and white patterned, nip-waisted dress that he had not seen before which accentuated her gentle curves and brought out the color in her blushing cheeks. "Shall we find a seat?"

Fred held the door open and they entered the romantically lit room. No more than fifteen tables graced the small space, but they were early diners and able to choose a table in the far corner that met Fred's requirements for privacy. The waiter greeted them, acknowledging his familiar patrons by bringing them the tea that she would drink and a pint of stout from the tap for Fred. The tiny establishment was run by a young Irish couple, and the food ran toward boiled dinners and cottage pies. This particular evening Maude deliberated before choosing fish and chips while Fred ordered an Irish stew. They settled back companionably, awaiting their meal.

"So how was your mother this weekend?" Fred brought up the subject about which she most wanted to talk. "You look more cheerful than you did last week."

"It's more my father that made the difference this time." Maude folded and unfolded her napkin unconsciously as she spoke. "He seems to be taking some control of himself and of the household. He is finally able to concentrate on keeping the bills paid and the grass trimmed, which takes the anxiety off of mother as she looks about and sees that things are being accomplished. I got her off of the divan on Saturday and into her wheelchair for a quick bit of fresh air since the day was so nice. She seemed cheered to get out and I hope we can do the same again next weekend if the weather keeps improving."

Fred was glad Maude was content with the small boons that had taken place with her parents, and thought that while her mind turned to pleasant things, he would take the opportunity to bring the subject back to them.

"I wouldn't mind accompanying you to Waltham any weekend, you know." He leaned across the table with an earnestness that he knew she had come to expect from him. "Especially if I wanted to meet your father and ask him…" Fred scrambled for words and fumbled in his pocket.

"Oh." exclaimed Maude, her hand suddenly fluttering up

by her throat. She stared at Fred across the table, clearly not knowing what to do but hold her breath.

"…ask him if I might marry his daughter." Fred opened the jeweler's box and three small opals seemed to catch all of the light in the room as they flashed up from their velvet bed. She hesitantly reached for the ring, but then pulled back. Fred caught the small tentative motion, and taking it as partial assent, quickly dropped from his chair to one knee and spoke the words of tradition.

"Maude Lindsay, will you marry me?"

A hush fell over the dining room, with the few patrons and wait staff held silent by the drama unfolding. A collective sigh escaped them as Maude sank to the floor next to Fred.

"Of course, my love, of course, with all of my heart." She leaned toward him until their foreheads touched, and with joy and relief he slid the ring onto her trembling finger.

He couldn't resist the tease, then, that sprang to his lips. "I apologize for displaying my affection in such a public place." And before she could protest he swung her to her feet and twirled her in the air, much to her surprise and to the delight of everyone else in the room. Fred was fairly certain that her laughter and tears absolved him of any crime.

When things had calmed down and the two had settled back in their chairs—still holding hands across the table—the waiter brought their meals and set them down with a brief, yet heartfelt congratulations. Fred picked up his spoon and blindly took a bite while continuing to gaze into Maude's eyes. His countenance went from overjoyed to horrified in an instant. He dropped Maude's hand and gagged in anguish, his mouth working in all the wrong ways.

"What's wrong, Fred?" Maude's look of concern was undone the second she looked at his plate. She clearly didn't mean to giggle, but couldn't help it. The waiter had inadvertently switched their meals. She had been given

Fred's stew and he, her fried seafood. On what was, undoubtedly the single most wonderful night of his life, Fred was relegated to gagging into his napkin. Damn, he thought with tears in his eyes, he hated fish.

# Chapter Nine

July 1892

"In the last couple of months, I've been spending more time in the country than I have in town." During renovations Gertrude had divided her time between Boston and Hingham while plumbers crawled through the house. But with the advent of quiet on the re-modeling front, she now found that the pace of life in Hingham held much greater appeal to her than that of the city.

Gertrude lifted her glass of lemonade, peering through the condensation at the trees surrounding her home. She would never get tired of sitting outside, surveying her property with an appreciative eye. She knew that her friend Idell, however, was not of the same mind. "I adore you for coming to visit again," Gertrude teased. "But I know you only keep coming to the sticks to convince me that I belong back in town."

"Wrong, dearest. I keep coming to make sure you stay sane." Idell looked pointedly Gertrude, who wanted to laugh. Idell thought Gertrude was in danger of jeopardizing her career if she lost touch with her Boston connections. Not so Edith Torrey who had also made the trek to Hingham, accompanying Idell on this particular trip.

"Well I find it quite charming," the younger woman enthused. "And I slept like a top last night with this wonderful country air." It seemed that Edith was not immune to picking up Idell's idioms in the English language. And thank God, she was also not above wanting to play tourist. “Can we see some of the town? I've read a couple of guide books and found some interesting Hingham facts. Did you know the town boasts the oldest continuously used Meeting House in the entire United States?” This question was aimed at Idell, who purported to hate history. Right on cue, Idell groaned.

Gertrude suppressed a giggle. “That would be the Old Ship Meeting House, and it's lovely.” Gertrude looked pointedly at Idell. “The woodwork is even older than what we have here, and, Idell, don't you adore being surrounded by old woodwork?”

Idell wrinkled her nose at the teasing. “Is it my fault that I'm a city girl through and through? I prefer plaster walls, thank you, and if you hadn't installed the water closets, nothing you could have said would have enticed me to visit.”

The extensive work done at Rocky Nook over the past year included a second floor bathroom for Gertrude's guests, and a third floor facility for the household help. The coal fired furnace in the cellar and the cast iron radiators that were now in every room of the house would make the old relic warm and cozy for her winter trysts to the property.

George, although not entirely won over by the house, seemed to be coming around to its charms, and Gertrude was eagerly awaiting his next visit this coming weekend. Her summer after that—despite Idell's fears—was a whirlwind of singing engagements, all local, which would seriously curtail her time with George. She sighed out loud to think that it would be fall before she would be able to make plans with him again.

Idell misinterpreted the sigh and sought to mollify her friends. “Oh, what the heck. I’ll play tourist. We can take a jaunt downtown, and I'd actually enjoy a tour of Melville Gardens.”

“Gertrude, you performed there last year, didn't you?” Edith spoke of the forty three acre park that was chock full of amusements and massive Victorian structures which currently held the town's best restaurants and venues for entertainment.

At Gertrude's nod she continued.

"How wonderful to be able to sing so close to home." Edith's career had not progressed as Gertrude's and Idell's had, but she was content and had begun teaching piano and taking singing pupils at home, to supplement her income.

It certainly helped that she still lived with her mother and father. Gertrude knew that her younger brothers, Fred and Arthur, had long since moved out and there was plenty of space in her parents' home to allot a room for her piano and teaching. But one problem marred her contentment at present, and that was the possibility of the elder Torrey's moving to Wellesley in the near future. It would bring Edith too far away from her students and she was not happy about having to build up clientele in a new area. Also, moving in with Fred was out of the question. He had just recently become engaged, and the wedding, although not yet scheduled, seemed to be coalescing to take place in the winter months. Arthur was not a candidate for roommate either, due to the fact that he already had three very untidy and boisterous young men living with him.

Gertrude tried to stave off Edith's melancholia with a bright enthusiasm for their excursion.

"Let's be off, then. We can do a short tour, some shopping and… Oh, I know, we'll finish at the Clam Bake House in Melville Gardens. You'll love their fried clams. If we stay late enough, we might even be there when they do their illumination. Can you believe they have twenty outdoor electric lights? It looks just like a fairyland."

It was easy to win Edith over, and eventually Idell got caught up in her companions' zeal as they prepared for their outing. Gertrude called her handyman to hitch up the horse. She had become quite adept at handling her own conveyance, and so dismissed him as her friends tucked themselves in and she took the reigns. Gertrude clicked her tongue, flicked her wrists and off they went.

The first thing that Gertrude pointed out, heading south on East Street, was the imposing Agricultural Hall, a large gray, three story Victorian beauty.

"What's that used for?" Edith craned her neck, upward.

"That's Agi, uh, Agricultural Hall," Gertrude answered. "I haven't attended anything there, yet, but they're supposed to have wonderful harvest fairs and farm competitions throughout the summer."

They trotted on, by the Public Library building, yellow and stately on the common, before turning right onto Main Street, down the shaded slope of Pear Tree Hill. Gertrude pointed out the stately mansions that graced Bachelor Row before the three entered the town square.

The Old Ship Meeting House was the first important edifice on the rise to their right, and Gertrude made sure her companions saw it.

"There's the Meeting House you were reading about, Edith." But she kept the horses moving. Idell would not thank her if she stopped to give Edith a longer look. She continued verbally cataloguing the town for her friends. "On the left— that lovely white, clapboarded building—is Loring Hall, where lectures and local entertainment takes place. Next on the right is the illustrious Derby Academy building." She indicated an edifice high up on Cemetery Hill, it was a coeducational school funded by Madam Sarah Derby in the 1700's, and it was running at full capacity these days.

Gertrude next pointed straight ahead. "You can't miss the tall spire of Saint Paul's Church at the apex of Main and North Streets. It makes the other buildings in the square appear minuscule."

Gertrude pulled up to the siding before reaching North Street, and tied the horse off to a post. It was a beautiful day to walk around and sample the charms of the many individual establishments.

The women alighted, and with Gertrude in the lead, headed straight for Hennessy's where Gertrude picked up a much needed button hook. Idell took her time at W.W. Hersey's which had a fine millinery, and ended up ordering a new bonnet to be delivered to Boston the following week. Gertrude couldn't help but feel smug that the city girl had found something fashionable in little old Hingham. The next stop the ladies made was to the Humphrey Brothers emporium where Gertrude made a purchase of Ceylon tea.

The day was fine, the company lively and when the woman moved on and became replete from their late afternoon clam bake—alas, missing the evening lights—they declared the day to be one of the best.

Gertrude was sorry to see her friends depart the next morning, but was eager for the weekend and George's presence.

Procuring the place in Hingham had not, as she had hoped, made their liaisons any more frequent, but the privacy that her home afforded more than made up for the sporadic nature of their time together. She had employed a cook and a household servant, both of whom resided in the third floor apartments. The part-time gentleman who fed her few animals, mowed her fields and hitched her horse, lived down the road and kept very much to himself. She had chosen her staff with care, wanting no hint of scandal to attach itself to either herself or George.

But still she felt like stamping her foot. If he would just get on with his divorce, she would be free to employ whomever she wanted, entertain as she pleased, and eventually have her parents move in with her. All would be well if he would simply be forthcoming with his timetable, and she wasn't going to sit idly by waiting any longer. This weekend she would make it clear to George that she expected a detailed commitment from him so that she could proceed with plans for their future.

# Chapter Ten

*August 5, 1892*

*Hingham Journal, August 5, 1892*
*"We are pleased to report the following pertaining to Miss Gertrude Edmands of Rocky Nook: Her health is wonderfully improved. "*

This small bit of information was buried deep on page two of the weekly paper due to the spectacular story sweeping the country regarding Lizzie Borden of Fall River, Massachusetts who had, purportedly, the previous day murdered both her mother and father with an ax.

Gertrude knew she should welcome this bit of luck, knowing that the Boston papers would not notice this small one line announcement in a local weekly with their zeal to capture the ax murderer story of the year.

"You've gotten lucky, my girl." Idell poked Gertrude where she lay on the divan. "If this news of your recovery had come out on any other day, those sharks in Boston would be all over the reason for your supposed decline. And now that we've had you back out in public to perform admirably at that Cohasset fete, it's time to get you back onto some bigger stages before nosy Boston people begin to wonder and ask questions."

Gertrude was aware that in the few short months she'd lived in Hingham, the native residents had gotten used to her being out and about; gay with her friends in town. Certainly they had noticed when, last month, she had canceled all of her local engagements, sequestering herself in her home. This explained why, with her first public appearance in this latter part of summer, the newspaper had pronounced her well.

She was very lucky that only two people knew the real reason for her absence from public. Idell and eventually, Edith had been called back to Hingham only a week after they had departed during the first of July. They received an earful of Gertrude's misery. And commiserating over her heartbreak, concocted a tale of illness to cover however much time she would need to recover and come back from an unscheduled hiatus. Her household staff had been sworn to secrecy, and Gertrude was allowed, for a short while to wallow in self-pity.

It still frightened Gertrude how wrong she had been about George; how fooled and foolish. She had always depended on her own judgment to guide her in life's big decisions, but this time her intuition had let her down. No, that was not quite right. Her heart had let her down. She had solely followed that fickle organ when letting George into her life.

Thinking his name now conjured more anger than hurt, and Idell had told her this was a sign she was getting past the melancholia which had sapped her strength.

Indeed, she could now actually allow herself to think back on the weekend of George's arrival. It seemed so long ago when it appeared that the world was about to become her oyster.

****

"Hello." His call from the yard sent her rushing from the new, brick terrace and into his arms.

"George," she cried, raising her face to his for the taste of a long awaited kiss. "I'm so happy you're here. I've driven the cook mad with the evening menu. Do you remember those artichokes that you adored when we were in Montreal? Well, I've had a man scour Boston to procure some and Cook has stuffed them with mushrooms. We also have fresh haddock right from the wharf in Hull, and a banana mousse that I've concocted, all by myself, without any assistance." Gertrude knew she was babbling, but George's smile told her it was all right.

"And I can see the proof of that pudding right here on the lapel of your frock." He laughed, fingering her lace collar where a dab had escaped the bowl. He stuck his finger in his mouth and sampled the flavor in a very provocative manner, sending Gertrude into a fine blush.

"I don't care who sees you misbehaving at my expense." Gertrude shook off her embarrassment and became bold. "Maybe we'll save some of the pudding for later in the evening," she dared.

It was George's turn to look shocked and Gertrude turned toward the house with a small, self-satisfied smile. "Shall we see you unpacked?"

The afternoon passed in a similar fashion, both of them teasing and being teased in turn. They took a walk behind the barn, to lament the lack of strawberries that announced the apex of summer, then took a quick spin in George's brand new and extremely flamboyant Benz automobile. It wasn't until their supper repast was placed on the romantically candle-lit table that Gertrude dismissed her two women and the conversation turned serious.

"George, really, I need to know how we're going to proceed with this. I can't keep waiting here in Hingham for you to have a clear spot on your calendar. I've turned down two engagements recently just to accommodate your schedule," Gertrude huffed. "Have your lawyers given you any more indication of how long it will take to disentangle your financial interests from those of your wife?" She spoke of the boarding house on Commonwealth Avenue that

George and his wife Adeline owned together.

"It's not as easy as that, Gertrude." George spoke with some authority. "These things take time."

"It seems to me that you've had adequate time." Gertrude retorted, a little more sharply than she intended. "It's been two years after all."

George coughed on a piece of fish and brought the damask napkin to his mouth, pursing his lips in an aggrieved manner. "And what would you have me do, my dear? My life will be in an upheaval if I rush these things. What we're doing here seems by far the simplest way to conduct ourselves. You have this lovely retreat where we can meet, undetected, and no one gets hurt or is the wiser because of it."

Gertrude slowly lowered her fork, a mushroom still poised on its tines. "Do you mean to say," she spoke casually but deliberately, steeling herself for an answer she didn't want to hear. "That you wish us to continue as we are now, for an indefinite period?" She held her breath.

"That's precisely what I'm saying." George's complexion smoothed back to serene. "And there's a good girl, seeing the reason in it. I'm glad that you are so sensible." He lowered his eyes and attacked his artichoke, pulling it apart with his fork and knife.

Gertrude's pause was significant, but George seemed not to notice, and she chose her next words, carefully. "So what we have here, between us, is very convenient for you. A country respite where you can let loose and unwind from the demands of your profession without upsetting the status quo of your Boston household."

"Exactly so," he agreed.

George had yet to detect the dangerous undercurrent in her question.

"And I'm glad that you brought this up." He popped a bit of food into his mouth and chewed introspectively. "I've been meaning to warn you of the delicate parameters of our trysts, but was fearful you wouldn't understand."

Oh, Gertrude understood alright. Finally. George had been putting off this discussion because he didn't want to ruin a good thing or make the situation difficult for himself. After all, the whole relationship was about pleasure and convenience. *His* pleasure and convenience.

"I'm touched by your foresight and compliance," he continued. "Maybe in a couple of years when my daughter turns twenty, a different arrangement might be attempted, but for now, I see no reason to rock the boat, as our friend Idell would most likely put it." He wiped his lips delicately with his napkin, and seemed surprised when Gertrude quietly pushed back her chair to stand, shakily tucking a loose strand of hair behind her ear. "What are you doing, Gertrude? Aren't you going to finish?"

"Yes George, I am going to finish. I'm going to finish something that I obviously never should have started." Her voice rose with each clipped word she dared utter. "I've been a fool."

When he looked puzzled, her ire gathered steam. "You never thought we'd be doing anything more than this; having a bit of fun without anyone being the wiser."

A small protest looked to be forming on his lips, but she cut him dead.

"No. Do not speak. I can see the truth of it now. Although how it could have taken me this long has me ashamed. I'm a blind idiot." Her gaze locked onto his for a final, incendiary moment before she threw down her napkin and turned her back. "But I won't be any longer," she snapped. Gertrude squared her shoulders. "I want you gone first thing in the morning. Before I awake."

She choked back a small bubble of hysteria, depending instead on anger to finish what had to be done.

"I've wasted two precious years of my life with you." Her head shook back and forth of its own volition, the curls George purported to love dancing on her shoulders. "I believed you when you said you loved me and that you'd never loved your wife," she scoffed. "I actually thought you would leave her for me. How could I have been so naive?" Her voice rose. "Idell warned me, but I was so sure. You were so convincing." She held her head high and without a further word—although many wanted to spring from her lips—Gertrude walked from the room before George could utter anything, be it lies or platitudes.

****

George sat, finishing his meal. No need to waste good food, he whiffed. Damned inconsiderate of Gertrude to re-think her position after all this time. He'd taken this valuable period during his busy schedule to travel to Hingham, and Gertrude knew the strain of the trip always disagreed with him. It was quite stressful for him, in fact, making excuses as to where he would be. He had been looking forward to relieving some of his tension later, in bed. George sighed. This was very unfair of Gertrude, and damned inconvenient. It would make things difficult for him after all this time, trying to find someone new with whom he could take his leisure. It wasn't easy, at his age, to attract and woo young girls. Yes, damned inconvenient. George continued to eat, and when he did head up the stairs hoping that Gertrude had changed her mind, he found her bedroom door locked and his belongings in the hallway. Yes. Damned inconvenient. He hoped the bed in her guest room was comfortable.

****

Gertrude had arisen the next morning after a sleepless night, and thankfully George had been gone. His clothing and his smart car were absent. The only thing left behind, the scent of his cloying toilet water. She'd felt drained and listless, wandering the house for hours before sending off a missive to her friends.

And now, weeks later, she needed to put it all behind her. She looked up into the face of Idell, and became filled with resolve.

"So tell me what's next?" Gertrude asked.

With the help of her friends, she had pulled herself back from the brink and now handed Idell carte-blanche for her future.

"Next, we find you the performance of your life." Idell nodded with certainty. She seemed so sure. And because of that, Gertrude didn't even question her.

*Boston Herald, September 3, 1892*

*"Building Fund Concert. A last minute addition, Gertrude Edmands sang contralto songs by Robaudi and Maud V. White. The way in which she reverently retained in her face the expression of the Cradle Song, till the last note of the postlude sounded, was not only worthy of imitation by all singers, but the result of her own deep feeling about the piece."*

# Chapter Eleven

September 1892

"Are you sure you need to take the trip this weekend?" Fred was feeling low. His two best friends were out of town for a few days, he was scheduled to work tomorrow for a special shipment, and Maude had suddenly decided to head back to Waltham. Her mother had passed away three weeks earlier and she had not returned home in the interim to see how her father was faring.

"I really must go Fred. You understand, don't you?"

Fred gazed up at the worn ceiling of the trolley they'd boarded which would take them to West Cambridge. From there, Maude would catch the Watertown Branch passenger train to Waltham.

"Of course I understand, my love." He bucked up for Maude's sake, and brought her hand to his lips for a quick kiss. "Your father needs you more than I do, right now."

The funeral had been difficult for them all. Even though Mrs. Lindsay's death had been a long time coming, she had defined that household, and Mr. Lindsay—for the few short months Fred had known him—had shrunk in size as his wife lingered.

Over the summer, Fred had made it his mission to help ease things for the whole family. He had accompanied Maude to Waltham most weekends to trim hedges, paint house shutters and assist in lifting Mrs. Lindsay—who was always gracious even in her failing state—to different favorite positions throughout the house. Maude was comforted that her Mother clearly adored Fred and seemed more at peace that he was around to take care of things when she was gone. Fred, for his part, tried to keep everyone as buoyed up as possible during her mother's final decline.

Even now Fred attempted to dream up ways to make Maude smile and keep her from worrying about what she'd find when she arrived home.

"And how many times will you be checking with the seamstress on that wedding frock of yours?" He teased her over the dress that was likely to cost more than the two of them, combined, could earn in a month. Maude was not in any way vain, but she had insisted that her dress was to be custom made to her specifications.

Maude slapped at him playfully, seemingly willing to perk up a small bit. "You'll see, Mr. Torrey. This is something I've dreamed of ever since I was a little girl and you cannot make me feel differently about it. I will be the most beautiful bride that you've ever laid eyes on, you mark my words if I'm not."

"Maude, you could be dressed in old burlap sacking and you would still be the most beautiful bride in all of Boston." Fred sighed contentedly when the compliment brought the intended, sweet smile to her lips. He leaned back in the uncomfortable seat, and would have spoken more, but he could see that Maude was quickly retreating; mentally preparing herself for the trip home.

It would be difficult for her to arrive alone, for the first time, to the absence of her mother. The two had been very close and Maude had vacillated between quiet tears and a detached remoteness ever since her mother had succumbed. Fred had never lost anyone close to him, but he was entirely sympathetic toward Maude, and would give her all the time she needed to adjust.

They had not yet set an exact wedding date, but he was

hopeful that it would still occur before the end of the year.

He had, since the advent of their engagement, busied himself trying to locate a flat that would accommodate them both, with a spare room for guests or eventually for a child they might have. An appropriate space had been found, for sale, just this week on Huntington Avenue and Fred had given the current owner a sum of money as down-payment. This would enable him to take possession of the property as soon as he was sure Maude liked it. If she agreed, he would move in when his current lease expired at the end of the month, which would give him plenty of time to paint and make modest renovations before Maude moved in, after the wedding.

"So, Monday, when you're finished with work, will you meet me and I can show you the flat on Huntington? I want to make sure it meets with your approval before I finalize the deal."

"I'm sure you've chosen something splendid, Fred. You know I trust your judgment in these matters." Their trolley was just pulling up to the West Cambridge stop and Fred lifted her small bag easily as they both got to their feet.

"I'd still like to show it to you. It won't feel like it's going to be our home until you've at least seen it."

"All right then." Maude capitulated, but with only enough enthusiasm to let Fred know she was listening. Her mind was already in Waltham. "I'll meet you at your office after work. Monday."

Fred would have liked more enthusiasm, but considering what she would be facing when she arrived at her family home, Fred easily forgave her lack of ardor.

They alighted from the car and were immediately engulfed by a fog so thick they were unable even to see the station siding ahead. The bad weather had rolled in, unexpectedly, from the not so distant waterfront. The gloom adequately emulated Maude's mood, and Fred shivered as they walked the short distance to the train. He handed her bag to the porter.

"You have to be the strong one, Maude." Fred grappled with his words. "Your father hasn't done well with his grief. Someone has to bring a sense of normalcy to his situation, and there's only you to do it." He bent forward for a quick kiss, knowing that she didn't hold with public displays, and was therefore surprised when she clung to him briefly and returned his embrace.

"I wish you'd go with me, Fred. You could lend both of us your strength." Fred felt badly that he was sending her off on her own.

"You know I can't. I have to work tomorrow. But, hey." An idea lit up his brain. "How about I come out first thing on Sunday morning?" His arms had snaked around her waist like he never wanted to let go.

"It would be a quick, one day trip," Maude bit her bottom lip but looked hopeful.

"For you, I'd do anything." Fred kissed her again.

The porter, trying to be discreet, gave a meaningful cough which signaled that it was time to depart.

"I have to go, Fred." Maude disentangled herself with difficulty. "But now that I know you're coming to get me on Sunday, I won't fret so much." She beamed. "I won't even have time to miss you." She teased and reached out to him this time, squeezing his arm and leaning in. Fred inhaled her soft fragrance.

"Goodbye my love," he whispered in her ear. "I'll miss *you*." He felt the lingering touch of her hand on his sleeve as she quickly turned, mounted the steps and disappeared into the car. He watched her shadow move between the train windows to settle in an empty seat. Fred hoped she was able to see him wave and throw a kiss, though the heavy fog made him unsure. He was gripped with a melancholia that was very unlike him, and knew tomorrow—indeed, all the hours until Sunday—would seem interminable.

Slowly he walked back the way they had come. He forced

himself to think past the weekend, focusing instead on their new flat and what had to be done before Maude moved in.

He'd just turned the corner to the trolley stop when he heard it. At first he wasn't sure, but then the hairs on the back of his neck all stood on end. Without a doubt, a train was approaching the station much too rapidly.

There was no sign of it in the dense fog, but the roaring was getting closer and closer. Several people on the siding were looking around, fear and concern showing on their faces. Where was it coming from? Should they run? The ground shook under Fred's feet. Damn the fog. The roaring was much too close.

What followed was an explosion so loud, Fred crouched, covering his head. He was sure the earth must have opened up, or buildings begun to topple. But when nothing fell to earth around him, and he saw that he remained whole, he spun in confused circles. That's when his eyes focused on the fire down the track that burst to life and cut through the murk.

Oh, God. The train. Maude's train. It was on fire. Fred ran toward the flames, joined by other horrified individuals, only to be thrown back by the heat and smoke emerging from the chaotic pile.

"Maude." he screamed into the inferno. "Maude."

His words choked in his throat, heavy with thick black smoke. And the night devolved in a scene of horror that would haunt him for the rest of his life.

*The Cranberry Press, September 17, 1892*
***A Terrible and Fatal Accident at West Cambridge, Mass.***
***A Train Telescoped, With Much Loss of Life.***

*A through freight express train, west-bound, on the Fitchburg Railroad, ran into a passenger train standing on the out-bound track at West Cambridge, Mass. Junction, telescoping the rear car, killing eight persons outright and injuring nearly forty others, three of whom died next day, and seven others were thought to be fatally hurt. While standing near the crossing, the express freight train, which was bound west, came thundering along, and just as the passenger train started to cross to the Watertown branch the freight train crashed into the rear of the passenger train. The cars were piled up on one another in indescribable confusion, completely blocking both tracks for fully one hundred yards. C.F. Lawson, engineer of the passenger train, and one of the best men on the Fitchburg road says: "I cannot account for the accident, except that the night was so foggy that the engineer of the freight did not see our brakeman until it was too late to stop his train." As soon as the crash came there was a wild rush to get out of the cars.*

*Frantic men and women rushed about in a purposeless way, shrieking and groaning. Two alarms on the fire bells were hurriedly sounded. Then the work of rescuing the dead and injured was begun. The station was turned into an emergency hospital, to which those taken from the wreck were removed and cared for. One by one the dead bodies were brought in and laid upon the floor.*

# Chapter Twelve

April 1895

"I do wish you would come." Edith attempted to coax Gertrude one more time. "You haven't met my family, but you've heard so much about them that none of them will seem like strangers." Gertrude put down her trowel and pushed the large brimmed hat back away from her face, looking up at her friend who was perched on the edge of the stone bench.

"Edith, I just can't. You know May is an extremely busy month for me. It would be too much confusion to try to make a Thursday evening wedding and then be in Springfield on Friday ready to sing without having practiced with the assembly beforehand." Gertrude was actually relieved to have a valid excuse to be absent at the wedding of her friend's brother. Too many mitigating circumstances would make her comfort in attending, questionable. Edith guessed at one.

"Could this possibly have to do with James Bartlett?" At Gertrude's strained look, she knew she'd guessed correctly. "No one at the wedding would dare to confront you or bring up that subject. I'm surprised you would think otherwise."

Gertrude was indeed mortified, yet conversely, extremely honored by the conduct of the Mr. James Bartlett in question, not to mention the cheeky effrontery of that young William Haskell Coffin.

James was an accomplished vocalist turned composer whose main attribute, in Gertrude's opinion, was that he was extremely fair complexioned, in contrast to George who was a bit on the swarthy side. Gertrude had briefly, with insistence from Idell and against her better judgment, begun seeing Mr. Bartlett the previous year.

James, or JC as he was known to his friends had shown a vigorous interest in her, and without any encouragement on Gertrude's part, had begun calling on her after performances. He pestered her to accompany him to dinners, to attend openings of this one's gallery or that one's party. Gertrude, somewhat charmed and having no other plans, simply fell in with his arrangements and got dragged from museum to soirée, night after night, without once having her highly strung emotions become the slightest bit involved.

Apparently, the same could not be said of poor Mr. Bartlett. He began telling mutual friends that he and Gertrude were certain to become engaged, joking that he would be lord of a fine country manor. He was not being pompous, Gertrude realized, just extremely smitten. As soon as she gleaned the extent of his affections, she cut off her availability. She didn't want to lead him on. Heaven forbid. If she had learned one thing about affairs of the heart, it was that both parties were better off using total honesty. Much to Mr. Bartlett's chagrin, Gertrude remained, thereafter, aloof to all entreaties.

His tendresse, unrequited, caused the gentleman much pain. How much of it was real, and how much artistic license, Gertrude was unsure, but he carried on, abjectly, for weeks, to all within his circle and hers.

When his friends were utterly sick to death of listening, and told him to get over it, he resorted to the only thing he could. He composed a song in her honor, dedicated it to her, and published it for all the world to see. Not only that, but his 17-year-old scamp of a friend, Coffin, had, without her authorization rendered a likeness of her on the sheet music, staring romantically up from a book and pillow, while reclining on the grass. "*A Dream*" caused quite a sensation and now her name was being romantically linked once again with James, and speculation was rife about a prolonged, deeper affair.

"It's not that," Gertrude responded sharply to Edith. "If I want to squelch rumors, the more public appearances that I make without Mr. Bartlett, the more the stories will be put to rest." She paused meaningfully. "The truth is, I'm simply too busy to fit it into my schedule." She felt bad as she took in the disappointed pout of her companion, but in reality there were other reasons why she didn't wish to attend.

Idell, who had always managed to lift her spirits and help deflect any unsavory suitors was currently touring Europe with her husband. The couple had departed the previous fall from New York, taking the *SS Teutonic* to Liverpool.

Gertrude, after much coaxing from Idell, had joined them briefly in London over the winter, making her first trans-Atlantic voyage to Europe. The couple had enthusiastically shown her all the tourist sights: London Bridge, Elizabeth Tower, Buckingham Palace and the unparalleled St. Paul's Cathedral. They also made a tour—to assuage Idell's husband's curiosity—of the streets where Jack the Ripper had plied his evil trade. Strangely though, the smell of London street-food ranked the highest amongst all the wonderful things that Gertrude witnessed.

Idell had even managed to procure three highly sought after tickets for the opening night of Oscar Wilde's new play, *The Importance of Being Ernest.* It was performed at the St. James Theatre in mid-February, on a frigidly cold night in London. The crowd that attended would have braved a full-on winter blizzard to have their names connected to such a prestigious opening night.

Gertrude and Idell had, weeks before, poured through the pages of the latest edition of the *Delineator,* then gone forth into London to procure gowns in the newest style of nipped waist and exaggerated, broad shoulders. Gertrude's was a confection in winter green, and Idell's flamboyant in crimson. Luckily, both were built with slender middles and ample bosoms that showed the new couture off to perfection, and knew they looked stunning, blending in with the other finely attired women of London who attended.

Gertrude departed soon after the splendid performance, but Idell and her husband weren't due back for several months yet, and Gertrude found herself reluctant to attend this wedding solo, without the support of her dearest friend.

Justifiably, she also felt that attending Arthur's wedding would feel odd, never having met the young man. She was aware that Arthur had been seeing his young woman for a few years, but in deference to the still raw feelings of his older brother, Fred, who had lost his fiancée in a horrific accident, they had postponed the wedding until now. And there was the final reason that Gertrude was unwilling to go.

Edith now lived on Huntington Avenue with Fred, in the flat that he had purchased for himself and his then wife-to-be. She had moved in shortly after the train accident to care for her brother who was unable to come to grips with the death of his fiancée. Edith had, with much nurturing, eventually succeeded in bringing Fred back from the brink of despair, but was unable to infuse into him any enthusiasm for life.

For some time now, Gertrude had the feeling that Edith was trying to maneuver her into meeting Fred. His loss had occurred at the same time that Gertrude's relationship with George had unraveled, and somehow Edith, who had been fully aware of the disastrous affair, thought that Gertrude and her brother might become a balm for each other's disheartened souls.

Gertrude, increasingly, was only embarrassed at the youthful indiscretion she had believed to be love. In no way did her loss remotely compare with the wrenching sorrow of Edith's brother, Fred, having his fiancée ripped from his arms as they stood on the brink of their lives together. Gertrude brushed the dirt from her skirt as she arose from the flower bed having made up her mind on all scores.

"I will send a gift." She sought to placate Edith. "And tell Arthur and his new wife that they are more than welcome to stop here on their way to honeymooning on Cape Cod. I would love to meet them…after my busy weekend is over."

# Chapter Thirteen

December 1906

"I will not go alone." Edith was beside herself, flinging her small bag across the front parlor and slamming the door behind her. In an uncharacteristic show of anger, she stomped smartly across the room and invoked a mild epitaph at her reflection in the mirror.

Fred lifted his face out of the washbasin in his room, his visage covered with shaving cream as he worked around his full beard—his normal addition for the winter—a straight razor clutched in his hand. He was unaccustomed to his mild sister raising any kind of a fuss, and quickly entered the parlor to see what had precipitated her tirade.

"What's happened to get you all into a lather?" He queried, and such was her agitation that she missed his rare attempt at a pun.

"Idell promised she would accompany me to Gertrude's performance of *The Sphinx* if I procured the tickets," Edith explained angrily to her brother. "So I purchased them and now she tells me she can't attend."

She threw the small pieces of cardboard and the handbill onto the worn table.

Fred wiped the soap away with a towel and slowly walked over to pick up the discarded advertisement.

*December 1, 1906*

*"The Sphinx, a comic opera written by William Maynadier Browne with music by Lewis S. Thompson, will be performed at the Jordan Hall on December 14, 15 and 17th under the auspices of the Ellis Memorial Club a well known Social Service Organization..."*

His eyes skimmed farther down the page.

*"...to Miss Gertrude Edmands has been assigned the contralto role. Miss Edmands is well known locally and the country over as a leading contralto."*

Fred sighed and put down the paper. "There's no chance at all of your friend, Idell, accompanying you?"

"No." Edith seemed to be coming to grips with her disappointment after her initial outburst, and sought to make the appropriate excuses for Idell's lapse. "She completely forgot what weekend we had been discussing, and she, her husband and her daughter have purchased train tickets for Iowa to visit Idell's parents. There's nothing to be done about it now. I just dislike going on my own."

It was obvious to Fred that, short of being a total cad, he was required to offer his services as escort. He fumbled with the towel, cleared his throat and otherwise looked uncomfortable. Never actually having said a word, Edith clearly divined his intent and jumped on his hesitation before he could re-think his altruism.

"Really, Fred? Really? You would go with me." She ran and give him a quick impulsive hug. "You don't have to, you know. I can always stay home."

Fred barely had time for a shrug before Edith was off again.

"We'll have to bring your suit out of mothballs and see if it still fits. The last time you wore it was at Arthur's wedding nearly twelve years ago. At the very least it will need a good cleaning."

Fred was resigned but happy he was able to do something for Edith. She rarely went out socially these days, a single woman on her own always felt a bit out of place amongst the married couples and their children. She much preferred to visit her friend Gertrude in Hingham.

Fred seldom went out either, but for far different reasons. Recently he had preferred coming home from work to immerse himself in his reading. He was riveted by the events taking place in Russia; the evolving revolution, and specifically a deep fascination with the Bolsheviks and Vladimir Lenin. Fred had his ear to the ground where the Boston working man was concerned and he knew the future favored those with ties to organized labor. He was interested to see how the mass worker's revolution overseas would proceed.

Edith, however, was unaware of Fred's new found interest in the Bolsheviks, and was more inclined to be concerned with matters closer to home. In particular, she felt the need to be supportive of Gertrude who, from all the news Edith offered up, Fred gathered had been going through some trying times of her own lately.

In the spring of 1903, Gertrude's father and mother, along with the stalwart and ever loyal Martha Smith had moved from their home in Somerville to Gertrude's estate in Hingham. Gertrude's sisters and their families had remained in Boston and there was much visiting back and forth between city and country. All in all, it had been a slow but joyful period in Gertrude's life where she worked little but enjoyed the family times she had missed during the previous fifteen years of extensive engagements and travel. To fill in the monetary gaps she had taken on some vocal students at the urging of Edith, who had achieved great success in the teaching genre.

Gertrude, well rested and—according to Edith—restless, had just begun making inquiries and agreements to start a new round of appearances in town when the family was rocked with devastating news. Hannah Edmands was diagnosed with consumption. The awful truth was confirmed by examining the results of a new innovation called an x-ray which was just now becoming available in Boston. They had feared for her health over the previous few years, and the diagnosis was the worst they could have received. Gertrude had canceled her planned engagements and stayed close as her mother's health deteriorated. In the spring of 1906 her mother passed away at the age of 68.

For the next several months, Gertrude had felt rudderless, Edith gossiped. She'd made a half hearted attempt to sell her Rocky Nook to a gentleman from New York who had shown up on her doorstep, exhibiting some interest. Gertrude was only acquiescing to the pressure from her sisters that she and her father move back to the city, but the deal dissolved with apparent apathy on both sides. In the end, Gertrude remained in Hingham, happy that the sale had not coalesced as she and her father found solace in the kindness of their neighbors and the peace of a poignantly beautiful country summer.

As soon as her father had seemed stronger—and much to Fred's detached amusement—Gertrude saw to it that his duties on her gentleman's farm were extended to the care and feeding of a new flock of chickens, which, surprisingly, he took to with relish. Gertrude, and Edith when she visited, enjoyed the fruits of his labor in fresh eggs.

As the remaining family healed, Gertrude once again gained enough strength to venture out into her professional circles, and that's when she'd procured a coveted role in the upcoming production of "*The Sphinx*". To which now, Fred would be in attendance.

****

The night of the performance was cold and clear—most thankfully unlike the unusual blizzard conditions in Nevada that had the nation abuzz. Upon removing their coats and having them checked, Edith beamed approvingly at Fred, who looked resplendent in a borrowed tuxedo, which became a necessity after Edith found unacceptable worn spots on the elbows of his long-suffering suit.

Edith had purchased a gown. Although used and not quite at the height of fashion, it was a reworked blue confection, overlaid with tulle and white beading, designed by the famous—or so Edith had assured him— Frenchman, Jean Paquin. It fit her to perfection, as well it should. It had cost her a pretty penny, but the result was clearly worth it. He could tell she felt elegant and stylish, even though she was on the arm of her brother.

The lights in the lobby flickered, letting them know they had only a short amount of time to find their seats. Fred kept a fixed smile on his face for the benefit of his sister, who seemed to be enjoying the crush of people, and hoped he could slink into oblivion once they reached their destination. Perhaps he could grab a little sleep. He was quite sure, never having attended an operatic performance, that he wouldn't be able to follow a thing.

Once settled, however, and with the show underway, he found his attention instantly engaged by the woman Edith surreptitiously pointed out as Gertrude, playing the teacher at a seminary in Cairo in the opening scene. She was good; very, very good, thought Fred. And also quite beautiful. He couldn't keep his eyes from her, and found himself laughing at the onstage antics, despite his prediction.

The story began when the entire student body at a women's seminary in Cairo—having been romantically swept up by a band of Bedouins—were compelled to find a remarkable sphinx named Hathor. The sphinx would pose a riddle unto each of them, which if answered within twenty four hours, would assure them of happy marriages. The students, before embarking on their journey to the sphinx, were joined by Professor Papyrus and his valet, Ptimmins. Papyrus wants to find the marvelous sphinx for its own merits. Ptimmins is invited along for being touted—erroneously—as an expert riddle-solver. In reality the valet is nothing of the kind, relying on a book called

*"Happy Evenings at Home; 2,000 Riddles with their Correct Answers",* for his supposedly superior knowledge.

Enter an evil magician, throw in an impossible love connection between the professor and the sphinx and panic ensued as a riddle that had never before been posed became the only solution for true love. The happy ending, after a delicious romp, was all that one could expect and more, and the entire performance had held Fred rapt.

The audience loved it, Fred loved it, and Edith couldn't thank him enough for accompanying her. Fred was able to assure her, without any untruths, that he was happy to have attended. Strangely enough though, his thoughts kept creeping back, time and time again, to the dark-eyed woman who was friends with his sister.

*Boston Evening Transcript, December 18th, 1906*

*"...Gertrude Edmands, who played Pteecha, the principal of a young ladies seminary, gives a splendid exhibition of finished work."*

*Hingham Journal, December 20th, 1906*

*"Mr. Thomas Edmands of Rocky Nook reports that he lost thirteen valuable hens to thieves on Saturday night. The fowl were dressed on the premises."*

# Chapter Fourteen

July 1914

Gertrude sat, ramrod straight, at her desk. As many times as she went over the household figures and budgets, she knew she could not maintain the property any more than five or six additional years under the present circumstances. She was running out of money. She had been ignoring the faint pricks of mental discomfort each time a large bill had to be paid, reasoning that another engagement would take care of the cost of a new roof, or the sills on the barn. But now it was time to face the fact that her engagements were too few and far between to support the household, not to mention that she was getting paid at a much lesser rate in the waning years of her career. The roles she had won easily just eight or nine seasons ago were snapped up by fresh faced women; the new crop of voices emerging on the scene. And her house was not as self-sustaining as she had dreamed when younger and more optimistic. The sale of fresh eggs and strawberries did very little to alleviate the plethora of bills that cascaded in each month.

Not one to be beaten down, Gertrude had a few ideas. It was time to call a "family meeting" which would include her father, Martha, and Mary Kirke, a girl she had engaged four years ago who had quickly—despite her abrasive personality—made herself part of the family and nearly indispensable with her wonderful cooking and alert, organizational skills.

“Mary,” Gertrude called, knowing that the other woman was always nearby. Less than ten seconds later, she popped her head into the office.

“Yes, ma'am?” Mary kept to the appropriate title even though Gertrude had, on many occasions, given her permission to drop formality and call her Gertrude.

“Could you go and find my father and Martha? I'd like everyone, including yourself, to come to the keeping room for a discussion.”

“Of course, ma'am, right away.” Mary scurried off, clearly perturbed by the worried look that she had perceived. Mary knew Gertrude was not one to let things upset her. And that was true. She faced most problems head on without fuss or fanfare, never doubting the outcome would be anything but positive. But this time mere grit didn’t seem like it would help.

Gertrude didn't have long to contemplate, as Mary gathered the others and they joined Gertrude at the same oak table that had graced the room for all the years of her tenure, and well before.

“I'm sure this will come as a surprise to all of you,” Gertrude began, looking at the beloved faces before her. “But I've come to the conclusion that at our present rate we will not be able to sustain the expenses of our home for many more years.” She waited to see how this would sit with her companions. When she noted only curiosity, she briefly realized that perhaps she had been the only one hiding her head in the sand, and continued. “Therefore, I have some proposals to make that will affect us all, but allow us to continue living here as long as we are all willing to work just a little harder.”

This brought raised eyebrows from her father, a look of slight discomfort to Martha who was approaching the venerable age of 74, but not a blink from Mary.

“I've thought this over quite hard, and we need to do

several things. First and foremost, I will begin advertising myself as a singing instructor and widen my student base. I will need help from you, father," she turned a loving gaze toward her patriarch, "as you are a better pianist than I."

He nodded, clearly pleased that he would be able to help.

"Secondly, we have plenty of room in this house and I believe that a paying border or two might not be such a dreadful idea."

And here was the most difficult for Gertrude to consider, as she liked her solitude when at home, and the comfort of having just family around her. But this, too, met with no rebuttal.

"And thirdly," Gertrude's eyes took on a sparkle that they all knew meant something new and very different was about to be undertaken, "I propose to open the front rooms up to the public and run a tea room. We will serve tea and sandwiches on weekdays and Saturdays."

Then she dropped an even bigger bomb shell. "At the close of the Saturday sittings I will entertain the assemblage with a small concert. I believe that my reputation is still good enough that we will have many takers." She looked around, daring anyone to contradict her predictions of success.

"That seems a sound plan," Mary folded her hands in her lap and nodded. "And I would be happy to act as server. I once had a job at a pub in Quincy you know." Mary's enthusiasm was lacking spirit, but that was par for the course, and didn't upset Gertrude at all.

"And Martha," Gertrude continued, "I know that you are still capable of culinary genius in the kitchen. Between you and Mary, you should be able to work out the nature of what is to be served. I believe that if we have a choice of two or three food offerings with a nice selection of English and Ceylonese tea, we will leave our customers quite satisfied."

"What would you have me do in connection to your tea room, my girl?" Thomas Edmands, although eighty three, still cut a dashing figure and Gertrude knew he was quite capable of any task and more than willing to lend assistance.

She already had something in mind for him. “I'm thinking that many ladies attending would probably enjoy having a ride to their luncheon in your new Model T, Papa.” Gertrude grinned because she knew here was something her father would relish. The car that Mr. Edmands had purchased only a year before was his pride and joy. He performed all of the errands that the household could dream up, and Gertrude knew that running a personalized livery would have him beaming with pleasure.

“That's splendid, my dear. I will gladly take on the role of chauffeur.”

They all became quiet for a time, reflecting on what this would mean for each of them and for the future of the house. There would be many details to be ironed out, and much work to be put in to the front rooms to make them suitable, but they knew that if this was what she deemed necessary to keep the household intact, then it would be done.

Mr. Edmands broke through their respective reveries. “Have you thought what you will call your tea room?”

Gertrude had not given it a single thought, and said so. “It never crossed my mind, Papa. Do you have any suggestions?”

“Not a one,” he puzzled. “But I'm sure that, given time, we will find something eminently appropriate.”

# Chapter Fifteen

September 1918

Despite the wretched heat, the lack of rain, and the intense war rationing which had doubled the price of eggs to forty-nine cents a dozen and butter to fifty-one cents per pound, Gertrude's endeavor, the Rocky Nook Tea Room, had proven to be an enormous success. Of course, having their own chickens and, recently, two cows, certainly helped. The burden of food cost was not quite as great for Gertrude, and she could charge very good prices for her freshly baked goods served in the tea room, thanks to Martha who still cooked them.

It was the beginning of September and hot was an understatement. Scorching ninety degree days had dried things up, almost completely. Gertrude was never happier to have several sources of water to keep things running. She had the well in the summer kitchen—which was dipping perilously low—and the deep well under the barn that was blessedly still half full and went toward keeping their attic cisterns topped off.

They had installed an additional washroom for their clients up front near the Tea Room, so the source of water was much welcomed.

Additional changes had come to the Hingham establishment. As well as water and electric lights, the advent of a telephone now graced the keeping room, allowing them to take reservations by phone. And certainly the saddest of circumstances was the death of Mr. Edmands the previous year at the age of eighty six. He had gone peacefully in his sleep. Gertrude was comforted by the fact that he had seen the success of the Tea Room and passed on believing his daughter would be financially sound. She missed his good cheer, but kept busy running the household and the business so she had little time to pine. In her quiet moments, she still found herself talking to him and pondering what his advice would be on various problems that arose throughout the day. She found this situation not alarming at all. On the contrary, she found it quite soothing.

They still had a man in the house, albeit not one who bestirred himself over much to be social. Frank Jackson was their only boarder at present and kept to himself, smoking his ungodly cigars and confiscating every newspaper that appeared on the premises. If ever there was a man who was current on all of the world events, it was Frank. When he deemed to join them at mealtime, he kept them fully abreast of the progress of the Allies overseas—stating with a certainty that the war would soon be over, every Red Sox win—with equal certainty declaring that the Boston team would be playing in the World Series, and just this evening he had brought up a rather troubling bit of news.

According to the Boston Globe, on August 26th two sailors aboard the *Receiving Ship* at Commonwealth Pier had contracted an illness that was being suspiciously eyed as a possible Spanish Flu. On the 28th of August, eight more men had been hospitalized, and then on the 29th fifty-eight additional men had succumbed. None of this had alarmed anyone but the doctors, who had been cataloging symptoms that rattled their hearty Boston composure. But now the papers were reporting that an average of one hundred and fifty new cases each day were appearing, and that the illness had crossed over from the military into the general public. Not only that, but the rate of death for those afflicted was said to be close to 20 percent. This sent a shiver of fear throughout the household, and Gertrude to the telephone.

"Sadie, it's Gertrude." She spoke with familiarity to the operator on the line. "I need to speak to my friend Edith in Boston, will you ring her for me?"

"Certainly Gertrude." Sadie had placed this call many times before and was well acquainted with Edith although never having met her. One of the many benefits of being an operator was the ability to listen in on people's telephone conversations, and Gertrude knew it was not above Sadie to glean all of the information available to her and turn it into gossip which she could spread town-wide. She chatted Gertrude up while connecting the lines.

"When is Martha going to cook another batch of those scones that you served in the Tea Room last week? My mouth waters just thinking about them, and I wouldn't mind having half a dozen to bring home."

Gertrude's mind was far from scones but she made the appropriate responses. She'd do well to pamper Sadie, who with her ready chat, was actually excellent advertising. Gertrude promised to drop off a free half dozen at her next opportunity.

"Thanks, honey. Here's your party." The handset at Gertrude's ear began ringing as her call was put through.

"Hello?" Edith's voice, tinny and clear, came over the wires all the way from Boston.

"Edith, it's Gertrude. I've just heard the news from Boston…about the influenza. I understand that it's spreading rapidly, and I fear for you my dear. I know this is sudden, but I think it prudent that you and your brother close up your house for the time being and come to Hingham. We've had no news of any illness here, and I wish to safeguard you at all cost." Although Gertrude had never met Edith's brother, Fred, she was well aware that her friend would be reluctant to leave without him, and had therefore immediately extended the invitation to include them both.

"Gertrude, that's very generous of you. But of course I'll have to talk it over with Fred. You know how involved he's been lately with his men's groups and meetings. I'm not sure he will consent to leave town, nor do I think he's concerned that this illness will spread our way."

"Edith, I'm begging you to take me up on this. I can't abide the thought of you falling ill. Please discuss this with your brother as soon as you possibly can."

"He's out for an early meeting right now, Gertrude, but he should be home in a few hours. I'll speak to him as soon as he gets in. And sweetie, please don't worry about me. I'll be just fine."

Since Idell had moved permanently to Iowa, Edith had become Gertrude's greatest friend and there was no way that Gertrude was going to let this rest. If she had to go to Boston and drag Edith back to the country, she would do it.

****

Edith, unable to sit still while waiting for her brother to come home, quickly grabbed her purse and walked to purchase food for the evening meal. Her mind refused to quiet. She knew that Gertrude would be relentless in her appeals and that Fred would not want to go to Hingham for an unspecified amount of time. She hated to be caught in the middle, and the problem was that both Gertrude and Fred had amazingly strong personalities. Neither would be able to see the others' point of view and she would be left to founder in no man's land. A sigh escaped her as she picked up a tomato. She would do her best to convince Fred, but she feared that she already knew his answer.

****

Fred was deep in thought as he turned onto Huntington Avenue. He had finally succumbed to the pressure from his comrades and given his name and address to the Boston chapter of the Industrial Workers of the World. He was not yet a full fledged member of the organization which was now a hundred thousand strong nationwide, but he had been regularly attending meetings since February. His intense interest in Bolshevism and the plight of the working man had led him toward the closest thing to socialism he could find in America. Having its inception in 1905 with a meeting of 200 working men, the IWW's goal was to promote worker solidarity and overthrow the widespread power of the employing classes. The members, known as Wobblies, believed that the trade unions of the time were ineffectual because the controlling upper classes had learned to use them, pitting one union against another for their own purposes.

In the first meeting Fred had attended, the speech given by John Ballam was very convincing.

"*...the trade unions aid the employing class to mislead the workers into the belief that the working class have interests in common with their employers.*"

The motto of the IWW had become: "An injury to one is an injury to all." And Ballam's speech resonated throughout the hall supporting this sentiment.

"*There is no building of any size, there is not a subway which has been put through, there is not a railway line which has been built, but what is cemented with the blood of the workers, the actual physical blood of the workers cemented in stones and built into the structure.*"

Fred had seen too much of this bloodshed first hand. Workers in the lumber industry he toiled for, were killed or maimed all too often on the docks or in the warehouses. He also knew, from experience, that the widows and families of such men were never justly compensated for their losses which resulted in young children turning to the streets to try to secure a living for the rest of their families. It was an ugly undercurrent in Boston and one not mentioned by fellow workers for fear that any dissent would have them on the streets as well. Unions had been born to uphold the rights of this working class, but the IWW was correct that the privileged classes had found ways to corrupt the higher-ups in the unions and had turned them to their own advantage.

Fred's hesitation with joining the IWW had not been a disagreement with their beliefs; he thoroughly embraced their ideals and mandates. The problem became, once your name was connected to the IWW, your livelihood and your very life could be in danger.

In August of the previous year, labor organizer Frank Little had been forcibly taken from his boarding house in Butte, Montana by six masked men and lynched from a railroad trestle. The masked men had never been apprehended, in fact they had never even been pursued. Such was the danger to an IWW worker and the apathy of President Wilson in allowing the American Protective League to use whatever means necessary for them to disband and arrest—at any time—groups that smacked of communism. The current number of IWW workers residing in federal prisons was thought to be upward of fifteen hundred, and Fred was not anxious to become one of them.

Another problem Fred foresaw was now that his address had been given to the organization, leaflets and propaganda would be delivered to his house. He had so far successfully avoided having to discuss the agenda of his meetings with Edith, who hobnobbed with a gentler class of individuals and would likely be appalled at his involvement. He would presently have to find a way to assure her that he was no radical. He was convinced that everything the IWW espoused was more than reasonable and certainly no less that what every American worker deserved.

He slowly walked up the stairs to the flat, pondering the best way to approach Edith about things she might see and hear now that he'd committed to the path of the IWW.

He smelled supper cooking, and as always, was more than

appreciative of the things Edith did for him.

"Hey," he called out as he opened the door. "That smells good."

"Pork loin was on special today at the butcher and I picked out some lovely vegetables at the green grocer." Edith laughed when his stomach growled loudly from across the room. "I'm glad you're hungry. Go wash up." She shooed him away, and had food on the table by the time he returned.

"I spoke to Gertrude on the telephone today," she told him.

Fred smiled. He always liked hearing about life in Hingham and Edith's charming acquaintance, even though he had still never found the time to make the trip a few towns south to meet her. He picked up his fork and took a bite.

"She sure has been a good friend to you," he acknowledged around his mouthful. "Has she asked you out for another visit?" Even though the house became a shambles when Edith left, and he had to take all his meals down at the corner pub, he never begrudged her the time away.

"Actually, this time she's invited us both." Edith glanced up from her plate while Fred chewed happily and reflected on an appropriate, yet dismissive answer.

"That's very kind of her, but things are really busy at work right now, what with so many of the guys having gone off to war, and a desperate need for good lumber."

He shrugged and also threw in, "and I'll be heading to a few more meetings at night."

Edith pursed her lips. "I've heard that the city might start curtailing some of the meetings around town due to the influenza," she stated. "I purchased and perused several local newspapers while I was out."

"No," Fred mumbled around his pork. "That's all hearsay. Nobody's really worried about it yet." He had heard talk of it at the lumber yard and had overheard a few conversations at the meeting earlier, but nothing had sounded definitive. He did admit to himself that he had yet to glance at the papers to see what the fuss was all about.

"It's not hearsay, Fred. Today's Globe and Herald stated the numbers being admitted to hospitals has increased dramatically in just the last day."

"So is this what Gertrude put into your head? That we'll be safer out in the country?"

"Yes, she has," Edith scowled. "She says that there have been no cases in Hingham yet, and that we would be much safer there. That we should be expedient in our departure."

"And I couldn't agree with her more." Fred's response clearly surprised Edith but she wouldn't like what he had in mind. "So you'd like to go?"

"Well, yes. I thought it would be the right thing to do."

Fred was privately elated that things had worked out so perfectly. Here was the excuse he needed to get Edith out of the house for an unspecified amount of time, and continue his involvement with the IWW without arousing her suspicions. Now he just had to break the news that he would not be going with her.

"I think you should pack up as soon as possible. I'll feel much better that you are out of the city if this turns into an epidemic. But you do realize that I can't go with you." He let this hang in the air while she digested his words with her last bite.

"I knew you wouldn't agree," she sighed. "You had no intention of accompanying me from the moment I opened my mouth." She placed her napkin gently on the table. "And I am supposed to leave without you? What if you get sick? Who will be here to care for you?"

"I'm never ill, Edith. I have a strong constitution and I doubt I'll even miss a day's work."

"Not true." she cried, trying to make him see reason. "You had that awful flu earlier this year, don't you recall? I nursed you for ten days and you were weak as a kitten afterwards. What would you have done if I weren't here by your side?"

"It was my first illness in fifteen years." He reasoned. "The chances of me succumbing again are against the odds. You, however, are susceptible to every cold that comes along and I highly agree with Gertrude that you should join her and avoid the contagion at all costs."

"I knew I wouldn't be able to make you see reason." Edith started to clear the table, but her backbone remained ramrod straight. She had something up her very pretty sleeve, and Fred knew it. He didn't have to wait long to find out what it was.

"I need you to call Gertrude back and thank her for the invitation." Edith stared him down.

Oh, he was aware of what she was doing. She figured there was still a slim chance that Gertrude could convince him of the sagacity of her request.

He sighed. "Shall I tell her that you'll be coming?"

"Yes. Tell her I'll be on the first Greenbush train Tuesday morning."

That meant when Gertrude failed to convince him, it would give Edith four days to try and talk him into it, but deep down she had to know that even that extra time would prove futile. "You can telephone her now. I told her to be expecting a call this evening."

Fred arose from the table reluctantly, knowing he had to do as he was bidden. Edith never asked much of him, but the set of her chin as she exited to the kitchen told him that she meant business this time. He picked up the handset and requested the connection from the operator, musing as the phone began to ring that in all the years of hearing Gertrude's name, this would be the first time they had ever spoken.

"Hello? Edith, is that you?" The slightly husky but lilting voice carried to him over the phone. He cleared his throat.

"Uh, no. Gertr…Miss Edmands, this is Edith's brother,

Fred."

"Oh. Is Edith all right?" She interrupted, immediately anxious. "Has she become ill since I spoke to her this afternoon?"

"No," Fred assured. "She's fine." He gave a polite laugh. "She's just busy clearing up the table after supper and asked if I would call you." He cursed under his breath at having been put in such an awkward position. "I hope I'm not interrupting anything?"

Gertrude paused for a moment clearly puzzled that it was Fred on the telephone, but being so in tune with Edith, she quickly put him on the spot.

"So you're not coming." She said bluntly.

"Well…I…uh…no. No, I won't be coming, but Edith will be out on the first train Tuesday morning." Blast it, how had the woman come to her conclusion so rapidly? "I want to thank you for your kind invitation, but my business schedule doesn't allow me take advantage of your generous offer." There, that was well said, thought Fred.

Gertrude snorted. *Snorted.* He had heard it. "If this influenza takes hold, you won't have a place of business to go to, nor the health to attend to it." She took him to task and Edith would be proud. "I do say, Mr. Torrey, your sister must be severely disappointed."

Fred was not used to having his decisions questioned, and was quite taken aback.

"I know what I'm about Miss Edmands, and although Edith is a little frustrated at my decision, I assure you that my judgment is sound. I thank you for taking my sister in, but will, myself, abstain from accepting your invitation."

And to that piece of his mind, the blasted woman had the audacity to chuckle.

"I certainly didn't mean to question your edict, Mr. Torrey. And rest assured, I will make sure that I take good care of your sister."

"That's grand." Fred's tone, although remaining polite,

couldn't hide his relief that Gertrude had let the idea of him going to Hingham slide. "What matters here is that we are both concerned for the well being of Edith. Once again, I will say my thank-you's and ring off."

"Very well, Mr. Torrey. I will say good evening to you, as well."

****

Gertrude put the phone gently back into its cradle, absently tapping her lips with her index finger. She wondered how long Edith would be forced to stay in Hingham if there was a major outbreak, and what more the two of them could do to convince her brother to join them. Only time would tell, but she tingled a little with anticipation. She had liked the slightly belligerent sound of Fred Torrey, very much.

# Chapter Sixteen

November 12, 1918

Dearest Fred,

I wish that I could have been with you in Boston yesterday to observe the Armistice. When you rang up last night and described the celebrations taking place in the streets, it made me miss the city terribly. Sometimes country life can be so isolating. Perhaps I will be able to come home soon as I hear that the epidemic is slowing. You can't know how relieved I am that you have remained well. Your stories of the young people you know who have passed away stay with me long after we are through talking. I think you have been very brave to carry on and continue working.

You will think it odd that I am writing to you only a day after we spoke at length on the telephone, but what I have to ask you would not do well as fodder for the gossips in Hingham who get their best information from our local operator.

I will be blunt, as I know that you care little for the niceties of small talk. I need you to send money—Oh, Gertrude would swoon in mortification if she knew that I was telling you this.

Things are rapidly deteriorating here. Whereas previous to the influenza, financial ends were just being met, circumstances have changed. Shortly after I arrived, the only paying boarder packed up and moved farther west in what he deemed a necessary exodus to avoid illness. We reluctantly came to the conclusion that no new boarders should be sought until after the contagion concluded. In a like respect, the Tea Room has been closed for two months, and Gertrude will not open again until the danger of infection has passed. To top it all off we are—don't laugh picturing your city sister—collecting eggs and milking cows because Gertrude's handyman, an odd gentleman at best, refuses to come out of his house and risk La Grippe.

I have wheedled and cajoled Gertrude for weeks now to allow my assistance, assuring her that a loan would be perfectly acceptable until she gets back on her feet. You know how stubborn she can be, but I finally broke through her prideful defenses and she has agreed. She does not know that our finances are handled together by the bank and that any deduction I make must also have your approval. It would cause her great anguish if she thought anyone else were privy to what she sees as her shortcomings in handling her affairs.

Please, my dear, would you put your mind to this delicate matter without fanfare? I trust your judgment to determine how much is appropriate for helping my dear friend without compromising our own financial integrity. A postal money order would be just the thing, or a direct wire of funds into her account at the Hingham Institution for Savings. Do let me know how you will proceed, but if we speak by phone we must be most circumspect.

I miss you terribly and hope that I might return to Boston as soon as we feel it is safe to do so.

Your Loving Sister,

Edith

Edith had posted her letter a week ago Tuesday and didn't

expect to hear from her brother until the following week. She told Gertrude that she had made discreet inquiries to her banker by post, and that without going to Boston, it would take a bit more time to know exactly how much she could loan.

****

The budget had been analyzed and Gertrude considered they could get by on thirty dollars per month, the unknown being how cruel the winter months would be. The Fuel Administration had allotted each house six tons of coal for the winter, but if they had to use it all, the cost for more could be as much as an additional forty dollars for the season. This meant an added eight dollars each month added to the budget, for a total expenditure of nearly forty dollars per month. Edith had said not to worry, that her banker would get back to her soon, and Gertrude hoped that was so, and that with a small lifeline to tide them over, things would be back to normal by the spring.

She and Edith had just come in from the barn, and laughingly washed up at the kitchen pump. They had been cleaning the coops and were covered in the detritus of chickens. Both wore kerchiefs around their heads and old sensible shoes, but looked a sight with straw poking out in various spots on their clothing and smudges of unknown nature decorating their garb. The weather was unseasonably warm and they were still able to do without their coats, or they would surely have ruined several layers in their diligence.

“Aren't we a pair?” laughed Gertrude. “Should we clean up and have some tea or head back out for another round, this time with the cows?”

Edith gave an exaggerated sigh. “Let's get the chores finished. Once I'm done, I'm done for good. I plan on using that big copper tub in the attic for a very long soak.” She started out the back door when the front knocker sounded, startling them both.

"What?" Gertrude tilted her head. "We haven't had anyone come to the front door in months," she puzzled, glancing at Edith as they segued toward the unexpected summons. "And I hope they're not expecting tea," she giggled. "We're hardly in our Sunday best."

Edith chortled right alongside her as both women pulled off their head coverings in unison. Gertrude ruffled her curls and threw back the bolt, opening the door.

"May I help you…?" She sputtered to a stop.

Gertrude was rarely at a loss for words, but here, at her door, was a very fine looking gentleman poised on her doorstep with his hat held politely in his hands. His generous mouth swooped upward at Gertrude's greeting, and she could not keep herself from sending her eyes discreetly upon his whole pleasing visage.

Stiff creases graced the front of his smart suit-pants, and his white shirt was as highly starched as any she had ever seen. He also had the most brightly polished shoes she'd encountered since the war began. Edith, close behind, gave Gertrude a small nudge in an unspoken acknowledgement that this was an exceptionally good looking man.

"Miss Edmands?" The gentleman under speculation glanced questionably at the two of them.

Dressed as they were in their barn clothes, Gertrude understood. She would also have doubts as to whether the once famous opera singer could be this unkempt female answering the door. She squared her shoulders and stood erect.

"I am, sir. To whom do I have the honor of finding at my front door?" Gertrude called on her years of public aplomb to elevate herself above her soiled clothing.

"Ah, indeed," the visitor nodded agreeably. "Ambrose Fletcher, Miss Edmands. I'm very pleased to meet you." He shifted his hat into his left hand and stuck out the right to shake hers.

"Fletcher," Gertrude repeated. "The name is familiar sir. Would you be related to a Bertha Fletcher of my acquaintance?"

"Indeed, ma'am. That would be my dear mother," he beamed.

Gertrude took a new look at their caller and then turned to Edith. "Forgive me, sir, for not introducing my good friend Edith Torrey from Boston. Edith, this is the son of one of my dearest clients at the Tea Room, and if I'm not mistaken Mr. Fletcher, you are an officer of the law in our fair town."

"In a way, yes." He clearly preened at her description but gently corrected. "In actuality I am the town detective." He acknowledged their raised eyebrows as a normal reaction to his disclosure and seemed to look speculatively at Edith. Specifically at her hands, which—Gertrude wanted to giggle—were unencumbered by rings.

"I'm sorry," she coughed to hide her glee, having been too amused at that distraction. "Where are my manners? Would you care to come in?"

"It looks like you are in the middle of something." He eyed their disheveled clothing again.

"Indeed we were, sir." She gave a practiced moue of displeasure. "I must admit that the man who helps us with our odds and ends is no longer available and we have just been cleaning out the chicken coops."

Her explanation had him nodding in understanding. "We have yet to wash down the milking area or muck out the horse stall so we don't smell quite as badly now as we will a little later if you'd care to stick around." Gertrude gave a pointed, mischievous glance at *his shoes* this time, mimicking his earlier—not so discreet—perusal of Edith. Edith gave a snort behind her that she quickly turned into a strangled sniff, and Gertrude wondered at their boldness.

Ambrose laughed a full, hearty male sound, clearly appreciating that he'd been called out. "I do believe I will pass on that," he allowed. "Although being party to your company would be quite enjoyable, dressed as I am I don't think I would be a fit guest for your animals. But would it be possible to be invited back to your tea room in the future?"

His appreciative look took in both of them, but focused on Edith, who Gertrude could see was in a fine blush. She answered for them.

"We would look forward to seeing you, sir," she said smartly. "And I'd be pleased to admit you on the arm of your mother."

His intoxicating smile got even broader. "Which brings me to the reason for invading your doorstep." He finally turned his full attention to Gertrude. "I'm here at the behest of my mother to find out when you might be re-opening your business. She doesn't have many excuses, at her age, to leave the house, and your tea room has become an important part of her weekly social agenda." The mood turned slightly somber as did hers. She knew they both contemplated the disruption that the flu had brought to everyone's lives. Gertrude hated letting anyone down, but gave Mr. Fletcher the bad news.

"Unfortunately, in good conscience I have to wait until spring to see if an additional outbreak will occur. The newspapers say that the illness is waning but doctors warn that another wave could be right around the corner. I don't have anything definite that you can tell your mother, but if there have been no new cases in Hingham by April or May, I would consider starting up again, then."

"That's better news than expected." He smiled. "She was afraid that you might abandon the venture altogether." Mr. Fletcher placed his hat, thoughtfully, back on his head. "And will you be singing again?" He didn't wait for her answer, but continued. "My mother has raved about your voice, and I would very much enjoy hearing you."

Gertrude told him that she planned on it, as he nodded to her answer, a little absently. Then as if he couldn't help himself a minute longer, he turned to Edith.

"And you, Mrs. Torrey, do you sing as well?" He used the married prefix—Gertrude noticed immediately—quite obviously making sure he hadn't jumped to conclusions on her marital status.

Edith quickly corrected him. "*Miss* Torrey if you please," she colored up nicely. "And yes, I have sung professionally, but not to become well known like Gertrude."

She paused for a moment, which had Gertrude cocking her head, then dismissed whatever had distracted her. "I haven't...," She stopped again, this time with a puzzled look on her face. Now Gertrude heard it, too. Something floating on the wind had Edith listening with intense concentration.

"Does anybody hear that whistling?" she asked, peering around Mr. Fletcher where he stood on the portico. Gertrude and Ambrose both glanced to the road where Edith was looking to see a solitary figure approaching down Summer Street, just emerging from the trees.

"Oh my." Edith exclaimed softly. "Am I hallucinating?"

As the wind brought them another cascade of notes, Edith's face suffused with emotion.

"Fred?" She raised her voice, joyfully, brushing Mr. Fletcher aside to quickly step out into the yard. She raised her hand and waved it above her head.

"Over here," she yelled to the jaunty individual, interrupting the gay tune and receiving a face splitting smile for her troubles.

"Edith." He picked up his pace, and Edith flew across the yard, launching herself into his arms.

Ambrose Fletcher's eyebrows rose as he witnessed the mid-lawn collision and he turned slightly to Gertrude for some kind of verification.

"Her brother, if the name cried out is correct," she intoned thoughtfully. If she wasn't mistaken, Mr. Fletcher looked instantly relieved.

"Edith hasn't seen him for over two months. They share a

flat in Boston and he sent her here to be away from the influenza."

"Well, it's certainly nice to be witness to such a happy reunion." Ambrose watched with a satisfied cast to his face. "I myself have no siblings. It is just Mother and me." He cleared his throat. "And what about you Miss Edmands, do you have brothers and sisters?" Clearly he was trying to draw his attention away from the reunion.

"I have two sisters who are much older than me. They both moved to Chicago a few years back and I don't see them very often." This did not make Gertrude sad. She remembered little of her sisters in childhood, because Gertrude had been immersed in her singing from such an early age that she had little time for play. The siblings had enjoyed a few good years of back and forth visits while their parents lived in Hingham, but after her mother's death, the sisters had moved to Illinois to be closer to their own children who had settled there. For that reason, Gertrude too, mused longingly at the close bond that was obvious between Edith and her brother.

Edith was, at that very moment, tugging at Fred's hand, urging him quickly toward the front door.

"Gertrude," she was breathless and flushed with happiness as she approached. "Gertrude, I want you to meet by brother, Fred." She pulled him forward without ceremony and waited while Gertrude came down the steps.

Her first thought was that he was very tall. She, herself, was fairly diminutive, and Fred seemed to tower over her. He was dressed impeccably in pressed beige trousers and a button down shirt. Not nearly as dapper as Mr. Fletcher who still stood, expectantly on the stoop, but Gertrude was unable to bring her eyes away from their newest visitor.

"I'm so very pleased to finally meet you Mr. Torrey." Gertrude managed to speak and held her hand out in Fred's direction. He took it while boldly meeting her eyes and giving her a confidant smile.

"The pleasure is all mine. I have seen you once before, in concert, so I feel as if we've already met. And of course I've heard all about you from Edith, over the years." He looked her over before releasing her hand and turning back to his sister to tease. "And exactly what have the two of you been up to this morning?" His glance said everything about the soiled state of their clothing and Gertrude became mortified all over again.

"Oh dear," she exclaimed. "Wouldn't you just know it? We haven't had company in weeks, and the one morning we decide to clean the barn we have two visitors."

She remembered Mr. Fletcher then, and flustered in a way she hadn't felt in years, quickly rectified her social faux pas to introduce him. "I'm so sorry. Mr. Torrey, this is Mr. Ambrose Fletcher who was just calling on us at the behest of his mother."

Mr. Fletcher slowly took in everything about Fred before lifting his hat in acknowledgment of the introduction. "Mr. Torrey." He said politely.

"Mr. Fletcher." Fred inclined his head slightly in return.

Gertrude, looking at the difference between the two men, wondered that just minutes before she had been admiring the cut of Mr. Fletcher's suit and his elegant style. She wanted to laugh out loud. Compared to Edith's brother, he looked to her, now, as slightly effeminate. When Ambrose turned back to her with the intention of leaving, she found that she didn't mind in the least.

"Well, I must be off ladies, Mr. Torrey. I will tell my mother to look for an advertisement for your re-opening in the spring."

"No need Mr. Fletcher. I will personally ring her up and let her know."

"That's very kind of you. I look forward to seeing you again. Both of you." He gave Gertrude his most charming smile and then reached for Edith's hand, giving it a small squeeze before—with a final bow—walking back to his automobile parked in the drive.

Edith, although clearly intrigued by the handsome detective, dismissed him with a brief wave, and attached herself to her brother again. "How long can you stay?"

Gertrude assessed the small bag at his side which indicated that this was not just a day trip.

"Two or three days, if you'll have me. I've got some time coming to me at work for all the extra hours I've put in during the sickness." He gave them a serious look. "I've also made sure, as much as I can, that I haven't carried any illness here with me. There have been no new cases of the flu at work for over a week, and I've kept to myself so that I could visit."

To Gertrude, it looked like he was choosing his words carefully.

"I've also forgone the last two meetings of my men's group for those very reasons. Attendance has been way down since the influenza hit anyway, so no one will question my absence." He perked up. "So if it's all right, I'd like to stay. And I'll make myself useful." Once again his gaze rested on their soiled clothing. "I'd be more than happy to help you ladies out in the barn." He raised an eyebrow at Gertrude.

Her smile blossomed instantly, although she wasn't sure if it was because of his offer of help or just the fact that he was staying. Suddenly the day seemed brighter. Working in the barn for the afternoon took on a whole new complexion.

"We'll be very pleased on both accounts, Mr. Torrey." She turned to hide her unaccustomed blush. "Edith, why don't you see your brother settled and I'll tell Mary that we have one more for supper this evening." She gestured for them to go ahead of her into the house, but Fred held back until Gertrude preceded him. She couldn't help but think, "Nice manners."

Aloud she said, "It will be nice having you join us. I'm sure the work will go much faster with your help." *And your muscle*, she added to herself, looking at his arms, appreciatively.

****

Fred followed Edith up the front staircase, surreptitiously placing a small envelope into her hand. He looked back to make sure he hadn't been spotted, and an unfamiliar twinge caught him off balance. Gertrude had turned away and her small figure was back-lit in the midday sun that streamed through the windows. She was stunning.

He stood, stalk still and a blunt feeling gripped his belly. He must have made some small noise because she turned to look up at him, questioningly. He successfully shook off his brief confusion and cleared his throat.

"It would please me, Miss Edmands, if you would call me Fred." He knew by her reaction that his eyes must have momentarily held a glint of something she had not seen from a man in quite some time. "May I call you Gertrude?"

"Yes…yes, of course…Fred." She swept from the hallway, clearly flustered, and a rare tingle set up right behind his breastbone. The feeling was new, and just a bit disturbing.

****

The rest of the day passed in a blur. Chores were accomplished and laughter was abundant. Gertrude was amazed, but the three worked side by side in perfect choreography as if they had been doing it all their lives.

Edith was the first to call it quits. "I'm done in." she exclaimed after carting the umpteenth load of manure to the back field. "It must be time to clean up." She paused for another moment. "And I'm starving."

Gertrude stretched and agreed. "I think you're right. We're finished for today." She glanced at her watch and was surprised to see that it was after five o'clock. “Oh, dear. We have just enough time to clean ourselves up before Mary puts supper on the table.” She glanced at Fred, feeling a slight panic. “Don't even think of getting to the table a minute later than six or she'll make our lives a misery.” Edith held her eyes wide in agreement, but Fred, glancing back and forth between them, was puzzled.

“Does Mary have a problem if you come to the table late?” The thought was clearly absurd to him. “You do know that for years, Edith cooked my meals and would keep them warm for me no matter what time I arrived home from work,” he praised his sister. “Does the woman not work for you?”

Gertrude and Edith burst into laughter.

“Sometimes I wonder who's in charge.” Gertrude led the way across the yard. “But we learned, early on, if we wanted a pleasant meal, we needed to follow her rules.” She tapped her lip with one, soiled finger. Mary is very…dedicated…? Insistent…?”

“Bossy.” Edith chortled.

Gertrude suppressed a snort. “Whatever you call it.” She playfully poked Fred in the ribs. “Just don't be late for supper.” She whipped her kerchief from her head and shook out her chestnut curls.

****

Amongst the lushness, damp tendrils clung to Gertrude’s face and Fred found his fingers itching with a sudden urge to smooth them back. This was the second or third time he'd entertained confusing thoughts about Gertrude. Damn if something wasn't wrong with him. He hadn’t felt this way in years. Not since… No. He would not let himself think of Maude. It always sent him into a melancholia to imagine what might have been, even this many years later. He pushed the thoughts away and quietly followed the ladies to the house.

Later that evening, after being shown to his quarters to clean up, he'd enjoyed a lively supper. And as he arose to help clear the dinner table, he congratulated himself on bringing his wayward thoughts back under control. He had employed the diversionary tactic of flirting with Mary as she served, but she was a hard young woman and none of his teasing had any effect. On the other hand, both Edith and Gertrude had noticed what he was trying to do and egged him on, hiding their faces in in their napkins every time his efforts fell flat. Well, he'd see about that.

"Mary, the meal was delicious. I want you to relax now and take a seat while I put the dishes in the sink." He reached to remove a plate from her hand and inadvertently entered into a small tug of war. She stubbornly refused to let go.

"It is my job, sir," she informed him coldly, "to clean up after the meal."

He glanced over at Gertrude, who clearly had all she could do to stifle her amusement. She'd surreptitiously told him that Mary's apathy toward men had been apparent since the woman had first been employed, but she had proven to be so capable—if not quite delightful—working in the tea room around the many women who regularly attended, that they had decided her mood could be ignored.

Fred, getting his first taste of what Mary was like, didn't know how they put up with it. Heaven help him for the duration of his visit. He wasn't sure if he could keep his mouth shut regarding her attitude.

Gertrude reached for the offending plate, and loosening Fred's grip, gave it to Mary before taking Fred by the arm.

"Come on, Fred. We'll adjourn to the sitting room and you can bring us up-to-date on what's been happening in Boston. The kitchen is Mary's domain and she won't thank you for getting in the way."

Mary sniffed as the plate was handed over to her and

turned with a flounce, but Fred's trouble were only just beginning, and they had nothing to do with Mary.

The spot where Gertrude held his arm jolted with burning awareness.

# Chapter Seventeen

May 1919

*Boston Daily Globe May 2, 1919*

*Lettish Red Flag Parade Leads to Bloody Melee Which Rages for an Hour, Many Women Taking Part...an international labor May Day Riot started through the attempt of the Lettish Workmen's Society of Boston to hold a red-flag parade in Roxbury as a climax to a revolutionary mass meeting in the Dudley Opera house yesterday afternoon...two policemen were shot, one stabbed and many bruised in Roxbury Battle...several others were clubbed and stoned and attacked with ice picks... angry Crowds seek reds.*

"Oh God. Oh, God no." Fred ran for his life as the crowd erupted in screams and gunshots. Momentum was moving the panicked mass of workers east toward Cliff Street but Fred struggled against the tide in the opposite direction. All he could think of was to get home...and to get there as fast as he could. He broke free of the mob and spotted the sign for Ruggles Street. His breathing became a tight fist in his chest as he bolted toward it, ripping off his red arm-band as he fled. He was three miles from his house and he hadn't run like this in years, but the adrenaline was propelling him forward faster than he thought possible.

He approached the crossing at Shawmut Ave. and had to

slow down to catch his breath. The crowd noises were behind him but he sensed more danger at the intersection and willed himself to look before leaping out into the street. Sure enough, several blocks away, police with paddy wagons from Boston were screeching towards him to back up the Roxbury precinct.

Without forethought he dashed across Shawmut and took a fast right onto Westminster. He heard shouts behind, but no one followed him as he moved away from the melee. He knew he would eventually come to Tremont Street and if he could keep from being intercepted there, he could make his way to the railroad tracks and then home.

His lungs were on fire but he dare not stop. If he were found on the street even without his armband, his working-mans clothes could implicate him as a parade participant. Sweat poured down his face as he wondered what had gone wrong.

In his head he clicked off the names of the groups participating in the parade, starting with the Lettish Workman's Society. He had also recognized signs proclaiming the presence of the Central Branch Socialist Party, the Young People's Socialist League, the Amalgamated Clothing Workers, the United Hebrew Trades, the Women's League, Cutters Local 73, and of course his comrades from the IWW. These were groups that had met together many times without a problem. What was it that had caused this gathering to deteriorate into chaos?

He remembered seeing a police presence, and voices raised in anger from the front. A disquiet had filtered back through the crowd as it became apparent the police were ordering them to disband for a lack of proper permitting. This, in itself, should not have created a problem. They were used to being ordered to disperse and always assented with alacrity. They didn't want the police seeing any threat of revolution in their actions. Their organizations had always worked toward peaceful protest.

Then Fred remembered. *A rock.* A rock had come out of nowhere and hit the person standing next to him, and before he knew it, people outside of his group started throwing things and shoving them. He had seen the flash of more than one knife before he broke free to run. What did it mean? American laborers had been celebrating the May Day holiday for almost thirty years and never once had it erupted as things had exploded today.

He slowed his pace and willed his heart to decelerate. It was midday on Thursday and because of the holiday, he was starting to see groups of strollers out taking the spring sunshine. He took a right onto Tremont Street, and received only a few stares from the passersby. He heard sirens in the distance, but felt better walking normally to blend in, until he spotted Northampton Street. Crossing over and feigning a nonchalance that he certainly didn't feel, he ducked onto Northampton and, quickly again, made his way to the Boston and Providence tracks. He didn't relax again until he entered The Baseball and Bicycle Grounds where he finally took a minute to sit on a bench with his head in his hands to catch his breath.

He was too old for this. Up until this moment, the violence that—purportedly—surrounded the movement had seemed nebulous. Fred simply believed in equal rights for all Americans and the IWW had seemed a rational route for him to take. The idealism he had held in his youth, however, had worn thin and he just now realized that the risks he took being part of the IWW had not translated into any progress that he could see. Today proved to him that even the general population must think of them as radicals and were not, as the organizers had assured their followers, behind their cause.

A shiver of fear went down his spine. His name was now part of the IWW records. He was certain after today that the government, using their rights under the newly passed Sedition Act, would be confiscating everything from the halls of the local chapter, and his address would be included.

He increased his pace as he neared home. What would be the odds of government officials coming to find him and taking a look around his home? Pretty damned good if the rumors he'd heard bandied about were true. He would have to destroy anything in the house that smacked of socialism. Terrible, hushed stories had already reached his ears about illegal search and seizures, unwarranted arrests and forced deportation of radicals. Had he put himself, and unwittingly, Edith in serious danger?

His body was just about wrung out as he mounted his stairs. He opened the door and things felt surreal; oddly normal, as he watched Edith bidding one of her students goodbye. She raised her eyes to smile at him, a hand still on her small pupil's back, when the smile disappeared from her lips.

"Goodbye, Norman. I'll see you next week at the same time." Her gaze never left Fred as she led the boy to the door and shut it behind him with a soft click.

"What's happened, Fred? Why are you hurt?" She raised a hand to his temple and wiped away a small smudge of blood.

"Huh," he grunted, bringing his hand up to the spot. He must have been hit by a rock while fleeing and winced as he became aware of the slight sting.

"It's nothing," he assured her. "But I wouldn't mind a cold drink."

"I'll get your drink, but don't think you can keep anything from me. You have to tell me what's happened. You're out of breath and bloodied. And worried." She sought to compose herself and headed into the kitchen.

****

Worried was the mildest word Edith could come up with for the fear that she read on Fred's face. She was no fool. Since she had come home a month ago, she had seen evidence of that in which Fred had become involved. Gleaning information from the leaflets he left lying around and reading between the lines with what the newspapers were saying, Edith surmised that her brother was, at best, involved with socialism and, at worst, an anarchist.

She had, to this point, dismissed the thoughts of anarchism but now filled with dread at Fred's appearance. Could it mean that he had become so radicalized? Edith returned to hand Fred his drink.

"Why don't you start by telling me where you've been?" She asked calmly.

He took a few sips and the tension began to leave his shoulders when he ascertained that she was not about to go into histrionics.

"I wish I could say that I was at the Red Sox-Yankees game at Fenway."

"But you can't." She clipped. Edith wanted no part of him trying to lighten the seriousness of his situation.

"No, I can't, and I'm sure that you'll be reading about it soon enough, so I might as well tell you." He ran a hand through his thick, already disheveled hair. "I was part of a group in Roxbury this morning, meeting at the Dudley Opera House. We talked about labor rights and cheered for ourselves and got riled up and took to the streets for our annual parade. Only this time, something went wrong." His eyes took on a haunted cast.

"The police were involved and people started getting angry and before you know it, things got out of hand," he cried. "Edith, it was like I was stuck in a horrifying Fatty Arbuckle or Buster Keaton police-chase movie, except this was really happening." He put a tentative hand to his cut, then laid the side of the cool, perspiring glass against the abrasion.

"All I could think of was just to get home as quickly as possible. So I ran." His eyes glazed over as she saw him re-live his escape. "I got lucky. By the time I started up-town a whole force of police were headed in to join the scrum." His face looked so devastated that Edith finally sat down.

"Well, you're away from it now, so it's over, right?" she questioned, knowing by his look that it wouldn't be that simple. There was more to come, and she braced for it.

"I'm away from the actual skirmish," he told her. "But a few months ago I became a member of the local IWW and they have all of my information; my name, where I work and where I live."

"And you're afraid that they'll come here after you." Edith swallowed her fear to keep her rational brain engaged. Some part of her must have known it would come to this. She had begun expressing her concerns to Gertrude, discreetly over the phone and more in depth in a few recently exchanged letters. Gertrude had cautioned her to stay out of it.

"Your brother seems like a sensible sort," she had written. "He's made his way in the world just fine up 'til this point. I'm sure you have nothing to worry about. Let him go about his business."

Good advice until now. Gertrude was always so sure of herself in tough situations. What would her friend do with this new problem if she were in their shoes? The answer came to her in a flash.

"You're going to have to leave town for a while," she told Fred decisively. His mouth dropped open. Clearly he had not thought that far ahead.

"Leave town?" he repeated incredulously. "That's ridiculous."

"No. It's not," she scowled at him. "Just until things die down. And you should probably leave today. These things have a way of escalating quickly. The authorities will want to put the public at ease by rounding everyone up they can who was involved, and if your name is in those records, they'll certainly come looking here, for you."

"But what about you?" Fred spluttered, unable in his surprise to disagree.

"Pah," she chided. "What will they discover about me…an aging spinster piano teacher? I'd like to see them try to connect me to any Bolshevik plot."

Fred had to know that her reputation was spotless, and that she would, in all probability, be safe remaining. "But where will I go?" he questioned abjectly. "I'll be without a job; indigent for the first time in my life."

Edith could see the seriousness of his situation taking hold.

"Who would take me in? I don't know if you're aware or not, but before our brother Arthur and his family moved to St. Louis last year, he and I had a falling out over the organized labor issue. Arthur won't welcome me for an extended visit, especially under these circumstances."

His concerns bit at Edith's heart.

"Where will I go?" he questioned. And this was another first for him. Edith never remembered him—with the brief exception of when Maude had died—putting himself in her hands.

"Don't quote me on this," she pondered. "But I think Gertrude will be willing to put you up. She still hasn't hired anyone to help around the estate and you proved to be very useful when you showed up in the fall. I'm going to place a call to her right now."

Fred barely nodded, and seemed far too docile, which worried her. But she trusted her instincts and headed to the phone.

"Do you have a fire in the stove?" he asked suddenly, coming out of his stupor before she rang up Gertrude.

She looked blankly at him, wondering if the rock had temporarily disturbed his sanity.

"Yes, I do. But what does that matter?"

A decisive look came over his face. "I need to burn the documents and reading material that I've collected over the years." His self-disgust was evident. "It's as if my eyes have suddenly been opened and I realize that the last twenty five years of my life might just as well have never happened. But it's funny," he continued. "Instead of feeling cheated, I somehow suddenly feel lighter, freer than I have in a long time." He gave Edith a nod. "Let me know what Gertrude has to say and then I'll start packing." He left the room, she realized, to dismantle his existence.

Edith listened to the phone ring and ring. She bit her lip in consternation, hoping that someone was home. "Pick up, pick up." She willed either Gertrude or Mary to be there. The two women were on their own now. Dear Martha, at her advanced age, had succumbed to the flu after insisting upon traveling to Boston to care for her ill grand-niece and nephew. It was an event made even sadder by the fact that public funerals had no longer been held during the epidemic, so there were no final goodbyes.

Eight rings, nine, and finally a breathless, "Hello? Gertrude Edmands here."

"Oh, Gertrude, I'm so glad you're home."

"Edith dear, it's good to hear your voice. Mary and I were just trellising some new rosebushes when I heard the ring."

"You'd better sit down. I have a huge favor to ask."

"All right. Just let me remove the pins holding my hat, and I'm all yours." There was a brief pause. "Fine. I'm seated, now. What's on your mind?" She probably imagined a student whom Edith was unable to cope with, or a neighbor that wouldn't stop pestering. She had a surprise coming.

Edith chose her words carefully, because the Boston and Hingham operators would be privy to her conversation. "Fred needs a place to stay for a while." Edith began in a rush. "I can't tell you for how long but it's quite important that he go on vacation right away, due to *the issues we have mentioned in our correspondence.*" Edith prayed that Gertrude would understand without having to explain further over a public line.

"Oh my. Is it very bad?" She could almost hear Gertrude

race through all of the things that could have gone wrong with Fred's life, and she must have come to a fast conclusion. “How quickly would he like to come?”

Edith looked at her watch. It was four o'clock. “He could be on the six o'clock train tonight if that would be all right.” Her voice broke with emotion for the first time.

Gertrude must have heard the catch. “Nonsense. We don't want him to take the train *in his state.”* She playedup the conversation for possible eavesdropping by Sadie. “I'm getting ready right now to drive in. I should be there in a little over an hour. Tell him to be ready to leave right away. I assume that's what you want?”

Edith gave a huge sigh of relief. “I'll miss him, Gertrude. But it's what needs to be done.”

“Then I'll see you soon. Sit tight, everything will be fine”

Edith entered the kitchen and her mouth dropped open in astonishment. A pile of books, two feet high sat on her counter. They were being fed into the oven one by one by Fred, who looked quite calm under the circumstances.

“Could you hand me another, Edith?” he asked.

Absently she picked the top one off the pile. “*Revolutionary Socialism, a Study in Socialist Reconstruction” by Lewis Corey.* She gave the book to Fred. “Gertrude is coming in her automobile to get you,” she told him.

“Right now?” He raised an eyebrow. “Wouldn't she rather I take the train?”

“No,” Edith assured him.” She insisted on coming and said she'd be here in an hour. I'll put the rest of these in the fire so you can go pack.” She thought the situation over quickly and called to him as he headed toward his room. “Why don't you pack enough for a couple of weeks, and we'll see how things go from there.”

“That sounds like a plan.” He disappeared into his chamber and over the crackling of paper in her stove, she heard him drag down his old and dusty suitcase from the top shelf of his closet. When was the last time he had used it? In all the years that they had lived together, it had always been Edith who had gone away, never Fred. He had, many times, put her on the train for a singing engagement or to visit Gertrude, but never once had she been the one to remain at home alone.

She asked herself the question, could she cope without him? *Get a grip, my dear,* she admonished her internal trembling. It's only for a couple of weeks and you can't look hesitant in front of Fred. If he thought for a moment that you were unhappy about being left alone, he would refuse to leave. She shuddered to think of a confrontation between Fred and any authorities who might show up at their door. No. Better her than him. This was undeniably for the best.

It seemed like very little time passed before the knocker sounded. Edith glanced cautiously out the window, relieved to see Gertrude's Model T parked by the curb.

"Fred, she's here," Edith called and went to the front door.

****

Gertrude breezed in, exuding comfort and confidence, bringing Edith into a reassuring hug. "Things will be fine. You'll see." Gertrude refused to see the doubt in her friend's eyes. "Will you tell me what's going on, now that we don't have Sadie for an audience?"

"I'll fill you in all the details once we're on our way." Fred stood in the doorway, filling it with his broad shoulders, a suitcase in one hand and a duffel bag across his back. He looked every bit the man who had fascinated her a few months earlier, and he appeared even more rakish with a day's growth of beard on his face and a cut above his eye.

"I expect that you will." Gertrude admonished succinctly, hoping her face didn't reflect the heat that had suddenly risen up, unbidden within her. She turned quickly to her friend. "He'll be fine in the country, Edith. You should wait a few weeks and then come visit once you feel the need for secrecy is past. I'll call you in a few days to find out if anything more has happened here."

****

Fred marveled at the composure with which Edith's friend accepted the situation, completely without explanation.

He fussed with his bags, watching the women say their goodbyes. And while they were at it, he tried hard not to notice the way Gertrude's driving coat so lovingly hugged the ample curves of her back-side.

# Chapter Eighteen

May 1919

She shouldn't have been surprised. It had been two days since Fred left with Gertrude. Edith gently parted the lace curtains again and surreptitiously looked out. Yes, they were still there. Two of them, black, shiny and new. Two Chevrolet Touring Cars parked by the curb outside of her house. And each automobile held three men wearing dark, low slung fedoras. She had noticed them this morning on her way to the market. They were still there when she returned from her errands, and there they remained two hours later. What were they waiting for? She wasn't sure. Perhaps they were thinking that Fred would appear, or maybe they were attempting some intimidation. If that was their plan, they were succeeding admirably.

She paced the floor and looked at the ormolu Empire clock on the sideboard. Her eleven o'clock student would be arriving soon, and at least that would take her mind in a different direction. As it was, she had approached the telephone over a dozen times, wanting to call Fred, but had quickly snatched her hand back each time. She had read how the government could listen in on your telephone calls. Even though her rational self felt that Fred's involvement would not warrant such drastic measures, she reminded herself that there were two, not one, but two obviously federal vehicles sitting outside her door.

She peered out again and saw her student heading up the sidewalk. A curious boy, he stopped and stared at the polished automobiles, not bothering to disguise his interest. Edith panicked when it looked like he was about to approach the lead car, and didn't the little scamp walk forward with just that intent. Without thinking, she threw open her window and affected a stern tone, calling down to him.

"Jeffrey. You're late young man. Hurry up the stairs now so that we can get started or I'll call your mother."

Her admonishment had the desired affect and Jeffrey quickly abandoned his curiosity and segued to the door. Edith let out a sigh of relief and gently closed the window. Her heart couldn't beat any faster even if she'd run a race, she thought, and tried to regain a calm visage. She needed to ready herself for teaching.

By the end of the day, Edith had taught six students and purposely allowed herself no time to look out the window. Her last pupil departed and she began cleaning up sheet music, scoffing at her fears. Surely the cars had long since gone.

With hands that could not keep from shaking, she went to the window and pulled back the curtain. Her knees gave out and she slumped to the floor. They were still there. Dear Lord what was she going to do? She glanced at the phone again. No. She couldn't use it. Think, think. A slow uneasy smile came to her lips. If she dared walk out again, she could go two blocks to the druggist who was still open and use the pay telephone at the back of his store. Her spirits rose. That was a grand plan of action. She refused to cower in her house like a prisoner.

With hands still unsteady, she pinned her hat to her head and tugged on a short jacket. Making sure she had proper change, she picked up her draw-string reticule, took a deep breath and made her way onto the street. She did not so much as glance in the direction of the offending conveyances, but primly and with purpose, walked down the street.

As soon as she was out of sight she quickened her steps. By the time she reached the drug store she gasped for breath, but felt better for her brisk excursion. Entering the cool interior of the establishment made her feel even better. She pulled off her gloves, and with heels clicking on the wooden floor, made her way to the back and found the pay phone unoccupied. She gave the operator her request and waited as the phone line rang in Hingham, the only sign of impatience, her rapidly tapping foot.

Gertrude picked up on the third ring.

"Gertrude Edmands here," she stated.

"Oh Gertrude. I'm so glad that you're at home. I…I need to talk to Fred right away."

"Has something happened?" Gertrude had to have heard the tremor in Edith's voice." Are you able to talk?"

"I'm on the pay phone at the local druggist. I can't vouch for the privacy of my home phone at the moment, those…visitors that we thought might arrive when we last talked are making a nuisance of themselves."

She was doing her best to keep any interested operator from gleaning the true meaning of their conversation, and Gertrude followed her lead. "Do you want me to come and get you, Edith? I'll leave right now. I fear that you shouldn't be facing this…company on your own."

"No Gertrude, but thank you, dear. I think keeping a regular schedule will be the least suspicious thing to do. I just need to speak with Fred to find out how he would like me to handle our "guests", you understand."

"I understand perfectly. He's in the tea room, working on a few renovations before we re-open. I'll just be a minute getting him."

Edith had calmed considerably hearing her friend's voice. She was relieved to regain some of her composure. It wouldn't do to start crying with Fred or he would come back to Boston lickety-split, and her visitors would get what they wanted. Her foot slowed to tap out a more patient beat.

"Edith." Fred's comforting voice crackled over the wires, nearly undermining Edith's determination not to cry.

"Oh Fred," Edith sighed. "Did Gertrude fill you in on my problem?"

"She told me you had visitors but no details."

"They arrived this morning in two cars. I can't be sure of the time, but they were definitely there when I went out to do my shopping. There are six men, which is quite an intimidating number, but they haven't come to the door. I imagine that's because I've had students come and go all day and they were reluctant to interfere. I do believe they will feel free to call upon me tonight and I wondered what you would like me to tell them about your absence?" Finding the right ways to modify her choice of words was starting to wear on Edith and she lapsed into silence, waiting for her brother to speak.

"Tell them the truth, Edith." Fred was also choosing his words carefully. "Tell them that I came home, looking unwell on Thursday, threw some things into a bag and left with a friend. You didn't see who it was that picked me up. Right? I didn't tell you where I was going. Let them have a good look around. Invite them to have some time in my room if they want. I don't think they'll stay long." She could hear the strain in his voice. "I'll be worried about you."

He knew that once they hung up, she probably wouldn't be able to call again until the next morning. He and Gertrude would likely fret all night. Edith sought to allay his fears.

"Don't worry too much, Fred. I'll call you first thing tomorrow and let you know how things go. Please say goodnight to Gertrude for me. I must ring off. The druggist is signaling that he is about to close the store." She waved back at the white-coated gentleman motioning from the front. She hesitated for a moment. "Say a small prayer for me, will you?" she asked, blinking back tears.

"I will sister." Edith pictured his dear face lined with

worry. "Talk to you soon."

She slowly replaced the phone back in its cradle, murmured a vague goodbye to the proprietor on her way out, and set her feet determinedly toward home.

****

Gertrude took one look at Fred's face and went to the counter to pour him a glass of whiskey. She knew he usually drank nothing stronger than beer, but felt he needed something with a little more grit to get him through the night. As an afterthought, she poured one for herself.

"What did she say?" Gertrude placed the glass in front of him and sat down holding her own.

Absently he swirled the golden liquid. "Six of the bastards have parked out in front of the house all day."

She knew he was so absorbed in his thoughts that he was unaware of the strong language he used. Gertrude allowed him this slip with her reply.

"And what do you think the bastards will do now?"

He turned his head with a start and gave a raw chuckle.

"Ah, Gertrude," he clenched the glass in his hand and paused in thought for a good long time. "I wish to God I knew." The whiskey had to burn as he tossed the entire contents of the glass down his throat.

****

Edith arrived home before dark and shivered as she passed the black cars. She expected it wouldn't be long now before the occupants made their presence known. Entering her home, she turned on all of the electric lights and started for the kitchen to make her supper. She hadn't even crossed the room when the knock came.

Edith smoothed her damp palms on the sides of her cotton dress and quietly opened the door. The first thought that hit her? There were only three. A hysterical laugh threatened to bubble out of her throat and she fought hard to suppress it. They must have figured that three large men in dark clothing, no, make that two large men and one fairly diminutive individual, would be enough to frighten her, and had left the others to amuse themselves outside. Had they drawn straws? She forced herself to become calm and brought a most polite smile to her lips.

“May I help you gentlemen?” She was proud that her voice didn't quiver and that her gaze was direct.

The small one in had to be in charge, she surmised, as he pushed forward of the others. The remaining two reached to remove their hats from their heads as soon as she spoke, but boss-man was clearly not giving her any polite concessions and simply thrust his identification at her. She took it while pointedly looking at his hat but he showed no inclination to remove it.

“Cuthbert Hamilton.” She read from the small leather folder. One of the large men actually snickered and Mr. Hamilton snatched back his ID and quickly corrected her.

“Cuddy,” he growled. She refused to be intimidated and held her hand out again.

“I'm quite sure it said Cuthbert, and I did not have the opportunity to see what agency you represent, sir.” She paused significantly. “Are you gentlemen with the Zion's Watch Tower Society?”

He turned the full force of his weasely eyes on her with displeasure and reluctantly handed back the folder.

She was a little less bold the second time around. “I see, you are Federal Agents.” She took a tentative step back into the parlor. “Would you care to come in gentlemen?”

The ferret stepped through the door almost pushing her aside while the other two—obviously brought up with better manners—let her precede them into the room.

“To what do I owe the pleasure of your company this evening?” Edith relied on her years of propriety to dictate her behavior with the boorish man.

"We're looking for Fred Torrey." Stoat-face didn't waste time with niceties. "Are you his wife? His girlfriend?" He sneered.

Edith was sure that the agent knew full well that she was Fred's sister. They would not have approached without fully researching things first. They would also know that the house was in her name as sole owner. Fred had transferred title to her a year ago, and it was just dawning on her why he had done so. She looked down her nose and let disdain drip from her words.

"I am his sister, *sir.*" She placed emphasis on the title to let him know that she used the term loosely.

He was not in the least bit put off. "Where is he and when did you last see him?"

"Two days ago, in the late afternoon," she informed him. "He came in as I was finishing up with a piano lesson." She kept her voice hard, emotionless. "He packed a small valise and then walked out of the door. When I looked from my window he was stepping into a Model T and that's the last I've seen of him." So far Edith had told no lies.

"So you have no idea who was driving the car and where he went?" he continued.

"That is correct." Edith crossed her fingers in the fold of her skirt and promised to say numerous "Our Father's" at church the next day, figuring it was best to cover her bets with both pagan and Catholic doctrine.

"So you won't mind if we search the premises?" Now Mr. Hamilton was beginning to act like the badger he resembled, wanting to root through her house. She recalled Fred's advice and tried not to choke on her response.

"Be my guest, Mr. Hamilton." She gave him a serene look as well as a reason to be excused from his detestable company. "And if you don't mind, I haven't yet had my evening meal. I'll be in the kitchen if you have any further questions."

She opened the icebox and stared into its dark interior for several minutes, not actually seeing any of the food inside. Her mind was focused on the noises from Fred's bedroom where they were obviously turning things upside down.

"Damn." She muttered, then added another "Our Father" to the list she owed. Edith grabbed the first thing that her hand settled on and turned to the table clutching a block of cheese. A cold supper it was, then. She sliced herself some of the bread she had purchased at the bakery that morning and sat with bread and cheese in her hand, forcing herself to eat. The rummaging men took their time and she watched the minutes tick by on the clock while she willed the food to go down her constricted throat. Twenty minutes, thirty…Edith had just gotten up to put the teakettle on when one of the two larger men appeared at her kitchen door.

"Ma'am," he intoned politely. "We have one more request before we leave if you'd join us in your front room."

Edith wiped her hands on the napkin she was clutching and followed the giant out of the kitchen. She noted with calm detachment that none of the men, including Mr. Weasel had anything in their hands to show for their search. *Thank you, Fred,* she whispered in her head, before turning her attention to the leader of the pack. He began speaking without polite preamble.

"I insist that you call us if you have any contact with your brother." He pinned here with his beady eyes. "Or if you happen to remember his where-abouts." This last was said in a way that let her know that the agent didn't for a moment believe her story. Mr. Hamilton tossed his card onto the table, not making a pretense of civility by handing it to her. Edith felt herself grow cold. This was an enemy whom she would be unwise to antagonize. She thought to ally herself with him the best she could.

"And you, Mr. Cuthbert," she retorted deliberately. "If you find Fred before I do, tell him that he's not welcome back until he pays me the two months rent he owes." She felt her parting remark might finally have made a dent in Mr. Hamilton's haughty demeanor as he actually touched the brim of his hat when she opened the door and wished the trio a good evening.

She closed the door behind them and leaned her entire weight on it in order to prevent the collapse that she knew would eventually come.

# Chapter Nineteen

May 1919

Almost a month had passed since the day of the parade and Fred was not happy. He sat on the bale of hay in the loft of the barn where it was quiet and he could think. The news from Edith was both good and bad. Since that horrible evening when she had dealt with the Federal Agents, they had not confronted her again, but she was aware that every day or two, one of the black sedans would park across the street for an indeterminate amount of time. She couldn't use her own phone to call them for fear of a wire-tap, and so used the phone down the street or communicated through the mail. She wouldn't even let Fred or Gertrude send anything to the house directly, afraid that someone would open her correspondence. Everything was now done through the mother of a pupil. God only knows what she had told the woman.

"Damn it all." He cursed out loud, running his hand back through his hair. He had fully expected this to blow over in a week or two at the most, after which time he had planned to go back to his boss, beg for forgiveness and get his position back. Now that weeks had elapsed, he was pretty certain his job was a thing of the past. He could hear himself now.

"Hey boss, I know I've been gone for a month and that the Feds have been by asking for me. They might have even told you that I have ties to an organized labor party. So what do you think? Can I have my old job back?" Sure. That would go over like a ton of bricks. He wasn't going to waltz back in and expect to start collecting wages again.

And wasn't that just the problem. Between Gertrude, Edith and himself, he had been the one bringing in the majority of the money supporting everything, and now he wasn't. In order to have Edith maintain the flat in Boston, he couldn't touch another cent of their savings. He had enough ready cash on hand to see himself through two, maybe three months. With her students and their bank account, he figured Edith had about two years before she would have to worry. Gertrude was another matter, entirely.

He had paid her a stipend for the month when he arrived, even though she hadn't wanted it, but he couldn't give her more and still have enough to start over someplace else. The good news remained that she was within a few weeks of having the tea room up and running and her voice pupils were starting to trickle back in, but it would be a burden for her to feed and house him while she was living so close to the bone. He had to leave, go someplace far away where no one knew him and get a job. But, hell, he liked it here. It was easy and it was close to Boston in case he needed to go back for Edith. He had also fit seamlessly into the daily routine in Hingham, doing odd jobs around the farm, eating, sleeping soundly. Gertrude had made it simple for him, demanding nothing and leaving him to work things through.

Ah, Gertrude. There was the biggest issue, if he was to be honest. She was constantly nearby and he was finding it damned hard to deny his attraction. He found himself listening for her voice, watching her move, and he looked for any excuse to get close and make her laugh. He felt like a simpleton. When was the last time he had been bothered like this by a woman? He couldn't recall. Certainly the more distance he put between them the better, before he did something stupid they would both regret. He pictured a few things he'd be regretful for and his body tightened uncomfortably. Shifting on his hay bale, he made up his mind. This was ridiculous. The sooner he could leave, the better. Gertrude could put an advertisement in the paper this afternoon for a new boarder. That would help her finances, and keep him from making an ass of himself. She wouldn't even realize what a close escape she'd had, from his unwanted attentions.

****

Gertrude watched Fred coming toward her from the barn. He walked like a man with a purpose. She continued to hang clothes on the line as if unaware of his approach, when instead she was acutely aware of everything about him. Her life seemed to have taken on a new sharpness since he'd been around.

She looked forward to getting out of bed in the morning just to see him at the breakfast table. She noticed things about him that she shouldn't. He only shaved every other day, and on the off day—which she liked better—there was a patch of gray right in the middle of his chin. He buttered his toast from left to right and spread it all the way to the edges. He smelled good. And wasn't that the most disturbing thing of all. Gertrude felt like a dog, always trying to catch his scent. She was surprised he hadn't noticed.

Even now, as he was striding across the lawn, her breath started coming a little faster and her nose began to twitch. He made her feel so young.

Gertrude kept busy with laundry, pretending to be totally unaware of his presence, which he must have noticed, for he purposefully started up a small, off tune whistle to warn her of his approach. She turned and smiled. His whistle faltered. What had him in such a twist?

"Need some help?" he instinctively picked up the basket and held it so she didn't have to bend to retrieve the wet things.

"Thank you, Fred." She hoped the blush on her cheeks didn't show.

"I…umm…I've got a problem, Gertrude." He stared at the clothespin she was fixing in place.

"What kind of problem?" She was momentarily non-plussed. Fred did not tend to be someone who unburdened himself on a whim. She turned her attention to him, laundry momentarily forgotten.

"It's something I've been putting off thinking about, but I can't ignore any longer." He ran his free hand back through his hair. "You know as well as I do that I've probably lost my job in Boston by now." He paused significantly and looked her way.

"Yes, I assumed that was likely. And?" Her eyes fixed to his face, urging him to continue.

"And be that as it may, I have to make sure that I can support Edith in the future."

"Absolutely," Gertrude commiserated. "Edith's well-being should be high on your list of priorities."

"Exactly," agreed Fred. "So you will understand why I can't stay here any longer. I can't pay you rent for another month because I need the money I have left to get started in a new situation."

Gertrude wasn't stupid. She had known this was coming. Fred was a proud man. And keeping that in the forefront of her mind, she attempted to placate him, treading lightly.

"But Fred. I've been meaning to discuss this very thing with you." She began to hang the laundry again, purposely keeping sheets between them to give him privacy over his thoughts. "You have been such a big help to me over the past few weeks. The tea room would never have been ready for opening without you, not to mention the fence you mended in the goat pen and the repairs to the plumbing in the attic, and don't think I didn't see you up on the barn roof fixing that hole where the shingles came off this spring."

Fred acknowledged with a grunt that he had accomplished

those things and tried to interrupt but Gertrude kept right on going.

"I would have had to hire a man to do all that and it would have cost me a lot of money, so now hear me out." She paused for a quick breath. "Would you consider staying on as my live-in handy man? I'd give you free room and board, and once the tea room gets up and running, we could discuss what I could afford to pay you."

Fred stood, seemingly dumb-struck. Gertrude could tell he was flummoxed and unknowingly came around the latest sheet and began patting his hand where it held her basket. "Of course you can take some time to consider the offer, but I think when you mull it over you'll see the sense in it." She paused. "If you agree, we could have Edith pay us a visit and bring out the rest of your things."

****

She sounded downright pleased at the prospect…and blast it all, it made sense, and made *him* feel good too; especially good because the daft woman was touching him with her small warm hand.

Trying to ignore her touch, he cleared his throat and glanced down at her. Was this really what he wanted?

"I *will* have to think about it." He said, attempting to sound brusque, but it was too late. Gertrude must have seen a glimmer of something in his eyes and knew he would be staying.

"I knew you'd see sense," she replied, and with an effort that seemed to end the conversation, she bent and picked up another shirt, continuing to hang the laundry.

Later that day, with his permission, she sent word to Edith, via the alternate address they'd been using.

*Dearest Edith,*

*Your brother has agreed to stay on to become my "Man Friday", if you will. I am quite thrilled with this arrangement as he has been a tremendous help around the farm. We are hoping that you will come for a visit as soon as possible and bring the rest of his belongings with you. Don't take the Greenbush train to Hingham. Fred thinks it's better to take the Old Colony to Bridgewater to throw anybody off a possible trail. If all looks clear, we'll wait for your call and meet you there with the car. We know that you will take every caution not to be followed. I look forward to seeing you again.*

*Your loving friend,*
*Gertrude*

# Chapter Twenty

June 1919

*Gertrude Edmands re-opened the Rocky Nook Tea Room this week. There will be a one hour morning sitting beginning at 11AM, and an afternoon sitting at 2PM, daily. On Saturdays, there will be held a two hour tea and concert beginning at 3PM. The Tea Room will be closed on Sundays. Miss Edmands has let us know that reservations are required.*

Gertrude had restricted attendance in the tea room to forty, ten tables of four, and was beyond pleased when she sold out for her first Saturday afternoon. She was going to sing *Ah Mons Fils* from *Le Prophete* by Giacomo Meyerbeer. It had always been one of her favorites and she hoped to do it justice after her long hiatus.

Fred had wished her luck much earlier, declaring his intention of staying outside to direct the parking of cars. Mary, as was her habit of late, hadn't said much beforehand as the two women bustled about the kitchen making food and decanting tea. Her never joyous employee seemed to get more sour with each passing month, and if she wasn't such a genius in the kitchen, Gertrude would have long since let her go.

The new girl, Annie Spring, engaged to serve the clientèle on Saturdays was a different story altogether. Young and bright, she added a welcome and enthusiastic presence. She had been recommended by Ambrose Fletcher, who seemed to have taken an active interest in the re-opening of the tea room. He'd even pitched in to help Fred with the arrangement of tables a week before, and while toiling it had occurred to him that with Gertrude singing on Saturdays, Mary would be hard pressed to take care of all the cooking and serving by herself.

Ambrose immediately informed Gertrude that he and his mother knew a woman in her twenties—with whose family they were well acquainted—here in Hingham who was looking for a job and would be a perfect fit. He had arranged for a meeting between Annie and Gertrude the very next day, and Gertrude had hired her on the spot. Annie's lilting Irish brogue was rich and warm, she had serving experience, and Gertrude was certain she would instantly make her guests feel welcome.

Which led to her epiphany that she couldn't express how relieved she was that Mary had been relegated to the kitchen. The cook's dour tendencies seemed to have become stronger recently, and Gertrude was glad the patrons of the tea room wouldn't be subjected to Mary's dark moods. She couldn't understand the reason for Mary's ill humor. With the re-opening of the tea room, her wages had been increased and Gertrude always made sure she was praised highly on her menu choices and cooking.

She was becoming more certain that the woman's poor attitude was somehow connected to Fred. For what reason, Gertrude couldn't be sure. She wouldn't visit that thought right now. She needed to clear her mind to sing in just a few minutes, and to stop her hands from shaking.

****

Fred was nervous because Gertrude was nervous. He had been singularly in tune with her moods lately, and had easily picked up on her agitation earlier in the day. He was doubly frustrated because there was no way he could comfort her. Hell, if he were the one who had to sing in front of a bunch of people, he would have upchucked several times by now.

The last of the cars had been parked almost an hour before and he knew Gertrude would begin her performance soon.

He eyed the small number of men milling around the yard—probably only six or seven—who had brought their wives and decided to wait the two hours in the fresh air. Could he possibly slip past them into the sanctuary of the barn? He was feeling so shaky, he desperately needed a little something to calm himself down. That little something was a bottle, yet to be disturbed, which he had hidden at the bottom of the horse's hay bin a few weeks past. A short nip would go a long way toward making him forget his worries for Gertrude.

He greeted a couple of the men he recognized from earlier that week as he sauntered toward the barn door. But as soon as he pulled open the portal, he was approached by one of the more vocal gentlemen who he remembered as Pete.

"I've always been curious to see inside this barn." Pete looked at Fred, obviously looking for an invitation. Fred sighed to himself. There went his solitary comfort.

"Sure, sure." He motioned for Pete to go on in, and much to his chagrin, all of the other men followed.

"It sure is a big one," the one with glasses stated as he stepped through the door.

"Good lot of storage," said another, looking up two stories into the loft.

"Do you know how old it is?" This came from Pete who smiled his appreciation of the structure.

Fred gave in to their prodding. "We think it was built just after the house was finished, so, somewhere in the mid to late 1700's. The previous owner was unsure of the exact year." His career dealing with lumber helped him voice his thoughts. "Nobody around here has been able to cut trees that big, though, in an awfully long time." He pointed to the enormous beams that were easily a foot thick. Each man nodded in approval and the small talk continued.

They turned out to be a jovial bunch and the topic of conversation moved from the barn, to the weather, to the price of flour, and eventually to President Wilson and politics. It wasn't long before one of the men snorted and voiced a popular opinion.

"If Congress has its way, we'll all be drinking tea like the women." He inclined his head toward the house. "That new law they passed after the armistice?" he stopped and shook his head.

"What new law?" a couple of the men asked in unison.

"Don't you know?" he answered. "Starting the end of this month, all our liquor will be limited to two and three quarter percent alcohol. Just piss." He spit onto the dusty floor.

Some of the men looked puzzled, but Fred recalled reading about the temporary Wartime Prohibition Act. It hadn't mattered much to him at the time. He wasn't a heavy drinker and he had been distracted by his involvement with the IWW. But now he remembered.

The idea of the bill was to save grain for the war effort but it hadn't actually made it into law until after the war was over. Damned if it hadn't even taken effect yet, not until June 30th. He had read that people had begun referring to July 1st as the "Thirsty-First".

The displeasure that ran like a current throughout the group was universal at the injustice of it all, and Fred, caught up in the moment, offered a share of his largess to the other gentlemen.

"Would anyone care to join me in a drink while we're still able?" He went to the hay bin and pulled out his bottle of Jim Beam Whiskey. Smiles all around told him he had made the correct offer.

****

Inside the tea room, the women seemed to be thoroughly enjoying Gertrude's performance. She shouldn't have worried, thought Annie Spring standing at the back of the room. She sings like an angel. Annie glanced around to make sure that all of the women still had tea, then relaxed to give full attention to her employer. What a lovely woman Miss Gertrude was, and she liked that fine Mr. Torrey, too. Now, there was a situation just waiting to bust open. She stifled a giggle. The attraction between the two was as palpable as the teapot she held. Annie smiled. She really was going to enjoy working here.

Hopefully, the tea room would become a big success and her hours would be increased, eventually elevating her to a coveted position as live-in help. By the look of things, she might get her wish. There was a full house today, and they had sold out all during the next week.

The only pickle in the barrel was Mary, Annie huffed. There was a sour number if she had ever seen one. Not that she would be telling Miss Gertrude her business, but she thought that Mary was a bad bit of trade. If she was in charge, Mary would have gotten the sack a long time ago, and perhaps if Annie made herself very useful…well, she was new and would keep her mouth shut for now. But make no mistake about it, she would show Miss Gertrude her own skills in the kitchen and eventually her employer might be prodded into putting Mary Kirke out to pasture.

****

Fred listened to the talk swirl around him about alcohol and prohibition. He had never been that interested before, but now he was listening with full attention. Talk was, that as long as two and a half years ago Congress had called for an amendment to the Constitution that would ban sales of all alcohol. Not only that, but the bill had actually passed by the end of that year and hung in limbo, waiting around to be ratified. It finally had gotten all the necessary votes in January of this year by 36 of the 48 states. It seems the men in the barn knew all about it… that, and that Wilson was against the bill. They doubted, with Wilson's interference, that it would ever become law. Fred was not so sure, and said as much to his cohorts.

"You seem to have a lot of faith in the strength of our president, but I wouldn't be surprised if he's overruled on this one."

He had witnessed many things during his years in the city, he told them, and this is what he knew; men in the house and senate—men in charge—usually got what they demanded and the common man be damned. If someone high up in government really wanted a ban on alcohol, then sure enough it would be coming. It was just a matter of time.

He looked around him. The men were all enjoying their drinks. And why shouldn't they. A small germ of an idea began to take shape in Fred's head; something he was going to have to think on. There were opportunities everywhere. One just had to be ready to take advantage.

****

The ladies were making their way down the driveway, clucking like the hens in the yard. The group in the barn became aware of the commotion and one by one drained their glasses with guilty smiles.

"Fred, thanks for your hospitality." The one named Joe, or was it William, clapped him on the back. "Maybe we could do this again next week before the new law takes effect."

"It was a great way to kill some time," Pete agreed. "I'll be here next Saturday." There were murmurs of agreement from the other men.

"You'll all be welcome." Fred was magnanimous, holding court at the barn door as the men departed.

He had forgotten all about his earlier attack of nerves, and belatedly wondered how Gertrude had fared. Was his lapse of attention due to the alcohol he had consumed, or from the idea that was beginning to form and take root in his brain?

# Chapter Twenty-One

November 1919

On October 28th, all his new friends realized that Fred had been correct in his assumption about the power of Congress. The 18th amendment, implemented by the Volstead Act was passed. Wilson, as expected, had vetoed the bill but Congress overrode his veto and Prohibition was to become a law on January 17th of the New Year.

Since that day in June, Fred had begun making plans. He had taken steps to renew his acquaintance with an old pal, Hugh, whom he'd known from the docks. The gregarious Scotsman had opened a bar in Dorchester after returning from active duty in France, and Fred had been able to purchase several cases of full strength liquor from Hugh before the Wartime Act had gone into effect. It had been a wise investment to make with his remaining cash. Fred had already doubled his money. Now, every Saturday a small group of husbands and drivers convened in the barn and paid him well for their libation. If things continued for a few more months in the same vein, Fred would soon have the means to invest his money in Gertrude's property, helping with some of the bigger expenses around the farm which had been ignored in the lean, previous years.

Fred's original seven barn attendees had quickly grown to a dozen. He recognized several prominent citizens who had started dropping in, by their first names: Mason, Daniel,

Albert. The group, as always, talked politics and pondered the latest developments by the government.

"What are you going to do, Fred, once the law has passed?" queried Pete. "I sure will miss our Saturday afternoons."

The other men murmured their agreement.

"Well, I've given it some thought." Fred smiled. "If you care to read it, the Volstead Act only makes it illegal to buy and sell alcohol. It doesn't make it illegal to *have* it or *drink* it." He saw the puzzled looks around him and sought to explain. "If I can manage to get a hold of some more liquor before January 17th and tuck it away, we should be good for a while. The only problem is, I can't sell it to you."

His words met with more confusion.

"So what are you going to do?" asked Joe amidst a chorus of groans. "Give it to us for free?" There was chuckling throughout the room.

"No. Not free, but you won't be buying alcohol from me, either." Fred once again brought silence to the room. "I will, however, have to charge each one of you a membership fee every month to maintain your good standing in my new men's club." He waited for this to sink in. "We'll continue on Saturdays just like we do now, but everyone will pay dues. We'll elect a couple of guys to write up an agenda, have some lively political discussions—he saw the light beginning to dawn on the assemblage—and keep minutes of our meetings just in case we come under scrutiny." Fred was smiling by this time.

"And after all our men's club business has been taken care of, when we're sure we won't be disturbed, who's to question it if I bring out refreshments?" He clasped his hands at the nape of his of his neck and sat back to enjoy the excitement in the room. It was risky, he knew, having to procure the alcohol, but his friend Hugh had assured him that sources were far from drying up. In fact, business was booming.

Fred briefly thought about the potential risk to Gertrude,

but quickly dismissed his unease. If he kept her in the dark there should be no repercussions where she was concerned.

The only possible fly in the ointment was Ambrose Fletcher who, as good as his word, brought his mother to the tea room weekly. It bothered Fred to have Detective Fletcher around, and worried him even more that the police station on Joy Lane, where Ambrose worked, was less than a quarter of a mile away. It bothered him, too, that the detective seemed far too interested in Edith when she visited. Fred was uncomfortable with that on so many levels. He knew it was only a matter of time before Fletcher started finding excuses to stick around, maybe accompanying his mother for a Saturday performance. He would have to be very watchful if that should happen.

Before breaking up his little party, Fred assured everyone that things would remain just as they were until the first of the year. There was no need to rock the boat prior to the law taking effect. If the men knew, in the meantime, any other discreet individuals whom they thought could take part in the "club", he wanted their names so they could be thoroughly vetted before being allowed to participate. The men eyed their watches and made their last requests for drinks before the tea room emptied out.

****

Gertrude looked over the assemblage after her solo was complete. She couldn't have been more pleased with the way things were turning out. Her teas during the week were not always full, but were very well attended. But her Saturday teas—with concerts as an added draw—were sold out every week in advance. She was in better voice than she had been in years because of all the vocal exercise and was becoming quite well known in the community. As a matter of fact, everything was just about perfect. Even Mary had become more amiable lately. She wondered if that had to do with the one thing that wasn't to Gertrude's liking.

She let the bothersome thought enter her head. There was no way around it. She was not imagining things. After Fred's initial month in the household and once he had become an employee, he was keeping his distance. This development pleased Mary no end and bothered the heck out of Gertrude.

Fred had weaned himself away from attending meals in the kitchen or dining room, and most times took a plate up to his room. He reported to Gertrude the goings on with the property each day, all the while addressing the wall slightly above her head. He was pleasant but not fatuous, present but not attentive. It was driving Gertrude mad. If he had calculatedly set about to cause her agitation he could not have done a better job. She had begun finding excuses to engage him in conversation; had purposely in the last week tried to incite him to anger—with no luck—and was itching for an excuse to spend a prolonged amount of time in his company.

Annie had noticed the changed atmosphere as well. Last week Fred had barely acknowledged their presence while repairing a light fixture in the tea room before walking out.

"Whatever has gotten into Mr. Fred that he's acting so strangely?" She finally asked, clearing tables after one of their sittings.

Gertrude nearly wept with relief that someone else had observed what she thought she might have imagined.

"So you've noticed too." Gertrude had desperately needed someone's opinion on this.

"Pshh. I've noticed all right," Annie had readily agreed. "The man has a right stick up his arse if you ask me." She clasped a hand over her mouth, appalled that she had just said out loud what was supposed to have stayed in her head. "I'm begging your pardon Miss Gertrude. I didn't mean to say it so's you could hear it."

Gertrude had snickered when Annie didn't realize that

she'd compounded her error.

"It's fine Annie. You are entirely correct, and I don't mind you saying so. Mr. Fred *has* got a stick up his ass, as you so aptly put it, and it's about time we figured out why it's there."

The picture had so amused both women that the snickers turned into spasms of mirth and then became uncontrollable laughter when Annie inadvertently snorted. As they entered the kitchen with dirty teacups, the pinched look on Mary's face from their unexplained behavior renewed had their hysteria and it was a good long time before they'd been able to calm down.

Gertrude recalled the episode with a smile as she moved around the tea room to say goodbye to her clients.

"Mrs. Hersey, it was so good of you to come." Gertrude extended her hand to a formidable woman donning a large hat. "Mrs. Vickery, it was nice to see you, as well." She ushered the pair toward the door. A hand on her arm made her pause and she waved to the ladies before turning to see Mrs. Loring still seated at a table.

"Dear Miss Edmands," the august woman implored. "I wonder if you would have a moment to chat with me."

"Why of course, Mrs. Loring. If you'll excuse me for just one moment, I'll say goodbye to my other guests and be right back to join you." The woman seemed prepared to wait for an audience as she had yet to don her coat.

Gertrude eventually finished up at the door and went back into the tea room. Mrs. Loring looked anything but comfortable and Gertrude wondered what the problem could possibly be. She and Annie had—in the previous months—supplied numerous patrons with everything from recipes to advice on their choices of tea, and Gertrude had every expectation that the conversation today must be similar. She was therefore surprised when Mrs. Loring looked around the room as if to make sure that there was no one listening in. She spotted Annie coming in the back way.

"Could you dismiss your girl for a short while? I'd rather speak to you in complete privacy."

Gertrude was now intrigued, and with a quick flourish of her hand she urged Annie from the room. "I'm at your disposal Mrs. Loring."

"Well, it's a bit awkward what I want to ask. I hope you'll forgive me for being so forward, but I just didn't feel comfortable asking Mr. Loring's help." She paused to fuss with her empty teacup.

Gertrude tried to compose her face into what she deemed an approachable look. "What is it, my dear?"

"I wonder if you would be able to…" Mrs. Loring lowered her voice to a whisper even though there was no one else in the room. "Do you think I could get…?" She cleared her throat and began again. "What are the chances that…?" She finally got it out. "Could you procure me a bottle of that which Mr. Loring has been enjoying on Saturdays in your barn?"

Gertrude was struck dumb. What had Mrs. Loring just asked? She pondered her response—perhaps for too lengthy a time—and noticed the prolonged silence was beginning to worry her guest, so she smiled as serenely as possible.

"I'll just need to leave the room for a moment," she patted Mrs. Loring's hand. "You understand," she added a squeeze and the woman looked relieved and expectant at the same time.

"Of course. Of course. Take all the time you need. And dear," she whispered conspiratorially. "I've brought my largest reticule." She patted the over-sized bag in her lap with a smug little smile and Gertrude backed from the room, her mind churning with possibilities.

She leaned against the smooth woodwork in the keeping room, willing her heart to slow down, and nearly jumped out of her skin when Annie cleared her throat from the opposite threshold.

"Are you feeling all right Miss Gertrude?" She had a

worried look on her face and Gertrude knew she must look a fright. Without thinking she crossed the room and grabbed Annie by the shoulder.

"Annie, what do you suppose the men do in the barn while we're having our concert?" They had both been aware that men would come and go, but they had previously given it little thought.

"Well, I suppose they talk, and look at each others' automobiles, and you know, do what men do when they get together." Annie thoughts were clearly inconclusive and Gertrude pinned her with a stare.

"Okay. More to the point. What do you suppose Mr. Loring and the rest are enjoying out there that can be procured in a bottle?" Gertrude became specific.

Annie's hand went to her mouth. "You don't suppose…" she started.

"Oh, yes. I do suppose." Gertrude was becoming so angry she was amazed that sparks weren't bursting from her eyes. "I suppose that Mr. Torrey has been doing something in the barn of which we have been blissfully ignorant."

"Yes, Miss Gertrude." Annie agreed quietly and unlike her normal self, seemed suddenly at a loss for words.

"I also suppose," Gertrude continued with her voice rising, "that Mr. Torrey owes us quite an explanation, wouldn't you say?"

Annie would not be present to witness Fred's explanation but simply agreed with her on principle. "Yes, Miss Gertrude."

"It's settled then," Gertrude gave a curt dip of her chin. "I will see to Mrs. Loring but you will have to clear up the rest of the tea room on your own today." Her face was now flushed and furious. "I will be going to the barn to have a talk, which is probably long overdue, with Fred."

Without waiting for Annie to answer, Gertrude swept back into the tea room. Her color was high, but Mrs. Loring probably assumed that Gertrude had rushed to the barn to find her a bottle of whatever she had in mind. She'd be sorely disappointed when she found that wasn't the case.

Gertrude used her years of public performance to appear calm. "I'm so sorry to keep you waiting my dear lady, but I can't seem to locate the item you've requested. I apologize…but perhaps if you come back next week…" Gertrude was so incensed at that point she had no idea what she was saying or whether it was intelligible. She just saw the relief on Mrs. Loring's face and assumed she had said the right thing.

"Well of course Miss Edmands. I will most assuredly be back next week and we can complete our, umm, business transaction at that time." She grabbed Gertrude's hand and pumped it up and down in a very unladylike fashion. "Thank you, my dear. Thank you very much." She bustled out the door without looking back.

If the jubilant woman had glanced around, she would have witnessed the look of determination on Gertrude's face as she slowly counted to one hundred.

By the time Gertrude reached that number, she figured all of the cars in the driveway had to be gone, and marveled at her own tightly held composure.

She would walk sedately to the barn, find Fred, and—forcibly if need be—remove the stick from his ass.

# Chapter Twenty-Two

November 1919

Gertrude looks good, thought Fred, watching her walk toward the barn. *Huh*, he pondered, she looks especially good since she's still dolled up in her concert clothes. *Strange*. Why would she be coming to the barn in her fancy outfit?

Fred took a closer look and noticed that her hands were clenched into fists by her sides, and grunted. This was no social visit. Something was causing her distress and she was coming to him for…advice…help? Funny that something would bother her so much she couldn't wait until things inside were cleaned up to seek him out.

As that thought crept into his head, it reminded him of something *he* hadn't cleaned up, and he smacked his hand into his forehead. The whiskey bottle and a dozen glasses littered the barn floor through the door directly behind him. *Shit.*

He quickly positioned himself across the entryway, stretching his legs out in what he hoped resembled a relaxed pose. Whatever was bothering Gertrude would be small beans compared to how she'd react if she found out about his extracurricular activities. She closed in and seeing the high color on her face, gave her his most nonchalant smile.

"To what do I owe the pleasure, boss lady?" he quipped. But when she was a mere few feet away, he got a good look at the fire in her eyes and quickly changed his stance to alert. Gertrude was angry. Very angry.

"Are you all right? Has someone done something to make you upset?" His ignorance was short-lived as she stepped in close and poked him in the chest.

"Yes. You. You son of a bitch." She drew back her hand and slapped him, hard across the face with all of her strength.

Fred's head snapped back, but he instinctively reached for her hand before she could deliver a second blow. His normal calm quickly gave way to a growing ire of his own, and using his free hand to mollify his stinging cheek, he glared at Gertrude as if she had lost her mind.

"What the hell was that for?" His voice boomed in a way that would, at one time, have had his subordinates running for cover. Gertrude didn't flinch. Cold as ice she responded.

"Let go of my hand you miscreant." Her words dripped with disdain.

"Like hell I will," Fred responded, pulling her even closer. "I'll let go when I know what's going on," he paused, "*and* when I'm sure you won't hit me again." He could feel his face beginning to burn, and was so spitting mad.

"I'll tell you what's going on," Gertrude ground out. "Next week, *Mrs.* Loring would like a bottle of whatever *Mr.* Loring is drinking in the barn."

She shouted the words right into his face and something flickered in his gut. And that something wasn't the repentance that Gertrude expected. Hell no. It was more like a powerful surge of lust, finally being released after weeks of suppression. And it must have shown in his face because Gertrude was suddenly looking at him in a totally different way, understanding suffusing her eyes as she tugged on her hand to escape.

Fred felt like he had suddenly lost his mind. He should have been making excuses, explanations. Hell, he should have been groveling with apologies. Instead, his mind refused to function properly. Here was Gertrude, sparks shooting from her eyes, closer to him than she had been in weeks. So close that… Was he really going to do this? Damn right he was.

Without further ado, he grabbed her around the waist and pinned her up against his achingly, needy body. *God*, she was soft in his arms. His mouth descended, his desperate need unleashed as he crushed any remaining words from her lips.

****

Gertrude was instantly lost. The feel and taste of Fred filled her senses, and his kiss went from punishing to all consuming in the course of a few seconds. His hands roamed her back. Her fingers buried themselves deep in his hair. Gertrude could tell he wanted her desperately. Now. In the barn. And when he drew her deeper into the shadowed doorway, tightening his hold, she became frightened at the depth of her feelings.

She used all of her strength, both mental and physical, to pull away, panting. He gave her room without releasing her, and all she could do was stare, transfixed at his mouth. Swallowing convulsively, she slid her hands to his chest where they lay trapped between them, and flexed her fingers into his steely muscles, gaining a few seconds to ask herself what the hell she was doing. She acknowledged, with what little brain she had remaining, that this was what she'd been waiting for, for weeks. She was more than ready for this and sought the right words, but Fred rolled his head back and groaned.

"Gertrude," he breathed out. "I'm appalled at my lack of self-control, and I know I've behaved abominably." He loosened his hold further. "You came to me, angry at my betrayal of your trust and here I've compounded it by compromising you in an entirely different way."

He continued before she could speak. “But in truth, I’ve felt like kissing you for weeks, and it’s taken all of my willpower to hold myself in check.”

She couldn’t find her voice while she was still pressed against him in such an intimate manner. *Oh, Lord.* Had she just snuggled even closer?

Gertrude swallowed dryly, again, and willed herself to relax. Wasn't this where she'd wanted to be for weeks, as well? Held securely in Fred's arms? She had to let him know that what they were doing was okay, but there needed to be some conversation first, and she needed to calm down. Gertrude took a deep breath and looked up into Fred’s deep brown eyes.

“I do believe I'm in need of what Mr. Loring's been having in the barn.” She ducked her head and murmured the last against his neck.

“I’m not sure I’m hearing this properly,” Fred gritted, and pushed a curl back, behind her ear. “You need what…?” His voice was hoarse, emotional.

“A drink,” she reiterated. In truth her legs were shaking, and she reluctantly pushed herself away, hoping the space would restore sanity.

****

Fred saw the tremor as Gertrude moved. Had he scared her? Hurt her? His brow furrowed, and another groan was inadvertently ripped from his throat. He had to stop himself from reaching for her again. He was a mass of uncertainty. An additional apology formed on his tongue, but before it came out, Gertrude stunned him into silence. Standing on her tip toes, she softly brushed his lips with hers. Without waiting to see if he followed, she entered through the barn door and threw the request, once again, over her shoulder.

“Yes. I need a good stiff drink.”

Fred couldn’t tell what hit him. His hand absently touched

his mouth as he followed her, bemused. Inside the barn, in the dim, late afternoon light, he watched her pick up the nearly empty bottle of liquor and lift it for a quick swig. At that moment he knew he was lost. He couldn't hold back. He had to kiss her again.

Fred covered the distance between them, but this time his touch was gentle as he took the bottle from Gertrude's trembling fingers and pulled her into his arms. She turned her face up to him willingly, and his tongue teased a drop of alcohol from her lips before urgently exploring further.

She opened beneath his tender onslaught like a flower.

He stood as long as he could, supporting both of their weights, before finally collapsing back against a sawhorse table, bringing her with him and nestling her firmly between his legs. There were no lies between them now. She could easily tell the effect she had on him, and he wasn't ashamed. She was a beautiful, strong woman, and he desired her in every way.

Each gave what they could offer, and took what they needed for themselves. They were too old for games, and young enough that need was still a driving force. It had been a long time for him, and Fred was going to savor every moment, and hopefully give Gertrude pleasure beyond her wildest imagination. Just not here. Not now, in the barn. She deserved better. He pulled back reluctantly.

"You're not mad anymore?" he questioned, turning her face up to witness and relish the hazy look in her eyes and the swollen pink of her lips.

"I'm still furious." Gertrude's husky words were belied by her hands which blatantly explored his shoulders.

Fred's chuckle rumbled deep in his chest before he lowered his head again. "Then I guess furious is good."

He wasn't aware when the light had totally gone with the setting of the sun—so intent was their absorption with each other—until Annie's hesitant voice penetrated their self imposed cocoon.

"Hello in the barn?" she began tentatively. "Miss Gertrude…Mr. Fred…are you in there?" Annie queried, and at the sound of Fred clearing his throat, she became bolder. "I'm certain to be wondering if you've killed each other dead by now."

Laughter bubbled up in Fred's throat, and he answered her from the darkness. "No Annie, we haven't killed each other." Fred's deep voice surprised him with its mellowness.

He heard a sniff. "So you say, Mr. Fred. But I'll be hearing from Miss Gertrude if you please. She's the weaker gender and the one most likely to have been done away with." Annie sounded quite imperative.

A snort escaped from Fred, who disagreed heartily with which one of them was the stronger, and apparently Gertrude thought the same.

"I beg to differ with you Annie," Gertrude's voice rang out toward the door, clearly amused. "If there was any killing to be done, it would have been me putting this scoundrel six feet under."

Annie's reply sounded relieved. "Ah. Well you both seem grand, so I'll be on my way. And just for your own edification, you wouldn't catch me in that barn after dark."

Fred knew that Annie probably crossed herself superstitiously before turning away with a final admonishment. "And Mary says supper's on the table, about to spoil, so if we *want* no deaths here tonight you'd better stop what you're doing and be getting in."

Fred listened as Annie's steps retreated down the driveway. "Before we go in, we should talk about this." Fred removed Gertrude's hand from his thigh. "But it's not going to happen if you keep touching me like that." She was clearly using it as a diversionary tactic to glean more kisses.

"You want to talk about what's been going on here, now, or what's been going on with you and the other men in the barn." Gertrude put her hand right back.

Fred sighed. "Neither is going to be easy." Trying to

ignore her fingers to the best of his abilities, he filled Gertrude in on exactly what had happened since that first Saturday afternoon. He left out nothing, including the amount of money that had been garnered to date, and how he planned to proceed. Gertrude had several questions when he was through, but started off with the one that must have bothered her the most.

"Was this the reason you've been stand-offish lately? Both Annie and I have noticed that you've been avoiding the house."

"I'm not a very good liar, Gertrude," Fred admitted. "If you had shown any curiosity about the men on Saturdays, I wouldn't have been able to keep anything from you, and I didn't want you to be involved. I wanted to keep you safe from any problems that might arise."

She gave a small huff. "I think it will go better now that I know." Gertrude surprised him. "I can make sure that nothing up at the house interferes with your little club, and…," she dimpled up at him, "if Mrs. Loring is any indication, I can make a little money on the side as well."

"Well, we'll see about that." Fred still had the idea that she should remain uninvolved.

After more discussion, interspersed with a lot more kissing, they pair finally agreed that it was time to go in for supper. The air was fresh and crisp, as it was wont to be in early November. Fred slipped his arm around Gertrude as they walked to the house. He hadn't forgotten that there were two things she had previously thought they might talk about.

"Now, as to what *just* occurred in the barn," he teased.

Gertrude came to an abrupt stop and looked up at him, expectantly. "I told you I've been wanting to kiss you for a very long time, so I'm giving no apologies."

He could see the wheels turning in Gertrude's head as she pondered her response. "None necessary," she smirked. "I've been feeling the same way." She never failed to surprise him. "So where do we go from here? Do you…I mean to say… will we…"

"What is it Gertrude?" He was teasing her in earnest now. "You just have to ask." His smile in the dark was clearly infuriating her.

"Will you be coming to my room tonight?" Her face was on fire as she blurted out the question that burned to be released, and she trembled in his arms as she waited for his answer.

Fred reluctantly backed away, so that in the moonlight he could look directly into her face. He lost any trace of banter and lowered his voice to a mere caress.

"Ahhh. As much as I'm a fool, and will kick myself as I lay awake tonight in my solitary bed thinking about you, I won't be joining you. I plan to court you as a *lady* deserves to be courted."

Gertrude sighed. In appreciation of the sentiment, or in disappointment that they wouldn't bring things any further tonight?

He squeezed her hand, then leaned down and whispered even more softly in her ear. "But when I do come to your room…and make no mistake about it, I will be bedding you, there will be nothing ladylike in how I approach that."

His eyes sparked down at her, and Gertrude's intake of breath let him know that he had said just the right thing.

# Chapter Twenty-Three

January 1920

*Boston Evening Globe, January 3, 1920*

*COMMUNISTS IN 33 CITIES ROUNDED UP*

*"...Raids were ordered in 33 cities over the United States and promptly at the hour of 9 last night, the operatives moved with clock-like precision in the roundup of Communist workers and sympathizers."*

*"REDS" SENT TO DEER ISLAND*

*"...between 700 and 1000 men and women believed to be "Reds" were rounded up in the big raids in New England last night...Deer Island will be the great detention pen for New England "Reds", and, according to local officials, within a few days will have as guests the largest bunch of "Red" sympathizers of any place in the country. The first batch went down the harbor this morning on the steamer Monitor..."*

Fred's hands were wet with dishwater as the telephone rang four, five, six times. He cursed, rapidly wiping them on a towel that had been draped over his shoulder. Gertrude needed to find somebody, fast, to replace Mary who had walked out in a huff last week. Her departure had become inevitable, as she seemed unable to handle Fred's elevation back to "person of interest" by Gertrude.

Annie was planning to work more hours, but with the burgeoning success of the tea room, more hands were needed. For now, Fred filled in, not just handy-man any more, but house-boy. It wasn't that he minded housework… Hah, who was he kidding? He hated it.

Fred answered the phone.

"Edmands residence and the Rocky Nook Tea Room," he intoned politely.

"Fred." Edith sobbed in relief. "You're there."

"Well, where else would I be?" he quipped, belatedly registering the distress in her voice. "Wait. What's going on?" he demanded. "Is everything all right?"

Edith took a moment to compose herself, but still sounded strained.

"I was worried. I thought for sure…" Her voice caught again.

"Take a deep breath, Edith and try to tell me what's wrong."

A few moment's later, having followed his instructions she was finally able to speak. "Have you seen the morning papers?"

"No. No yet. Gertrude hasn't arrived back from the grocers and she usually picks up the…" His words were interrupted as he caught sight of Gertrude, standing stock-still in the doorway, pale as a ghost with the newspaper held out in front of her. It trembled in her hand.

"Ah, she's just come in, Edith. And apparently she's been afflicted with the same thing that's ailing you."

By this time Fred wasn't sure he wanted to know.

Gertrude stepped closer and turned the paper so that Fred could see the headlines. *Communists in 33 Cities Rounded Up.* He sat down hard.

His voice was devoid of emotion as he spoke into the phone's mouthpiece. "Why don't you talk to Gertrude while

I read this?" He handed the device over and began skimming the article.

It was as bad as it could possibly get. Palmer's Raids were apparently not yet over. Not by a long shot, and they seemed to have taken on a new life under J. Edgar Hoover. The article Fred was reading informed the public that the U.S. Department of Justice had amassed over sixty thousand names of Bolsheviks and sympathizers using the enrollment records of suspected Communist organizations. Fred was pretty sure that one of those organizations would be the IWW. The Feds were making arrests and detentions without warrants, this time with the blessing of the Labor Department who had previously been a source of protection but had obviously caved in to some high handed pressure. The LD had also agreed that those detained would not get their constitutional right to an attorney until well after a case against each person could be established. Fred swore, then sat quietly while Gertrude said her goodbye's and came over to place a hand on his shoulder.

"Edith's taking the train out. I'm going to pick her up." Gertrude caressed him gently. "Will you be all right?"

"Well, if they haven't come for me yet, I assume they're not able to find me." He swallowed his disgust.

"That isn't what I meant." She knew that guilt riddled him for the dangerous position in which he had placed Edith, and the sympathy in her eyes almost had him undone. Unable to speak, he nodded his head and gestured her to the door. She gave him the privacy he needed, quickly leaving to pick Edith up at the Bridgewater train.

Fred's thoughts wandered through the faces of all the men and women he had met through the organization over the last few years, some highly radical, but most just common people like himself searching for a better way to work and live. He, luckily, had been able to escape. He couldn't help but wonder. How many of the ones who couldn't, were on Deer Island right now?

Fred attacked his chores as if doing penance for the rest of the day, straining his muscles to the point of exhaustion. He was thankful they had closed the tea room down this week after the busy holidays. He couldn't imagine trying to hold whiskey-court with his mood so grim. He wanted sweat that froze in the winter air. And pain. And numbness.

Conversely, there was no fear. At least not for himself. If the Feds came for him, he would be able to handle it. His trepidation was saved for the women. Would he ever forgive himself for involving Edith and then Gertrude? It was doubtful that any direct harm would come to them, but who knew what collateral damage could be sustained. He had to sit with them tonight and devise a plan. A plan that would help them survive if anything should happen to him.

There was another piece of bitterness, as well. The one that haunted him all afternoon while he worked. He had been dreaming, lately, of asking Gertrude to marry him, and now, in good conscience, he could not. For the past month and a half he had blissfully been playing a game. A game where he wooed Gertrude, made her fall in love and then asked for her hand in marriage. But now that couldn't happen.

Even if Gertrude still wanted him, there were two insurmountable problems. The first was that he could be deported at any time, tarnishing her good name if she were attached to him. The second; if he wanted to remain anonymous, he couldn't put his name to any documents that had to be filed with the state, and that included a marriage license. He rubbed his tired eyes with one hand while absently stroking the flank of their remaining milk cow. Farm life had become entirely agreeable. He hated that something could spoil it at any minute. Conversation at the supper table tonight would not be easy.

****

Gertrude arrived back home with Edith to see Fred, perched high on a ladder planted haphazardly in the snow, clearing ice from one of the barn gutters. He briefly raised a hand, but that was all the acknowledgment they received. If her mood was pensive, Gertrude thought, she could only imagine the thoughts that were swirling around in Fred's brain.

Edith preceded her into the house, both silently acknowledging that Fred wouldn't be in until he was good and ready to talk things over.

Edith excused herself to unpack, and Gertrude started the evening meal. This was one time they were certainly thankful for Mary's absence. The housekeeper would have relished the sour atmosphere, but Gertrude was still trying to be optimistic. Surely the witch hunt in Boston would die down quickly. After successfully rounding up so many in yesterday's raids, wouldn't the Feds be through hunting? The sooner that happened the better.

It had been such a very long time since she had been pursued and adored by a man, that the thought of Fred being forced to leave made her heart stutter. Fred was the consummate suiter, meeting all her womanly expectations. *Well, most of them*, she smiled to herself. He still held off on fully consummating their relationship, but showed her every consideration from flowers and small gifts, to blatant compliments that made her blush.

He used every opportunity to whisk her into a dark alcove or a cobwebbed outbuilding and kiss her silly. She had long since abandoned the pretense of pushing his hands away from parts of her body that ached to be touched, giving as good as she got and boldly caressing him back. It was only a matter of time before she broke through his odd, old-fashioned resistance to feel warm skin under her hands instead of worn flannel.

Gertrude had been patient this long, and would persevere—under these new circumstances—for as long as it took Fred to come to grips with his fugitive status. And to overcome the certain grief he must feel, mourning for a past and friends that would be, no longer. What she would refuse to do, was to let him bury himself in remorse. She shook her head, vehemently.

Gertrude believed Fred was safe here, and she had to let him come to that realization. Once time passed and he understood that no one was coming for him, he might be able to bury his demons.

Fred finally came through the door well after dark. He looked cold and tired and Gertrude suggested he clean up before supper. Edith was at the table absently polishing a spoon and the smell of beef stew permeated the kitchen.

"I'll only be a short while." His voice was gruff and the ladies exchanged a look as he disappeared up the stairs.

"There's something on his mind besides the raids," said Edith quietly.

Gertrude, too, had seen his eyes, dark with purpose. "You don't suppose he's planning on going away?" She shivered at the thought.

"He's so full of pride, it's hard to tell." Edith eyed her friend knowingly. "But I'd say if he has the choice, he'd rather stay around."

She was clearly giving Gertrude an opening to admit that something had been going on with her brother, but Gertrude was not quite ready yet.

"I'd rather he stayed," she choked out. "I don't think I could replace him." And that was as close to an admission as she would get.

Fred came back down, and Gertrude served up the stew in silence. It wasn't until they were eating the last of yesterday's squash pie that Fred spoke up. With quiet deliberation he put down his fork, picked up his napkin and wiped his mouth.

"Edith needs to know what's been going on."

For a moment, Gertrude thought he meant to divulge their personal secrets and her hand fluttered to her chest. She understood, quickly, when he launched into an explanation of the men's club in the barn, that it was not his intent.

Clearly it was hard for him to confess these sins to his older sister, heaped on top of the ones that had made him leave Boston. But if Edith was shocked, she hid it well and simply nodded as he continued talking.

"The reason I've told you all this is because I have cash that I've been amassing and I need you to take it and put it in the bank." He took a large wad from his pocket and placed it on the table in front of Edith.

Gertrude was stunned. She had no idea that Fred had made so much money. If she was honest with herself, she would admit that it looked like a lot more than she had taken in from the tea room.

Edith may have been overwhelmed, but she hid it well and became eminently practical. "I think Gertrude should put it in her bank account. If I put it in ours, I'm not so sure that it wouldn't be noticed by people who might be monitoring our affairs."

Gertrude was proud and dismayed at the same time that Edith had come to think like this. Certainly Fred had never meant for her life to become so complicated.

"You're right." Fred pushed the money toward Gertrude. "We're all a family now and we need to take care of each other. If Edith needs money, I know you'll get it to her."

Gertrude hesitated to touch the pile, but he did not relent. "Not only do I want you to take this money, but if something should happen to me…"

Gertrude envisioned him in a cold, hard cell on an island in Boston Harbor, and her eyes teared up.

Fred cleared his throat. "And you can't afford to keep up with this place, I want you to go to Edith in Boston. The flat is completely paid for, and with the proceeds from the sale of this house, the two of you should be able to make do for the rest of your lives."

"Now Fred. Nothing is going to happen to you," Edith

scolded. “But if it does, of course I want Gertrude to stay with me.”

Gertrude swallowed hard. It was more difficult for her, all this talk of her future entwined with others. She’d never had anyone to depend on but herself. Oh, her father had been supportive in his way, but Gertrude had forged her financial independence at a very early age. She had also never been privy to any close, sibling-like relationships. Her tears spilled over. “Edith is right. Nothing is going to happen to you, Fred.” She said it in a way that demanded compliance. “But if it does, I'll give things up here and live with Edith.”

****

Fred was satisfied. If he was removed from their lives, they would manage, but he wasn’t about to get too complacent because Gertrude's flooded eyes had pinned him with a hot stare. He waited to see what she’d say next.

“That doesn't mean you can sneak off to God knows where and leave us to our own devices.” Ah. So she feared he’d leave and wanted to make sure of his exact intent.

Fred held up both hands in front of him. “They'll have to pry my fingers from your doorstep to get me out of here. I promise.” He smiled for the first time that day, and Gertrude gave him a small, watery grin back, mollified, if not content.

It had been a long day, and an even longer evening. The food had been enjoyed when Edith finally excused herself. “Now that we've solved all of our future problems,” she yawned. “I'm going to bed. Do you mind if I skip out on the clearing up, Gertrude?”

Fred spoke up. “You go on, Edith. I'll help Gertrude with the dishes.”

“Thanks, Fred,” Edith sighed, dropping a kiss on his cheek before she left the room. “Our friend Idell would say you're a sport.”

Gertrude arose, clattering the plates together hastily

before Fred gathered the dishes from her hands and deposited them on the counter.

"You and I have a little more to get straight," he said, lifting her chin with his finger.

He was pretty sure she wouldn't want to hear what he had to say, and her response confirmed it.

"Can it wait until morning?" she asked

"No, it can't." He moved her gently into the circle of his arms, but kept her inches away from his body. "This is as close as you get," he warned. "If I hold you closer I'll just start kissing you, and then I'll be sidetracked for the rest of the night."

She moved to test his theory or undermine his intent, but Fred would not allow it, and held her back.

"No, let me say this." His serious voice quieted her. "I've been courting you for six weeks now, and I think I've been doing an admirable job." Gertrude started to speak but he raised a silencing finger to her lips. "And it's all been leading up to something that I know, now, can't happen." He saw confusion in her eyes and sought to explain.

"Gertrude," he whispered against her hair. "I love you. I think I've loved you since I saw you covered in chicken feathers the first time we met." She pulled back and he let her see the sadness that he knew was coming from his eyes.

"I've been trying to do the honorable thing, trying not to…you know…let things get totally out of hand before I asked you to marry me."

Gertrude gasped, but before she could get her hopes up, he stumbled on.

"But now I can't."

The hopeful light in her eyes clouded over, and fat tears, renewed, spilled down her cheeks as he slowly told her the reasons that she could never be his wife. He felt like such a cad as he went through the whole fugitive and license issues. It all made him sound like such a criminal.

As his explanation ran down, he found himself rubbing

Gertrude's back in small, mesmerizing circles.

"Are you through now?" she asked. Her voice came out small against his chest where she'd managed to nestle.

Fred looked down on her in surprise. He hadn't known what to expect but this no-nonsense reaction certainly wasn't it.

"I suppose I am," he said with some hesitation.

"Good. So now I'll tell you something." She looked up at him, determination glowing on her face. "I don't care about becoming your wife." Her finger actually came up and jabbed him in the chest. "I don't care about respectability." Jab. "I don't even care who knows I love you." Another jab, this one even harder.

"Ouch." He grabbed the offending digit, unclear on where Gertrude was going with this.

"If you are faint of heart, you should leave this house the day that Edith goes back to Boston." There was no slowing her down, now. "Because if you remain," she skewered him with her dark fathomless eyes, "I will be coming to your bed the very night we are left alone."

She reached up and pulled his head down in a forceful kiss, sealing his fate. "And there will be nothing ladylike about it."

Fred smiled. She had said she loved him.

# Chapter Twenty-Four

January 1920

"I'm going with you."

"No. You're not."

Edith stood next to her bags that were on the kitchen floor, packed for the trip back to town, and Fred knew she watched as the two people she loved most, yelled at each other. But he couldn't help himself. As he and Gertrude fought, toe to toe, it was obvious that the tension between them had built to such a point that verbal explosion was their only release. Edith must fervently wish they would just stop and get on with things.

"I am, and you can't stop me." Gertrude glared and punched Fred on the arm. He started to grab her, then glancing Edith's way, prudently changed his mind. They must look like raving lunatics. He tried to calm himself and reason with the heathen woman.

"The part of Dorchester I'm headed to is not a proper place for a woman," he rationalized. "It's a rough crowd at Hugh's pub and I won't have time to be looking out for you."

"You won't need to look out for me." She had lowered her voice as well. "I'm well past the point where any man is going to try to bother me."

Fred was amazed that she wasn't aware of her own appeal. At an age where many woman looked worn out, Gertrude was still in full bloom. Her rich hair, with no apparent gray, curled and teased. The small crow's feet emanating from the corners of her large, expressive eyes, still had the ability to captivate, and her lush figure begged for attention. His hands twitched every time he looked at her.

"You're a pretty woman, Gertrude. A man would have to be half blind not to notice you."

She ignored the compliment and forced his hand. "You said yourself that Edith and I would need to be able to take care of ourselves if anything happens to you. Don't you think it prudent that I meet your friend Hugh, just in case?"

"If anything happens to me, you won't need Hugh. You won't be selling liquor, you'll be selling Rocky Nook," he said reasonably.

"And what happens if you go to Dorchester and you don't come back?" Gertrude played a trump card. "Either Edith or I would have to come looking for you. You'd rather we stumbled around not knowing a soul and inquiring at every gin joint on The Neck?" She waited, as if for that to sink into his obstinate head.

"Of course not," he spluttered. "I wouldn't expect you to come after me at all." His voice had begun to rise again.

"Really? We'd just sit out here for days or weeks, wondering what happened to you?" She matched his tone. "If you think that's going to happen, you're crazy."

"No, you're crazy." he yelled. "You're both crazy." He swung his arm in an irate arc, including Edith in his proclamation although she hadn't participated. He was venting his frustration because, dammit, he knew he'd lost.

"Fine. Do what you want," he turned in disgust. "But I'll be leaving in five minutes." Fred grabbed Edith's bags and slammed out the door.

****

"That went well." Edith's dry tone elicited a smothered chortle from Gertrude, who hurried to get her hat before following her friend to where Fred sat, fuming behind the wheel of the car. She had obviously won this round, but at what cost? He looked so angry.

The trip to the Bridgewater train station, as Gertrude lamented, was done in silence. And not a comfortable silence, but one that tied everyone up in knots, with not a clue in sight as to how to break it. Fred and Edith sat in the front seat, and Gertrude fretted in the back. The only sound that filled the car was the crunch of ice under the wheels as the vehicle traversed the winter roads.

Time dragged by slowly, and Gertrude was never happier to spot the steeple of the New Jerusalem Church on their approach to the station. For Edith, at least, the tension-fraught journey was over. But Gertrude still had a trip to Dorchester to undertake.

Fred parked the car and hopped out without a word. Gertrude and Edith followed, pausing to embrace on the siding, allowing Fred the opportunity to find a porter for the bags and cool down. By the time Edith and Gertrude reunited with him, he was able to give his sister a wan smile and a peck on the cheek.

"Don't let your guard down," he warned in a brusque and brotherly fashion. "Gertrude and I won't be home until after dark tonight, so I'll expect a call first thing tomorrow morning to know you're safe." The drugstore opened at eight AM and Gertrude knew he would worry if her call was even a few minutes late.

"I will call, Fred." Edith looked up at him earnestly, "And listen to me. Don't be so hard on Gertrude. She's been on her own for a long time and finds it tough to put her well-being in anyone else's hands." Edith gave her a knowing smirk. "Even yours."

"Off with you now." Color crept up Fred's neck. "I'll talk to you in the morning." He waved goodbye as she followed the porter, then turned back toward the car with a sigh.

"Don't be so hard on you?" he scoffed toward Gertrude,

passing her by with his shoulders hunched. “What about me? I’m the one who feels like I’m being squeezed in a vice. You know, I have more on my plate than any reasonable man can stand.”

Gertrude judiciously kept silent as she slid into the front seat. The balance of the journey was not going to be comfortable unless they both changed his approach. She was aware that he could just as easily turn the automobile toward home, as allow her to accompany him to Dorchester, and was wondering what to say to bolster her case when Fred’s voice cut through the silence.

“We'll have a bite to eat when we get to the pub,” his tone was firm. “But you will stay close to me at all times.” His decision, although forced by her, had ultimately been made, and Gertrude was happy.

“That sounds lovely Fred,” she answered with a docility that he had to know, was false. If he looked at her, she would be sporting a small, self-satisfied smile, and that would not do. He was still on edge about the Feds, and having her come with him ramped up his worries, which was a shame. But there was no way she would let him go to Dorchester without her.

“I suppose I can always take out my frustration by busting anyone's head who looks at you twice,” he told her.

“Yes,” she agreed demurely. “You could.”

It looked like that thought cheered him considerably, because after a few miles, he actually began to whistle.

Gertrude felt the tension leave her body. Fred couldn't carry a tune to save his life but she would gladly listen to him for the rest of the trip if it meant an end to the uncomfortable silence. She wasn't going to push her luck and be smug.

She worked the rigidity from her neck and henceforth, began to engage Fred, chatting about road conditions, the sweep of the wind through the pine trees and the beauty of the snow covered Blue Hills. Even though Fred was not effusive in his replies, she took his grunted responses as a sign that he was over the majority of his anger.

****

Dorchester Neck, or Southie as it was sometimes called, was not so much an unsavory neighborhood, as a working class Irish-American enclave. Hugh—Fred's friend—was Scottish not Irish, but felt right at home due to a mutual Gaelic descent with his neighbors and a common bitterness toward the English.

Fred's mood darkened as he parked the car at the curb. He quickly got out and went around to Gertrude's door before she had a chance to alight. He tucked her hand into his, possessively, and held tight, tugging her close to his body as they entered the pub that was dimly lit, smoke laden and filled with staccato noise.

From one corner came a raucous laugh and from another a spate of swearing that clearly had Gertrude momentarily stunned. “I’ve heard all those words before,” she whispered up into Fred’s ear. “But never strung together in quite such a fashion.”

He wanted to laugh, but he also needed Gertrude to know that this was serious business, so instead of a smile, he simply nodded and pulled her farther into the room. He wound his way through densely packed tables, his destination being the bar up against the back wall.

The smell was equal parts spilled alcohol, stale cigarettes and wet, woolen overcoat. But if Gertrude's senses were overwhelmed, she did not say anything about it. A few non-accidental brushes against her by inebriated patrons had Fred growling, but he kept a hold of her and continued his way through the throng. Halfway across the room they were spotted by the bartender.

“Fred,” the broad man behind the bar called out while pulling a draught.

"Hugh." Fred raised a hand in salutation, leading Gertrude the rest of the way toward the large man.

"That time again, is it?" Hugh's thick, rich brogue reached out, and by the rapt look on her face, his accent immediately appealed to Gertrude's musical ear, and as her eyes took Hugh in, he could tell she was surprised. Fred had told her Hugh had served in the war, but apparently she'd pictured him different. Older perhaps? Hugh was a spring chicken just approaching thirty.

****

"What's this, my man? You've got a wee bit of something clinging to your arm." Hugh's eyebrows went up in disbelief. In the ten years that he had known Fred, never once had the man been with a woman. Sure, he had witnessed Fred leave the pub a time or two with a doxy in tow, but this was a lady, and he'd brought her here when they had business to discuss.

"Hugh, I'd like you to meet Gertrude, my…uh…boss," he finished lamely.

"You're boss, eh?" Hugh was having none of it, and stared at Gertrude in a blatantly ungentlemanly fashion until Fred gave in.

"Well, yes, but she's…we…"

"I'm a bloody romantic, Fred." Hugh savored the angst on his friend's face. "Give it to me straight, man," Hugh demanded, loving that he could put Fred on the spot and relishing the other's obvious discomfort.

"All right, if you must." Fred practically growled. "She's my woman." Fred looked daggers at him, which did nothing to discourage his teasing, satisfied to be wearing Fred down. Gertrude, on the other hand, had color moving up her face at Fred's pronouncement, not realizing that it was just a load of cave man, chest-thumping going on here between them, so he thought to quickly diffuse things.

He gave her a broad, welcoming smile and she freed herself from Fred's crushing grip, offering him her hand.

"I'm pleased to meet you, Hugh, although how you've been friends with this scoundrel for so long, I can't understand."

Hugh leaned across the bar and took her proffered fingers and lingered over them. "Ah, there's no excuse for it except I'm a glutton for punishment." He turned to his friend. "Fred, her voice is like aged whiskey. I think I'm in love."

Fred snapped back but with good nature, "Yeah? And you can get your bloody Scottish hands off her right now, you lout, or I'll see to it that your wife hears you're mauling strange women."

Hugh withdrew his touch slowly, "Gertrude, you know he's not nearly good enough for you. I can tell you've a genteel soul. I pity you the first time you have to witness his awful temper. When the man's riled, he's a sore sight."

Before Gertrude could respond, Fred nearly choked with laughter. "My God, it's not her you should be worried about." Fred pulled Gertrude closer. "When she lets loose, she makes me sound like a Sunday school teacher."

Their banter continued in the same vein for a good many minutes, giving them all a chance to appreciate and assess the new dynamics, until Fred finally announced that they would find a seat so they could sample Hugh's famous Shepherd's Pie.

Hugh saw Gertrude look around, and it was clear to him Fred hadn't told her how they worked. Unbeknown to his woman, Hugh's boys had already been alerted, taking their car from the front and spiriting it off to load the requisite cases. All Fred had to do when they finished their meal was to pass money into his hands and they could be on their way.

Hugh, satisfied that everything was running smoothly—and anxious to continue talking to Fred—eventually whistled to one of his helpers in the back to take over at the bar, coming around to join Fred and

Gertrude at their table. He took a seat.

****

"Can I speak freely in front of the lass?" Hugh queried.

"Gertrude is up to her ears in this," Fred admitted with no little amount of trepidation. "She won't be repeating anything she hears."

Gertrude interjected with her own thoughts on the matter. "I'll be coming in with Fred on all his runs," she stated. "I think it looks less suspicious to have a man and a woman out for a drive, late at night, than a man on his own."

This was news to Fred, but he couldn't find fault with her reasoning. Hugh obviously thought the same thing.

"Good," he nodded. "The less suspicion we can arouse, the better. I just wanted to tell you that I don't know how long I'll be able to keep accommodating you. We have to close down the bar at the end of the week when the new law takes effect." He looked melancholy at the prospect. "I'll be open to serve food, and for now anyway, *our* business will remain the same. But," his voice took on a serious note for the first time that evening, "Josie's pregnant and I have to start thinking about my future, so I'll not be taking so many chances. If anything should happen to me, she and the bairn would have to fend for themselves and I can't be having that, you understand."

Fred clapped his buddy on the back and smiled. "Tell Josie I'm so happy. You need to do what's best for both of you. Don't worry. I'll find a way to make things work when you decide you've had enough."

They talked longer into the night and Gertrude began to nod off as the food and smoke began to take their toll. Hugh noticed.

"It's time to take your wee bit of baggage home, Fred. You'll have to be leaving her to sleep on the table if you wait any longer."

"I can see that," he agreed with a smile. Fred slipped Hugh a wad of money and clasped hands, thanking the big man and promising to see him again the following month before drawing Gertrude to her feet. She came awake long enough to tell Hugh what a pleasure it had been to meet him and that she hoped he and his wife would come visit Hingham some time soon. She also assured him that, yes, she was capable of making it out of his establishment without being carried to the car, which amused Fred no end as he supported most of her weight on the short walk from the bar.

Gertrude smiled as she settled into the leather seat, and murmured before dropping off to sleep. "You have a very nice friend, Fred."

She conked out and was already unaware when the automobile started, and dead to the world for the entire trip home.

Fred, on the other hand was fully awake. For two reasons. The first was that he never lost focus of his driving while hauling a load of liquor. He could not afford to be weaving about or calling attention to himself in any way. The second was, when he and Gertrude arrived home, they would be alone, and Gertrude had made her intentions toward him very clear. Had she been serious? And would she follow through?

In Fred's heightened state, the trip to Hingham seemed to take forever, yet conversely took no time at all. Gertrude had slumped over in her seat, somehow managing to nestle her head in a very sensitive spot between his hipbone and thigh. Every time she moved in her sleep he had to suppress a groan. By the time they reached Weymouth, he considered driving the car to the top of Great Hill, to wake Gertrude up in a most urgent way, but mentally chastised himself.

"You're not a callow youth, dammit," he muttered under his breath, "and she's a lady. You can't be taking her—especially for the first time—on the front seat of your car like some undisciplined oaf."

Fred forced himself to think of her limited experience with men. Gertrude would be mortified, of course, if she knew that Edith had shared her past with him. From what he had been told, Gertrude's only lover had been that arrogant bastard, George Parker. And wouldn't he love to get his hands around that man's neck.

The affair had lasted just under two years before Gertrude had woken up to the fact that she was being used, and in the long, ensuing interval, she had, according to Edith, been unable to trust any other man. No one had been close to her since, so as only the second lover in her life, it was his duty to make this right. Hell, it needed to be right for him too. He'd had his dalliances over the years, but nothing special. He hadn't loved a single woman that he'd ever taken to bed.

His thoughts went to Maude. This was a place he rarely allowed himself to go, but his thoughts flew to his past, unbidden.

He and Maude had been so young and so idealistic. He recalled the shy way they had decided to wait for the physical aspects of a relationship until after they were married. He had thought they had all the time in the world, and they'd be better for their restraint. How wrong he'd been.

So here he was, many years later, about to be intimate with a woman that he loved, who loved him in return, and if he didn't get to it fast, but do it right, it was surely going to kill him.

He finally approached the driveway at Rocky Nook, turned the car into the drive and came to a stop. He squared his shoulders, then put his hand out, stroking tousled curls where they lay across his leg, and attempted to slow his breathing.

"Gertrude." Fred's voice sounded odd in his ears. "It's time to wake up. We're home." He shook her gently, and she stretched like a cat.

"Oh my." Was her sleep filled voice huskier than usual?

"Did I doze all the way home?"

****

Gertrude opened her eyes and was instantly awake, feeling Fred's leg and a little more beneath her cheek. "Oh, my." she repeated, this time with a different inflection. With as much dignity as she could muster, she forced herself into an upright position and stammered an apology.

"I'm so sorry, Fred. I… It must have been very uncomfortable trying to drive…like that."

"You don't know the half of it," he groaned teasingly. She heard his sarcasm and blushing crimson, Gertrude quickly changed the subject.

"Will you need my help bringing the liquor into the barn?"

"I'm leaving that for the morning." His green eyes bored down into hers, causing her breath to catch. "I have more important things to take care of tonight."

"You do?" she squeaked. No, she couldn't have squeaked. She'd never squeaked in her life.

"I do."

Fred lowered his head to capture the lip that she had been worrying with her teeth, and without hesitation, she kissed him back. Fred's arms encircled her like steel and she loved the power she'd unleashed as he dragged her across the seat into his lap.

Ravaging her mouth, he pushed the car door open and easily lifted her, striding toward the house. As they reached the step, her legs slid from his arms and she trailed down his body before being pressed up against the door, his desire evident and all-consuming. She trembled in his arms. Fred drew away and ran a hand back through his hair, making it stand on end.

"God, Gertrude. I feel like an animal," he panted. "I'm not giving you enough time." He held himself back while she allowed herself a secret smile, opened the door and preceded him inside. The small electric bulb left glowing in the entry didn't allow enough light for him to see her face, but he could not mistake her actions. Setting her purse on the side table, she reached deliberately, possessively, to his hips and drew him forward, the hard length of him nestling into the softness she was offering.

"I've had plenty of time, Fred," she whispered into his chest. "Now, please take me to bed."

He took her hand and led the way upstairs, not bothering with the lights, but hesitated, silently asking if it was his bedroom or hers that she would prefer. She sensed his indecision and moving around him, made her way to the second floor staircase that led to the attic. She wanted his scent all around her. She wanted his bed.

In his room, in the darkness, he would have heard rather than seen, the gentle whisk of her dress as she drew it off her hips and dropped it to the floor. Gertrude knew, because Fred moved forward then, finding her warmth, nuzzling her bare collarbone and running his thumbs up her sides. He quickly slipped the straps of her camisole from her shoulders and traced the flimsy cloth from her body until she stood, naked before him.

Kissing her deeply, his tongue teased and stroked, while she could tell he battled mightily to rein himself in. But Gertrude denied him his restraint, urging him on with her fierceness, meeting him, matching his movements. She dug her nails into his back and sank her teeth into the side of his neck until he lost all control and abandoned himself to her needs.

They tumbled to his bed and his hands were everywhere, making her body thrum with need until finally they became joined. His movements above her were fierce yet gentle, and she reveled in his unbridled restraint.

Earth-moving minutes passed, and Gertrude was glass about to be shattered. She had never felt this way in her life;

this rise…this lift…this coming apart. The world suddenly tipped. The world stopped. Fred and Gertrude clung to each other and spiraled to the stars.

The only sound in the room, minutes later was their mingled breathing, attempting to return to normal. Fred tried to roll off her, to spare her his weight, but Gertrude refused to let him move. She wanted to hold on to this feeling as long as possible…as long as forever.

She sighed her happiness against him, and it must have pleased him because she saw the glint of a smile on his face above her.

Minutes passed in silence, and wordlessly she stroked him from shoulder to hip, enjoying the way his muscles tensed beneath her fingertips.

Suddenly, he was moving again, and God help her but she was right there with him.

# Chapter Twenty-Five

January 1920

Edith was tired. There had been a long hold up resulting in a several hour delay at the train station in South Braintree, and by the time she reached Boston, darkness had settled in. She stretched her legs and hailed a cab, thankful that the driver heaved her two large bags into the back. A nice bath once she reached home, and she was headed right to bed. There was no food in the flat—she had assumed she would arrive early enough to pick something up—but luckily she had eaten her fill of bread and cheese on the train that Gertrude had packed for her this morning.

She briefly wondered what was happening with Gertrude right now. She would bet that Fred, at this very moment, was probably giving her a piece of his mind. It was unusual seeing her brother so flummoxed, having come across a strong willed woman who would stand up to him, but the thought made Edith happy. The two were perfect for each other, and she'd known it all along.

If they'd only listened to her, years ago, they would have been happily married by now, with children, and none of this foolish Communist involvement would ever have happened. She harrumphed. The clock could not be turned back no matter how much she wished it. But as long as the two of them moved forward from here, things would be well.

The cab pulled up in front of her door and she paid the

driver before getting out. This might have been a mistake because his chivalry disappeared, not inclined to help her with the bags once money exchanged hands. She struggled to move the heavy objects with her uncooperative muscles, and once the foolish things were on the curb, she slowly caught her breath then dragged them to the door while the cab pulled away. She fumbled in her purse for the key.

"Miss Torrey." A hand reached out and touched her shoulder.

She screamed and jumped, dropping the key. Turning toward the voice did nothing to alleviate the rapid beating of her heart. Behind her, on the doorstep was Cuthbert Hamilton, his oily smile only inches away. She could smell the stale onions on his breath.

"Mr. Hamilton." She drew away from him as far as possible on the stoop. "You startled me, sir." Edith strove for calmness in her voice, but in truth, she was petrified.

"I didn't mean to, Miss Torrey." His leer let her know he most certainly had. "I've been waiting for you all evening so we could have a little talk. Why don't you pick up your key and we'll go up to your apartment." His voice had turned cold. He expected no argument.

"I would prefer that we conduct our business right here Mr. Hamilton." Edith matched his clipped modulation, wanting to appear strong.

"I wasn't asking." He growled, grabbing her upper arm. "I don't need an invitation or a warrant to get you upstairs." He cited the mantra of the Palmer Raids. "You'd better comply or I'll make this very unpleasant." The strength of his grip was bruising her arm. "Now get down on the ground and look for the goddamn key."

Edith felt faint, and hoped that Mr. Hamilton had brought his gentle giants with him tonight, but with a glance around, her expectancy faded. The streets were empty and they were all alone.

The small man's patience was growing thin as he twitched

and nervously looked about. Clearly having enough of her indecision, he forced her to her knees where she groped around with shaking hands for the fallen key. Once she found it, he wrenched her to her feet.

She tried several times to fit it in the lock, but her hands refused to respond. Hamilton grabbed it from her while maintaining his hold. The successful click of the lock sounded loud in her ears. Oh Lord, what was going to happen now?

****

Cuddy was enjoying himself. If the bitch would hurry and get in off the street, he knew he'd be able to enjoy himself even more. He liked the way the lady trembled. He liked the fear in her eyes. He gave her another little push just to feel her reaction.

"M…m…my bags," she stuttered.

He let go of her long enough to kick her bags into the foyer. "You'll see to those later." He shoved her forward through the door, gesturing with his head that she was to preceed him to her flat, and snickered that she might not make it up the stairs. This was the way he liked to feel. Strong and in charge. He looked forward to the interrogation he would be conducting; looked forward to terrorizing the lovely Miss Torrey and getting answers from her about her brother.

They emerged into her flat.

"One light," he snarled when they entered her sitting room. "I prefer to do my business in the dark."

She gasped and did as he ordered, but gave him a pained look once the light fell on her face. "Please, Mr. Hamilton, I have a great need to use the washroom. I've had a long trip…and…"

"Yes, we'll be talking about that long trip Miss Torrey." His eyebrows raised. "Go use the toilet but make it fast. I'll be standing right outside the door in case you try anything stupid."

She made a small keening sound and his gratification intensified. This was so easy.

Why his whole career couldn't be this simple was a source of discomfort and anger for Cuddy Hamilton. His superiors didn't like him, his underlings didn't like him and he had yet to bring in any really big fish for the Department to prosecute. True, he didn't go out of his way to endear himself to anybody, but wasn't that the way Federal Agents were supposed to work? Apparently his style didn't comply with office policy, which brought him to the reason that he was here. This was a last ditch effort. His boss was dying to let him go, and told him if he didn't come up with something fast, his days with the Department were coming to an end. The papers were already on his superior's desk, waiting to transfer him to the new Prohibition Enforcement Agency. Cuddy didn't know what the job entailed, but he knew he wasn't going to like it. If he could just shake down this one dame…

He heard the toilet flush and rapped his knuckles on the door.

"You've been in there long enough, sister. You have thirty seconds." He looked at the stout door and knew he wouldn't have a chance of knocking it in, but she didn't know that.

The door swung open and Cuddy gave her little room to walk by, crowding her, intimidating her with his nearness. He could feel her fear, and it fed him, but he backed off the slightest bit. It wouldn't do to work too fast. He didn't want her dying of a heart attack before he got to the good stuff. That wouldn't work for anybody.

"Sit over there." He indicated a straight, ladder-backed, arm chair in the shadows against the wall. She wasn't going to be allowed to get comfortable. His prey moved toward the darkness and settled herself on the edge of the straw seat.

"Now, if you cooperate, and answer my questions, things

might not have to get ugly." He was lying. She was a good looking woman and he couldn't wait for an excuse to rough her up. He was already tasting and savoring her terror as she nodded in fear.

****

Unable to look directly into his eyes, Edith focused instead on the dense hairs that connected his two thick brows near the crest of his forehead. The first line of the Lord's Prayer played over and over again in her head.

"Now. Let me start with an easy question. Where have you been?" While he waited for her to answer, he pulled a length of rope from his pocket, caressing it in an obscene way.

"I've been visiting my friend, Idell," Edith lied. "She lives in Iowa."

"And is that where your brother is?" He stroked her cheek with the rough hemp, snapping it on her sensitive skin when she was too slow in answering.

"No," she finally choked out, able to be honest but horrified as she endured the sting of the rope.

With a deft movement, he brought the coil down from her face and looped it around one wrist and then the other, binding her fast to the chair. He pulled the rope tight and clearly his debauched excitement mounted with the small scream she could not suppress.

He rubbed the front of his trousers, making sure she was aware of his arousal and grew incensed when she was unable to hide the look of disgust that crossed her face.

"So you're too good for me, my little captive?" He laughed maniacally. "I'll have you begging on the floor before we're done." He brought his face down to her level.

"Where is your brother, Miss Torrey?" he demanded, and was so close she felt spittle spray from his mouth.

"I don't know," Edith whimpered and was unprepared for

the blow that lashed out, striking her on the side of her jaw. As her head snapped back, his hand snaked up and grabbed one heaving breast.

"You don't know, my pretty lady? Or you won't say?" His hand grew rougher, causing her to gasp. "How about I help you remember?"

He took a vicious hold and squeezed hard, bringing tears to her eyes. Edith knew there was no way she would betray Fred, but wondered how much she could endure. This was pain she had never experienced, and she knew with a certainty that Cuthbert Hamilton was capable of inflicting so much more.

"I don't know," she yelled into his face, causing him to draw back and release her chest. "He's gone, and as far as I'm concerned he's never coming back. You can kill me if you want, but there's nothing I can tell you." She forced herself to look him right in the eye, and she knew at that moment he was not going to kill her; he was going to have her begging for mercy, instead.

He closed the small distance between them, and grabbing her chin, forced his obscene tongue into her mouth. She gagged. He pulled away to slap her face and then, with deliberate concentration, rubbed his throbbing erection back and forth over her arm where it lay trapped on the chair. Unable to move, she was forced to endure the evil contact and summoned what she hoped was a look of contempt. He pulled away, slapped her again and pinched hard at her breasts.

"Just wait until I have you naked in front of me." He leered. "There are so many things I can do to you." His wet lips came down on hers once more and her already roiling stomach couldn't take it.

Without warning, Edith retched and her meager lunch of cheese and bread rose up, spewing into his startled mouth. He leaped backwards in horror and disgust, the acidic contents from her stomach leaking down the front of him.

“Oh my God. My God.” He swore and spit the nasty liquid from his mouth. Edith continued to retch but a small part of her was able to gloat at his discomfort.

“You did that on purpose, you foul woman.” He slapped her, harder this time. Vomit dripped down into his shoes as he cursed; then cursed again.

“You think you've saved yourself?” He brought one finger up under her nose, then with a suddenness that startled them both, he reached down with his splattered hand and wrenched the neck of her dress open from throat to waist with one vicious pull.

Her abused breasts tumbled forth and he stared at them…waiting. He swore, and swiped at them, but it was no good. Edith could see it. His previous arousal was gone, and he was seething with his impotence. Edith thought then, that he’d kill her, but as she dared look at him, she could see he was close to losing the fight with his own nausea.

“I need to get away from this awful stench,” he gagged. “But don’t worry bitch. I'll be back to finish this,” he promised, wiping ineffectually at his soiled shirt while he stifled a retch. “Don't think you can get away from me.”

To Edith’s relief, Cuddy picked up his hat and nearly ran from the apartment. Sounds of his departure, accompanied by his physical distress in the hallway rang blessedly in Edith's ears. He reached the street. The bottom door slammed and the lock snicked behind him. She was safe.

Edith was able, eventually, to slip the loosened rope from around her wrists and grope her way to the upper door. She slammed it closed and threw the bolt. Her face and her body stung from the punishing blows Cuddy had rained down, but she wasn't about to stop moving. She crept on all fours to the sanctuary of her room and, retrieving a clean nightgown, made her way to the bathroom and scrubbed every inch of her aching body. Eventually she had to face the scene in the parlor. The chair, the rope and the contents of her stomach brought the nightmare back, and tested her strength. But she squared her shoulders and went at the room with a vengeance until everything was clean and the smell of vomit and vermin had been entirely erased. The chair would greet the trash man on the curb the next morning.

# Chapter Twenty-Six

January 1920

Edith stood quietly in the cold, her back propped against the back door, watching her breath dissipate in the mid afternoon sun. She could still hear Fred and Gertrude inside, fighting over what to do.

They had picked her up at the corner drugstore, throwing caution to the wind when her desperate call had reached them. She wouldn't explain over the wire what had occurred, but the tone of her voice, or rather the lack thereof, she knew, had Fred frantic.

Luckily there had been very few people in the small store this morning, so Edith had paced the well stocked aisles, unquestioned during the hour it had taken for Fred and Gertrude to arrive. She had waited for them, her face hidden under a wide hat with a dark veil, numb to everything.

Earlier that morning, at dawn, it had taken all of her courage to exit the apartment, but she knew it was impossible to stay. The thought of the malignant agent returning was too much to contemplate. After clothing her tender body, she turned out the lights that she'd left blazing all night, glanced out the window to make sure the street was clear, then dragged herself across the room and clicked the door shut behind her.

At the bottom of the stairs, she picked up her already packed bags where they had been kicked in the foyer, and ordered her legs to carry her down the street.

The wait had been long, but a sense of unreality gripped her and she'd barely been aware of time passing. When Gertrude came in, leaving Fred behind the wheel, Edith had almost broken down, but controlled herself long enough to exit the store. In the comfort of the back of the automobile, tucked deeply in the shadows, she had finally allowed quiet tears to come. They'd streamed silently down her face, working their way into the cut on her lip, stinging, but she'd been calm enough. She needed to stay calm. Her face was a mess; she had risked a quick glance in the bathroom mirror before leaving, and when Fred got a good look, it was going to be difficult to keep him under control.

She knew that Gertrude and Fred, in their silence, had given her time to settle in before asking what had happened, and they'd nearly reached Hingham before she'd been able to speak. She began in a low and modulated voice, retelling the events of the night before, leaving out the more graphic details so as not to incite Fred any further. She'd seen his knuckles, white on the steering wheel, and that there would be plenty of time—once they Gertrude's house and her face coverings were removed—to witness his fury full force.

Not an hour later, Edith had left the house to get away from the arguments within. She'd closed the door behind her and leaned on the cold, yet sun-drenched siding.

Fred wanted to go back to Boston right away, recruit a few of his old friends to find Cuthbert Hamilton and kill him. Gertrude was more rational, knowing that Fred would end up in jail—or worse—if he started trouble in town, and tried to convince him that getting in touch with Hugh, who could make a few inquiries, would be a better plan.

Annie, who had arrived just as they returned from Boston, had sat Edith down at the table and seen to her wounds once it became apparent how extensive the damage had been to her lovely face. She'd tisked and tutted and tended to Edith while putting in her two cents, agreeing with Fred as the debate escalated. Something should be done right away to that horrid man.

Edith closed her eyes to the sun. The frigid air felt good on her battered face. She almost fell asleep, so little rest did she get the night before.

“What the….?”

The loud male voice startled her. Instinctively she dropped and crouched on the ground, covering her head with her arms to cower in fear.

****

“Miss Torrey.” Ambrose Fletcher hurried forward as Edith dove, seeing the physical devastation before she was able to cover it up. “What happened?”

He was appalled at the bruising to her face. He might look like a dandy, but he had witnessed plenty of fights in his life, and he knew a beating when he saw one.

Edith raised her head. A shudder moved through her entire body. “Oh, Mr. Fletcher. It’s you.”

Ambrose wondered who she might have expected as he reached out a hand and stroked her hair. At his touch, something must have let go inside of her. Huge, choking sobs made their way to the surface and bubbled over as her body rocked and shuddered with some kind of delayed reaction.

Ambrose bent and gathered Edith up from the ground. He held her gently while the storm raged, and absorbed her tears onto his fine woolen coat while he got a good look at the damage. Her eye was black, her temple purple. There were several cuts on her swollen lips and a nasty abrasion raked across her left cheek. Whoever had done this had made a thorough job of it, and his detectives mind started cataloging details. When she was finally able to calm down, he kept hold of her elbow and walked her away from the house.

“Do you want to tell me about it, Edith?” He gently and

purposely called her by her given name.

"You can't help me, Mr. Fletcher," her eyes, wet with tears, avoided his. "It happened in Boston, which is surely out of your jurisdiction."

But with a little cajoling she finally relented and explained to him how she had been set upon by a stranger as she reached her home last night, and had implored Fred and Gertrude to come get her this morning, so great was her fear.

Ambrose didn't believe her for one moment. The wounds to her face looked methodical, professional, not the work of a random assault. He brought her cold hand up to rub it, and got another shock. There was no mistaking the rope burns around her wrist.

"Somebody bound you." He stroked softly at the marks, his voice hard with anger he couldn't manage to tamp down, but his gentle touch must have had her undone. He could tell she purposely left out the name and the true intent of the intruder in her home when she then told him everything that had been done to her.

She relived the humiliating events of the previous evening, stumbling unevenly through her words. And he bore witness to it all.

For Edith's sake, Ambrose maintained a calm exterior, murmuring words of sympathy and walked with her as she talked, beginning to calm down. Inside he seethed. He needed to know who had done this to her.

He was a patient man, very systematic. He had already uncovered quite a bit about the Torrey's past, Fred's in particular. He had made it his business to investigate Gertrude's family friend when he had first moved in. Fred's name hadn't been hard to find. Fletcher surmised that Edith's beating might have something to do with either Fred's past indiscretions, or his current ones, but the seasoned detective didn't hold with tactics like these. Whether they had come from a ne'er-do-well acquaintance of Fred's, or from the law, he would find out. All he needed was a name.

He hadn't thought, when Mary Kirke had visited him a few weeks ago, filling his ears full of her hatred and suspicions, that he would have to become involved so soon.

He turned Edith around and headed back to the house. Now it was time to have a talk with Annie Spring.

# Chapter Twenty-Seven

April 1920

"I shave it off every year. April First."

Fred was surprised at Gertrude's reaction to his missing beard. Apparently she had become so used to it over the long winter that she'd forgotten he had it only during the coldest months. She looked him over carefully.

"Hmmm. I'm going to miss it. You look so young." Gertrude sometimes fretted that she was four years older than Fred. She reached up and stroked his smooth chin, then leaned in and lightly moved her cheek against his.

"If you don't stop rubbing on me, woman, I won't be able to get my chores done this morning." Fred eyed her half in jest, half in hope.

Gertrude sighed. It was Saturday morning and Fred knew she needed to help Annie in the kitchen before preparing for her afternoon concert. She clearly regretted having to pull away from him, extinguishing the small spark in his eyes, but there just wasn't any time.

Not only did she have *her* preparations to make, but Fred had to accomplish any number of things before entertaining his men's club this afternoon. Tomorrow they would be bringing Edith back to Boston after a two and a half month sabbatical. They would spend the whole day with her, changing locks, stocking her house with food and making sure she felt comfortable enough to be left alone. There was no time to dally this morning.

Back in January, Edith had written or called her docket of students to cancel lessons, but with her recent round of inquiries earlier in the week, she was happily reporting that all but one of her pupils would be continuing their lessons.

Fred wouldn't have let her go, but he'd made sure it was safe for Edith back in town.

Using caution—as Gertrude had argued the morning they picked up his sister—had proved the proper thing to do. Still, they had debated loudly and for several days on what course of action to take before Fred had finally agreed to see Hugh and put him on it; to find the whereabouts of Cuthbert Hamilton.

Gertrude had been fiercely anxious the day he went to Dorchester. She was unsure if he would go against his promise and look for the weaselly man, and indeed it had taken all of his resolve, not to. But when he returned, he'd assured her that Hugh had put an end to his nonsense, reminding Fred that he had been removed from Boston for almost a year, and informants you could trust came and went far more rapidly than that. Hugh would take care of it.

When Fred and Gertrude had made their February pick-up in Dorchester, Hugh had no news for them, but he had finally contacted them two weeks ago and asked if he and Josie could take them up on their invitation to visit. He had news to impart. Fred knew that could only mean one thing and had told Hugh to come as soon as they were able. They'd arrived on a Saturday morning. Hugh thoughtfully brought Fred's monthly allotment with him.

"Hugh. It's lovely to see you again." Gertrude had met their guests at the door and been swept into an altogether inappropriate bear-hug by the big Scotsman. The very tiny, but very pregnant woman by his side had punched him soundly in the ribs.

"Give it up, Hugh. Can't you see your embarrassing the poor woman?" She had a brogue, but most definitely Irish.

Not Scottish.

Gertrude had caught her breath after having it squeezed out. “You must be Josie. I'm so happy to finally meet you. I've heard all about you from Fred.” She clearly put the woman at ease. Fred grinned like crazy right beside her.

“And what fanciful stories has that big lug been putting in your head,” she’d teased. “I'll deny them all.”

Everyone had laughed and started talking at the same time, but Gertrude had looked so pleased. Fred had known this would be an easy and enjoyable visit no matter the news from Boston.

Gertrude had linked her arm with Josie's and brought her into the kitchen to meet Edith, and Annie who had finally been engaged full time and happily ensconced in a room of her own on the third floor.

The women had spent the next ten minutes enthusiastically talking food and recipes while he and Hugh exchanged generalities in the corner. Fred had eventually brought their bags upstairs, with Hugh assuring him he would fill them in on everything he had uncovered as soon as the afternoon's concert and men's club meeting had wrapped up. It seemed both Hugh and Josie had been looking forward to attending the gatherings, respectively.

Later, he’d learned from the couple that Josie had been thrilled with the tea, immediately having been surrounded by elite Hingham women wishing to find fodder for juicy gossip from the big city. And Josie—in the same spirit—had recounted every near-scandalous tale from Dorchester that she could recall, making up a few others just for the fun of it. She’d been in full swing when the concert was finally announced and the women hushed and hurried back to their seats for the main event.

Gertrude had chosen to sing the part of Orpheus from *Gluck's Orfeo ed Euridice.* Originally written for a male, female contraltos had been performing the role for a number of years. Gertrude had never sung it, but had purchased

Clara Butt's recorded rendition for her phonograph and had enjoyed it so much she sent away for the sheet music. She had fretted to Fred for weeks that she hoped she could do it justice.

From the opening lines, Josie told him she'd been enthralled. The power and control in Gertrude's voice had sent chills up and down her spine; the emotional arias, tears to her eyes. She'd even boasted that her baby had moved within her, as if the music had traveled to her womb. She'd wished that Hugh had been witness to the performance.

But Fred knew better. Hugh had been happy right where he was. The barn-club was his kind of gathering. With a glass in one hand and a cigar in the other, he'd obviously been just as comfortable holding court on hay bales as he was proselytizing from behind his bar. And the stories he told of Dorchester were not nearly as clean as the ones—Fred later learned—that had been recounted by his wife.

When all the patrons had left for the day, Josie and Hugh agreed it was one of the most enjoyable Saturdays they had spent in a good long while. But the real reason for their visit couldn't have been held off forever.

That night at supper, the mood became more somber and all eyes had turned to Hugh who spoke first across the table to Edith.

"First off, I'm sorry, lass, that you had to meet such a one as Hamilton."

Fred could see Edith's slight tremor as Hugh said the name.

"Here's what I've found," he'd paused as if to put his thoughts in order. "First off, no one likes the man, so it wasn't too hard to get people talking. I didn't do any of the questioning myself, but the gents I put in charge know their business. Turns out he's a nasty streak of pish. Begging your pardon ladies." Hugh had apologized for his crass, Scottish turn of phrase and started again.

"Hamilton has been with the U.S. Department of Justice for just over three years and has made a bad name for himself with his colleagues. Some family connection to a senator got him his position, and he lords himself over anyone of lesser rank. He plays rough and dirty and lets his temper rule his actions. In the last six months or so, men in the department have refused to work with him on the grounds that he's unethical. *He's* unethical." Hugh snorted. "This from a bunch of the most cold-hearted choobs you could ever dream up. Anyway, he rattled one cage too many without anything to show for it, and they've transferred him to a different agency. One where they hope he can't get himself into too much trouble. He's been sent over to the Prohibition Enforcement Agency."

The irony of the situation had not been lost on either Fred or Hugh. Gertrude had just looked distraught.

"Now, Gertrude, the chances of him being assigned anywhere near us are remote," Fred had soothed, and Edith agreed. Fred had attempted to bring the conversation back into safer territory.

"So what you're saying, Hugh, is that Hamilton was working alone and without proper jurisdiction when he went to Edith's flat."

"That's right," Hugh had agreed, and pointed toward Fred. "*You* are a quiet file as far as the Department is concerned. Hamilton was just trying to raise something from dust to save his career. There's no one else interested. They have their hands full with illegal immigrants. They aren't following through on anybody like you right now, born in the States."

He'd looked at Edith. "No one else is going to approach you, and he's out of the way and will never bother you again."

Edith had clearly mulled it over. Eventually she nodded and took a deep breath.

"That's good, then." She'd looked resolutely at Fred.

"That means I can go home."

Hugh and his had wife departed the following day, and it had taken Edith another week and a half to convince Fred she would be safe and that she had no intention of staying in Hingham any longer. As much as she liked the country air and Rocky Nook in particular, she had finally become aware of how things currently stood between him and Gertrude, and that she would not be putting a damper on their time alone. She was, of course, positively thrilled with their relationship and wanted to give them the privacy that they deserved.

****

Edith had begun saying her goodbyes to all of the tea room patrons throughout the week and got the comforting feeling that she would be missed. Ambrose Fletcher, in particular, had been more than attentive and she would be sorry not to see him anymore on his weekly visits. When she'd extended an invitation to several of the women to come and visit in Boston, she'd made sure to include one to Mable Fletcher—the detective's mother—in that group.

"I'm sure that my Ambrose would be willing to drive me in some Saturday or Sunday." Mable had assured her. "It will do him good to take a day off to enjoy himself. I've never known anyone to take such a full time interest in his work." She'd added this last with pride. "Thank you, my dear."

The morning before her departure, and prior to the 11 o'clock tea, Edith sat in the garden cutting the first spring daffodils to place on the tables, when she heard an automobile pull up the driveway. Shading her eyes with her hand, she recognized Ambrose's vehicle and wondered what he could want. She thought back to that horrible day when he had pulled her from the snow and she had made a mess of his nice coat. She had come a long way since then, and it comforted her to know that the gentle detective had been there to help alleviate her worries.

"Mr. Fletcher," she called, as he alighted from his car and walked toward her. "It's so nice to see you again."

He swept the hat from his head. "And you as well," he told her with a smile. "You look charming this morning."

She knew that a blush stained her cheeks, and whether it was his presence, or thinking of the unspoken bond they'd shared when she'd been so needy. Words tumbled from her lips before she could stop them.

"I was just thinking back to that horrible morning when you had to pick me up from the ground." She blinked down at the flowers in her hand. "I realize we haven't talked about it since, but I want you to know how thankful I am that you were there." She played with the damp stems, her voice lowered to a mere whisper. "I also apologize that you had to witness my collapse. It was such an emotional moment…not something I'm prone to."

His visage became serious and his voice, stern in his rebuttal. "Miss Torrey, I don't know anyone who could have endured what you did that dreadful night, and still been able to carry themselves with as much dignity."

It was high praise from the detective and she knew it. "Thank you, Mr. Fletcher," she responded softly.

"Ambrose," he prompted, and when she hesitated he added, "If my mother and I are to come visit you, we should be on a first name basis."

"You're right…Ambrose." She smiled. "And you can call me…"

"Edith," he interrupted with authority.

She laughed, which was clearly the effect he wanted his boldness to have.

"Now, Edith, I have something of importance to tell you before you go back to Boston. Come walk with me." He offered his arm, and grasping toned muscles under her fingers, she stood, feeling small and dainty next to the fine detective. He steered her deeper into the jonquils.

"I very much want you to feel secure when you get home, and for that reason I've asked a couple of fellows I know in Boston to make sure that your flat gets some extra attention. The men I've talked to are more than willing to walk by your house each day. And so as not to alarm you, have promised always to be wearing beige fedoras so you'll know they are the good guys."

Edith gave an inadvertent shiver. Not black fedoras, like the awful agent had worn.

"If they pass you on the street, they'll give you a wink and a small salute, and you may turn to them at any time you might feel the need. It's not much, but it's the best I can do from a distance."

Edith didn't know what to say, and overwhelmed with gratitude she turned toward him, putting both hands on his arm, and feeling brash, went up on tiptoe and placed a small kiss on his smooth-shaven cheek.

"Thank you, Ambrose," she dropped her eyes, instantly embarrassed. "You can't know how comforted that will make me feel." When she stole another glance at him, she swore that a little extra color bloomed on his neck. That she had in some way affected him, pleased her no end. What a charming man, and so very thoughtful. There was no doubt that she would be looking forward to his Boston visit.

****

What Fletcher didn't tell Edith was that—once he had the name of her attacker from Annie—he had done some investigating regarding Cuthbert Hamilton. The man's transfer, tantamount to a demotion, had already taken effect by the time Ambrose's inquiries had born fruit. Still, Fletcher hadn't been totally satisfied. A demotion was not punishment enough for a creature as vile as Hamilton. He'd needed to send a message, letting Hamilton know that his actions were not without consequences. With a few calls to the right people, Ambrose had made sure that the man in question highly regretted his January nights' work and was acutely aware of what would happen if he ever, ever, darkened the door of Edith's flat again.

****

Edith settled back into her Boston life with little difficulty. She felt safe, having already witnessed the beige fedora men walking by her apartment. Mothers of her students, who thought she had been ill and recuperating in the country, brought gifts of food and assurances of their children's continued allegiance. Life had returned to normal more rapidly than she thought possible. There was only one thing that puzzled Edith and niggled in a bothersome way at the back of her head. The framed photograph of Fred that had been taken at Christmas time was missing from her bedside table.

# Chapter Twenty-Eight

January 1921

*Boston Sunday Globe, January 9, 1921*
*DRY AGENTS TAKE 90 IN MARSHFIELD RAID*
*Descend on Webster House with Drawn Revolvers.*

*Marshfield...the biggest and most sensational raid here in years occurred about 10 o"clock tonight when more than a score of prohibition enforcement officers from Boston...swooped down on the Webster House.*

*The man who claimed he was the proprietor...was held on a charge of having liquor in his possession illegally and also on a charge of conducting a gambling nuisance...The authorities believe that nearly all of their prisoners gave fictitious names.*

"It's getting too hot for me here in Dorchester, Fred." Hugh played with a fork that had been laid on the table in anticipation of the evening crowd. "I hate to tell you this, man, but I'm closing the place up. Josie and I are moving to Canada." He waited, looking up to see Fred's reaction. "I've got relatives up there and with what I've put away I can do a bit of bar tending and take care of my family without jeopardizing their safety."

Fred had known this was coming. Ever since the night that Hugh held his son for the first time, the big Scotsman's heart had clearly no longer been in the game. Fred understood. He clapped his friend on the shoulder.

"Don't worry about it. I'll find another way. You just keep your family safe," he assured him.

Fred and Gertrude had made some decent money over the previous year. Not enough to assure their future, but enough to get by until he figured out something else. Fred thought he'd done well, masking his disappointment, but apparently Hugh saw through it.

"Now don't think I'm leaving you out in the cold." Hugh seemed affronted that Fred would have so little faith. "I'm going to make sure you have the right introductions before I go. It just depends how deep you want to get yourself into the quagmire," he said cryptically. "My connections will keep you going, but I've heard that there have been some raids down near you recently, so if you want to consider a different line of work, tell me now."

Fred already knew his answer. "I'm sticking to this until I find it becomes too dangerous. So far, we've kept things small and handleable, so I feel pretty safe with what we're doing."

"Okay," Hugh acquiesced. "Now I'm going to give you some good advice." The giant got down to business, tapping his index finger on the table in front of Fred.

"You need to get rid of the bloody Model-T. Get yourself something that can hold a good, large, concealed load." He stood up. "It's time for you to see some of my trucks and what we've done to them." He sauntered to the back door.

As they walked through, Fred asked Hugh how many of his customers would be privy to the new arrangement. Hugh stopped and grasped Fred's shoulder with a look that was solemn.

"You're the only one. We've been through a lot together, and I have faith in you. The other guys, lowlifes who I deal with, can't be trusted. I'm not about to put my suppliers up the chain in any danger. They know me well, and if I vouch for you, they'll take you at my word." He nodded abruptly, knowing nothing else needed to be said.

Fred followed the Scot out into the evening dusk and they spent the next several hours going over the trucks with their extraordinary hidden compartments. Fred's eye for construction was keen and he took what he needed from the details he was shown. Immediately, of course, he began mentally cataloging his own modification.

Before heading back to Hingham, he and Hugh agreed to meet in New Bedford the following Saturday night in order to make the necessary introductions. Then Hugh made one last suggestion.

"My final suggestion is to have Gertrude see her doctor sometime soon."

Fred looked askance at Hugh, stopping dead in his tracks. "Her doctor?" he barked. "Do you know something that I don't?"

The Scotsman's teeth gleamed bright in the moonlight, so wide was his smile. "I do." He paused for dramatic emphasis, then gave out to Fred's stunned expression. "I know that if your lady pleads a nervous condition to her doctor, she can get a prescription for whiskey that's legal and aboveboard," Hugh chortled. "She'll be entitled to a half pint every ten days, to which you should be taking full advantage, stockpiling just in case your main source dries up."

Fred laughed in relief and agreed with his friend that it sounded like a good plan. He knew Gertrude would acquiesce to the prescriptions, but how would she feel about his future trips to New Bedford to pick up their liquor? He had to go home and let her know the change in plans. And she wasn't going to like it.

****

"No. You're not going." Gertrude was adamant. She paced her bedroom where Fred sat, tentatively, on the bed after interrupting her putting laundry away.

It was one thing, him heading in to Dorchester once a month for what appeared to be an innocent monthly visit with his friend. It was another thing entirely to drive down to New Bedford with a truck in the dead of night to meet strangers on a dock while carrying wads of cash. Gertrude shuddered. It was not going to happen.

"We need to keep going, Gertrude." Fred tried to reason with her. He came to his feet. "We've put away a lot of money, but it's still not enough to get us through more than a handful of years. If we stop now, we'll be back to broke before you know it."

"No," Gertrude shook her head. "The danger is too great. And if we're looking to conserve our money, we shouldn't waste it by purchasing a truck." She turned his financial arguments back on him.

"The truck will be an investment," he growled, massaging his temples. "And we can use it as advertising; put the Rocky Nook Tea Room name on the side. It will help business," he ended lamely.

Gertrude stopped arguing and thought about it. It would be handy to have an additional, reliable vehicle, and the advertising would be nice.

"Would I drive it?" she asked pointedly, even though it would let Fred know she was caving in. Damn him, he knew she was a pushover for a nice vehicle.

"Well of course," he agreed instantly, "not to New Bedford, of course, but certainly around town and…"

"Now wait a minute." She stopped him. "What if I wanted to go to New Bedford with you? Not to the docks," she hastened when she saw his mouth turn down, "but to take care of other business while you conduct yours."

She could see him wondering what, exactly, could justify her accompanying him.

"What if…." she paused and carefully pondered an idea that might just satisfy them both. There was no way she was going to be left behind in Hingham to fret every time he went south on his mission.

"What if we buy a truck, do your modifications and make the pick-ups, but on the trips homeward, we also carry a load of something legal to satisfy anyone who might want to take a look?"

He looked slightly intrigued.

"For instance?" he questioned.

"Relish." she stated with pompous certainty.

"Relish?" Fred gave what she could only consider a disgusted whiff of disbelief. "And how the heck are a few jars of relish going to help us out?"

"Now have an open mind, Fred. Try to keep up," she told him, smiling now because she knew—once she explained—she would get her own way.

"I am intimately familiar with New Bedford," she reminded him, unable to keep the pleased grin off her face. "If you remember, I used to sing there all the time. And there's a wonderful establishment called the Fountain Relish Company down on North Second Street," she added. "They sell the most delightful relishes and sauces you've ever tasted. I deem it quite reasonable that I'd want to use their products in the tea room. I could call ahead and order several cases of, say, ten or twelve different products. That should fill up a good size portion of a truck, wouldn't you think?" She looked to Fred for his approval.

He blinked, clearly contemplating whether her plan sounded brilliant or foolish. She waited.

"Yes," he drew the word out slowly, stroking his chin. "And once we've got all this relish, how many years do you think it will it take before we use it all up? Because if we keep it up, by the time we've made three trips, we'll have enough relish to fill the barn." Still not fully comprehending, or entirely on board, he finally sat down again on the edge of the bed.

"Who says we ever have to use it?" Gertrude asked coyly,

coming to stand in front of him. She wiggled herself in-between his knees, creating a nice heat between them. Placing both hands on his shoulders, she leaned in. “Who says we even, ever, have to unload it?” Her eyes sparkled with triumph, and arousal at her wanton proximity to Fred in the light of the mid afternoon. “We buy one load, and then just keep carrying it around.” She let her hands wander to his neck. “Unless someone actually stops us and sees it, it's a good excuse every time we go.”

Fred finally saw the plan, even though clearly distracted by her ministrations. He reached up to stroke the sensitive underside of Gertrude's wrists. “Chances are we'll never get stopped,” he agreed, his voice gone husky. “And even if we do, we can always just rearrange the crates the next time to look a little differently.” He paused, his breathing gone irregular, and Gertrude knew she’d won. She dropped light kisses across his cheekbone.

“I still don't like the idea of you coming along.” He tried his best to resist her, but Gertrude's proximity was destroying his resolve. He attempted a glare.

“Well, you won't be going with me for my first meeting,” he voiced around the small kisses she was now planting on his lower lip. “And you'll never be allowed down on the docks.” He said firmly. “Do I make myself clear?” His voice strove for control but became a distant echo to them both as Fred suddenly growled, flipped her over onto the bed and surrounded her with his hard body.

Gertrude gave over to his dominance. The rest of the discussion would have to wait.

****

Fred met Hugh on Nash Road, in the outskirts of New Bedford, at dusk. Together they drove in the Scotsman's truck to their destination. The meeting place was at the end of Cove Street where the water in the Acushnet River was still navigable to small lobster boats. It was full dark when they arrived, and Hugh filled him in on everything he needed to know.

"You'll be meeting Stan and Douglas," he said. His face that had been in shadows suddenly glowed as he struck a match to light his cigarette. "And nobody has any last names here, you understand." He took a long draw.

Fred nodded.

"They bring the load in from the schooner, Arethusa. It's anchored just outside the limits. When they come in, you hand them their money, they help you load up, and you're on your way. The whole thing takes just a few minutes, but pay attention. It anything looks wrong, they'll be gone fast, and so should you."

Fred paid strict attention as Hugh continued.

"Before they leave, they'll give you the time of your pickups, whether you decide on once a week or once a month. And you can't be early or late. If you miss your window, you're out of luck for that month. If they have problems on their end and they're not here for you, you leave and come back on the next pick up date. No exceptions to any of the rules. Got it?"

Fred understood. It all sounded very straight forward. "Are the pick-ups always at night?" he asked, keeping his voice low, like Hugh's.

"Yeah. So far the Dry Navy hasn't started patrolling at night or on Sundays. But we don't know how much longer that'll last."

"Dry Navy?" questioned Fred.

"Just a friendly term for the Coast Guard." Hugh took another haul of his cigarette before pointing out toward the river. "And here come our friends, now."

Fred couldn't see anything. The lobster boat obviously wasn't showing any running lights, and he wondered how Hugh knew it was there. He finally, minutes later, heard the deep thrum, thrum, of the engines and his own senses went instantly on alert. This was it. This was for real, and a lot more dangerous than what he had been doing in Dorchester.

The boat, painted a dark color, stopped 50 yards from shore and silently dropped a small dinghy, loaded with cases, into the water.

Brief greetings and introductions were made. Hugh told the pair that this was his last run, and outlined their new customer's needs. A deal was quickly struck and Fred had his schedule as fast as that. As Hugh had said, the transaction took only minutes. No useless chatter, just business and a quick get-away. Fred barely had time to be nervous as the unloading and loading occurred, and the boat pulled away. But his detachment changed once he and Hugh were alone in the truck, and in possession of all the alcohol.

"Now we just have to hope for the best," Hugh told him. "This is the tricky part because the Feds have no qualms about the hours they work. If they've gotten wind of a shipment or delivery, they can be out any time of the night, patrolling the shore, and you better have your excuses in order."

Fred held his breath as they traveled back up the dirt road. He expected to see head lights any minute, and wondered whether or not he really had the guts to do this by himself.

As always, for Hugh, things went smoothly. The saying was; "luck of the Irish", but Fred thought it should be "luck of the Scots". They made it back to Dorchester in record time, with no problems at all.

And then it was time to say goodbye. Sadness at seeing his friend off was tempered with well-wishes for the man's future. They gave each other a rare clap on the back. Fred wished Hugh the best of luck while suddenly experiencing a strange, empty spot within his chest. Hugh looked to be struggling with the same, neither having anticipated that their final parting would be so difficult. Finally, not giving in to the thickening in his throat, he gave a cough and said goodbye. There were no plans for any future meeting as the men parted company.

The loss of his good friend to Canada had Fred melancholy on the trip home, and in order to curtail his downward spiral into nostalgia, he forced his mind to his own future. He pondered numerous ideas that would help save his hide should he be waylaid on his next trip.

Gertrude, of course, was waiting up for him when he arrived home in the small hours of the morning. He took her, sighing, into his arms and carried her up to her room. And with her warm body wrapped around his, Fred purged the night's business from his head.

Gertrude fell asleep on his chest and Fred was content. They'd gotten a little carried away and skipped all necessary conversation. *Ah, well.* Tomorrow would be soon enough to fill her in on the details of his trip.

# Chapter Twenty-Nine

June 1921

*Boston Daily Globe, June 29, 1921*

*FAKE RAID UPSETS CHAMBER'S OUTING*

*...One Cut, Several Bruised in Fracas. There were numerous stunts yesterday afternoon at the annual outing of the Boston Chamber of Commerce at Pemberton, and all but one of them, a fake liquor raid, were in the hands of the Committee of Arrangements. The raid, however, was planned without their knowledge...When the originators put it into effect during the dinner at Pemberton Inn...it resulted in one man receiving a cut head from a flying missile and others receiving bruises from flying fists...*

"Tempers are high. Are you sure you want to make the trip with me?" Fred had just finished the morning paper and was feeling uncomfortable about Gertrude coming to New Bedford. He had made several excursions by himself, simply because they had still been using the old Ford and making very small pick-ups once a month. But now they had the new truck—painted with it's bright Rocky Nook logo—ready to take on a larger load and he was feeling anxious.

They had purchased a half ton Model T Van—although Fred had pined over a Mack AC which was entirely too big and inappropriate for their needs—and were set to make their maiden voyage with it that afternoon. He had completed the modifications for hiding their cases only two days before, and although he was absolutely certain of his disguised compartments, Fred had been trying to talk Gertrude out of coming ever since.

"I've done fine by myself so far. There's no need for you to go."

"I know there's no need," Gertrude answered, pinning her hat in place and attempting to placate him. "But I've already made the call to the Fountain Relish people and they have my order ready. I've also made our reservations at the Bancroft House and my bags are packed." She smiled at him, reassuringly. "I'm looking forward to this." She put her hand on his arm. "It's been a long time since I've been out of Hingham."

Fred couldn't deny that Gertrude had been patient, waiting through all of his excuses. In truth, the pick-ups made him nervous. Each time, he had felt very exposed, waiting for the boat to meet him and then driving away at such a late hour, up the solitary road, almost advertising his automobile's presence with what always seemed like overly-bright headlights.

He went over the new plan in his mind and realized that it really was far safer than what he'd been doing on his own.

Upon arriving in New Bedford, they would pick up their order of relish late in the day, then head to the Bancroft House where they would check in under Gertrude's name and have a leisurely supper. At the appointed hour, he would leave her safely at the hotel and arrive at the waterfront to do his first, large transfer; a four month supply this time to try and create a stockpile in the barn. It should take him less than an hour to load the truck and get back.

He didn't like the idea of leaving the new van, unchaperoned, on the street overnight afterwards, but he supposed the worst thing that could happen—because the alcohol would be well hidden—would be to have someone steal their relish.

If all went as planned, they would come back again in six weeks and do it all over, at which point Fred would have enough put away before winter to avoid any trips in harsh conditions.

On his previous middle-of-the-night treks back to Hingham—trying to avoid detection—he had been forced to use back roads that made his excursions much longer than necessary. Being able to drive back tomorrow in daylight on the main roads would cut the trip time in half, and the possibility of being stopped to practically nil. All well and good, except he still hated to involve Gertrude.

The woman foremost on his mind clearly had no such fear.

****

Gertrude was looking forward to the opportunity to get away with Fred and leave the cares and woes of the household behind. Upon her direction, Annie had employed the services of a friend to help serve tea at both sittings today, and that same woman was spending the night at the East Street house to help tomorrow.

Gertrude sighed in relief. It had been a long time since she'd had a couple of days to herself. She climbed up into the new truck, and attempted to relax. Until they reached the border of Hingham, Gertrude wouldn't believe she was actually getting away from the tea room.

With the changes to their liquor circumstances, she had been under a lot of pressure lately, and hadn't had to prevaricate over much when seeing Dr. Chapman this spring. Gertrude always prided herself for maintaining control and had therefore been thoroughly surprised when she told the doctor of her nervous condition and immediately broken down into tears. The only excuse for such poor behavior, in her mind, was that Fred had been headed for a pick-up in New Bedford that night.

The dear doctor had been so kind to her then, patting her hand and telling her he had just the thing to ease her condition. As she sat on his hard, leather examining table, she had all she could do not to choke with laughter on her falling tears, because sure enough, he handed her a prescription for Old Hermitage Sour Mash Whiskey, 100 proof, and she had been speechless. Doctor Chapman had mistaken her silence for shock.

"It's all right, Miss Edmands," he had assured her. "Medicinal purposes only. Just present this to Ernie Lincoln over at Hunt's and he'll fill it for you with no problem. You'll get a half pint every ten days for the next six months, and then I'll see you again to determine if it's been helpful." He had regarded her kindly as she'd ducked her head and tucked the piece of paper into her reticule.

"Thank you Doctor Chapman." The smile she'd given him was full of relief that the appointment was over. "I'll see you in six months."

Gertrude had walked all the way to J.L. Hunt and Company at Thaxter's Bridge before realizing—in her flustered state—that she had left her car in the square. Giggling, she figured it was probably for the best. If anyone had seen her filling her prescription, it would have been instant grist for the gossip mill, and Lord knows there was enough of that already. Annie had let slip that a few of the tea room clients had begun speculating on her relationship with Fred. She was certain that talk was starting to spread, and only her good reputation and the popularity of the tea room kept her from becoming a pariah.

Right now, however, she could leave all her trepidation over gossip behind. She and Fred were on their way to New Bedford. The open road through Weymouth was just ahead, and she was determined to enjoy the beautiful summer day.

It wasn't long before Fred was able to completely thaw her

out with his teasing, losing a lot of what seemed like his own anxiety in the process. By the time they reached 47 North Second Street in New Bedford; Gertrude was more relaxed than she'd been in months. So much for alcohol being the prescription for her troubles. All she'd really needed was fresh air and Fred.

The relish company was just as she remembered. The smell of vinegar and spices filled her head, and the boards of the antique pine floor creaked comfortingly beneath her feet. The proprietor was charming and efficient and soon had them loaded up and on their way to the Bancroft House.

Gertrude hadn't stayed there since the time—so many years before—when she had met George Parker and began the slippery slope into her dreadful two year love affair. Well, love on her end, lust on George's. Now, here she was with Fred, and it was assuredly love on both sides.

She went to the front desk to check in while he dealt with the bags in the truck. "I have reservations," she said pleasantly to the small man behind the desk. "Mr. and Mrs. Edmands, for one night." The lie came out easily, and the clerk filled out his paper work and handed her the key just as Fred appeared by her side.

"You can leave those for the bell boy Mr. Edmands." The desk clerk said helpfully. Fred looked down at him, his visage suddenly harsh as thunder, and the young man became flustered under his cold gaze.

"I'll take them myself," He snarled, turning away quickly. Gertrude elbowed him as he passed. He sounded like an ass, but she understood. There was no way the clerk could know how much it bothered him not to be able to use his own name, but if all went well, Fred would get over it.

Gertrude gave the employee a look of apology before thanking him for his help, then followed Fred to the lift. She took his elbow when she caught up with him, remaining silent and watching the arrow count down the floors as the elevator approached. She held her tongue, waiting to hear if he'd make excuses.

"I'm sorry for being an idiot," he finally spoke, but his jaw lost none of its tension. "It just rubs me the wrong way to…"

Gertrude cut him off with a brush to his cheek. "I know," she said. "You don't have to explain to me. I understand, and it doesn't make me love you any less." The lift arrived at their floor with a subtle "ding".

Fred's shoulders lost their rigidity. "What have I ever done to deserve you," he asked, devouring her lips with a quick, hard kiss before the doors slid open.

They hurried to their room, and it wasn't until several hours later, moods much improved, that they enjoyed a sumptuous meal in the well-appointed dining room.

****

Fred's meeting was on time. He had told Stan and Douglas to look for the new truck, so neither would be disturbed not seeing the old Model T.

There was some joking about the crates of relish in the back, and how Fred could be useful at a catered affair. In return, Fred skewered their masculinity right back, suggesting they were spending far too much time alone together in their boat. But the joking was quickly finished and they got down to business.

Stan actually praised Fred on his innovative hidey-holes, as the three packed them full with the new amount of alcohol requested before money changed hands.

"Can we make the next meeting six weeks from today?" Fred asked. "Same time, same number of cases?" They nodded their agreement, shook on it, then shoved off in their dinghy.

*That went well*, thought Fred, climbing into his truck. Whistling, he started back toward town.

He had gone less than an eighth of a mile up Cove Street when headlights snapped on, blocking the road as if in confrontation. *Shit.* His heartbeat accelerated and all feeling momentarily left his torso. He wanted to run from the truck. He wanted to lower his head to the steering wheel and pretend this wasn't happening, but he thought of Gertrude back at the hotel, and suddenly knew he had to be strong. He had to give his excuses, credibly, and make this work.

There was no getting away from it. Fred wasn't totally unprepared, having rehearsed what he would do in just such a situation, but now he was going to have to prove his acting skills; in front of a very interested audience.

He brought the truck to a full stop, pulse pounding in his throat, and watched four men emerge from a black sedan, two from each side. The men from the front of the car walked slowly toward him while the other two positioned themselves to the outside of the blazing headlights, making it impossible for Fred to see what they were doing. He was pretty sure the two periphery ones' had guns. *And* he was equally sure they were trained on him. Fred slowly squirmed.

"Hey." he called out in a surprisingly steady voice through his open window. "Hey, you there. I could have run right into you in the dark." He strove for what he hoped was a mildly impatient tone.

"Sorry sir," said the one approaching the driver side, all politeness but full of business. "Federal Agents." He identified himself. "We need to know what you're doing out here this time of night."

"It's a long story," Fred answered. *Good*, he breathed. *Remain calm.* This gentleman sounded like a reasonable human being, not a hard-ass.

"Come out of the car slowly and let us see both of your hands." The agent came back, still sounding reasonable. "Just a precaution, you understand."

"Yup," Fred replied agreeably. "But before I do, could I see some identification?" Fred matched the other man's pause. "A precaution for me too, being alone and all."

Reasonable Agent reached into his jacket and removed something from his pocket. He tossed it to Fred who caught it through the window, and opened it up to read. The guy's name was Jenkins.

Fred made a pretense of looking at the identification long and hard, even though he already knew that these guys were Prohibition Officers. He gave what he hoped was a relieved sounding sigh.

"This looks fine. Thank you, sir. I'll get out of my truck, slowly now, so as not to give you any worries." Fred eased the door open and stepped to the ground. He walked toward the officer, holding both hands forward, proffering the identification back to the agent.

"You had me scared for a minute." Fred shook his head. "I thought you might be looking for some trouble."

"No trouble. We're just here doing our job." He nodded at Fred's vehicle. "Mind telling us what's in the truck?"

"Relish," stated Fred, injecting a hint of exasperation in his voice. "God-damned relish." Anticipating, and then getting the look of confusion on Jenkins' face he'd been going for, Fred launched into his explanation.

"My wife has this little tea room in Hingham where she serves foolish do-dad sandwiches and such to the local ladies. She talked me into this trip to New Bedford to pick up relish. Have you ever heard of such a thing?" Fred was working the story, attempting to win sympathy.

"She got us booked into the Bancroft House." Fred reached up slowly and scratched the back of his head, rolling his eyes. "I'd never seen the place before, but when I got a load of what it was going to cost me for her little excursion, I told her that we could turn right around and go home."

Fred paused and saw what he perceived as a little softening from the men. "Well, one thing led to another and she got real mad and locked me out of our room. So I thought, fine. I'll leave without her and she can find her way back on the train."

One of the agents standing by the car gave a low chuckle, and Fred warmed to his story.

"I fumed for a while. You know how it is, and then I started driving. But I didn't hit the road home. Somehow, instead, I ended up down here by the water."

He looked sheepish now, changing things up. "I guess part of me knew I couldn't leave the Mrs," he demurred. "And after a while, contemplating my options, I started getting kind of lonely…if you know what I mean." He flashed the officer by the car his best, contrite smile and when Agent Jenkins gave him a look of understanding, Fred knew he had him. "So when you stopped me, I was headed back to town to tell the Mrs. that I changed my mind."

"Sounds to me like you're going to have a fight on your hands." The agent on the passenger side spoke up, commiserating with Fred. "I've got one at home that sounds a lot like yours. If I'd driven off, I'd have to do a lot more to get back in her good graces than telling her I'd change my mind."

Jenkins, who had been nodding along in agreement, eventually cleared his throat and got back to business. "I understand your problem and don't think I'm not sympathetic, but I still need to see some ID and open up the truck." He cleared his throat and rolled the stiffness out of his neck. "Once we're satisfied you are who you say, you can be on your way."

Fred did a frantic pat down of his pockets, exhibiting an apprehension that was not feigned. He didn't actually have a valid driver's license. He hadn't needed one in the city where he had no car, and by the time he fled to Hingham he couldn't use his own name to get one. He had to think fast.

"Dammit, fellas, I must have left my wallet in the room when the wife locked me out," he proclaimed indignantly, spluttering his apologies, not knowing what else to do.

"Well, what's your name?' The officer opened a small notebook and got ready to write with the nub of a pencil.

"Fred Edmands," Fred responded, unhappier about the lie now than he had been earlier in the day. To keep any further questions at bay, he walked to the back of the truck. "Let me just open this for you and you can have a good look inside." He was sure that his false compartment would escape scrutiny and the agents would be satisfied with the cargo of relish.

Jenkins groaned, seeing the piled up boxes, clearly not happy at the number before him. It must have looked like too much work. "Elmer. Scoot up inside there and shine your light on those cases." Jenkins gestured toward the crates.

The one named Elmer did as he was told, but it quickly became apparent to everyone that they would have to pry open every one to be absolutely sure there was no alcohol. Jenkins sighed again.

"Get the crowbar," he hollered to the men back at the car. "This is going to take some time."

As Fred suspected, it took the better part of an hour to go through all the contents, but once the agents were done, they looked no further.

****

Gertrude was frantic. Fred should have been back by now. She had paced her room for the past half hour and then come down to the lobby to pace some more.

She experienced vast relief when two hours after he'd left, Fred finally walked back through the door to the hotel. Gertrude could not help it, she flung herself into his arms, grabbing him around the neck as if she'd never let go.

"Huh, hum," said a voice behind Fred. "The little woman, I suspect. Looks like she might have forgiven you."

Gertrude's frantic kiss was cut off by an amused gentlemen—one of four—who had accompanied her fake husband into the lobby.

Fred whispered quickly in her ear that she should play angry and go along with whatever he said before he pried her off and turned away.

"Agent Jenkins, I'd like you to meet my wife, Gertrude Edmands." He swept a hand from Gertrude to one of the men dressed entirely in black. "Gertrude, dear, this is Federal Prohibition Officer Jenkins."

All the color left Gertrude's face. She felt it go. She also felt her knees weaken, but recalling Fred's whispered words she thrust off the weaknesses and sought to comply.

She slapped out at his shoulder, then fashioned her eyes into angry slits and perched on her tiptoes, leaning up toward him for a good smell. "Why did they come back with you?" Gertrude planted her hands on her hips. "Have you been drinking?" she demanded, throwing all of her worry of the past few hours into pretended ire.

"Hold on, hold on." Agent Jenkins interrupted. He must have thought it a good time to intervene.

Gertrude skewered him with a steady gaze. "Hold on? You want me to hold on?" she railed. "My husband is escorted back to me by Federal Officers and I'm supposed to hold on?" Her voice escalated. "Someone better tell me what is going on."

"Now honey, just calm down. Remember during our little spat you locked me out of our room?" Fred clearly feigned his sheepishness toward her. "Well these gentlemen found me driving without my wallet and license and they were duty bound to follow me back to make sure I am who I say I am."

She heard a slight cough, and turned, realizing the desk clerk—who had earlier checked Gertrude in—seemed to be thoroughly enjoying the whole conversation. Could he be used to their advantage? If he thought that the reason Fred had been cranky that afternoon was because they were in the middle of a fight…

Gertrude turned on all of her charm. "Kind sir, so that we

don't have to make the journey all the way up to our room and back, would you be so kind as to confirm my husband's identity?"

"Of course Madam," he preened. "It would be my pleasure. Sir?" The clerk addressed Jenkins. "I can vouch for these folks. That is Mr. Edmands and his wife. They checked in earlier today. They're here visiting from Hingham, and I've seen identification."

"Thank you, sir." Gertrude gave her most practiced smile to the clerk before turning back to the others, and letting fire relight within her eyes. "Is that it, then? Can my husband and I possibly try to salvage what's left of a very poor night of what is *supposed* to be a few days of vacation?"

An agent stepped forward, sheepishly, and introduced himself as Elmer. Twisting his hat around in his hands, Gertrude wondered what the heck was going on.

Jenkins gave him a sign that he should continue.

"Ma'am," he began, and if Gertrude wasn't mistaken, his adam's-apple came perilously close to choking him. "We had to have a look through the cases in the back of your truck." He quickly changed his tone to as business-like as possible. "It's our job, you know, to make sure no liquor is being transported in these parts."

The bluster then left him as quickly as it had appeared. "So we had a look at your relish, and in our haste…my haste…I, uh. A few things might have gotten broken."

Gertrude felt like laughing, and her remaining worry lifted like a morning fog, but she maintained her stern look as she questioned Elmer, making sure to pin him like a bug.

"How many of my jars were destroyed?" she spat, and the gentleman seemed suddenly lost for words.

Jenkins stepped in and answered for the tongue-tied agent. "We're not sure how many, ma'am, it was too dark to tell. But I'm going to give you my card, and when you ascertain the amount of damage, you send me the bill. I'll make sure it's taken care of."

Gertrude pretended to consider his offer before turning her considerable charm to Agent Jenkins, where she graciously thanked him for his help and concern.

****

Agent Jenkins was momentarily flummoxed by Mrs. Edmand's rich brown eyes, surrounded and enhanced by the high color on her cheeks. Temper or no, this was a fine woman, and he thought Mr. Edmands had made the right decision to return to her warm bed.

However, when they finally took their leave, and stood out on the sidewalk, as a group they decided that, beauty or not, none of them wanted to be in Fred's shoes tonight.

"Poor guy," Elmer commiserated. "He's going to be sleeping on the floor tonight, and hearing about this all the way back to Hingham tomorrow."

Another agent snickered. "Floor? He'll be lucky if he gets to sleep in the truck."

Jenkins laughed with the rest, but he was a cautious man, and although Mr. Edmand's story checked out, he thought he'd send a short dispatch to the Hingham police just in case anyone there would be interested in the events of the evening.

****

Safely back in their room, Gertrude and Fred stood numbly, holding each other, not bothering to turn on the lights. It had been a close call. Too close.

Fred comforted a trembling Gertrude, assuring her that despite the trouble, things had gone off as planned and that her relish had been a stroke of genius.

She pulled back from him, eyes aglow with tears. "Do you really think so?" she sniffed.

"You're a regular Mata Hari," he crooned in her ear. "But

more beautiful than she ever was." While he talked, his hands got busy on the buttons at the back of her dress.

His words, however, must have made her bold, because she moved slightly back and slowly caressed the material that he'd loosened, down over her shoulders, bringing her slip and brassiere off with it. And while his mouth hung open, she turned her back, lowering the material even further, finally grazing it off of her hips, baring her skin to his warm gaze.

When he reached out to touch, Gertrude pushed his hands aside, and turning, slowly dropped to her knees in front of him.

He held his breath as she worked the buckle of his belt free, and undid his trouser buttons with exaggerated slowness. He swelled beneath her fingers, and when the summer air, wafting in through the window finally had access to his body, Fred reached to draw her up.

He was momentarily confused as she refused to rise, but when she dug her nails in lightly he realized, with a groan, what she meant to do.

The flush that consumed his body was nothing compared to the fire that ignited when she finally drew him in. He shuddered with the force of her attentions, and looking down upon the incredible sight, sucked in a breath as a shaft of moonlight bathed her in brilliance. His eyes slitted and he watched her ministrations until he could stand it no longer and cried out, forcibly drawing back.

Her luminous eyes questioned him.

Fred forced himself to speak. "If you continue, this will be over before it gets started." He hardly recognized his own voice, as he held out his hand to her. "Please, my love. Come to bed."

Gertrude rose graciously from her knees, and still taking the lead, tugged him to the plush mattress where she turned and pushed him gently backwards.

Fred lay still, barely breathing while she climbed over him

and slowly lowered herself. There were no more words for either of them after that. They lost themselves to their own world.

# Chapter Thirty

July 1921

"I'm going to go out on a limb here, and guess that if those agents stop me again, they aren't going to buy the whole relish story a second time."

Fred was due to head back to New Bedford and make his next pickup that night. He was letting Gertrude know, in a round-about fashion, that she was not welcome on this excursion, but true to form, why wasn't he surprised that Gertrude had already made plans.

"Wamsutta Mills," she stated.

"Wam-what?" Fred asked, knowing he was not going to like the answer.

"Wamsutta Mills," she repeated. "Tablecloths and napkins." She spoke in a practical tone. "They're located on North Water Street and I could use two changes of linens for each of my forty tables. That should be enough cases for the agents to look through should they be so insistent."

Fred groaned. "But I don't want you to go."

Annie chuckled, standing at the sink doing dishes. "Mr. Fred? If you know what's good for you, you'll just give in. I know you and Miss Gertrude like to fight, but in the end, she usually gets her own way."

Fred snorted, but dammit, Annie was correct as usual. "What time do we leave?" Gertrude took his silence as acquiescence, and flourished a short list of things that she wanted to accomplish before departing.

"I'm leaving in one hour," Fred stated petulantly. "And you had better not keep me waiting if we have to go to that Mill place before we…what? Have you made plans?" He pondered whether they could find accommodations without any notice.

"We already have reservations at the Bancroft."

Fred wondered why he'd had any doubts. "And I suppose the Mill is waiting for us as well?"

"Of course." Gertrude went to finish packing and called back over her shoulder. "They had just what I wanted."

****

The mid-August trip to New Bedford was just as beautiful as their jaunt earlier in the summer, but the air was muggy so Gertrude had worn a new, revealing frock. She had boldly purchased a sky blue sheath, daring for the first time to go with a fresh, sleeveless style. The dress was also shorter than she was used to, showing off more of her matching silk stockings. She could tell, as she stepped into the truck, that Fred appreciated her new look, and preened under his constant surveillance.

She liked what she was seeing as well. His white lawn shirt, rolled up at the sleeves accentuated his tanned arms, and she loved watching the play of his muscles under his dark skin as he guided the vehicle down the narrow country roads. She stifled a contented purr, knowing that those muscles were hers to touch whenever she wanted.

She wasn't sure why, but Gertrude was less nervous about this trip than she had been about the one before. Part of it, she assumed, was because they were now acquainted with the Prohibition Officers, who had actually been quite amiable. Gertrude had been in touch for reparations as regards to the relish, and had not only received reimbursement, but a lovely note from the officers.

Another calming factor was that Fred had managed, in the ensuing weeks, to procure a pair of false drivers' licenses. The first one showed his address as East Street and confirmed his name as Frederick Edmands. That one would do if the same agents stopped him. The second was designed for total anonymity, with a completely fake name and address which he would use in all other circumstances. She didn't ask where he had gotten them, and knew he wouldn't answer even if she asked. There were parts of Fred's past that she still didn't have access too, and for now, that was all right.

****

Back in Hingham, having given Annie ample time to clean up after the eleven o'clock tea, Ambrose knocked at the back door to the East Street home.

Wiping her hands on her apron, he saw her peer through the screen, looking delighted to see him.

"Hello, Mr. Fletcher," she called out cheerfully as she pulled open the door. "It's lovely to see you, but if you're looking for Miss Gertrude, she's not in."

Ambrose well knew that Gertrude and Fred had left. He had waited patiently for them to do so for several weeks now, keeping tabs on the whereabouts of the new truck. He had actually come to talk to Annie.

"It's a shame that I missed her," he intoned smoothly. "Perhaps I could trouble you for a glass of something cold and a place to sit."

Annie seemed more than happy to accommodate him, probably owing to the fact that if it weren't for him, she might not have this job.

"Inside or out?" she suggested. "Whichever takes your fancy. And I'll have a nice glass of iced tea for you before you're settled."

"Outside sounds nice," he returned. "And bring one for

yourself, Annie. I could use the company." Ambrose wandered back out the door.

"I think I could be talked into that," Annie called to him through the screened window over the sink. "I've been rushed all morning. The lazy girl I hired for the day didn't show up. I'll be having a word with her mum, I will. You mark my words, I don't hold with people who promise you something then don't follow through."

When Annie emerged with two glasses and settled across the outdoor table from Ambrose, he began his questioning.

"So where has Gertrude gone?" He kept his voice mildly interested.

"Oh, she and Mr. Fred have gone for an overnight to New Bedford." If she thought this information inappropriate, it didn't register with her enthusiasm in the telling.

"Hmmmm," Ambrose took a sip of his iced tea. "Lovely in New Bedford this time of year. They must have some sightseeing in mind."

"Oh, no," Annie disagreed. "They've gone to pick up tablecloths for the tea room."

"Tablecloths? Surely our own Hennessey's would have those necessaries without having to travel all the way to New Bedford?" The detective hoped he managed to look suitably puzzled.

"Well, if she'd wanted one or two, that might be the situation. But Miss Gertrude is outfitting the entire tea room with all new linens. What with tablecloths and napkins she'll be bringing home quite a few cases."

"Funny thing, Annie, I seem to remember my mother—dear Mrs. Fletcher—telling me that just last month a similar trip was undertaken to buy relishes. I wonder that they didn't do all of their business at the same time."

"Don't think me spreading gossip Mr. Fletcher, but I do know that Mr. Fred and Miss Gertrude are sweet on each other and I think they like the opportunity to get away." Annie had the good graces to blush.

Ambrose put her at ease on that score. “They're both fine people, Annie, and well past the age where what they do is anybody's business but their own.” And having his answer, he drained his glass agreeably and changed the subject.

“The last time dear Mrs. Fletcher was here, she thought she lost one of her favorite earrings out by the barn. I wonder if you'd mind if I had a look around.”

“Go right ahead.” Annie picked up the glasses. “I'd help you look, but I've got way too much to do before the afternoon tea. I'll be getting back to the kitchen if you’ll excuse me?”

Ambrose picked up his hat and with a quick wave, gave Annie her leave and turned his feet toward the barn where he’d have a good long look around. It was a look that was well over-due.

****

The desk clerk at the Bancroft House greeted them upon their arrival, recognizing them immediately. Previously, upon their departure, they had left him with a splendid tip that he had more than earned, and this time he had them checked in and settled without any fuss at all.

Just like before, Fred went out around midnight, certain that the desk clerk would think nothing of it, unless, of course, he arrived back in the company of the Federal Officers a second time.

Fred had already ascertained that it was low tide, and instead of taking Cove Street after his pick-up, he would travel on the packed sand until he reached Gifford, making his way back to town using an alternate route. If the agents stopped him, so be it. He could always say that the missus had sent him on a mission to locate the officers to deliver a thank you for the replacement relish funds. It was a weak, but plausible excuse, and he thought that seeing tablecloths might just win him more sympathy anyway.

Once poised at his destination, Fred waited quietly in the

darkness until he heard the tell-tale engines. Pushing himself off the back of the truck where he'd been leaning, he peered into the night until the outline of the dinghy came into focus. Stan and Douglas were spot on time.

He could tell instantly that something wasn't quite right. Only Stan got out of the small boat. Douglas stayed where he was in the stern with what looked like a harpoon draped across his legs.

"Fred," Stan nodded. "Let's get your load in quickly, then we've got to talk."

Fred's curiosity was peaked, but he did as requested and hurried the cases under the secret floor.

"Push off, Douglas. Meet me down the beach after I finish with Fred," he instructed, then indicated that Fred should walk with him.

"I'll be short with you," he began. "Within a day or two, we won't be able to do any more runs. You'll be reading about us in the newspapers."

Fred's reaction was cautious. "Why, what's happened?'

"Somebody who knows too much has been blackmailing us and we've got to stop our deliveries before we're bled dry. We're giving things up here. The story will be leaked to the newspaper hounds as soon as the snitches find out they won't be getting any more money from us."

Fred immediately understood the situation. "I guess that's it then." He reached out to shake the man's hand.

"Just hold your horses Fred. We're not done yet." Stan reached to his back pocket. Fred was unnerved for just a moment until Stan pulled out what looked like a map, but turned out to be a folded chart.

"You live up in Hingham, right?" the runner asked. Clearly he knew from the logo on the truck. Fred nodded.

"Well we've got some other folks we do business with who also live in your neck of the woods. Are you familiar with the waters up your way?"

Fred had never paid a lot of attention to the Hingham

harbor area, but he and Gertrude had been on plenty of picnics on Planters Hill and World's End. He thought he knew where this might be going. He nodded again.

"Good. There's a nice secluded spot on the back side of World's End, headed into Hull," said Stan. Fred looked at the chart in the faint glow of a shrouded lantern at where Stan pointed to the cove.

Fred grunted. "I suppose I could keep a small boat there without much trouble. There's lots of tree cover and it would be well hidden."

"I like the way you think, Fred. And this is what I want you to do. In the next couple of weeks, get yourself a dozen or so lobster traps. Make sure the buoys marking them have a good distinct coloring and drop them in the water on the lee side of Rainsford Island." He pointed on the chart to the small island at the mouth of Quincy Bay. "I'll meet you one month from today at this spot off Worlds End," he tapped the chart, "and you can show me the markings on your buoys. After that, you'll need to seed your traps with money as well as a little chum, and wait for our drop to pull up your catch. We won't be able to keep an exact schedule, so check your traps often, and it wouldn't be a bad idea to take in some actual lobsters. If anybody's looking, they'll be satisfied if you have a few creatures aboard."

Fred's head was spinning by the time he got back into the truck. At the last minute he remembered to change his route and found Gifford Street with no difficulty. He couldn't say he was sad that this was his last trip to New Bedford, but why did the bloody rules have to keep changing?

He got back to the hotel without difficulty and Gertrude was waiting outside the door. Her eager smile upon seeing him made him light up inside. Fred remembered the last encounter they had when he returned to the hotel, and his body started an inadvertent hum. He stepped from the truck, locked it up and moved toward her with purpose. She reached for him and he reciprocated with a strong, warm embrace.

Before becoming totally distracted, Fred rested his chin on top of her head and cryptically greeted her.

"Looks like you're going to be serving lobster sandwiches in the tea room," he quipped, and thinking about the crustaceans caused his gorge momentarily to rise.

He hissed through his teeth. "Why did it have to be lobsters?"

*The Lowell Sun, August 13, 1921*

*ARETHUSA HAS THOUSANDS OF CASES OF LIQUOR*
*NEW BEDFORD, AUG. 13TH*
*...THE OLD HOOKER ARETHUSA HAS PEDDLED RUM...*

*The Arethusa is no myth, but is in fact a large schooner which has a load that is reportedly inexhaustible. The load is Bottled in Bond American Rye, Scotch and Irish, that would oil a rusty fliver...Gently easing back and forth just beyond the legal limit and within range of glasses from Massachusetts soil, is the wettest spot that has been within striking distance of the bay state since prohibition went into force...*

# Chapter Thirty-One

December 1923

Annie's lobster sandwiches had become quite popular with the ladies, not to mention the enthusiasm that met the tray-full that made its way to the barn every Sunday. Business was booming. Gertrude's bank account had become sizable and Fred constantly worried that something would go wrong. Perhaps his worry stemmed from the ease of the system that had worked flawlessly over the past two years. It was hard to believe that so much time had elapsed since becoming a lobsterman.

Life at Rocky Nook had taken on a comfortable cadence, post New Bedford. They all worked hard; he, Gertrude and Annie, but there was also a lot of time for play. They had nights out at Hull's Paragon Park, Sunday excursions to the Cape, and pleasant visits to Boston spending time with Edith when she wasn't in Hingham visiting them.

At the end of the long summer, Fred had even convinced Gertrude to ride the Giant Coaster at Paragon Park, and she'd loved it so much—squealing her joy from start to finish—that she couldn't wait for spring to try it again.

Some of his favorite moments had been spent picnicking at the top of Turkey Hill, a popular retreat in Hingham within walking distance of Rocky Nook, whose views stretched to encompass everything for miles around. From one's vantage point atop the hill, you could clearly see all the surrounding harbors, and into the heart of Boston itself, the magnificent Custom House Tower. Many a lover, Fred knew, young and old, retained fond memories of Turkey Hill.

Life was good and things were quiet. When they first started with the lobster traps, it had been decided that Gertrude would apply for the license, Fred being unsure whether his name was still suspect. She gained approval to have her dozen traps, but in the winter would be allowed only ten due to some arcane rule that had taken effect when the canneries had over-fished lobster a decade before. With that number of traps, Fred hauled in just enough alcohol to last each month.

Every trap they owned became the recipient of two bottles wrapped in burlap. This amounted to the bare minimum on which the men's club could get by. Luckily, they had stockpiled a number of extra cases from their pickups a few summers back, so if the winter months got lean, they could make do. And thanks to Doctor Chapman, Gertrude was still putting by her half pints. If anything went wrong, they had surplus enough to last a few months.

Fred worked the dozen lobster traps every other day. He had gotten very proficient. He usually baited them with chum, but once a month he baited them with cash, protected from the elements in a can sealed with wax. On the day he pulled up alcohol instead of lobster, he would leave Quincy Bay and head in, empty. Later that night he would make his way back under cover of darkness to retrieve the illegal load. So far no one had bothered him, questioned him, or tried to stop him, and for some inexplicable reason, he grew more anxious with each passing month.

Fred made it a point to read about the Coast Guard ships that patrolled the waters off the bay. Out of Boston was the Mackinac and the Tampa. Out of Woods Hole was the Acushnet. He knew the capabilities of the cutters versus the lobster boat that supplied him. The edge belonged to the men who made his deliveries. They were capable of running at twenty knots and the cutters were good for only ten to twelve knots sustained. Still, the article in the paper that morning indicated that luck was not always on the side of the faster boats. The headlines had proclaimed: *Six Rum Running Launches Seized... the seizure of six rum running launches...east of the Boston lightship was told by Captain W.J. Wheelor of the Coast Guard cutter Tampa.*

Fred could only hope that Stan and Douglas weren't one of the launches taken.

When the moon was full, or close to it, Fred knew not to expect anything in his traps. The runners were cautious with the extra light and avoided the brightly lit waters. On the reverse principle, if there were a thick pea soup fog, he might get his load a few days early, so the can with the cash had to be ready for the traps at all times. Last night had been the first night in a week that had afforded the perfect cover for a delivery, and sure enough when he had checked this morning, his traps had held more than crustaceans.

Fred hated leaving the old Model T in the bushes off the dirt road that circled World's End. He didn't like taking the small dingy they owned out though Hull Gut and West Gut after dark, and he especially didn't like a night like tonight where the temperature was still falling fast from ten degrees. Every bit of it, from start to finish made him wish for his warm bed at home. The only thing that sustained him, was that Gertrude would be waiting up, and her relief at seeing him was always followed up by more than adequate compensation for his evening's trials.

He pushed the boat out across the ice, testing with its weight, the sturdiness of his footing. Once the bow started breaking into slush, he hoisted himself aboard and pushed into deeper, unfrozen water.

It would be difficult tonight to get his bottles onto dry land without getting himself wet. He remembered the last time. His feet had been frigid blocks after their accidental bath in the icy water. His thoughts rushed ahead. Perhaps if he strung the burlap bags together, he could attach a rope and drag them across the ice to shore.

His breath froze in his nostrils as he started the engine and headed toward the Gut.

All was quiet except for the lonely tolling of bell buoys. He was the only craft foolish enough to be on the water in the arctic cold darkness, and he sped across the water as fast as his small amount of horsepower could carry him. When his destination was reached, Fred hauled his traps in as rapidly as his heavily gloved hands would allow. It still took twice as long as usual because, despite the protection, his fingers were numbed with cold.

When the last trap had been heaved over the side, back into the frigid depths, he gave himself a moment to recover. He hoped he wouldn't have to do this over another winter. If things continued to go well, they might just squeak out of this business before another cold season began. He fervently wished it to be so, heartily sick of this whole thing. And he just couldn’t help the nagging feeling that their luck was running out.

Coming back in, Hull Gut was rough going with a hard chop. When he finally came parallel to Nantasket Road, he sighed with relief that his night's business was nearly complete. Fred steered the boat to starboard and beached it onto the ice of the cove.

How he'd managed to get his cold legs to leap from the boat was something he'd puzzle out later, but right now he had to use what little brains he had left to slide the craft to shore and unload his bottles. He was getting too old for this.

Once the boat was was secure, he used one of his lines to tie the burlap bags together, and saw that the new method was going to work. He left everything on the beach and trudged up the embankment to start the car. He couldn't wait to load up and get home.

He was on his way back down the embankment, when his

tired mind registered the smell of pipe tobacco. He stopped, dead in his tracks. Fred's eyes quickly scanned the shrouded shoreline, once, then twice. There, to his left, the faint glow of a freshly lit bowl, much too close for comfort.

"Who's there?" Fred called out, glad now that he'd left the bottles down on the icy beach. "Show yourself."

The light from the tobacco remained stationary and Fred moved cautiously toward it. He approached, slowly, warily, willing the intruder to get up and leave before any confrontation. Finally, when he was no more than five yards away, a figure began to take shape, leaning back against a glacial deposit.

"What do you want?" Fred called angrily. He wished he had a weapon at his disposal. He looked around at his feet, but all the rocks were heavily encased in winter's grip. If the man was armed, he was definitely at a disadvantage. He blustered anyway and kept his forward trajectory.

"Out with it. What are you doing here?"

A soft laugh sounded in the darkness. "Why, I'm here to see you, Fred."

If Fred had any color left in his face after his exhausting night, it would have drained on the spot. The voice belonged to Detective Ambrose Fletcher, and the man who would certainly see him jailed before the night was over.

"Ambrose," resignation laced Fred's voice. "Might I say that I'm not very happy to see you?"

"You may. And I don't suppose you are. After a cold night on the water, I'm sure you'd just like to get home to your nice warm house, am I right?"

Fred had reached the detective by this time but instead of facing him, he placed his back to the boulder next to Ambrose, mimicking the other man's stance. "Yes, I'd like to be home right now." Fred couldn't keep the weariness that had seeped into his bones at bay any longer.

"You'll be home soon enough." Ambrose took a long puff on his pipe. "I just thought it might be time for us to have a little talk."

Fred had no energy left to hope, but the detective's words were soothing and a little life crept back into him. "You don't want to walk down the beach and see what I've caught in my traps?"

"Nope. As far as I'm concerned, that's none of my business." His voice was mild, uninterested, but he continued, "What is my business is the well-being of two very nice ladies whom I, and my dear mother, hold in great esteem." He paused to let his words sink in. "You know that Mother and I have visited Edith in town several times now."

"My sister said as much," Fred nodded. "She told us you took her out to lunch last week."

"That we did. She's a wonderful woman." Ambrose paused again. "Mother and I think quite highly of her, and also of Gertrude."

"As do I," Fred responded gruffly.

"I'm aware of that," Fletcher continued. "I'm also aware that at one time you made some foolish mistakes that endangered your sister."

Fred was shocked, and he struggled not to show it. "I know what I did, and I'm not proud of it."

"Good," Fletcher pushed away from the rock and turned, looking at Fred. "I'm hoping that you're a man who learns from his mistakes."

Fred remained quiet, waiting to hear what else Ambrose had to say.

"I've been aware for quite some time now, that there might be something going on that is a little out of the ordinary at Rocky Nook. And I want you to know that as long as it remains as quiet as it has been, I won't take the time to look for something that might be troublesome."

Up until this point, the detectives' voice had been mild, almost cajoling, and Fred was blindsided as Fletcher suddenly became as cold as the air around him. "But I will warn you. Don't do anything to put either of those women in harms way. What you're up to right now is not my area of concern, if you take my meaning." He punctuated his words by tapping the stem of his pipe against Fred's coated chest. "But if things should escalate, and I'm asked by any outside authorities to intervene, you will be one very sorry man."

The eyes that pinned Fred to the boulder showed none of the dapper weakness that usually characterized the detective. It was then that Fred realized the amiable buffoon was just an act. A damned good one, because it had fooled him for five years. He would never, ever make that mistake again. The detective was not one he wanted to have as an enemy.

Having said his piece, Ambrose Fletcher turned around and simply walked away. "Good evening to you Fred," he called over his shoulder as he disappeared into the shadows of World's End.

Fred was shaken. Shaken and castigated. Was this a good time to call it quits? It certainly seemed so. He hadn't felt quite like this since he'd been caught as a youngster by the headmaster, drawing with charcoal on the side of the school building. It was a feeling he hadn't liked then, and he certainly didn't like now.

With hands trembling from cold and emotion, he forced himself back down the beach, pulling his line in and gathering his catch. He loaded the liquor into the car, and drove home to discuss the future with Gertrude.

# Chapter Thirty-Two

April 1924

Fred nearly spit coffee across the room. One minute he was peacefully reading the morning paper, and the next he was on his feet, stabbing his finger at the small, obscure article on page five.

*Rum line extended to 12 mile limit*

*...legislation was passed yesterday to extend the jurisdiction of the U.S. Authorities to twelve miles from shore...*

It was no more than three lines in total. If the day hadn't been drizzly and he hadn't been dawdling, he would have missed it altogether.

Fred went back to the front page and scanned with greater attention this time. He found nothing. Had the newspaper done this on purpose? Had they buried the tiny article deep in the middle of the paper to keep it from being seen? He quickly grabbed his coat and ran out the door, intent on buying the morning edition of everything newsworthy that was available at Hennessey's. He would see what the other dailies had to say before he panicked.

****

Gertrude and Annie came up from under the barn where they'd been collecting eggs and emerged into the fine mist just in time to see Fred disappear down the driveway in the truck.

"That's odd," said Gertrude. "I thought he was going to do some planting this morning." She had requested a vegetable plot this year and Fred had obligingly bought carrot and beet seeds which she thought he meant to put in the ground today.

"Something's set him off," Annie observed, hurrying through the damp. "He left in an awful hurry."

"I guess we'll find out when he gets back." Gertrude shrugged and they trudged up to the house. She spotted the discarded newspaper on the table immediately upon entering.

Gertrude picked it up and noticed a coffee fingerprint, still damp, next to an article half way down the page. Her eyes moved quickly.

"Oh dear." she sat heavily. Now she knew the cause of Fred's distress. This was not what he needed on top of the dread that had hung over him these past several months.

After his encounter with Ambrose Fletcher, Fred had been so agitated that Gertrude was sure he would cease all his "rum running" activities on the spot. It had taken several weeks and many late night conversations before she could convince him that if Fletcher had meant to act, they'd both be in jail already. She rationalized that the detective had been giving them a warning to keep things low key, allowing them to continue as long as things remained small and circumspect.

It had taken a while before Fred could rationalize continuing his activities. But eventually he regained his composure—if not his confidence—and had continued pulling his traps, albeit with trepidation and a nervous stomach

Uncharacteristically it was Gertrude, not Fred who had wanted to keep on with the men's club and fortify the bank account. When one night deep in January, Fred had suggested that it might be a good time to sell Rocky Nook and move back to Boston, Gertrude had nearly stopped breathing. She was not ready to leave yet. The house had burrowed deep into her heart. Over the years she had memorized every knot in every beam, and the squeak in every board that her footsteps loosed from a floor-plank. She felt in her bones when the house emitted its haunting sighs in the middle of a wind-swept night, and reveled in the pungent smokiness that crept into the air during a damp day. No, she was not ready to go.

After long discussions, it had been decided that if they could continue selling alcohol through next Christmas, they would have enough money to stay in Hingham until they were older and much grayer. That had sounded good to Gertrude. Unfortunately it looked like the rules were changing again. With the offshore limit extended from three miles to twelve, the lobster boats would quadruple their risk from the elements and discovery by the Coast Guard. An impossible matter; insurmountable.

Gertrude waited for Fred and feared what he would say.

He arrived home more than two hours later and entered the kitchen with three soggy papers held loosely in front of him.

"They're all the same," he said in a voice devoid of emotion. "Every one has a small mention of the new law in the back pages." He drew one newspaper forward. "This one has it on the obituary page near the death notice of Eleanora Duse." He pulled another from the stack. "And this one is below the review for the new Douglas Fairbanks movie. I don't understand it. They must be hoping that runners won't find out about the law until it's too late. I hope Stan and Douglas are all right." He looked directly at Gertrude. "You know this is the end of the lobster traps."

Gertrude sighed. How he hated to disappoint her. Fred knew how much the house meant to her, but if she was honest, it was more work than they could handle if they didn't have a steady income to pay help. Still, Gertrude refused to give in.

****

Fred had taken plenty of time to think after picking up the papers and walking the harbor in the rain and had only one possible proposal to make. He knew Gertrude would not approve. He would plant the seeds of his new idea, then take a few weeks to make up his mind, whether she liked it or not.

"You know I've received a letter or two from Hugh, in Canada," he began.

"You've mentioned it," Gertrude murmured, still holding the offending article, shaking her head. "You said they're doing well." So great was her consternation that he knew she was listening only half-heartedly.

He wondered how long it would take for Gertrude to figure out where he was going with this. "He's got a job bar-tending at a nice resort up in Magog."

"Hmm," she said. "Funny name. Doesn't it reference a giant in English history, or have something to do with Babylon?"

Fred always wondered at the strange bits of information that floated around in Gertrude's head. "I don't know about either. All I know is that it's a resort town on Lake Memphremagog about 70 miles north of St. Johnsbury, Vermont."

Gertrude huffed. "And why are you bringing this up now, when we have better things to discuss?"

Fred could see he would have to spell things out.

"Hugh mentioned that if we ever were in need of any help, he would be in a good position to lend a hand."

"By lend a hand, do you mean loan us money?" she puzzled, coming out of her trance and staring at Fred.

He groaned "Gertrude, try to follow me, here."

He hadn't noticed Annie in the doorway, and her smart words seemed to break through Gertrude's fog, as his hadn't. "He means you can get your liquor from Hugh, up north," Annie stated pragmatically. "Which means that Mr. Fred will be taking the truck up to Canada, if I'm not mistaken."

"No, you're not mistaken, Annie," Fred continued. "That's exactly what I'm thinking."

Now Gertrude's thousand questions looked to be bubbling to the surface, but Fred kept talking. "I haven't sussed it all out, and I'm not sure if the risk is worth taking. But before I make up my mind, I'm going to wait a couple of weeks until I'm certain we won't be receiving any more deliveries in our traps. Then I'll decide." He rose from his seat and headed back outside, anxious to avoid whatever Gertrude had to say. Right now he needed solitude. "I think it's too wet to plant today. I'm going to go start that rabbit hutch we've been talking about." Fred was thankful for his escape, and strode toward the barn.

****

Gertrude sat for a long time staring at the rain falling outside the windows. Annie sat down beside her.

"It'll be a slow tea today because of the weather," she interrupted Gertrude's reverie. "A good time to catch up on your correspondence."

Gertrude knew better than anybody when Annie was up to something, and quirked an eyebrow in her direction. "Okay, Annie. Tell me. What letter should I be writing today?"

Her crafty friend gave her an impish smile. "Well, it occurs to me that Hugh works for a big resort up in Canada that probably has a fancy hotel and a fine restaurant," she began. "And it most likely caters to the rich with some first class entertainment." Annie paused, letting that sink in. "Now Mr. Fred, being a friend of his, might have reason for a visit, but not for anything I'd call necessary, so he could call attention to himself driving alone in a big truck, up and back to Canada, should anyone be noticing."

Gertrude figured she meant Ambrose Fletcher, and that Fred would need safeguards. "So you think I should go with him?" Gertrude speculated.

"No, Ma'am. I think you should go *without* him," Annie spoke definitively.

The shocked expression Gertrude could feel upon her face looked to be just what Annie had intended.

"Without him?" Gertrude repeated, feeling like she had been thinking one step behind everybody all morning. But as Annie sat there, smugly, she began to get the picture.

"Oh, Annie," she breathed. "It's a resort. I'm a singer. I could send the manager of that fine hotel a letter and ask for a job, singing." Her face brightened. "And what a fine and reasonable excuse to be traveling up and back to Canada. I'd certainly raise a lot less suspicion than Fred." Gertrude looked triumphantly toward her cagey, long time maid. "It's the perfect solution."

"Go write your letter," Annie nodded. "I'll take care of the tea room today."

# Chapter Thirty-Three

June 1924

*"Four and Twenty Yankees, feeling very dry,*
*Went across the border to get a drink of rye.*
*When the rye was opened, the Yanks began to sing,*
*"God bless America, But God save the King."*
- *Anonymous*

It felt like the longest five weeks of Gertrude's life. Since she had shown the letter to Fred, confirming her performances at the Canadian resort, he had retreated behind a mask of cold indifference. He had been to Boston for two extended visits with Edith, leaving Gertrude lonely and wanting, but when he was home, it was worse. Each meal was taken either away from her, or in painful silence. And every time she tried to approach him he moved away.

Finally, one evening at the supper table, a week before her departure, Fred deemed to speak.

"I'm coming with you," he stated blankly, bringing a bite to his mouth while focusing on a far spot on the wall.

"No, Annie's coming with me." Gertrude gave him the soft rebuttal and waited for his reaction.

Fred threw his fork on the table, scraped his chair back and strode into the next room. "Damn woman," she heard him curse. "Damn her, damn her. She'll be vulnerable, she'll be harassed, and she'll be caught." Gertrude knew he continued spouting for her benefit. “She'll be dragged off to some backwater jail in Vermont and I’ll be helpless to find her. Why won’t she listen?”

Gertrude pictured him dragging a hand, ineffectually through his hair. “Bah. There’s no reasoning with her.” He stomped off, and his tirade faded.

Gertrude ate the rest of her meal in silence, and after she was through clearing up, she retired to the parlor and sat quietly reading *Beau Geste*, a new novel written by P.C. Wren.

She was able to lose herself in the action for short periods of time, but Fred had returned, lurking just out of sight in the keeping room. His relentless pacing indicated that he wanted to come talk with her, but clearly was in need of some prodding.

“Fred. Please come sit down. You're making it impossible for me to enjoy my book.”

He didn't look the least bit repentant that he’d destroyed her concentration, but strode into the room with a ferocious look on his face. “I don't like this, Gertrude. I don't like you going. I don't like that I'm *not* going. I hate this whole thing.”

“I know, Fred. But I'm not doing it to make you angry,” Gertrude told him unhappily. “I'm doing it because it's the safest way.”

Fred looked like he would argue but she needed for him to finally hear all the arguments that had been piling up in her head for weeks.

“Just let me get this out, Fred. You haven't allowed me to reason with you, or talk about things, or get your opinions on how I should accomplish what I have to do. You've been so pigheaded in your objection that I've had to take care of all the planning on my own, and you know how much better I’d feel if you give me some help.”

Fred slowly sat down in the chair opposite Gertrude and met her eyes for the first time since May. She saw pain and frustration etched in their depths and if anything, his suffering made her regret that she hadn't forced the issue sooner.

"Will you listen to me now?" she implored. "Will you try to help me?" She waited for his verdict, barely able to breathe. The rigidity gradually left his body. "Tell me what you've got, so far?" He closed his eyes, giving in.

Gertrude almost burst into tears, such was her relief. She had felt so displaced over the past few weeks, not realizing how much she had come to depend on Fred, for physical support and for her emotional well-being. She dropped to her knees in front of him and placed her head on his lap while wrapping her arms around his waist. "Oh, how I've missed you, Fred," she cried.

A long moment passed before his big hand came down on her head and smoothed her hair, offering her the comfort she needed. She melted into him and with little encouragement she began telling him of her arrangements.

He listened stoically, gruffly acknowledging every now and then that she had done an admirable job of planning.

"But you've forgotten about extra gasoline," he offered petulantly. "I'll put a few cans on the truck that should see you through if you can't find a station."

Gertrude was puzzled, was that all he had to say after all this time?

"All right," she acknowledged slowly. "But Fred, even though I have the trip all planned, I'm still not quite sure what to do when I get there." She revealed to him her biggest dilemma. "How do I find someone that will supply me with whiskey?" Gertrude looked at Fred, trusting him to guide her in those most important details.

He finally relented. "I've given this some thought over the past few weeks—what I would have done if it was me, going." He gave a shake of his head. "Now I don't want to fight about this, but I believe your first trip should be a dry run."

"A dry run?" questioned Gertrude.

"Right. It's when you map out your suppliers and your routes, make your initial contacts, and try out the roads. But you don't actually have any liquor with you. That way, you feel comfortable the next time—when you do it for real—that everything will go smoothly. If you run into any troubles on a dry run, you can change your plans or give up altogether without any consequences," he stated calmly.

Gertrude contemplated. It did seem like a good idea. She would have enough to worry about the first time, giving a major performance in front of a crowd far larger than that of her tea room. But would it be sensible from a monetary standpoint to undertake such a long trip without making it count for more than her salary? She knew that Fred wanted reassurance and so she gave it to him without hesitation.

"A dry run sounds good, Fred. It might be just the right approach." Gertrude told him what he wanted to hear, but left leeway in her words to do what she thought was best. As she hoped, Fred heard only her agreement.

"Good." His voice filled with relief. "Now just one more thing," he continued in a serious tone. "When you get to the border crossing, I want you to stop for a while. Eat lunch or do some shopping but leave the truck where it will be highly visible to the border patrol. I want them to see it and know that you're relaxed enough to have them take a good look. Then, while you're eating or whatever you decide to do, try to make a connection with just one person in town. It could be a shopkeeper or a waitress, but somebody who will vouch for you. Someone you can inform about your singing engagement in Canada who will verify your story if the crossing agents get too nosy."

Gertrude swallowed hard. "So in case we get into some trouble at the check point on the way home…"

"…you have someone who knows your name," Fred finished.

Gertrude's mouth was suddenly dry as the reality of what

she was going to attempt finally sank in. She continued as calmly as possible.

“I actually had plans to stop at a local tourist spot I've read about at the border. Perhaps I'll be able to make a connection there.”

“That's just what I'm talking about,” Fred paused significantly, and she almost missed the dimple that appeared in his chin which meant he was feeling good enough to tease. “You've put most of my worries to rest, but I have one more.”

Gertrude waited for his punchline. “What's that?” she asked with an innocent air.

“Stay off the gas, woman. I won't have you wrapping yourself around a tree. You've the damned heaviest foot on the pedal.”

“Me?” Gertrude laughed, welcoming his humor. Fred knew she liked to drive fast and she dared taunt him for the first time in weeks. “Just because you drive like a little old lady, doesn't mean I have to. If we were in your hands going to Canada, we'd be on the road for a week.”

Fred's eyes took on an evil glint. “You don't like being in my hands?” He raised the appendages in question and ever so gradually moved in slow motion toward the places she most wanted him to touch.

Their time apart made her suddenly frantic with need, and she grabbed his hands, pushing them into her soft contours and relishing the feel of his strong fingers as they splayed over her bodice.

“Uh, huh?” he drawled. “How's the little old lady doing now?” He emitted a mock growl, scooped her up in his arms and in dramatic fashion that had her close to a swoon, carried her off to his room.

****

Gertrude and Annie left on a Thursday morning at six

o'clock. The truck was loaded with their luggage, Gertrude's music, food for the trip, and—as far as Gertrude was concerned—way too much extra gasoline, but Fred would not be denied.

They had closed the Tea Room down until Tuesday, eliciting well-wishes and excitement from most of her patrons for her trip north. Ambrose Fletcher had given Gertrude a small nod of his head when she'd told him the news. She figured he was pondering what new trouble she and Fred were getting up to.

The day was hot, but for the first six hours on New England Interstate Route 7, the roads were paved and it was easy going. They stopped, briefly in Turner's Falls for a quick picnic lunch before turning north onto New England Route 2 which would bring them out of Massachusetts all the way up to St. Johnsbury, Vermont. Unfortunately the road soon gave way to a dirt surface and the dust that was kicked up on such a dry June day was not conducive to the speeds that Gertrude liked to drive.

She sneezed. "At this pace we won't reach St. Johnsbury until six or seven o'clock tonight," Gertrude complained. But Annie the optimist would not be dissuaded from her good mood on their grand adventure.

"Pah," she chortled. "It could be raining," she came back cheerily, and Gertrude had to agree.

The day was beautiful and the scenery divine. And as they talked of this and that, Gertrude admired the burgeoning Green Mountains. Despite the unpaved road, the miles flew by. They didn't have to worry about being overtaken by darkness. The summer solstice was only two days away, and indeed—by the time they reached St. Johnsbury at just after seven o'clock—they drove down Railroad Street without a single street lamp having yet been lit.

Their destination was New Avenue House on the corner of Eastern Avenue. It lay just ahead of them. Never having stayed there before, Gertrude was pleasantly surprised by its grand brick facade. She parked the car on the curb and was met by a bellman who quickly whisked their luggage inside. Both women were looking forward to a full hot supper and a good night's sleep.

Annie, always chatty and following Fred's suggestion to the letter and beyond, made sure to tell everyone they came in contact with that Gertrude would be singing that weekend in Magog.

After a wonderful evening lingering over Baked Alaska in the dining room and eight full hours on the most comfortable of feather mattresses, they arose leisurely at seven, packed, ate a light breakfast and were on the road once more.

From St. Johnsbury, Magog was less than seventy five miles. Gertrude had inquired and found that the tourist spot in Derby Line, where she planned to stop at the Canadian border, was called the Haskell Free Library and Opera House. It straddled the boundary between the United States and Canada, with the room on the first floor being a free lending library and the room on the second floor being the Opera House which made money to support the library.

As Fred had instructed, when they arrived in Derby Line, Vermont, she pulled the truck into a highly visible parking spot just across the street from the border patrol building, with her brightly painted Rocky Nook logo pointing directly toward their large glass front office.

The ladies made a grand show of alighting from the truck, stretching and gawking before slowly making their way to the library. The door they used was on the United States side of the line. Upon entering, Gertrude marveled at the cool hush of the interior, and neither she nor Annie, taking in the comfortable atmosphere, were in any hurry to move.

They were quickly approached by a diminutive middle aged man in a black wrinkled suit whose demeanor was all smiles.

“Can I help you ladies with anything?”

Gertrude extended her hand enthusiastically. “The library

is very grand." She paused to make sure the compliment registered. "But what we'd really like to see is the Opera House. Would that be possible?" She gave him her best smile and the man was instantly charmed.

"Oh, you haven't seen grand until you've seen our Opera House," he beamed. "We usually do tours on the weekends, but since we're not very busy today, perhaps…," he peered around until his eyes lit upon a stout woman who stood near the main desk.

"Helma, I'm going to show these ladies the second floor. I shouldn't be long." Almost before her scowl reached them, he had steered Gertrude and Annie to the stairs, where they climbed to the upper chamber.

"Oh," Gertrude's startled exclamation resounded as they entered the four hundred seat auditorium. "It resembles a smaller version of the Boston Opera House," she informed Annie in an amazed but hushed voice. She gazed upward at the plaster cherubs and scroll-work and Gertrude felt an instant affinity for the room.

"Are you familiar with the building in Boston?" asked the small man who had granted them a tour, and clearly Annie wasn't about to keep quiet.

"Is she?" Annie chortled. "My dear sir, this is Miss Gertrude Edmands. She's a famous opera singer." Her smug brogue sounded bright in the granite hall, and the demure gentleman looked astonished.

"Miss Edmands? Oh, my." His face became wreathed with smiles. "What a pleasure it is to meet you. I'm such a devotee," he told them. "And although I've never heard you perform in person, I've enjoyed your splendid voice on a friend's phonograph." He looked as if he were about to swoon and Gertrude moved closer in case she needed to catch him.

"I never thought I'd meet you in person," he warbled. "Might I say that I'm honored and thrilled? I find your singing to be magnificent." His manner was quickly becoming effusive. “Dear ladies, wait until my wife Helma hears this.”

Gertrude smiled in embarrassment and realized that here was the impressionable person Fred had been anxious they meet, and he was more than they could have hoped for. Annie, of course, left nothing to chance.

“She's singing tonight and tomorrow night at the Magog Resort, you know. You and your missus should go up there to see her, and bring all your friends.”

Lord, the woman was shameless.

“I will most assuredly do that,” he enthusiastically rejoindered, and Gertrude felt terrible that Annie had put him on the spot. She thought to rectify her guilt immediately.

“My good sir, if you write your name down for me, I will leave it with the proprietor and make sure you get complimentary seats in the front of the house.”

Gertrude's words offer had him almost apoplectic. The poor man was so overwhelmed that his hands shook as he extracted a pen and paper from his pocket and proceeded to write down his name.

“Thank you.” He pressed the paper into her hand. “Thank you so much. The missus and I will attend tonight. You can count on it. We're only an hour away, you know.”

Gertrude nodded and turned, heading back down the stairs. “I hope you enjoy the show.” she said, sincerely, “But despite how close we are to our destination, we really should be going now. There is much to prepare for our first show.”

They reached the library floor once again and she continued. “I want to thank you so much for taking us around.” She smiled broadly at their host.

“The pleasure was all mine,” the small man gushed. “And I'll see you tonight.”

It took all of their willpower for Gertrude and Annie to make it to the truck before dissolving into an undignified fit of giggles.

“That one won't be forgetting you anytime soon.” Annie prophesized. “But let’s hope it won’t come in handy.”

Gertrude took a few moments to compose herself before re-alighting from the truck. She crossed the street to the border patrol office and spent all of a minute and a half explaining her business in Canada before the uninterested officer waved her on.

The final hour on the road to Magog, afforded them brief and tantalizing glimpses of Lake Memphremagog which was a good thirty miles long. Each time the brilliant blue of the water shone through the stately pines, it took Gertrude’s breath away. It was the most delightful scenery of the entire trip, and even though she was sorry that it was over so rapidly, she was glad they reached their destination before the unbearable heat of mid-afternoon.

The Magog International Resort rose before them, nestled into a rising hillside, fronted by the sapphire blue waters of the lake. Easily four stories tall, its majestic facade of white clapboards was surrounded by covered porches sporting green wicker tables, chairs and settees. A magnificently tended profusion of flowers cascaded over a front walkway that led to a wharf, where a paddle steamer named *The Lady of the Lake* had just pulled in, letting an excited group of travelers disembark. Everything was splendid.

Gertrude suddenly felt small and insignificant in comparison to all the grandeur, and a shiver of trepidation passed through her bones. What had she been thinking to believe she could pull off either of the monumental tasks that lay ahead?

# Chapter Thirty-Four

June 1924

*Daily Kennebec Journal*
*CLEVER QUEEN OF THE BOOTLEGGERS AGAIN EVADES LAWS GRASP*

*Frankly Admits Gets Thrill Out of Game. Raises Turkeys on Vermont Farm When Not On Road*

*Mrs. Hilda Stone, to whom the border liquor patrol has given the name "Queen of the Bootleggers", has won another skirmish with the law. She walked free today after her fourth arrest in as many months, but prohibition enforcement officers retained as souvenir of the encounter an automobile with skillfully devised compartments for carrying liquor. Not so much as a spoonful of beverage was found in the car as evidence.*

"I located Hugh," Annie whispered, running up to Gertrude where she stood backstage. Gertrude grabbed for Annie and squeezed her fingers.

"Thank God," she breathed. "Did you tell him that I'd meet him after my performance?" She nervously smoothed the skirt of the gold lame, Chanel dress that Edith had insisted she buy in Boston last week.

"Yes. And stop fussing. You look perfect and everyone's going to love you." A dimple appeared in Annie's cheek as she teased. "Your little Mr. Opera House is in the front row and you'll never guess who he's with." She attempted to coax a laugh from Gertrude.

"Who?" Gertrude sighed distractedly.

"That enormous woman who was in the library this morning. She must be his wife. What did he call her? Helga…Helma? Anyway, she's dressed all in gray and looks like an enormous battle ship."

Annie was correct, she won a chortle from Gertrude. "Stop being so mean, Annie." She was distracted for a single moment before, once again, looking at her watch. "Five more minutes before I go on. When you head to your seat, thank them for coming and have Hugh send them whatever they're drinking. We want them to be very happy."

Annie nodded and scurried away, leaving Gertrude to her nerves.

The room where she was to sing was not the auditorium she had imagined, but a large room filled to capacity with small tables. Done in tasteful shades of mauve and gray, it was obviously emulating the brand new art deco style that had just emerged in Paris. The stage where she would sing took up one side of the room. It was flanked by enormous pleated curtains, and opposite, between two sets of entry doors stretched an enormous bar, under-lit and elegant. During a quick practice in the afternoon, Gertrude had found the acoustics of the room exemplary and the accompanying pianist brilliant. She wasn't full of confidence, but she was determined to give the best show that she could.

The stage director finally gestured for her to take her place. The house lights dimmed and the curtains parted. Not a sound could be heard in the vast room except the slight tinkling of glasses. The first notes from the pianist rose tantalizingly.

Gertrude sparkled where she stood in the spotlight, her dress picking up the brilliant reflections from overhead. With a pause, she gathered herself and slowly raised her eyes to the audience. When her voice finally rose in song, she knew it was only seconds before she captured the crowd. She could feel the energy flowing her way as she trapped them in a spell that would last until the echo of her final aria.

****

Gertrude finished with a flourish and the patrons sprang to their feet. Cheers erupted, the like of which Gertrude had not heard in many years. Tears of gratitude sprang to her eyes at being able to share this moment with such an appreciative crowd, and when the curtain finally dropped, she was unable to move.

It had been a magical performance. Every now and then she had been a part of one. They didn't happen very often, but when they did, you climbed as close to heaven as you could ever get, standing on this earth. Gertrude was humbled. She had never thought to feel this way again.

"Miss Gertrude." Annie's voice penetrated Gertrude's haze as she was finally able to move to the wings of the stage. She found herself wrapped in Annie's embrace with the housekeeper's words buzzing around her.

"I never knew. All the time I've heard you sing in the tea room and I never knew you could do *that*. Oh, Miss Gertrude. You were amazing."

"Thank you, Annie," she returned the hug and took a deep breath, trying to settle back into herself. She squeezed the other woman's shoulders. "Now take me to see Hugh before I collapse."

That was easier said than done. Gertrude emerged into a room filled with well-wishers, waiting to touch her and have their programs signed. She was surrounded by joyous humanity, all looking to have the spell she had woven while on stage continue just a little longer. She talked, she smiled, and all the while Annie moved her inch by inch further in the direction of the bar.

Gertrude was unaware when they finally reached their

destination until the wind was, unceremoniously, squeezed from her lungs as she was lifted off her feet and swung in enormous circles by the biggest man in the room. Hugh's voice rose, exultant, above the clamor.

"Gertrude. You're a charmer and an angel, lass. Doona be tellin' me that dunce, Fred, has been keeping you at home when this is what you should be out doin'." He finally placed Gertrude on her feet and looked around. "Where is the oaf, anyway?"

Gertrude laughed at his exuberance and suddenly missed Fred with a stabbing awareness. "I wish he was here," she cried with heartfelt emotion. "But I asked him to stay home. This was something I needed to do without him."

Hugh was quick to catch the underlying tone, and rapidly led Gertrude to a seat at the bar, shooing people away with his protective air.

"Don't fash the wee lass," he scolded the patrons still clamoring for her attention. "She needs to sit and revive with a pint." He pulled a quick glassful and set it down in front of her. Eventually, his scowls disbursed everyone around and the two friends had an opportunity to speak.

"When I saw your name on the marquis this week, I thought to be seeing Fred. Am I right in thinking that you'll be wanting a little something from Canada to bring home?"

Gertrude made her mind up at that moment. This would not be a dry run. If Hugh could make a connection for her, she would take a load home on Sunday. Fred would not be happy, but once she had succeeded, what would he be able to say?

"Absolutely, Hugh. I've made this excuse to be here and I shouldn't waste it." Gertrude surreptitiously told him how many cases she was looking for, and he promised he would arrange things tonight. They would meet up with his friend, a man named R.J., tomorrow to complete the transaction.

"I don't know if you've heard the name before, but R.J. works for one Hilda Stone." He fed Gertrude this information in an undertone. “She's known as the queen of the rum runners up here, and she's a right one, she is.” It was a high compliment from Hugh, and even if Gertrude hadn't heard the name before, she felt better already, knowing that another woman was involved. She yawned and quickly glanced at the Scotsman to see if he had witnessed her rudeness. Hugh laughed.

“Ah, yes. I saw that, ye daft bit of fluff. Off with you, now. I'll not have you falling asleep on my bar.” He brought his head closer. “Meet me in front of the hotel at ten tomorrow morning and we'll make things happen.”

Gertrude impulsively leaned up and kissed his cheek.

“Achh. Now I'll have to be doin’ a penance when Josie finds out I've been kissed by a lovely lady tonight.”

“I've got a better idea,” Gertrude grinned. “Instead of a penance, find someone to watch your son tomorrow night and have Josie come to the performance. I'll leave her name with the manager so she'll have a good seat.”

“Hah. You're a right wonder. She'll be so excited I won't hear the end of it all day,” he snorted. “She'll probably be expecting a new dress out of it as well.” His eyes glowed warm. “Thank you, Gertrude. I'll see you in the morning.”

Annie materialized at her elbow and she stumbled to their room in a delirious cloud. The first evening had gone well. She could only hope for the same tomorrow.

****

Gertrude woke up slowly and looked around. Annie was already gone and it was only, she squinted at her watch, nine o'clock. She threw the covers off and leapt from bed. She had to meet Hugh in an hour and she hadn't yet had breakfast. At that moment the door opened and Annie entered with a waiter behind her. The cart he pushed was filled with tantalizing smells and Gertrude couldn't wait to lift the silver lids to find out what was hidden beneath.

"Annie, you are a life-saver. I don't know what got into me sleeping so late, and I have to meet Hugh at ten."

"Do you want me to come with you Miss Gertrude?" Annie inquired, glancing under her lashes at the mustachioed waiter who was setting up breakfast. "Because if you don't need me, Armand gets off in an hour and has asked if I'll walk with him near the lake."

Gertrude smiled in impish approval. "No, I don't need you, Annie. Go and have a good time. I'll see you when I get back."

Armand looked appreciative and placed a kiss on Annie's hand before quietly closing the door behind him.

"Isn't he just lover-ly?" Annie swooned. "And his name… Armand, can you be believing it?"

Gertrude chuckled. "Just don't get too carried away. We're only here for one more night," she warned, as she tucked into her huge breakfast.

She ate with relish then dressed rapidly, arriving at the hotel entrance two minutes before ten. Hugh was already waiting.

"We'll be meeting R.J. up the river. I've asked the valet to bring your car around and if it's all right with you, I'll drive."

"Of course," Gertrude told him. "You know where you're going. And it's a truck now, not the old Model T. You're going to like the modifications that Fred has made." Her eyes sparkled with mischief as she watched Hugh's face when the vehicle was brought around the corner.

"Bloody hell," he intoned. "Is the man daft? You'll not be anonymous in that."

"Which is exactly what we're counting on to work for us," Gertrude informed him. "With a high profile truck and an honest reason to be in Canada, we're hoping that the border patrol will think we'd be crazy to try anything."

"How about I think you're just plain crazy," Hugh muttered, slipping behind the wheel. "I sure hope Fred knows what he's doing sending you up here to do this on your own."

Gertrude felt a twinge of remorse for deceiving Hugh, but not enough to deter her from her plans.

They traveled a few miles up the Magog River, driving slowly, reaching a picturesque bridge and damn that spanned the water.

"How lovely," Gertrude intoned.

Hugh paused so she could take in the view before the car moved on.

"See that carpet factory?" Hugh pointed down into the notch as they rounded a bend. "Hilda rents one of their outbuildings and fills it with stock. R.J. oversees the distribution. We don't get into any trouble up here because it's all legal. The risk becomes yours, going back into the US." He looked over at her. "You're sure you want to take the chance?"

"That's what I'm here for," Gertrude answered decisively. "Let's get this done."

R.J. was another charmer, and after holding her hand a little too long, he assured her that he could more than meet her demands, and that he'd be at the hotel to catch her show that night. Gertrude enjoyed his down-Maine accent—one that sounded like he never left the woods—and wondered if he'd ever heard an opera in his life. She vowed to find him after the show and see if he enjoyed it.

As for the loading up and exchange of money, she couldn't believe it was so easy. Once R.J.'s guys started packing in the cases, everything went rapidly. Perhaps they had blown the dangers of this scheme out of proportion? It seemed so much safer than the clandestine meetings in New Bedford and the pulling of lobster traps in the dead of winter. They should have been doing this all along.

Hugh and R.J., much to her delight, were quite taken with the secret compartments that Fred had fashioned and, knowing he'd be pleased, Gertrude promised to pass on their praise. It was less than an hour before she was back at the hotel and saying goodbye to Hugh.

"I'll see you tonight." He tipped his hat to Gertrude as they left the now precious truck in the hands of the valet. "Josie's really looking forward to the show."

"And I'm looking forward to seeing Josie again," she told him, and feeling lighter than air, Gertrude waved Hugh off with many thanks, and went back to her room to prepare for the night's show.

****

"Bloody bastard." Annie slammed into the room, belatedly noticing that Gertrude was tucked partway into the closet, rummaging through clothes. She clapped a hand over her mouth. "Begging your pardon Miss Gertrude." She threw off her hat and attempted to regain her composure.

Gertrude didn't know whether to laugh, or be outraged for Annie who was obviously in quite a state. "What happened?" she finally managed to choke out.

"Armand, the bloody bas…, no, I won't say it again. Well it turns out the arse is married," Annie lamented, throwing herself on the bed to glare at the ceiling. She covered her face with one arm while she continued. "The morning started out so lovely. The sun was shining and Armand asked if he could hold my hand while we walk down by the lake. Things couldn't have been better." Her eyes took on a dreamy cast as she recalled it. "He had some poetry or another that he's spouting at me, not that I'm noticing because his eyes are saying something altogether different." She paused for dramatic effect which Gertrude fully appreciated.

"We finally stop and he turns to me, waggling that lovely mustache, and comes in for a kiss." Her pause was significant. "When suddenly, out of nowhere, this banshee comes screaming towards us, wielding her purse and hitting him about the head. And do you know what the bloody…man does?" she asked. "Do you?" she questioned again. "He hides behind me and let's me take the blows!" Annie pointed to a small red mark on one cheek. Gertrude, wanting to laugh, murmured instead, in sympathy.

"So once I've sorted things out, and finally understand from all her babbling that she's his wife, I understand her dilemma and I help her whack the living daylights out of him." Annie peeked over her arm. "And that's my morning for you."

Gertrude couldn't help it. She sat heavily on the bed and burst into laughter, picturing the scene in vivid detail. Annie eventually joined her until the two women were hoarse.

Gertrude patted Annie on the shoulder to commiserate, still spluttering, and for the next hour they took turns coming up with evil things that they would like to do to the hapless male. By the time they went down for lunch, both women were hoping that Armand would be the unlucky waiter to serve them their mid-day meal.

****

The show that night was spectacular. If not quite as magical as the evening before, it still rated with the top ten performances of Gertrude's career. She had gone on, confidently draped in a form fitting gown of silk and glass beads redolent of a Mariano Fortuny. The room was once again filled to capacity, but this time it didn't bother her in the least.

She completed her show with plenty of time after to hob-knob with the crowd, which included a dapper R.J.—leaning across the bar from Hugh—throwing appreciative glances at her beneath lowered lids while he polished off a snifter of brandy.

Gertrude glowed under his regard, but turned away to catch up with Josie who had come to join them, and it was a good distraction from his attentions. Especially when Josie brought out the Kodak's of their young son and Gertrude was able to respond to them with the proper enthusiasm. All thoughts of border crossings and handsome purveyors of alcohol were pushed aside to bask in the joy of seeing her dear friend who relished in her new domesticity.

****

Gertrude and Annie got an early start the next morning and planned a short trip back to St. Johnsbury. The long travel day would be Monday, but by then they would be well away from the border and out of any possible danger. Both women were unusually quiet and became more so as they approached the border crossing at Rock Island. Annie fidgeted to the point where Gertrude's nerves became fraught.

"Annie, this won't do," Gertrude reprimanded. "We have to look happy and carefree, just as we did when we came into Canada on Friday. Remember, we have a perfectly good reason for our trip. It's not like they should have any suspicions unless we give them one." Gertrude pulled the truck up in front of the border patrol office and yanked the hand brake with a little extra verve. She stepped from the truck and Annie, not wanting to be left behind, accompanied her in.

"Good morning, sir," Gertrude was perturbed to see that it was not the same gentleman who had waved her through so easily two days ago.

"Ladies," the officer removed his hat and took his feet off the desk in a leisurely fashion. "I'll need your identification and the reason for your travel today." He glanced out the window at the truck while Gertrude and Annie procured their papers.

"I performed this weekend at the Resort Hotel up in Magog," Gertrude said levelly. "Now we're headed back home." He glanced briefly at the items he was given and passed them back in a desultory fashion.

"You a singer?" he asked without much interest.

"Yes, opera." Gertrude responded, unreasonably miffed at his lackadaisical attitude. Annie kicked her foot, reminding her to maintain her smile.

"Why the big truck?" he asked, inserting a toothpick into his mouth and emitting a small wet noise that grated on Gertrude even more.

"Our only other option is a very old Model T that hasn't been driven farther than from our home to Boston in a good many years."

Having taken the point from Annie's blow, she forced herself to sound amiable. "We feel safer driving the truck. It's much more reliable, you see." Gertrude hoped her voice was sincere. She opened her eyes wide to gaze innocently at the officer.

"Okay." He sucked the toothpick again, handing their papers back and dismissing them. Gertrude was astonished. He wasn't even going outside to take a look. "Have a safe trip." He sat down and resumed his reading.

Gertrude and Annie walked sedately back to the vehicle, when in actuality Gertrude wanted desperately to break into a run and disappear as fast as possible.

She noticed a small, breakfast cafe across the way where three men sat in the window, looking out at their truck. Well, they could look all they wanted. There was nothing to see.

Gertrude forcibly restrained herself from nervous giggles, but kept a proper, stoic expression on her face. Slowly she backed the truck from its parking spot and headed across the line into Vermont. Upon crossing, she dropped her shoulders in relief.

"Well that was easy," Gertrude allowed, but something nagged at her about the way the three men had watched. She shook it off. Certainly she had to be imagining things.

# Chapter Thirty-Five

July 1924

*North Adams Transcript*
*"Bootleg Queen" Wants Auto Back...*
*Mrs. Hilda Stone started proceedings to regain possession of the machine which federal officers declare is one of the cleverest for illegal transportation, with many secret compartments, they have yet to see. The prohibition men...intend to fight the proceedings.*

Fred was taking no chances. He'd felt like a fool, and totally betrayed when Gertrude had come back last month with a full load of whiskey. It had taken many days before he could bring himself to even talk to her.

But this time he'd be keeping an eye on things. He heaved his bag into the back of the Model T before giving some last minute instructions to the Hatchard boy who would be caring for the animals while he was gone.

"Just pay attention to the place and make sure you get the chickens in before dusk."

"No problem, Mr. Torrey," the teenager assured him. "I'll be over a few times a day to see that everything is okay. Don't you worry."

Fred pulled out of the driveway, more concerned with what lay ahead of him than what he'd left behind. He departed exactly one hour after Gertrude and Annie, and hoped to keep pace with them to arrive in St. Johnsbury around eight that evening. A room was booked for him at the St. Johnsbury House on Main Street where he would stay the night. Then he'd get up early to watch the women's hotel, and follow them the rest of the way to Canada. He anticipated no trouble on the trip up, but he was certainly going to be in for a fight once he made his presence known, and he'd stick with them on the way back whether Gertrude liked it or not. Fred didn't care that she would be furious he had followed them. He was not good at waiting, and he refused to leave things in her hands any longer. When he got to Magog, he'd find Hugh and lay low until it was time for the return trip on Sunday.

****

"Come see the lass sing." Hugh cajoled for the tenth time. He couldn't understand why Fred would drive all the way to Canada and then hide himself away. "She's naught but a wee thing. How much damage can she do when she finds out you're here?"

A noise of disbelief sprang from Fred's mouth. "You're kidding, right?" he rubbed his chin. "My situation isn't like yours with Josie." Fred was sure he'd never heard the other couple do more than coo, lovingly at each other. "Gertrude made my life hell last month, determined to get her way and do this by herself. If she had any idea that I followed her after finally giving in, I'd never hear the end of it. Nor would I be getting any…" Fred cut himself off quickly with a quick glance at Josie across the room.

"…getting any what?" Josie was not going to let him off the hook. "What do you think you won't be getting?" She was clearly amused. "Fred, you're a dunce. The woman adores you madly, and nothing you could do would keep her from your bed."

Fred preened and pouted at the same time. "Well, I'm still

not going to see her. The day she leaves will be soon enough for the fireworks to erupt. You tell me how she fared when you get home."

Josie was obviously delighted to be going to hear Gertrude again. Unable to convince him to accompany Hugh, the happy couple would be embarking, and he would be staying home to watch after their young son. A fine deal as far as Josie was concerned. She wished Fred luck with her little terror and fled before he could change his mind.

****

Gertrude was performing the songs of Katisha from the Mikado this weekend. Gertrude realized that any patrons familiar with the opera, would scoff as the curtain was drawn, wondering how—despite her Japanese dress—that a petiti American woman could perform such a role?

But their doubts would all be for naught. As the lights came down, Gertrude moved confidently and with evil dignity across the stage. Before the audience's eyes she became the old and appalling Katisha, giving them a show that wrapped them in its timeless fingers and revealed to them the power of her voice.

Gertrude felt it all right down to her soul as she sang. The magic had come once again.

At the end of her performance, as happened when she gave her all, Gertrude became drained. Tonight she had immersed herself so deeply in her role that she couldn't believe her heart hadn't actually been broken.

Annie was there to hand her a drink when the curtain came down on her final applause. She somehow found the strength to mill about amongst the crowd until finally coming, thankfully, to rest at the bar across from Hugh.

"Another marvel," Hugh's voice was unusually hushed at the emotion she had obviously evoked in him. He shook his head. "Fred should have come."

"No. He's better off at home," Gertrude disagreed. "He'd only make me nervous." She placed her empty glass on the bar in a deliberate way to bring Hugh back to business.

"So tell me. What time shall I meet you tomorrow?" she questioned.

"I haven't been able to talk to R.J. yet, but I'm sure it'll be ten. I'll send you a note if it's any different."

Gertrude reached across and squeezed his hand. "Thanks Hugh. I'll only be bothering you one more time after this. Fred and I have decided to get out of the business after my run in August. We'll have enough of a stockpile to see us through the holidays and by the time our inventory is gone, we should have plenty of money put away." Her smile was contemplative. "Maybe we'll come up next spring just to have a visit."

"If you do, you'll be seeing a new bairn in the house," he blushed appealingly.

"Oh! How wonderful, Hugh. I'm so happy for you," Gertrude gushed. "Where's Josie? I'd like to congratulate her too."

"She left a while ago, she was feeling tired so I told her to head home."

"I think I'll be off to my room, as well," Gertrude agreed. "I'll see you in the morning."

She spotted Annie across the room speaking with what she would call a "fine gentleman", so she made her way upstairs on her own.

Gertrude had been nearly oblivious of the time when Annie arrived back at the room. She had been deep in slumber, and simply rolled over at the slight disturbance. And now that the sun had come up, Gertrude was raring to go at seven in the morning, but Annie looked like she could sleep the day away.

Gertrude quietly swung her legs from the bed and put on her wrapper over her nightgown, tiptoeing toward the bathroom. Something alerted her to a note that had been tucked under the door, and she bent to retrieve it.

*Unable to meet you in the morning. Be at the warehouse by 10 and R.J. will take care of you. Sorry, Hugh*

She hoped that Josie was all right and that nothing had happened to the baby. No, Hugh would have said if it were something bad. She put the note on the desk and headed to the bathroom for a soak in the tub. She had a few hours before she needed to leave.

****

Damn, she hoped that R.J. wouldn't mind if she were a few minutes late. She had met some well-wishers in the lobby who wanted to talk all about the show last night and, despite repeatedly pointing at her watch and telling them she had an important meeting, they had refused to let her go. She finally had to be rude and walk away, backwards, smiling and shrugging. Now where was the valet with her truck? She checked her watch again. Five minutes to ten and he was finally coming around the corner. She hated being late.

She thrust the truck into gear and headed out of town. Luckily, having accompanied Hugh last time, the road was not unfamiliar, and after driving for a few minutes, she recognized that the bridge she'd so loved should be right around the next corner.

****

Hugh stood on the steps of the hotel. Where had the bloody woman gone? It was just gone ten o'clock—the time they'd agreed to meet—but the boy said that Gertrude had already retrieved her vehicle a few minutes before. Where could she have gone by herself? He signaled to Fred who had been waiting in Hugh's automobile across the street. Fred sprinted across the divide, frantically looking in all directions.

"I don't want her to see me," Fred hissed as he came close.

"Something's no' right, my friend," Hugh cut him off, his brogue thick with agitation. "The boy here says she's a'ready left. You need to go to her room and see if Annie knows aught about it."

****

Fred took the stairs two at a time, understanding that Hugh was not given to hyperbole. He flashed his fake license at the desk clerk, proclaiming himself husband to Gertrude and after being reluctantly given the proper floor number, dashed upstairs for her room. He pounded on the door.

"Be still," he heard from within. "I'll be there in a minute." Annie opened the door with a disgruntled look on her face that quickly became one of amazement.

"Mr. Fred. Whatever are you doing here?" she gawked.

He had no time for niceties. "Annie, where's Gertrude?" He pushed through the door.

"She must be down at breakfast," Annie said, clearly not understanding why Fred was tearing about the room looking as if Miss Gertrude would be under something.

His eyes spotted the smooth creased note, and his face drained of color when he read it. "Stay put," he yelled to Annie as he bolted out the door, clutching the missive.

"What is going on…?" she yelled, but she was too late. Fred had already left her far behind.

Fred vaulted toward Hugh as he pushed out the doors. He grabbed the Scotsman's arm and thrust the note into Hugh's hand.

"Let's go. Now," Fred growled. "You've got to know where she's gone."

Hugh managed to read while sprinting toward his car. "Bloody hell." he yelled. "I'll kill the bastards."

His long legs landed him at the driver's door even before

Fred had jumped into the passenger seat. He turned the key and slammed the vehicle in gear.

"Kill what bastards?" Fred asked shakily. He was afraid of the answer he would get.

Hugh looked grim. "There's them that way-lay customers coming to pick up liquor. They want the money used to pay the suppliers"

"And what do they do to the people they way-lay?"

Fred was aware of a significant pause before Hugh answered. "Usually rough them up a bit. But I've never had cause to know what they'd do to a woman." Hugh's foot went harder to the floor, but it still didn't feel fast enough to Fred.

"We'll get there," Hugh said, clearly as much to comfort himself as Fred. "We can only be five or ten minutes behind her at best. Don't worry, lad."

But worry was all Fred could do.

****

Gertrude stood next to the truck, her chest heaving. A large car blocked the road in front of her and the men who had emerged looked entirely disreputable and very familiar. As well they should. The pair had belatedly arrived at the warehouse the month before, helping R.J. load her truck.

At first, encountering the vehicle parked sideways across the dirt road, Gertrude had stayed in her truck and tapped politely on the horn. When that had elicited no movement, she had leaned on it a little harder and glared imperiously at the obstruction. That was when the two men had alighted from their car.

"Get out," the one in the worn gray suit had yelled, not sounding in the least bit like being disobeyed.

Gertrude had yelled back. "Move your car, gentlemen. I'm in a hurry."

"You're not going anywhere," the larger and nastier of the

two intoned. "Now get out of the truck."

Gertrude had sought to look compliant, waving one hand vaguely in their direction while with the other, groping around under her seat. Fred had made sure she had a tire iron in case of a flat, and it would come in handy now. Where was it? Where was it? Her fingers had fumbled and shook before finally curled around the iron's comforting coolness.

"Lady. We're not waiting all day. Get out of the truck or we'll come drag you out," Gray suit had snarled while grinding his cigarette out under his foot.

Gertrude had slowly opened the door and now stood, heart thumping, holding the tire iron aloft in one hand.

"Oh please, sister. Do you think that's going to stop us?" Large and nasty was moving very slowly in her direction.

Gertrude turned so that her door closed and her back was against it. She wasn't going to let either of them get behind her. Her only hope was to be able to swing the tire iron around in half circles to stave them off, and hopefully knock them out.

Hoping to alert someone, she reached in her open window with her free hand and leaned on the horn. All the while the despicable pair inched closer. Was she near enough that R.J. would hear her indication of distress?

*Don't panic*, she told herself. If you lose control you'll lose any advantage you have. Not that she was deluding herself that she had any. The two men were larger than her by far, and didn't look intimidated.

"What is it that you want?" Gertrude tried holding them off with a question.

"Well, first of all," one responded obligingly, "we want the money that you were going to hand over to R.J. And secondly…," his eyes skimmed over her quivering body and his tongue came out to lick his lips. "You're a mighty fine looking woman. Could be we won't dump your body over the falls if you act real nice to us." Both men laughed.

Gertrude felt dread in the depth of her stomach and swore

she'd die before either of the two ever touched her. *Oh God, help me*, she prayed. *Please let me live long enough to see Fred again.*

Tears stung her eyes but she denied them, filling her lungs and grasping the iron with both hands. She could do this.

*Not yet, not yet.* They were closing in, but Gertrude didn't want to swing too soon. She knew she had one chance to hurt them and then they'd be after her.

It happened swiftly. Gray suit lunged, and Gertrude swung high, catching him on the side of the face. At the same time she sent her foot up into his groin using the mightiest of kicks. He dropped to the ground, but before she had time to regroup, the tall one grabbed her arm and twisted it until the iron dropped from her numbed fingers.

"Goddammit, Goddammit, I'm going to kill the bitch." screamed the one in the dirt, clutching his crotch in agony. "Hold her, Ed. Hold her until I can get my hands on her."

Ed seemed to be doing just that as Gertrude struggled and kicked ineffectually against him.

"You are going to be real sorry that you ever messed with me." He rose slowly from the ground and wiped ineffectually at the blood running down the side of his face where she had smashed the tire iron against his jaw.

His bloody hand shot out and grabbed her by the neck. "What I'm going to do to you isn't going to be pretty, you bitch."

Gertrude attempted to kick him again, but he stumbled to the side, clearly still reeling from her kick to his jewels.

She felt Ed, holding her, start to look around with nervous movements.

"Let's just get the money first and then you can have her," he reasoned. "R.J. might have heard the horn and I'd hate to have him on our backs. The quicker we get off the road, the better."

It seemed like gray suit agreed. "Fine. What I have in mind for her can wait." His eyes glittered. "Where's the money, whore?"

Gertrude found enough moisture in her dry mouth to spit at him. "I don't have any money," she brazenly lied, when in fact it was hidden in one of the secret compartments.

"Hold her, Ed. I'm going to frisk her." The leer in his eyes set Gertrude to screaming as loudly as she was able. And when his hands began to move deliberately over her body she panicked but refused to be still.

He grabbed her chin. "I'm going to hit you into tomorrow unless you stop moving. And then you won't be in any shape for people to recognize your body when they finally come to pick up the pieces."

His words chilled Gertrude, but knowing his words made no difference to her outcome she renewed her screams and struggles. And lord knows her practiced lungs could conjure some loud screams.

****

Fred and Hugh rounded the corner, and what they saw chilled Fred's soul. A man was leaning back against the truck, holding a bloodied Gertrude up against him, while another groped up her legs, thrusting his hand between her thighs.

Fred was out of the car before Hugh could stop. His bellow of rage alerted them to his arrival and the tableau of three turned as one.

In slow motion, gray suit took his hands from Gertrude and reached to the inside of his suit jacket. Fred instantly registered that the man had a gun, but his anger and forward momentum didn't allow him room to stop. He watched in fascination as Gertrude, clearly also recognizing the danger, used the man holding her as leverage and kicked high with her hard shoe. Her heel connected with the gunman's elbow and his weapon was flung in a wide arc into the road.

Fred's roar filled the clearing. He launched himself at the

assailant and his fist connected with gray suits face, again and again while part of him was aware, despite his fury, that his friend had released Gertrude from the other's grasp and sent the man sprawling to the ground where Hugh held him with one big, booted foot.

Fred finished his work and dropped his man beside the first. "Are you all right?" His voice shook as he approached and ran his hands over Gertrude's neck, searching for the source of the blood that covered her.

"Not mine," she assured him taking a really good look at her assailants on the ground. She threw herself at Fred in a storm of tears. "You came. I don't know how, but I needed you, and you came."

If there had been any room for humor in the situation, Fred might have laughed. Gertrude thought she had conjured him from thin air, and couldn't quite make sense of it. But there was no time for explanations as he held her tightly.

A car approached from the opposite direction, and R.J. with two of his men emerged, appraising the scene.

"Damn it all to hell," R.J. cursed, not even attempting to curb his anger. "How could this have happened?" He turned regretful eyes to Gertrude. "I'm so sorry." His attention switched to Hugh. "We'll take care of things here, my friend. Bring the lady back to town."

R.J. was no longer the genial Maine bumpkin. "The bastards will be sorry they're alive when I get through with them."

"If it's all the same to you, R.J., I'll stay. Fred?" Hugh was momentarily able to draw Fred's eyes away from Gertrude. "Take her back in my car." He nodded down the road. "I'll be along with the truck and your load after I help R.J. clean up this mess."

Hugh looked grim but determined, and Fred knew it was on his behalf. Fred would never have been able to leave without knowing the two had gotten what they deserved.

He nodded to his friend, satisfied, and pulled Gertrude

flush to his side. Dazedly he led her away, allowing the men to do what needed to be done.

# Chapter Thirty-Six

July 1924

*The Bradford Era*
*Morning Musings...*
*This sent to us as a true story from the Vermont border:*

*Rum Runner approaches a farmer and offers him $50 for the use of his barn for one day.*

*"What do you want it for?" demands the farmer.*

*"Well, I'm bringing a carload of booze through tomorrow night, and I want to lay up during the day."*

*"All right," says the farmer, who watches the rum runner out of sight and promptly notifies federal agents.*

*The officers watch the barn all night, all the next day, and all the next night. Nothing doing, so they give it up and go home.*

*A few days later the rum runner appears and offers the farmer his $50.*

*"But you didn't use my barn," stuttered the farmer.*

*"No," replied the rum runner," but while you had the federal officers tied up here, I ran four loads down the back road. Here's your money."*

Gertrude wasn't going to sing Katisha.

Fred, Annie and eventually Hugh had tried to talk her out of singing at all after the disturbing events of the morning, but Gertrude was determined to perform.

She just couldn't sing the selfish songs of the old hag. She had to find something in her repertoire that uplifted and empowered; something with a true love story that would reach out from her heart to Fred's.

Inspiration finally struck late in the day, and she grabbed the obscure scores from her portfolio and rushed downstairs to find the pianist and the manager.

By show time, Gertrude was a wreck. Not only had she never sung these pieces on stage, but she was sure that no one in the audience would ever have heard of them. The last time *Alcina* had been performed publicly was more than a hundred years before. The manager, however, had assured her that he would write up the story line as she had dictated it to him. He would have copies made on his new Ditto Machine and pass them out to the audience prior to the performance. It was the best she could hope for. The time to worry was past.

Gertrude breathed deeply, and dressed in a simple black sheath, watched the curtain rise, and with all that lay within her, brought her passion to *Bradamante*.

For those in the audience who had yet to read the program, the anguish in Gertrude's voice still had to be deeply felt when she, portraying Bradamante, followed her lover Ruggiero to the enchanted island and bravely fought to release him from captivity. Inside herself, Gertrude recreated and purged all the horrific events of the morning, becoming powerful in her own right.

****

Fred, sitting at the bar, fell under the spell she was weaving, and it felt all too real. The despair and the joy in her voice, the danger and relief from the afternoon all mingled into one until no one else in the room existed except he and Gertrude. Fred had only seen her on stage one time before, and that time, so long ago, he had only been one of many to whom she sang. This time, Fred knew, her voice was just for him.

He had resisted giving in to emotions earlier, being strong for Gertrude, but dammit he was near to tears now. It struck him how close he had come to losing her. And without her, he would never be able to go on.

So immersed was he in emotion, that when the final curtain fell, he sat, unaware of everything, including the riotous applause, until Hugh clapped him on the back.

"She's a braw lass, Fred," his friend stated with quiet certainty, then cleared his throat, regaining his normal, booming authority. "Now come meet some friends of mine. I'd like to make proper introductions." He steered Fred between tables until they reached the far edge of the room.

"Fred Torrey, I want you to meet Hilda Stone." He gestured to a stunning young woman, carelessly wrapped in furs despite the summer heat, who looked at him with impish approval.

"So you're the one who's been knocking people down today." Her husky, cultured voice was at odds with her choice of words. "I sure could use another man like you on my side." Fred wondered what side that was, but bit his tongue. And while he assured her how pleased he would be to work for her, he also hastened to let her know he was already happily employed.

"I work for Miss Edmand's," he informed her, looking to the empty stage and not seeing her. He began scanning the room to see where she might be.

"Work for her, eh?" The sultry teasing continued, and when he realized he hadn't been paying the woman her due attention, he had the good graces to look embarrassed. Miss Stone let him off the hook.

"Don't worry your handsome head, honey. I see how it is. So these are my boys." She indicated her table-mates. "I think you've already acquainted yourself with R.J.," she smirked.

"Not formally," answered Fred, holding his hand out to the man who had come to the rescue earlier. "I want to thank you for your help today."

"Not necessary. You and Hugh had everything under control by the time we got there," R.J. assured him. "All we did was mop up, after." His eyes searched the room. "I'm glad to see the little lady suffered no permanent damage. I couldn't understand a damn thing she was singing about up there, but it sure was pretty." The pleasant Down-Mainer was back.

****

Gertrude finally emerged from the crowd, having spotted Hugh's head above the fray, and the first thing she did when she joined the small gathering, was to melt into Fred's side. She turned her face to him and Fred dropped a chaste but promising kiss onto her upturned lips. She was aware of an audible sigh from R.J. which he did nothing to disguise, and when Gertrude widened her eyes in his direction, he colored up nicely.

"Well, a man can hope can't he?" R.J. looked around him at the bemused faces. "Nobody told me the lady was already spoken for." He tossed back the contents of his glass and sat with his arms folded across his chest, clearly daring anyone to say anything. They all prudently held their tongues.

Introductions were made and Gertrude hit it off, instantly, with Hilda. They had their heads together for the rest of the evening, and found they had a lot in common besides rum running. Travel, fashion and farming took up a great deal of their conversation although by the time they said their goodbyes, Gertrude was no closer to knowing anything about the lovely woman. Did she live in West Burke, Vermont or Greenfield, Massachusetts? Was her husband a mill owner or a turkey farmer? The elusive Mrs. Stone remained just that. But she did promise Gertrude she'd be at next month's show, and that she, herself, would accompany Gertrude on the trip out to the carpet warehouses to make sure that all went smoothly. Gertrude couldn't thank her enough.

As the evening came to a close, Hugh accompanied her and Fred back to the hotel room, deftly maneuvering a slightly tipsy Annie back with them to pack her things. Gertrude was glad that the arrangements hadn't needed to be discussed. She and Fred needed to be together tonight, and Josie would be happy to have Annie take Fred's place on their divan.

****

Gertrude stretched like a satisfied cat. She peeked over at Fred's profile, relaxed in slumber on the pillow next to hers. They had certainly had a satisfying evening. They'd done a few things that made her blush thinking about them now. Should she wake him up? *No.* Better to let him sleep.

She moved to swing her legs out of bed and his hand shot out and grabbed her wrist. His eyes were still closed. “You're not leaving are you?” Fred's voice came out in a slow drawl as he insistently tugged her back under the covers. She snuggled down between his legs, raising an eyebrow at just how awake he suddenly was.

“Not if you don't want me to,” she purred, more than content to comply with his demands.

“I have to make sure you're satisfied with me so you don't run off after that man of Hilda's.” Fred's voice sounded as if he was only half joking.

“Who? R.J.?” Gertrude feigned innocence. “I imagine he's not half the man of the pugilist I *really* like. And I can't imagine he has anything better to offer.” She squirmed suggestively against Fred.

He seemed to agree because it took a long time before they were ready to go down to breakfast.

****

If they hadn't had responsibilities back in Hingham, they would have stayed a few more days in Canada. Having Fred with her was a delightful distraction.

When they arrived at Hugh's after checking out of the hotel—to pick up Annie, and Fred's car—they discussed a more leisurely trip for next month. Annie would stay home to take care of the tea room, while Gertrude and Fred made the journey. Annie, with a slightly hung-over constitution, assured them she had experienced enough excitement in the two jaunts she had already made, that she was content to stay behind.

She and Gertrude decided to drive in the truck, with Fred to follow them in the Model T. He would use his false, Fred Edmands license, and tell the border patrol he had surprised his wife by showing up at her performance. It was all very plausible but Fred still griped that he had a twinge of apprehension for what lay ahead. Gertrude and Annie scoffed at his concerns, reminding him how easy it had been to cross the border last time. They left amongst a flurry of kisses from Josie and Hugh, happily taking to the road, headed home.

Rock Island was upon them before the sun had climbed half way to midday. They pulled the truck into the same spot as the previous month and Fred pulled in beside them. They entered the cool of the federal office together and Gertrude was happy to note that it was the cheerful young man of their first trip into Canada whose boots were draped lazily across the desk.

"Welcome back, ladies," he called, genially as they came toward his seat. "How did your concert go?" He clearly remembered them and it made things easy as he waved the papers away that they held in his direction. "No need for those. I'm satisfied that I know who you are." He turned his head toward Fred. "And this would be…?"

"Oh." Gertrude exclaimed as if in oversight. "This is my husband, Fred." She hoped the young man didn't see the blush that brushed her cheeks, or maybe it might be good if he did. Referring to Fred as her husband felt bold and naughty at the same time, and men liked that sort of thing.

"Fred Edmands," Fred offered, holding out his hand and his license. "I followed my wife up as a surprise for our anniversary."

"Oh, how many years have you been married?" he asked politely, looking at Gertrude. Instantly flustered, she was unable to come up with a lie. Fred was more adroit.

"Five years," he said with definitive pride. "Five years last Friday."

"Well, congratulations." The officer handed Fred back his license. "You seem like nice people." He wrote their names in his log book. "Will I be seeing you again next month?"

"I have one more show in August, and that will be it for the year. My husband and I will be making the trip without our friend Annie next time."

"I'll probably see you then. A lot of the guys are taking their vacations at that time, and I'll be working most of the extra shifts." His gaze was rueful, but then he cheered. "Have a safe trip home." He waved them off and the three left the office with their hearts lightened.

****

Down the street, however, their arrival had once again caught the attention of the three men in the diner. Prohibition officer Cuddy Hamilton pushed to his feet, indicating that his two companions should accompany him outside.

As the Rocky Nook crew lingered in the office having their papers checked, Hamilton and his two co-officers walked into the street and stepped over the border into

Derby Line. They arranged themselves in the road outside of the Haskell Library, making sure they would be seen when they made their request for the truck to stop.

****

Gertrude started the truck and backed out. She'd only gone a few hundred yards before experiencing a quick, panicked deja-vu. Men were blocking her from continuing down the street. The only thing that brought her emotions under control was that they were in the middle of a populated area, and Fred was at her back.

She pulled to a stop and a highly unpleasant looking fellow approached the driver side door.

“Federal Officers, Ma'am. I have to ask you to step out of the vehicle.”

“We’ve just had our papers checked by the man in your office,” Gertrude assured him. “He said everything was in order.”

“We're not border patrol,” Hamilton replied, flashing his badge. “We're Federal Prohibition Officers.” He glanced behind her. “I want to have a good look at your truck.”

“Certainly, officer,” she scrambled down from her seat, gesturing for Annie to stay put. “I'll open the back for you.” She didn't want to look at her housekeeper who—she knew—would be displaying dismay as clear as day.

She went around back and opened the doors. Inside was a small pile of luggage and nothing else. She risked a look back at Fred. He remained in his car, obviously waiting to see if they would wave Gertrude on without any trouble.

“Why such a big truck for such a small amount of luggage?” His voice had a nasal, whiny tone that grated on Gertrude’s nerves.

“It's the only vehicle that my husband will let me drive all the way to Canada. We also own that Model T.” She pointed back at Fred, hoping she seemed more respectable, accompanied by her husband. “He joined me as a surprise the day after I arrived.”

“Arrived where?” he asked, moving closer in a way that was to meant to intimidate.

“I've been engaged to sing at the Magog International Resort. I performed in June, I've just finished a show this weekend and they'll be having me back again in August.”

He sneered and took Gertrude's arm, despite the fact she’d told him about her husband, watching. She attempted to pull away but he tightened his hold.

“I'm sure you won't mind walking around the vehicle with me just to make sure nothing's out of place.” He yanked her roughly and she tripped over a rock in the road, falling heavily against him.

She glanced over, panicked, toward Fred who had obviously seen enough. But before he got his door half way open, Gertrude was alerted to a large woman who emerged from the library emitting what could only be construed as a howl.

“Leave that woman alone you nasty man.”

*Oh, my*! Her avenging angel was Helma, of battleship proportions, who launched herself across the divide and grabbed Gertrude's free arm. The large native of Derby Line looked like she meant business

“I don’t know what you think you’re doing, sir, manhandling this woman? But this is Mrs. Gertrude Edmands, whose concert I had the pleasure to attend in Magog last month. How dare you accost her?” She hissed right in the agent's face, undaunted by his brutish demeanor. “I’ll have you know that I’m a very good listener in the quiet of the library, and I’ve heard stories whispered about you.”

Gertrude didn’t know whether she fervently hoped them true, or not true, depending on what the man wanted with her.

“Oh, yes. I’ve gleaned a few things about you, Mr. Hamilton, and if you don't want me to call the local authorities with my suspicions right now, I'd think twice about holding on to this dear woman in such a way."

Cuddy removed his hand from Gertrude slowly, and attempted to give a placating look to his attacker. "No need for histrionics my dear lady. I was just suggesting a look around her truck."

"Well look around the truck," she snarled. "But keep your hands to yourself."

Gertrude instantly noticed that without being able to intimidate, the fun clearly went out of things for Officer Hamilton. The two agents assigned with him seemed to have already assessed the situation, and chatting with the border patrol guard who now glowered in his open doorway, called over to their loose cannon associate.

"Cuddy, let's go. These ladies don't have anything." The two tipped their hats, and walked back across the border toward the diner.

Cuddy glared at Helma but her dark eyes never wavered. Turning to Gertrude he said, "I'll see you next month, Mrs. Edmands." His taunt was oily and Gertrude shivered. He spat in the dirt and followed after his companions.

On the way by the Model T—where Fred sat in furious silence—Cuddy showed his feral little teeth in a mock smile. "Mr. Edmands."

Gertrude gave a semi-confident wave to Fred, thanked Helma profoundly, letting her know that seats would be waiting for her at the next show, and climbed back in the driver's seat. She didn't dare go back and talk to Fred, or surely she'd break down in tears which would give the evil agent just what he wanted. Shifting into gear, she slowly drove away from Derby Line.

****

Cuddy watched the two vehicles move down the street, snarling mad that he'd been denied his fun. But something about the group just wasn’t right. He tapped his foot, stroking his chin. And why did that guy's face look so familiar?

# Chapter Thirty-Seven

August 1924

Annie watched the shadowy figure walk boldly down the driveway, illuminated by the full August moon. The obviously male silhouette moved in a vaguely familiar way, but Annie was unable to tell, from her vantage point at the second story window, who it might be walking toward the barn. Who would so brazenly stroll on private property at ten o'clock at night? She wasn't one to panic, but she kept her eyes glued to the exact path of the intruder, wondering if he were after alcohol or livestock.

When he switched on his flashlight and pushed open the door which led under the barn, Annie decided to act. She ran down the stairs in her soft slippers and, in the dark, rooted through the closet in the kitchen to find the heavy, hand trowel Gertrude used to cut weeds in the garden. Her fingers closed around the worn wooden handle and she hefted it with confidence, quietly stealing outside.

The burglar had left the lower level door ajar, and Annie inched through it holding her weapon at the ready. The chickens were broody and quiet, emitting small garbled clucks in their sleep. The air was still. She was momentarily surprised that the man was not amongst the chickens, but instead, in the back corner near the well. She watched in silence as he placed his flashlight on the ground and knelt by the hole, reaching for a rope that disappeared into its depths.

Annie inched forward, any small sound she made being overridden by the noise of the rope scraping on the rocks as he hauled something up.

Annie timed it just right. She waited until the intruder's hands were full of whatever he was pulling from the well before she lunged.

What she didn't see was the large rock sticking up from the dirt floor. Her soft-clad foot collided with the protrusion and she yelped in pain. It was all the warning the uninvited guest needed to drop the load back down the well, roll to his back, grab his flashlight, and blind her with its sudden beam.

She heard an audible, yet angry sigh.

"Annie, Goddammit. You just about gave me a heart attack." He eyed the heavy iron tool in her hand and ordered her to put it down. "Get rid of that thing. What are you trying to do, kill somebody?"

"The thought had crossed my mind," she snapped at him. "Just what are you doing out here anyway?"

Ambrose Fletcher, for one moment, looked nonplussed; something Annie had never witnessed before. The impeccable and polite detective who was always in control seemed to struggle for an explanation.

"Can I get up out of the dirt?" he prevaricated.

Annie became aware of her toe throbbing as her shock and anger started to dwindle. She grumbled sullenly at Detective Fletcher before lifting her foot to rub it.

"Of course you can get up." She dropped the tool. "Bloody fool, I think you made me break my toe."

Polite Ambrose was suddenly back to the fore, leaping to his feet and taking her arm, solicitously.

"Let's go in and have a look at it. Here, lean on me."

Annie, somewhat assuaged, narrowed her eyes and pinned him with a look. "Fine, but don't think this gets you out of an explanation."

****

Ten minutes later, Ambrose, having retrieved ice from the chest to place on Annie's damaged foot, went for honesty as he told her he was keeping an eye on Fred. He let her know that he'd long been aware of the Sunday meetings that were played out in the barn, and had—some time back—found the hidden floor where Fred kept his liquor.

But, he told her, what had most recently disturbed him was that last month he had watched Fred carry several cases into the basement of the barn. The stockpile on East Street, instead of remaining static, no longer fit in his usual place of concealment. To Ambrose, this had only meant that Fred was escalating his business. He couldn't allow that to happen, and it was a breach of the implied agreement they had made on a cold beach last winter.

"But this is their last time," wailed Annie. "The reason Mr. Fred bought so much was that after this trip, they're finished."

Ambrose let out a breath. He was glad. There had as yet been no trouble stemming from the alter usage of the Tea Room and barn, but time had a way of catching up with things, and he was damned happy they were closing down before disaster came knocking.

As for Annie, she had been very forthcoming and cooperative with him any time he had questions that needed to be answered, which much to his consternation, she now brought up.

"Why didn't you just ask me about what was under the barn instead of sneaking about?" She poked a finger at his dark-clad chest.

"I thought there was nobody home," he responded sheepishly. "The truck left for Canada again yesterday and since you went with them on the last trip, I assumed you were with them this time, too."

That had been a lapse in his usually thorough deductions and he mentally kicked himself.

"They took Edith this time," Annie sniffed. "She needed a vacation and Miss Gertrude was trying to coax her into performing a small accompanying part on stage." She smiled. "You should have seen the look of horror on Edith's face when Gertrude made the request."

The detective smiled too. He wouldn't mind hearing Edith sing.

Bringing his thoughts back to present, he reassured Annie. "Well, I'll keep an eye on you while their gone and…"

Annie interrupted him. "…and will you be doing anything about the liquor in the well?" She gave him the evil eye.

"No, Annie." He puffed a small bit of air from his cheeks. "If I get his assurance that this is the last time, then I'll look the other way."

Annie had to be satisfied as she showed him to the door.

****

In Canada, Gertrude watched Edith, at the next table, from under her lashes. Her dear friend was just coming down from a euphoria that she probably hadn't felt in many years. She had sung on stage, albeit only a small part to accompany Gertrude, but she had risen to the challenge and had to feel pleased with the way things had worked out. She was currently basking in the undisguised appreciation of one R.J. McKernon who was paying her an inordinate amount of attention, much to the amusement of his companions.

Gertrude's attention returned to Hilda Stone, at their own table, busy recounting yet another hilarious story, and trying to convince Fred and Gertrude that most of the rum running business was a a lark and a game, played against a hapless bunch of prohibition officers who were in no way smarter than any of them. Hilda didn't think this should be their last run. Instead, that it could be the beginning of a long and lucrative career.

Gertrude was ready to be won over, but Fred was adamant

that they were finished. If it were just him doing the runs, he admitted, he might consider it, but his guts couldn't take any more danger for Gertrude. Even now, he laughed, after she had finally relented to let him do the pick-up tomorrow by himself—much to the amusement of Hilda—he said his stomach roiled over the trip home the next day and the possibility of meeting up with that nasty federal officer again.

They all remained at their tables well into the wee hours of morning, enjoying the company longer than usual, and before breaking up, promised to meet again the next evening to say goodbye.

Gertrude could hardly believe this was it. She had gone from obscurity to the limelight and it would not be easy to go back to the Tea Room again. Maybe she'd close at the end of the year when Fred was through with his men's club. Surely she could pick up some small roles in and around Boston. She felt rejuvenated and ready to get on with a new chapter of her life.

****

Saturday, having a reprieve from being part of the pick-up, Gertrude spent a splendid day shopping with Edith, Josie and her little son, and oddly enough, Hilda, who refused to be left out of the fun. They all found themselves spoiling the boy, and were sorry when the afternoon came to an end. Gertrude promised, when saying goodbye to Josie, that they would visit in the spring after the younger woman had delivered her new baby, and help out around the house while the parents got used to yet another addition. Gertrude felt like a favored Auntie, and it was a surprisingly warm sensation.

The show that night was sung to a final, full house, all of whom roared their approval when the curtain came down. Afterwards, the manager extracted a promise that Gertrude would come back the following year. She readily agreed. It fit right in with what she envisioned for her future.

The goodbyes to Hilda and her crew at the end of the evening were heartfelt, Gertrude and Fred giving them all an open invitation to visit Rocky Nook. Hilda, in particular, seemed loathe to break up the little gathering, and Gertrude surmised that she rarely spent time in the company of other women.

"I'll let you know exactly when we'll be up again. Just tell me how I can contact you." Gertrude couldn't help but try to extract a little information at the very last moment.

"Let Hugh know." Hilda waved her hand airily. "He'll contact R.J. and R.J. will contact me. I'll see you again."

Gertrude could only hope it would be so.

****

"There's that truck again." Cuthbert Hamilton was on his feet before his two companions could react. "I'm going to have another look at it." He grabbed his hat from the table.

"Cuddy," the one nearest the door stood up, blocking Hamilton's way. "We went over this last month. The woman sings in Canada, we checked it out. They have a perfectly good reason for being here. I don't know what you think you're looking for, but you can't go harassing nice people."

Cuddy barely restrained himself.

"Now just sit down and eat your breakfast."

Hamilton glared at his companions and controlled his impulse to rush out the door, but refused to sit down, fixing his gaze out the window and on the truck as it stopped at the border office. This time, the man who looked so familiar alighted from the driver's door, and the woman he'd grabbed before stepped out on the passenger side. Damned if it all didn't look just as his fellow officers said. Innocent.

He was about to give in to his grumbling stomach when a second woman stepped from the vehicle. Cuddy's eyes narrowed and he felt his breath begin to come in small inaudible gasps. His tongue darted out to lick his lower lip and he found himself gripping the frame of the window.

My God. That was the woman from Boston. Edith Torrey. He'd never forget having his hands on her. It had been one of the most powerful experiences of his career. He was suddenly hard just thinking about it.

But as his lust took over, so did wariness. He'd sustained a pretty bad beating after his last encounter with Miss Torrey, informed with warnings that it had been administered on her behalf, and worse would follow if he ever made himself known to her again.  A slow burn began in his belly. He stared at the group, seething.

That man…that very familiar man. And just like that, the pieces suddenly dropped into place. Cuddy thought back to the picture he had taken from Edith's apartment. Remove the beard on the guy in the picture, and this was none other than Fred Torrey, who had slipped through his fingers five years ago. He almost crowed his delight. He would finally get his man and take his revenge. But this time he'd be smart.

Cuddy sat back down at the table, giving no indication of his agitation to his fellow officers. The Rocky Nook group emerged from the border office and got back in the truck.

He slowly ate the remaining bites of his breakfast as they drove away, and fastidiously wiped his mouth with his napkin, placing it—in a controlled manner—on the table.

"I'm going to have me a little walk," he told his companions before getting up and strolling out the door.

"Good riddance," mumbled one so that Cuddy could hear, and the other snorted in agreement. He knew his fellow officers didn't like him. They probably hoped his was a long walk and they wouldn't have to see him for the rest of the morning. Hell, they'd most likely be glad if he fell off a cliff and never came back.

Cuddy's destination was far closer than either of them surmised. He walked across the street and opened the door to the border patrol office.

"I need to see the last entry you made."

The officer reluctantly turned the book around, and cursing, Cuddy saw their place of residence listed only as Hingham, Massachusetts. He'd have to dig a little deeper to find out where, in town, the pair actually lived.

# Chapter Thirty-Eight

August 1924

*The Billings Gazette, 1924*
*Secure Cellar Whiskey Cache*
*...in searching the place, officers went into the cellar and discovered a trap door covered with about six inches of fresh dirt. Twelve quarts of the wet goods were confiscated. The cellar was demolished by caving in the sides and roof. One of the prohibition officers narrowly escaped getting buried by the earth...*

"Who did you say this was, again?" Ambrose Fletcher's hand wrapped tightly around the phone receiver, and he strove to sound like the small town dunce who federal agents often expected to talk to outside the big city limits.

"I'm a Federal Prohibition Officer and I need some information about a couple of your residents."

Ambrose had made the man repeat himself twice already, citing the crackly, static-ridden line.

"Oh. A Prohibition Agent," he intoned. "What can I do for you?"

The Agent's frustration showed. "I want you to tell me about two of your town citizens," he shouted.

Fletcher was fully aware of what the agent wanted. He was also aware that time had apparently caught up with the extra-curricular activities of Fred and Gertrude. He rubbed his eyes around the bridge of his nose. Why was he always right? On the phone, he prevaricated.

"We have over six thousand people in town," Ambrose supplied helpfully. "I can't keep track of them all."

"You'll know these two," the man said assuredly. "They run an establishment called the Rocky Nook Tea Room."

"Well now, I don't know about "these two", but certainly you're talking about Gertrude Edmands. She has an outstanding reputation in town. You know she's a famous opera singer? My dear mother enjoys going to hear her sing at the tea room. A fine, fine woman…"

"I'm not interested in what you're mother does," snapped the agent. "I'm interested in some suspicious activity that she and this fellow have been perpetrating at the border."

"Did you say you were border patrol?" Fletcher continued, sounding vague and confused.

"No, dammit. Not border patrol, Prohibition…*Prohibition*," the man yelled.

"So what can I do for you?" Ambrose maddeningly repeated his previous question.

"You can damn well tell me who the guy is that was traveling with her from Canada. They went through the border yesterday then spent the night here in St. Johnsbury and left about three hours ago."

It was clear to Ambrose that the agent already knew who Torrey was, so what was his game?

****

The previous day, Cuddy had followed the group at a discreet distance, making sure they were all settled in for the night at their hotel, before returning to his post at the border.

His intention had been to sneak out of his rooming house early this morning, pursue them closely, then way-lay them in some backwoods location where he would extract all the information he needed to put Fred Torrey in jail for a long time. The thought of what he might do to the two women, in the meantime, while a restrained Fred watched, had kept him awake and excited all night.

He had cursed his luck when one of the agents had knocked at his door before dawn, citing some suspicious activity at a barn in the next county. The job had kept him busy until he was able to make excuses and belatedly slip away. By the time he reached the St. Johnsbury House, the clerk had informed him the people he was pursuing had departed a couple of hours before.

It was then, he realized, that he would have to follow them all the way to Hingham. And all he needed from the small town police officer with whom he spoke, was an address.

****

Detective Fletcher wasn't going to give out any information unless he was obliged under the law, and this irate man on the other end of the line sounded as if he had more bluster than authority.

"Why don't you tell me what the man looks like?" Ambrose asked obligingly. "I'm going to take some notes." He picked up his pen and began to doodle.

"The fellow is about six feet tall, dark hair, clean shaven, but I have a picture of him from some time ago where he's wearing a full beard."

Ambrose's senses suddenly went on alert. "An old picture, you say?" He sat forward in his chair. "What year do you suppose it was from?"

"I came across it about five years ago. I was in the middle of an investigation at the time and I was interested in finding him then."

"You know, I didn't catch your name," Ambrose forced himself to sound casual, but the blood in his veins rushed to his head in anticipation of the answer.

"Cuthbert Hamilton," the agent bit out. "But that's neither here nor there. The important thing is whether or not you know this guy."

"What did Gertrude do?" Now that Ambrose was aware of who he was dealing with, he was giving out no information. He would have to play this one perfectly. Let the little weasel twist in the wind.

"I'm not concerned with the woman," Hamilton yelled again. "I'm concerned with her *companion* who I believe committed a federal offense by presenting false identification to the border patrol."

Ambrose's body went limp with relief. Cuddy didn't seem to have any idea that alcohol might be involved, he was only fishing. Perhaps it would be easier to deal with him than Ambrose thought.

"I'm a little confused, Mr. Hamilton. I thought you told me you weren't border patrol. Seems to me, I should be speaking to the correct department." He paused an appropriate amount of time as if deep in thought. "Why don't you have those gentlemen call me and I'll see what I can do."

Cuddy squealed like a pig, clearly outraged. "Why you piss-ass, little town, know-nothing cop," he blustered. "You'll give me the information I want or I'll make your life a living hell. I'll see that your badge is taken away for obstructing justice. I'll…I'll…"

At Fletcher's continued silence, the man could tell he was getting nowhere and slammed the phone down, cutting their connection.

Ambrose stared at the dead line, knowing one thing for certain. Hamilton was going to be a problem. He had obviously recognized Edith at the border and thank God she hadn't been made aware of him, or Fred would be in federal custody right now for strangling the agent with his bare hands. Ambrose pondered his next move.

****

Fred and the women took their time getting home. In St. Johnsbury, Fred had asked the hotel staff to put together a picnic lunch and they had stopped at a beautiful spot on the Connecticut River for a several hour respite. They savored the day, glorying in the sun, and as Gertrude lounged on a large, flat rock, she lamented that it was the last time this summer she wouldn't feel smothered by the needs of the Tea Room.

"These excursions have been so much fun," she sighed. "Despite the few moments of drama."

Fred thought that a vast understatement, but held his tongue.

"I'm afraid it's going to be a long winter."

With that, Fred could only agree. When the alcohol finally ran out, it wouldn't be easy closing down his men's club in the barn. He'd gotten very fond of his meetings.

Fred and Edith packed up the picnic things in the truck, bickering in a good natured way that only close siblings could, and felt blessed that his life included two such wonderful women. They got back onto the road, and headed home.

Darkness descended, and both Edith and Gertrude succumbed to the long day, sinking into deep slumber. It was well after eight o'clock when they finally arrived back on East Street, and Fred ushered both groggy women into the house before going back to the vehicle. He backed the truck up to the barn, and setting the brake, jumped down to finish the night's business.

"Evening, Fred," Fletcher's voice came out of the darkness, startling Fred with his nearness.

"Lord, Ambrose, you gave me a start." Fred immediately knew that he was in deep trouble. "I didn't see your car."

"I left it at the station. It seemed like a good night for a walk." The detective's voice came to him calm and controlled, as always. "We'll be taking your truck back to Joy Lane when we're finished here."

Fred was resigned, but had to ask. "What's this about, Ambrose?"

"Well, someone's interested in what you've been doing in Canada." Fred watched as the man lit his pipe and blew smoke out of the side of his mouth. "We had an agreement, you and I, that as long as things stayed small and local, I wouldn't interfere. But now it looks like someone's going to come snooping and when they do, you're going to be put away safely in my jail."

Fred was disconcerted to feel his hand shake as he ran it back through his hair.

"I understand. Shall I go tell Gertrude?"

"Nope. No need. By the time she misses you—I assume you were going to unload the truck—I'll be back to explain things to her." He looked pointedly over his pipe,

Fred's posture deflated and he turned to get back into the vehicle.

"Wait. We're not leaving yet." The detective stopped him. "There's something we need to do first. Follow me."

Puzzled, Fred followed Fletcher down the incline to the left of the barn, stepping through the door and around the chickens who were still active despite the late hour. Ambrose preceded him to the well, and knelt in the dirt, tapping out his pipe on a rock.

"We're going to bring this with us," Ambrose said over his shoulder. "If you've got anything else in the barn," He paused for emphasis, "I guess I'm just not aware of it."

Once again, Fletcher surprised Fred. Why take the small amount of liquor that was hidden in the well, and not the rest from up on the second floor? How much trouble was he really in? Fred's gaze dropped to the iron garden tool that lay in the dust at his feet and slowly bent to pick it up. Gertrude's hand trowel. He weighed it in his fingers as Ambrose's continued on his knees, his back toward Fred.

"How did this get here?" Fred asked.

"What?" The detective turned.

"This trowel," questioned Fred. "It's one of Gertrude's favorites, and I just wondered how it got out here."

Ambrose bent back to the well and chuckled. "Annie must have forgot she dropped it." He didn't explain further, so while the detective worked, Fred carefully placed the implement by the chicken coops, propping it against a box where Gertrude couldn't miss it.

"Here," Fletcher said. "Help me with these ropes." His business-like demeanor returned. "Is it just the one case in the well?"

"Yes, just one." If Ambrose didn't already know, Fred wasn't about to tell him that it was the only case that hadn't fit under the secret floor upstairs. As a matter of fact, Fred hadn't been quite sure where he was going to store his latest load. He guessed it didn't matter now. It would stay in the truck.

He bent down next to Fletcher and they easily hauled the case of whiskey from the well

"This case will get you a night in jail and a stiff fine, but I think the judge will let you off easy, considering that his wife is a regular patron of the Tea Room."

Fred didn't want to tell Ambrose that the *judge* was also a regular patron of the Men's Club. Other than a night in jail, that pretty much assured Fred that life would go back to normal very quickly. But why was Fletcher going to let him off so easily, when he knew the extent of what Fred really had?

On the detective's instruction, Fred carried the case up out of the barn, depositing it in the back of the truck.

"You drive," Ambrose told Fred. "Just back it to the top of Joy Lane when we get there, and I'll see that you get comfortable for the night."

"Ambrose, I…," Fred began.

Fletcher put his hand up to stop the words. "Don't thank

me, Fred, and don't go saying anything you don't want repeated," he paused. "Besides, once I have you in jail, you might not like me so much when I tell you that my night isn't over yet."

Fred puzzled over that one for the two and a half minutes it took to drive back to the police station, and for the couple of seconds more for Ambrose to turn the key in the lock and secure Fred behind bars.

"Coffee?" Ambrose asked, clearly fueling himself for what he'd intimated could be a long evening. The brew smelled old and acidic to Fred, where it sat on the one burner hot plate, but he nodded agreement.

"So here's how I see it," Fletcher handed him a stained ceramic cup full of muddy liquid. "There was a man who called me this morning from St. Johnsbury. He's an old acquaintance of yours." Ambrose actually took a sip of the vile liquid as Fred sniffed his. "He's never quite gotten over the fact that you slipped through his fingers five years ago, and he's most likely going to show up at your house in a few hours to set things right in his crazy head."

Fred eyes narrowed. "Who are we talking about?" He placed the undrinkable beverage on a small table in the cell.

"Does the name Cuddy Hamilton mean anything to you?" Ambrose released.

"Son of a bitch!" Fred slammed his hand against the iron bars. "That's the guy who attacked my sister." The gears turned in his head. "Oh, my God. Is that the guy who harassed us at the border?" He was incredulous. "I should have gutted him when he touched Gertrude." Fred could feel his blood pressure rising. "Ambrose, you've got to let me out of here." Fred yelled. "If he comes back, he'll kill Edith this time…or Gertrude." The howl in his voice sounded surreal to his own ears.

"Which is precisely why you'll stay right where you are," the tough Ambrose Fletcher gazed back at him. "This morning when he called, he was a good three hours behind you. In a little while, I'll go back to the house and keep an eye out for him." His voice was chilling. "I guarantee he won't be bothering any of you anymore when I get finished."

Fred spluttered. There was something not quite right, here. He searched his head for the answer but it had been such a long day. *A long day!* That was it.

"Ambrose. You've got to go now. He's not three hours behind any longer. We took an extra two or three hours in the late afternoon today having a picnic out in the western part of the state." He rattled the bars frantically. "He could be at the house right now. You have to let me out."

Fletcher's whole posture stiffened. "Damn, I'm getting too old for this," he barked. "I shouldn't have assumed I had time at my disposal." He grabbed his keys off the hook on the wall. "You, sir, are staying put," Ambrose growled. "I'll be back when I'm sure everything is all right."

Fred's anguished roar followed the detective out the door.

****

Gertrude turned the lights on in the kitchen and bustled about, unpacking baggage and hanging her special dresses so they didn't develop any permanent creases. It was a good half hour before she spotted the note folded on the kitchen table. The handwriting was unmistakably Annie's and she apologetically let them know that she had been unable to feed the chickens that day, having been called away to Mrs. Fletcher's sickbed before finishing her chores.

"Oh, dear. I'd hoped we could just have some tea and head off to bed, but we can't let the chickens go without," she tisked.

"I'll go out with you and help," Edith comforted. "It will go faster with two."

Gertrude lifted the electric lantern off of the top of the credenza. "Thanks, Edith."

They abandoned all thoughts of tea, and pushed back out

into the night, walking through the darkness toward the basement of the barn.

"That's odd," Gertrude puzzled. "The truck is gone. Is there any reason that Fred would have gone out tonight?"

Edith laughed. "You know Fred. Something must have struck him as necessary, and knowing him, it couldn't wait until morning. He'll be back soon."

"I guess so," Gertrude shrugged. They entered the bottom floor and she hung the lantern on the peg right inside the door.

Edith laughed at the confused chickens. "It looks like they want to be sleeping, but they know they've missed something today." She said of the dozen or so who were dazedly milling about.

"I'm pretty certain you're giving chicken brains a little too much credit, city girl," Gertrude laughed.

She walked over and raised the cover on the grain bin, scooping a load into a galvanized bucket. Edith followed suit. Moving back in that direction of the doorway, they slowly and methodically filled the trough. When she finished, and reached the end of the feeder, a movement just outside caught her eye.

"Fred, is that you?" As soon as the words left her mouth the shadow moved closer and she knew it couldn't be Fred. The size of the obscured figure was all wrong. "Who's there?"

She backed up, gradually, toward Edith who, at Gertrude's alarmed tone, also squinting into the darkness.

"Show yourself." Gertrude's voice held more command than she was feeling.

They were unprepared for the visitor who finally stepped in. Gertrude could only gape and shake her head at the agent who'd harassed them at the border.

"Good evening, ladies." The man eased forward, and a sound of abject terror was wrenched from Edith.

"Oh, my God, Gertrude. It's him," Edith screamed.

“That's the man who assaulted me in Boston.” Gertrude watched as her friend backed up as far as she could until she was flush against the bank of roosting boxes.

“Oh, shit,” Gertrude swore. This wasn’t good. “That's the agent who grabbed my arm at the border last month,” she told Edith.

Her gaze went from Edith to the agent and then back again, appalled that the intruder was one in the same with Edith's attacker. She unconsciously rocked the galvanized bucket she still had in her hands and, steadying her feet, consoled herself that the man was not nearly as big as the two who had attempted to subdue her in Vermont.

“What do you want?” She was pleased to find her voice came out steady.

“What do you think I want?” Ferret eyes slid up and down her body, as if assessing the strength she might have. Clearly he dismissed Edith, who stood impotent with fear, and reckoned that once he brought Gertrude under control, he could do what he wanted with his second captive. Gertrude drew in a calming breath. He was so wrong.

****

Cuddy’s heart started to quicken with excitement. Maybe he'd draw a little blood, first. How would it feel, punching the opera singer in her lush mouth? *Don't get carried away,* he warned himself. Just because he was lucky enough to come across the two women, alone, he still didn't know the whereabouts of Fred. He needed to feel out that situation before he made any moves.

“So do you think that man of yours is going to come to the rescue?” he taunted Gertrude. “What would you say if I told you I've already taken care of him?” He loved the look of terror that flitted quickly across her face.

“You couldn't have,” she spat at him, blustering. “He's twice your size. You'd never be able to overpower him.”

Cuddy withdrew his gun from his pocket and let her get a good look

"Oh, really? So how do you account for the fact that his truck isn't here." He fished for an answer, but a choked sob was all he got in response. Damn, the bitch didn't know where Torrey was. She thought that Cuddy really *had* disposed of him.

Well, he'd just have to make things fast. Despite the unknown whereabouts of Torrey, he was going to play with the two lovely women. He couldn't resist the palpable aroma of their fear. It fueled his desires. He'd have to move quicker than he would like, but he'd make sure the two never forgot him.

He indicated the dark recess of the barn to his right. "I want you both to move slowly in that direction."

"And you," he gestured with his gun to Gertrude. "Put the bucket down."

She started to refuse, but Hamilton pointed the barrel directly at her head. She dropped her meager protection, but in defiance, drew herself up and deliberately turned her back on Cuddy, approaching Edith who had gone around the well and backed up into the shadows.

She gathered the trembling woman in her arms. "I won't let him hurt you, Edith."

God, it was going to be so much fun breaking that one, Cuddy thought. He didn't know whether he should torment the weaker woman first and make Gertrude watch, or if—given unknown restrictions on time—he should just crush the little spitfire right off.

****

Gertrude had gotten lucky. Her fingers closed around her favorite garden tool as she'd walked away from Hamilton in pretense of soothing her friend. She had spotted it earlier, and, luckily, Edith had inadvertently placed herself right beyond the potential weapon.

"Don't worry," she assured Edith in a low whispered voice. "I'll take care of this." She hid the tool in the folds of her skirt as both women moved deeper into the barn, behind the well, as the man had directed.

Cuddy looked them over, and it seemed like he'd settled on tormenting Edith, first.

"You," he indicated to Gertrude. "Move over there, away from her." He then licked his lips at Edith. "And you," he pointed to the dirt at his feet. "Come stand right over here in front of me."

Gertrude gave her a silent hand to the back, in assurance, and Edith took two, then three hesitant steps toward the evil man. But that was as far as she got. Gertrude understood that Edith couldn't get her feet to move any further. Her terrified brain had begun to shut down.

"I said come here," Hamilton yelled, clearly angry that Edith wasn't listening.

Gertrude watched as her friend forced herself to take several more steps that moved her around the gaping hole in the floor, and toward the irate man. But apparently Edith still wasn't moving quickly enough for him. He snarled and reached forward to grab her arm.

Edith reacted without thought, stumbling backwards, away from his grasp. Her heel struck a stone sticking up from the dirt floor and she lost her footing, her arms cartwheeling as she went down, her body headed for the well. Hitting hard, she struck her head on the rocky edge, and before any of them could react, Edith's suddenly limp body folded in on itself and she melted down into the dark water.

Gertrude lunged forward, able to grab one ankle that was last to submerge. Her frantic gaze flew to Hamilton, wild with panic.

"Help me you fool. Help me."

She saw him snarl, but a blurred movement behind him

drew her eye. Seemingly out of nowhere, Ambrose Fletcher raised his hands and brought her galvanized bucket down on Hamilton's head with all his might.

"Hang on to her, Gertrude," he yelled as he spun the horrid interloper in place, hammering him in the jaw. The small man went down with just the one punch.

As Gertrude struggled to hold on, Ambrose threw himself in the dirt beside her and grabbed Edith's ankle below where Gertrude's hand had begun to cramp up. Together they hauled the sodden woman from the well. Blood seeped from a deep gash on the back of her head.

"Is she dead?" Gertrude was frantic, suffused with terror. She sobbed, remembering how earlier she had felt so blessed to have both Edith and Fred in her life. Now, she might not have either.

"She's bleeding, so she's still alive," Ambrose assured her. "Let's get her into the house and call the doctor." He dragged a comatose Edith to him, picked her up and gently cradled her in his arms. He strode forward with Gertrude on his heels, but before they reached the door, Edith began coughing and spluttered water all over his the detective's suit. Her lids flickered upward and Gertrude saw her stiffen in his arms.

"Shhh, Edith, you're fine. It's me, Ambrose." The detective hugged her close, and gave her quiet assurances while carrying her out of the barn and up the small, grassy incline. Her teeth chattered loudly in the night air, even though it was warm, and Gertrude had to chuckle that in her relief at being rescued, Edith made a small joke, even though tears leaked down her face.

"Looks like I'm ruining another piece of your clothing, Detective Fletcher," she shivered.

"You can ruin all the clothing you want, Edith," he murmured in return, and wasn't Gertrude surprised to see him, brush his lips across Edith's cold cheek.

She would have appreciated the scene more, had she not

suddenly been suffused with the remembrance that Hamilton had done something to Fred.

"Ambrose." she called from behind, choking on his name as terror rose up. "The man, Hamilton, he said he took care of Fred."

The detective slowed his steps and as she caught up, Gertrude saw a smile pass over his face. "Ah. For the first time tonight, my dear, I feel that I've done something right. Fred is safely locked away up on Joy Lane, Gertrude. He's fine."

A relieved sob escaped from her throat, and Ambrose, looking a little out of his league surrounded by two, weepy women, quickly cleared his throat and asked if Gertrude wouldn't hurry ahead of him to call the doctor.

She picked up her skirts and ran past him into the house to make the phone call.

****

Once Ambrose settled the bleeding woman on the couch to await the physician and stitches, he felt safe in leaving the recovering pair while he went back to the barn.

Outside the barn door, he drew his gun, making no noise as he glided into the semi-darkness. His caution was unnecessary. Hamilton was still prone in the dirt, crumpled and unmoving. And Ambrose knew what he had to do.

It didn't take long for the Hingham detective to take care of all the bad business, and when he emerged from the barn, he held the galvanized bucket in his hands, looking inside to make sure he had all Hamilton's belongings.

It was warm to have a fire tonight, but Ambrose would make sure to conjure an appropriate conflagration.

Now to keep the women company until the doctor arrived. Edith's bleeding was, at least, under control, so he had no fear that a number of stitches would have her right as rain.

****

Arriving back at the police station on Joy Lane, Ambrose pushed open the door and deliberately placed a pail behind his desk. Fred was instantly on his feet. When the detective reached for the keys on the wall and came over to open the door to the cell, Fred looked at him, clearly unable to ask the questions that Ambrose knew lay on his tongue.

"Everything is fine, and taken care of, Fred," he said. "What you need to do is go home and see to the needs of your women." Fletcher filled with a quiet satisfaction. "I'll just say this in answer to whatever you might ask. You won't be bothered by Cuddy Hamilton again."

Fred gave him his heartfelt thanks, grabbed his hat and had his hand on the doorknob when Ambrose stopped him with some final instructions. "And, Fred? When you're done with the ladies, I have one additional request."

The man hesitated and looked back at Fletcher, questioningly. "Go under the barn and make sure you fill in that goddamned well."

# Epilogue

Present Day

*Boston Globe*

*The body exhumed from a well in Hingham several weeks ago has yet to be identified. There were no accompanying artifacts to be found. Forensic specialists say the remains are in such poor condition, that the identity of the unknown individual and the cause of death may never be determined.*

# Afterward

For those people who like to separate fact from fiction, I will say right away that Gertrude and Fred were both very real.

When I moved into the Hingham house in 1979, rumors were still swirling around regarding the opera singer, and the "handy-man" who lived in the attic. Anyone from town, older than sixty, would wiggle their eyebrows and say "Oh…Gertrude and her live-in help." No one ever gave any details of the supposed affair, and at the time I was very young and didn't search for answers. I wish now, that I had.

When my husband and I began renovating the house, we came across one piece of stationary for the Rocky Nook Tea Room. I don't know if the Tea Room actually existed, or if someone made the stationary in hopes of starting a business. I don't even know the year the picture was rendered. It could have been from Gertrude's era or before.—Certainly not after, as I am aware of the house history after Gertrud's departure from Hingham.

The next bit of detritus that led to the creation of this story was a partial, mouse chewed prescription for Hermitage Whiskey that was made out to Gertrude Edmands. While pulling down an old plaster ceiling outside of the room that I believe would have been the tea room, a paper came fluttering down. It was written by a Dr. Chapman, and filled by J.L. Hunt and Company located at Thaxter's bridge in Hingham. The attending pharmacist at the time was Ernest

W. Lincoln. Of course, I'm not sure why Gertrude filled this prescription, but it suited my purposes to have another source of alcohol for the men's club.

As far as I know there was no men's club at all, but oddly enough, many broken whiskey bottles from the proper time period have been found in and around the barn, with the best "find" being an intact Jim Beam whiskey bottle, complete with a cork and glass stopper, that was found buried deep under musty layers of old hay in a horse trough.

A major piece of the story came while excavating the well under the barn. I needed a source of water for a vegetable garden and knew that if the filled in well were made active, I could attach a pump and solve the problem. Digging for hours, my hands became numb from the cold when I was suddenly afforded a moment of panic. At a depth of approximately eight feet, there emerged what resembled a human hand sticking up from the mud between my boots. After some tentative poking, it turned out to be a very well preserved leather glove. It had, nevertheless, been a momentarily startling find.

My mind was beginning to connect the dots with a possible story, but it still took some time before the tale came together.

There were a few wonderful discoveries and coincidences that occurred during the writing process, the first of which was how famous Gertrude really was. I had always known she was an opera singer and had given lessons at the house, but I had no idea that she had such an illustrious career. Finding newspaper articles that gave facts about her concerts and appearances was a boon to the story. I was able to include the pieces of music that she had performed and some of the venues where she performed them.

When I stumbled across the sheet music for *A Dream*, by JC Bartlett, I was astounded. This music had been written and dedicated to Gertrude, so in the story I added a little tendresse from Bartlett to her. It is also wonderfully synchronous that my maiden name happens to be Bartlett.

On the Bartlett side of my family, my father's cousin married a Torrey and that bit of family still lives in nearby Scituate. I'm sure that my second cousin, who is adept at genealogies, could probably find a quick connection between the Bartlett's and Fred.

This was not the last of the coincidences that tickled my imagination. Hannah, Gertrude's mother, had the maiden name of Buffum. Not a common name, but my older sister married a Buffum and my nephews retain that name.

Possibly the oddest twist came about while researching Hilda Stone. I ran across many newspaper articles stating various places that she lived, one of which was Burke, Vermont. My nineteen year old son, strangely, had just begun a brief internship on a farm in Burke the previous week—even though none of us had ever heard of or been to Burke before. Trying not to be oddly spooked, I had him and a friend scour the local libraries for additional information on Hilda, which they did with much joy at the adventure.

In the text, I have paraphrased many newspaper articles. If they have an *exact* date next to them, they are real, taken directly from newspaper archives. If the article has no date, you may assume that I either made it up, or moved it in time to suit my purposes.

The most horrendous, factual article was the train crash that "killed" Maude. Even though Maude was not real, when I knew the month I needed to have her leave the story, I researched disasters and this one fit the bill in every way, right down to being the exact train that would have taken her home to Waltham.

A lot of the ancillary characters in the book are real, or based on real people.

Gertrude's father and mother, Thomas and Hannah were real. Thomas was a musician and the head of the Edmands Band which played throughout Boston and the surrounding area.

Gertrude had two sisters, Eva and Alice, who were much older than her, but I can find no reference to them past their time living in Somerville, Massachusetts.

Martha Smith was their devoted housekeeper who actually followed the family to Hingham when they moved.

Fred and family, as described, lived in Cambridge on Dana Street. I kept Edith as a central character, even though there is no historic mention of her after childhood in real life. I used a few bits of information regarding his brother, Arthur, to bring him, briefly, into the story. Neighbors names were made up and jobs were fabricated and assigned based on existing companies of the day.

Idell Miles was real and quite the character on her own. (I might have to see if there's a story there that needs to be written.) George Parker was real, but not the villain and womanizer that I made him out to be. He just happened to be a person who was in the right place at the right time for Gertrude—although after the book was written, an elderly gentleman from Cohasset whose Grandmother had been best friends with Gertrude let slip; "You know she had a well known affair with a married man…" The story woven between Gertrude and George *is* a product of my imagination.

Another interesting aside on *A Dream;* the famous artist W. Haskell Coffin painted the picture of Gertrude on the sheet music. This wonderful picture kept me company at my desk through the entire writing process. It must have been one of Haskell's very first commissions as it was accomplished when he was only seventeen years old.

As much as I wanted Hugh and Josie to be real, they were brought forth from thin air, along with Ambrose Fletcher and Cuddy Hamilton.—Thank goodness he didn't exist. The savior of the day at the border, Helma—who was actually based on one of my great aunts, growing up—and her husband are also fictitious.

The police station on Joy Lane was also partially

fabricated. The building began its life as a police station on North Street, but after it was moved to Joy Lane, it was used only as a private residence.

Hilda Stone and R.J. McKernon were both real, and extremely fascinating people. Many accounts exist as to who Hilda Stone really was and where she hailed from, but at the end of the day, each time she was arrested for rum running, R.J. McKernon was arrested right alongside her.

The character of Annie was actually a compilation of two real people. Annie Jefferson worked for Gertrude from the 1920's until the 30's, when she was succeeded by Annie Spring. The reason I chose Annie Spring is because she was traceable as having lived the rest of her life in Hingham after Gertrude went back to Boston. She died on February 27th, 1993 and is buried in the Fort Hill Cemetery in Hingham.

Getting back to Fred and Gertrude and the end of their story, Fred Torrey died on January 1st, 1942 in Hingham. He is buried in the High Street Cemetery in Hingham.

Gertrude Edmands sold Rocky Nook on September 11th, 1943, and moved to Boston, where she lived until her death on April 19th, 1956. No burial place for her could be found.

www.ingramcontent.com/pod-product-compliance
Lightning Source LLC
Chambersburg PA
CBHW062022170626
46813CB00001B/259
*9780989433358*